SAME AS IT EVER WAS

ALSO BY CLAIRE LOMBARDO

The Most Fun We Ever Had

SAME AS IT EVER WAS

Claire Lombardo

DOUBLEDAY · New York

www.doubleday.com

DOUBLEDAY and the portrayal of an anchor with a dolphin
are registered trademarks of Penguin Random House LLC.

Book design by Cassandra J. Pappas
Jacket painting by Rachel Campbell © Rachel Campbell
All rights reserved 2023 / Bridgeman Images
Jacket design by Kelly Blair

Library of Congress Cataloging-in-Publication Data
Names: Lombardo, Claire, [date] author.
Title: Same as it ever was : a novel / Claire Lombardo.
Description: First edition. | New York : Doubleday, 2024.
Identifiers: LCCN 2023036860 | ISBN 9780385549554 (hardcover) |
ISBN 9780385549561 (ebook)
Subjects: LCGFT: Domestic fiction. | Novels.
Classification: LCC PS3612.O453 S26 2024 |
DDC 813/.6—dc23/eng/20230830
LC record available at https://lccn.loc.gov/2023036860

MANUFACTURED IN THE UNITED STATES OF AMERICA

1 3 5 7 9 10 8 6 4 2

First Edition

For Molly

PART I

Lost in the Supermarket

1

It happens in the way that most important things end up having happened for her: accidentally, and because she does something she is not supposed to do. And it happens in the fashion of many happenstantial occurrences, the result of completely plausible decision making, a little diversion from the norm that will, in hindsight, seem almost *too* coincidental: a slight veer and suddenly everything's free-falling, the universe gleefully seizing that seldom chosen Other Option, running, arms outstretched, like a deranged person trying to clear the aisles in a grocery store, which is, as a matter of fact, where she is, the gourmet place two towns over, picking up some last-minute items for a dinner party for her husband, who is turning sixty today.

This one is a small act of misbehavior by any standards, an innocuous Other Option as far as they go: choosing a grocery store that is not her usual grocery store because her usual grocery store is out of crabmeat.

Afterward she will remember having the thought—leaving the first grocery empty-handed—that such a benign change to her routine could lead to something disastrous, something that's not supposed to happen. This is how Mark—scientific, marvelously anxious—has always looked at the world, as a series of choices made or not and the intricate mathematical repercussions thereof. Julia's own brain didn't start working this way until she'd known him for a substantial period of time; prior to that she'd always been content with the notion that making one decision closed the door on another, that there was no grand order to the universe, that nothing *really* mattered that much one way or another; this glaring difference in character is perhaps what accounts for the fact that Mark dutifully pursued a graduate degree in engineering while Julia neglected to collect her English and Rhetoric diploma from Kansas State.

Now, though, they've been together for nearly three decades and so she did consider—just a fleeting thought—that so cavalierly altering routine could result in some kind of dark fallout, but at the time she'd been envisioning something cinematically terrible, something she wouldn't have encountered had she just forgone the crab instead of driving fifteen minutes west, a cruel run-in with a freight train or a land mine, not with an eighty-year-old woman assessing a tower of kumquats.

Julia doesn't recognize her at first. She doesn't consciously notice her, in fact, nor does she stop; she's headed industriously past the organic produce to seafood, contemplating a drive-by to dry goods to see if they have anything interesting in stock; sometimes the stores in the farther-out suburbs have a more robust inventory. She's considering taking a spin around the whole store, checking out what else they have that hasn't been subject to the frenzied consumption of the usual suspects at her usual grocery, when it hits her; the woman's face registers in her brain belatedly, clad in the convincing disguise—that invisible blanket—of age.

Hers has not been a life lived under the threat of too many ghosts; there's only a small handful of people whom she has truly hoped to never encounter again, and Helen Russo happens to be one of them. So why does she find herself taking a step closer to the endcap of the dry goods aisle, getting out of the flow of traffic so she can turn to look back? It's been over eighteen years, which is somewhat astonishing both given the fact that they used to see each other at least once a week *and* given the smallness of her world, a world in which something as small as altering one's grocery plans can be considered a major decision.

She is unsure, as well, what moves her back to where she came from, but Helen's not in produce anymore, has progressed to the bulk section, where she is weighing out a bag of pine nuts. According to their accompanying sign, they are $16.75 for a half pound, and she remembers becoming aware of such extravagances during the afternoons she spent at the Russos' house, the heaviness of the cutlery, the paintings that looked suspiciously like originals, the bottles of wine she'd look up when she got home and find to have cost $58.

She is here procuring the ingredients for celebratory crab cakes, one of her husband's favorites. The thought of Mark sets off a momentary swirling of wooziness. She's carrying around an empty basket and, feeling somewhat ridiculous, she tosses in a purple orb of cabbage. In some ways Helen looks predictably much older than she remembers; in others—her optimistic ponytail, the glint of the big blue beads around her neck—she hasn't changed at all. Julia takes a few steps, then a few more. Normally she is the queen of evasion, treats her trips to the grocery like sniper missions, seeing how many faces she can avoid having to interact with; this does not mesh with whatever gregarious phantom has overtaken her body now, impelling her close enough to see the pair of drugstore cheaters propped on top of the woman's head.

"Helen?"

When Helen turns to face her, there's a curious vacancy in her gaze; her eyes trail slowly up and down. Julia thinks to consider how she looks; she runs a hand through her hair. She worries, momentarily, that she'll be mistaken for some kind of miscreant; she's wearing what Alma calls her *clown pants* and one of Mark's old button-downs; she likes to think the combination has miraculously resulted in something extemporaneously stylish, but it's likelier taken her in the opposite direction. It can be hard to tell, in the suburbs, whether an eccentrically clad woman carrying around a single organic cabbage is nomadic or expensively disheveled. She begins to consider how much she herself has changed since last they met, and the volume of those changes hits her forcefully and all at once; she is, upon reflection, more changed than not. She becomes nervily aware of her pulse pumping in her ears. It's entirely within the realm of possibility that Helen won't even *recognize* her—that old worry, so familiar to her, that you haven't meant to someone as much as they meant to you—but then Helen speaks.

"It couldn't be."

The heartbeat sound recedes, overwhelmed by the surrounding

bustle, a woman arguing with the butcher, a man talking into an invisible earpiece, a child in a down vest singing shrilly about a baby shark. Helen's voice is remarkably unchanged; Julia is transported, not unpleasantly, to afternoons in the Russos' backyard, Helen—older, then, still, than Julia is now—imparting her parental platitudes, her pithy one-liners, her candid confessions, all with the confidence and ease of a person who actually enjoyed her life, astonishing to Julia at the time because she herself did not.

"I—thought that was you," she says stupidly.

"Don't tell me I haven't aged a day," Helen says, "or I'll have you assassinated."

Nervous, she laughs. "No, you look—"

"Because I have to say, you look *quite* a bit older, so I must look aeons older."

It's more surprising than insulting—and, to be fair, she *is* quite a bit older—but still she feels herself flush. "I think *aeons* is pushing it."

Now Helen laughs. "Well, you recognized me. That's saying something."

"You look terrific," she says, almost shyly.

"I remember you being a bad liar," Helen says. "Even your *grocery* cart isn't entirely convincing."

They both look down to regard the cabbage. "Just getting started," she breathes.

"How are you?" Helen asks. "Give me the rundown. The bullet points."

"Oh, I—" She's not sure what to say. It occurs to her that the last time she saw Helen was before Alma was in the picture, but it seems a strange thing to announce to a near stranger: *I gave birth! Seventeen years ago!* In fact, the plot points of her life over the last two decades are myriad; so much *bloomed* from that time, toxic and otherwise, tiny green shoots sprouting from ravaged land. A new job, another baby, a doubled-down commitment to her marriage, and then, after that, the way things relaxed into routine: the accrual of acquaintances and the maturation of her children and the adoption of a tiny black terrier mix named Suzanne, the embroidery of daily existence, fabric softener and presidential elections, the dogged forward march of time. The brightly colored billiard balls of her days—kinetic and pressing, constantly cracking against one another, rerouting and requiring her intervention—suddenly seem trivial. She hasn't seen Helen in eighteen years; it's difficult to account for anything.

"Same old," she says in lieu of all this. "Just—kids, work, et cetera." Her former self would be astonished to see her now, a woman with standing fellow-mom coffee dates and a special Nordstrom credit card and a relative sense of peace.

"*Kids*," Helen says. "Plural?" This was, she recalls, what being with Helen was like, constantly seeing your same old life from brand-new angles, finding dull spots that needed buffing or shiny ones you hadn't noticed: two children! A marvel! Helen lifts her eyebrows theatrically, and then her face opens in recognition. "That's right; the last time I saw you things were—percolating, were they not?"

She'd wondered if Helen would remember. Suddenly she's standing, once again, in the library on that horrible afternoon, seeing the woman for what she thought would be the last time.

"They were," she says. "They—did. A daughter."

"Goodness, I suppose that's what happens when you don't see someone for a hundred years, isn't it? And how's your son? He must be— He was—gosh, the tiniest little thing, wasn't he?"

"Less tiny," she says. "Twenty-four." Ben used to sit at their feet under the table, playing with the vintage trains Helen's husband, Pete, unearthed for him from the basement. She clears her throat. "And you? How are you? How's Pete?"

"Dead," Helen says easily, not missing a beat. "The latter, not the former, though I appear to be, as we have established, not far from it."

"Oh, God." Her sadness is immediate, and surprisingly close to the surface: Pete Russo waving down at her from the roof of their house, Pete Russo letting Ben make bongo drums out of his paint buckets. "Helen, I'm so—"

"I haven't seen you in ages," Helen says. "It's inevitable not everyone would survive."

"I'm sorry."

"I am too," Helen says, and for a second some of her hard-edged jollity slips away, leaving in its wake something tender and abandoned.

"How are you doing?"

"Oh, fine," she says. "It's been a long time. It'll be—Lord, five years, come August."

"I don't . . ."

"Julia." Helen smiles at her. "It's fine. Let's move on. How about yours?"

"My—?"

"Husband?"

"Oh." The reason she's here, having this unbelievable conversation, instead of home already, awash in the safe boring miasma of party preparation, where the universe surely intended her to be. How is she supposed to account for Mark, Mark whose life was very nearly ruined because of her initial run-in with Helen Russo, Mark who has not, thank God, died in the last eighteen years? "He's— well. He's actually— It's his birthday; that's why I'm—here." She lifts her basket inanely.

"Of course," Helen says after a beat. "The anniversarial cabbage."

She laughs on a delay.

Helen is studying her again, a new expression on her face, equally unreadable. "I should let you get back to it. It really is lovely to see you, though. You look happy."

"Do I?" She doesn't mean to ask.

Helen smiles. "You do."

Now would be an opportune time to tell Helen that she too looks happy; now would also be a perfectly normal opportunity for either one of them to make some effortful remark about *getting together* or *catching up.*

"Enjoy," Julia says ludicrously, gesturing to Helen's cart, which features—she notices now—its own somewhat comical sparsity, four key limes and the little parcel of nuts.

"Uh-huh," Helen says. She touches Julia's arm, and Julia is glad for her long sleeves, covering her goose bumps. "You do the same."

She does not recall collecting her groceries, waiting in the express line, putting them on the conveyor belt.

"Did you remember your reusable bags?" the cashier asks her with accusation.

"I remembered them in spirit," she says, but the cashier doesn't laugh.

S he doesn't feel herself fully exhale until she gets into the car. The crabmeat and the cabbage—she felt bad for it, couldn't bring herself to return it to its pyramid—cheerfully ride shotgun beside her. All of her most critical moments with Helen occurred over the course of a few months, but Julia's brain compresses them now, everything happening neatly in the span of a minute, crying in the car to languidly drinking wine on Helen's deck to the last time she saw her at the library, all of it in sixty seconds. She feels dizzy, opens her sunroof and inhales deeply.

On the drive here, she'd been responsibly—if not sort of wearyingly—listening to public radio, but when she gets out of the parking lot she turns on one of her daughter's playlists. Classic rock is back in, so every other song on the list is something she knows, Bowie and the Stones punctuated by bands with novelistic names, You Will See Our Smiling Faces on the Nine Train and Reckon with Your Racist Grandfather or Slight Right for the Sanitary Land-fill; she always gets the names wrong and it drives her daughter crazy. She admits she doesn't *get* much of the contemporary music Alma favors, but she has taught herself—constantly, desperately scrambling for her daughter to love her—to appreciate it, and she turns it up even louder, pushes down the window button so she can get some air.

She used to consider herself something of an expert, somewhat *cool*; she and Mark used to go to shows almost every weekend and she could recite the entire Pavement discography in order either of release or personal preference and she'd inured Ben to the same, by osmosis, playing her CDs much louder than she is now while she was driving him to preschool or on one of their daily madcap ventures around town, and this, of course, makes her think of Helen again, and the ghost of Helen's touch on her arm, the unbeliev-ability of the fact that she'd just approached the woman in the first place, but also of Helen back then, in the succulents room at the botanic garden, Helen sensing her desperation—the hollow-eyed, socially inept young mom in a Jesus and Mary Chain T-shirt she'd been—and plucking her out of the crowd.

The playlist gives way to "Smells Like Teen Spirit," and she cranks it, too loud—the man beside her, stopped at the light, is staring openly—but she turns it up a couple of notches more, merging onto the Eisenhower, glad for the excuse to move fast.

Mark is nowhere to be found when she gets home, which is fortuitous because the second she enters the kitchen she experiences a strange, sudden shakiness, a wobble at the edges of her vision that forces her to sit down hard on one of the stools at the island. She feels Suzanne's small forepaws pressing against her shins, the dog straining up on her hind legs to inspect her, affronted that Julia has not engaged in the usual homecoming fanfare. Suzanne treats Julia's every reappearance—whether she has been gone five minutes or five hours—like a sweepstakes, eyes wild and body vibrating with excitement. Suzanne is the most obsessed with Julia that anyone has ever been, more obsessed with Julia than Julia has ever been with another living being, including her children. It is flattering—if at times unnerving—to be loved this much.

"It's okay, tiny lady," she says to the dog. "I'm just a little out of sorts."

"That is not remotely what happened, but fine," Alma is saying to someone when she comes into the room, then: "Mom?"

She opens her eyes, lifts her head. Her vision clears; her daughter is resplendent and terrifying, Amazonian, with her dark unruly hair and her discerning green eyes. She has an empty mixing bowl tucked against her rib cage and a crushed La Croix can in either hand.

"Hi, Ollie."

The dog whines, and Julia leans down and lifts her up.

"Don't cry," she says into Suzanne's fur.

"You shouldn't police her emotions," Alma says, but then, frowning, asks, "Are you okay?" It's a rare display of interpersonal con-

cern as far as Alma goes, and Julia wishes for a second that she
weren't okay, that she could call upon her daughter for some kind of
nontraumatic assistance, splinter removal or a dislocated shoulder,
something that would require close bodily contact with this person
she's borne, so long as Alma is—such a rarity from her narcissistic
lioness—offering.

As it is, there isn't a way to navigate deftly. To allude to something physiological will make her daughter (who doesn't particularly enjoy her parents' live presence but also doesn't want them
dead) suspicious and to tell the truth—that she'd been steeling herself for an encounter with her husband following an encounter with
the woman who'd almost ended their marriage—is obviously out
of the question.

"Fine," she says, and Suzanne wriggles, goes flying off Julia's lap:
the dog, like a cat, like her daughter, has a specific set of boundar-
ies, desires constant attention but on very rigid terms. "Fine, fine,
fine."

She straightens her spine, rises from the stool and starts moving
again; there are never not things that need doing in the kitchen,
particularly when Alma has friends over, spills to be mopped or
dishes dried or refuse—two denuded apple cores, the purple rind of
an expensive wine-cured goat cheese—that will not make its own
way to the trash can.

Mercifully, Alma accepts this, ready, with that unbridled teenage confidence, for the focus to return rightfully and exclusively to
her.

"They called to reschedule my dentist appointment," she says.
"Dr. Gallagher had a death in the family."

"Oh, that's—"

"Which is actually good because we're doing an AP Euro study
group this week at the library—I mean good that it got canceled,
not good that someone died—so I was wondering too if maybe I
can use the car, so you won't have to come pick me up super late
every night?"

Alma had been a wildly clingy kid, but now she is a mostly autonomous and wholly inscrutable seventeen-year-old; she is mean and
gorgeous and breathtakingly good at math; she has inside jokes

with her friends about inexplicable things like Gary Shandling and avocado toast, paints microscopic cherries on her fingernails and endeavors highly involved baking ventures, filling their fridge with oblong bagels and six-layer cakes.

"I'm asking now because last time you told me I didn't give you enough notice," she says. She has recently begun speaking conversationally to Julia and Mark again after nearly two years of brooding silence, and now it's near impossible to get her to stop. She regales them with breathless incomprehensible stories at the dinner table; she delivers lengthy recaps of midseason episodes of television shows they have never seen; she mounts elaborate and convincing defenses of things she wants them to give her, or give her permission to do. Conversing with her is a mechanical act requiring the constant ability to shift gears, to backpedal or follow inane segues or catapult from the real world to a fictional one without stopping to refuel. There's not a snowball's chance in hell that she won't be accepted next month to several of the seventeen exalted and appallingly expensive colleges to which she has applied, and because Julia would like the remainder of her tenure at home to elapse free of trauma, she responds to her daughter as she did when she was a napping baby, tiptoeing around her to avoid awakening unrest. The power dynamic in their household is not unlike that of a years-long hostage crisis.

"We'll see," she says, and then, before Alma can protest: "You have company?" She hears at least two voices coming from the living room and is fairly certain that one of them belongs to Margo Singh.

Alma drops the cans into the recycling bin. "Yup." Her daughter has declined to provide any helpful insight with respect to Margo and, more specifically, the ties that bind them; any efforts Julia has made to garner details on their relationship have been met with derision, the silent suggestion that her views of relationships are far too rigid.

"She's not my girlfriend," Alma said recently. "But she's also— not *not* my girlfriend. Nobody calls it that anymore, Mom."

Julia had refrained, then, from asking *nobody calls it what?* Alma's Privacy, in an ever-shifting order of priority among Alma's Grades and Alma's Burgeoning Political Opinions and Alma's Minute Existential Desires, is a popular topic of late. Plus Julia likes Margo; she wishes the girl made a little more noise when she walked—she has a tendency to appear mournfully from the shadows like a gravedigger—but she seems to have a good head on her shoulders, and she seems to be making Alma happy.

"Lovely," she says. "Where's Dad? Is your brother here yet?"

Alma makes a little how-should-I-know hum. She sets her bowl into the sink, then seems to sense Julia's gaze and reaches for the dish brush. "What are you cooking?"

"An assortment," she says absently, opening one cupboard and then the next, pulling out items at will and depositing them on the island. "Those little quiches. Cucumber salad. Crab cakes." She's assembling her tools, the celery, the bread crumbs; she had actually, prior to the afternoon's interruption, been looking forward to the preparation, labor-intensive enough to feel impressive but not so much as to preclude her also doing nineteen other things simultaneously. She knows better than to expect much help from her children.

Alma turns to face her, affronted. "God, Mom, really?" She's behaving as though she's just been shot, and Julia looks around, startled, for some newly introduced trauma, but everything seems the same, the bowl in her daughter's hands dripping dishwater onto the floor.

"What?" she asks, alarmed.

"I told you I'm off seafood," Alma says. "I told you that *weeks* ago."

She considers this. She wishes—horribly, a not uncommon desire when speaking to her daughter—that she could simply evaporate from this conversation. She feels, too, unbelievably tired, stymied by gravity; so much of motherhood has, for her, been this particular feeling, abject disbelief that she's not only expected but obligated to do *one more thing*.

"Did you forget?"

"*Forget* is a strong word," she says, and she extracts a bushel of cilantro from the door of the fridge. In fact she does remember; she'd just been hoping that the conversation on what Alma referred to as *incremental veganism*, like many conversations with teens, could be swept under the rug within a few days, replaced by something uniquely, inexplicably pressing.

She inhales slowly, deeply, through her nose, until she feels the air expand at the base of her throat. She halfheartedly attended prenatal yoga classes before Ben was born, unaware at the time that the breathing exercises therein would aid her not during childbirth but instead, two decades later, in violence prevention against her teenage daughter.

"Why are you *breathing* like that?"

"Just—getting some oxygen," she says. "To my brain."

"You told me you'd think about our cutting out animal products as a family," Alma says, with an affected measure in her voice that makes Julia want to push her down a well.

"Honey, if you don't want to eat it, you don't have to. Plenty of other options."

"Are you *mocking* me?" Alma asks, and gestures to Julia's hands, in which she is holding—unthinkingly, like a volleyball or a severed head—her decoy cabbage.

She wants to laugh, fights the impulse to laugh, feels tears spring to her eyes instead.

"Why are you making that *face*?" Alma asks.

Mark's entrance is a merciful interruption. He's sweaty, back from a run, wearing his Lycra shorts and, strapped around his waist, the collapsible water bottle that she recently likened to a colostomy bag. He too bends to pet Suzanne, greeting her like he hasn't seen her in a decade; they have all, since her arrival into their family, rearranged themselves around Suzanne in this way, though it has been suggested that Julia has rearranged herself the most.

"What's that bracelet?" asks Alma. "You look extra weird today."

He lifts his wrist, encircled with a strip of molded purple plastic, the pedometer prototype they're testing at his work that Julia's been hearing about ad nauseam for months. "The commercial ones are historically inaccurate," he says.

"Maybe," Alma says, "but they don't look like *that*."

"Tough crowd in here," Mark says, putting his arm around his daughter; she mewls some protest but lets him, even leans her head against him, sweat and all. Julia herself has not been in such close physical proximity to Alma in ages; she emits a powerful radiant energy that keeps her mother, though notably not her father, whom she likes a lot more, at bay.

Mark comes to kiss Julia, and Alma watches them, repulsed. They are a family whose clock is always slightly askew, affections misplaced and offenses outsized. But it's better, she thinks—please, God, it must be better—than the complete absence thereof.

"Is this what we're having for dinner?" Mark asks, palming the cabbage like a crystal ball, and Alma lets out a monstrous sigh before disappearing from the room. They both listen to the dull thump of her socked footsteps stalking into the den.

"Improv," she says. "For your birthday."

Mark puts his hands on her shoulders. "What are you making?"

"Animal products."

"Can I help?"

"Nope." She makes her voice bright, turns to face him. "My gift to you."

"Plus all this." He indicates the spread before them on the counter, the firing squad of Malbecs along the sink, the groceries. She wonders if anyone else at the store had noticed her trundling up to Helen Russo, brazen in her clown pants. Mark has a hand at the nape of her neck, kneading gently. There must be some marital sixth sense that induces one party—unknowingly wronged—to suddenly behave with excess integrity, effectively increasing the guilt of the wrongdoer. It makes her nervous.

"Go shower," she says, and swats him with a dish towel. "Make yourself presentable."

She watches him leave the room, rakes a hand through her hair, tries to channel the energy she had an hour ago, her pre-Helen energy, focused on the task at hand. She'll julienne the cabbage, turn it into a slaw. Sometimes she catches herself thinking thoughts like these—*I forgot to pay the lawn guy; Suzanne's dog food delivery comes on Wednesday*—and she's amazed by her own ridiculousness.

"Life is a struggle for us all," she intones sometimes, to make

Mark laugh, watching the asshole day trader next door yelling at his contractor, or a squirrel suspended upside down stealing seed from their cardinal feeder, but they're no different, really; she has grown comfortable dwelling in her own ludicrous minutiae.

Julienne the cabbage, for fuck's sake; it is a point of astonishment, really, how improbably lovely her life has become.

2

Things hadn't been lovely back then, far from it, those foggy, cotton-swaddled days before she'd met Helen Russo, days so interminably long and paralytically monotonous that she couldn't distinguish one from another. Twenty years ago, one house ago. They'd moved from the city to the middlebrow part of a highbrow suburb, enrolled Ben at Serenity Smiles, which, she thought, sounded like the name of a not particularly expensive stripper, or a high-end rehab facility, though it was in fact—or as well—one of the most exclusive preschools in the area. She refused to call their town by its given name, had begun, irritating Mark to no end, referring to it as *Pinecone Junction. The Suburbs,* mecca for successful adults with incomprehensible job titles and their disillusioned stay-at-home spouses, oak trees and opulence and artfully disguised despair. They stretched on for miles, the street signs and the artisanally preserved cobblestone roads, station wagons and all-terrain strollers, acres of dense manicured foliage, palatable lawn signs, self-conscious displays of affinity for particular tradesmen, self-conscious showings of tepid political affiliation, plaques commemorating nothing at all, and you weren't even allowed to *drive* normally; not infrequently she'd find herself on a street with a speed limit of 15 mph, like something out of olden times. Everyone liked to think their suburb was the best suburb, but really they were all the same, slight variations in proximity to the lake or degree of amorphous "diversity" or "historical significance" but ultimately a wash. Their street was called *Superior,* but her amusement about this, after a few months, had worn thin, along with almost everything else.

What had happened? Who knew. The world started falling apart, or she and Mark forgot how to talk to each other, or perhaps it was just her temperature dropping, settling back to where it was comfortable. They'd left the city around the time Ben started walking, and he was now fully and confidently mobile, if not especially graceful, and also miraculously fluent in both English and a bit of Spanish, which they taught on Wednesdays at Serenity Smiles; Julia, meanwhile, felt static, like she'd been embalmed. She wasn't sleeping; her internal monologue had taken on a caffeinated, nervy quality, the unpunctuated warbling of a crackpot, and she was aware—in her rare interactions with fellow adults—that her external monologue might be exhibiting some of the same mania.

She'd begun to notice that when she wasn't waiting for something to happen—something pedestrian, like Ben waking up from a nap, or sometimes something implausibly awful, like an asteroid falling from the sky—she felt entirely unmoored, brooding, usually while staring pensively into the middle distance like a disenfranchised Victorian nursemaid.

She didn't hear Mark enter the kitchen.

"Are you okay?" Like he'd found her tangled in barbed wire. It was his favorite question to ask her of late, always with an ingratiating softness to his voice.

She straightened. "I thought I saw something stuck in the garbage disposal."

Mark shuddered a little. He had a visceral antipathy for any kind of mysterious food product, things rotten or globular or simply unidentified. He touched her shoulder lightly as he passed en route to the coffeepot, did not ask any follow-up questions regarding the disposal, the potential for dark mystery therein.

"I wish this week could just skip right to Friday," he said, seemingly unaware of both the childishness and the banality of this statement, stirring sugar into his coffee. "I woke up already overwhelmed. Doesn't that seem like a bad sign?"

Julia, on the rare occasions she slept, frequently awakened preemptively dreading whatever was to come and retroactively dreading what had already elapsed, but because Mark was wearing a tie and had a master's degree, and because Julia's woes were frequently foregrounded in dealings with Duplo architecture and coerced carrot consumption, Mark was more vocally allowed to rue his responsibilities; that was just the way the world worked. She had long since stopped trying to envision his days out of both boredom and jealousy.

How *dull* their life had become, zero to platitudes in ten seconds flat; surely this put them in the running for some kind of sleepy Olympic victory. *Remember our honeymoon in Greece,* she did not say. *Remember when we had sex standing up in an alley in Corfu while a rat watched; remember when we had sex in the bathroom of a Frank's Nursery & Crafts; remember when we had sex in a—*

"Jules?"

"Mm." She blinked, was met once again with his furrowed concern. "Yes, definitely a bad sign."

The furrow deepened; apparently she had missed some intervening remark. "I asked what you were doing today," he said.

"The same thing I do every day," she said. "Oh the wonders that await."

He looked at her over his shoulder. "I ran into Erica when I was cutting the grass the other day; she mentioned she'd like to get her son together with Ben. Why don't you call her?"

"Who's *Erica?*"

"The woman who lives a few blocks down, the one who goes jogging with the toddler in the little cart behind—"

She wrinkled her nose. "The one with the face?"

"Julia, come on."

She stared at him, this man who wanted to fix everything. The solutions to his own problems tended to be less complicated than hers; they always had been. She was so lonely it had started to feel like a corporeal affliction.

"What would I do with her?" she asked.

"I don't know," he mused, his back to her, poking around in the fridge. "Mom things."

It instantly enraged her. "What do you mean, *mom things?*"

"I just mean—you could go for a walk. Or maybe like a book club?"

"Ah, yes, *walking.* A storied *mom* tradition."

"You know what I—"

"I would rather die than join a book club."

It was boring to rue the suburbs; she was aware of this. She pictured the anthropology of her life like layers of shale, jagged and delicate, crumbling, but all, fundamentally, indistinguishable shades of gray. She lived elsewhere. Then she did not live elsewhere. It was all the same, really; everywhere, eventually, became elsewhere. It was a cliché to be this person; she got bored just thinking about it, the sadness over nothing, the fact that she was resentful of the easiest life in the world. And yet she couldn't help herself.

"Okay, Julia, forget I—"

"I just don't understand what you mean by *mom things*. That's like saying *oh you know, one of those things people who wear sweaters do. One of those things right-handed people do.* It's not like being a *mom* is a different—species or something."

"You know what I mean, Jules. It might be nice to—have some other people around."

"I have you," she said, and he softened.

"Of course you do," he said, and then he did come over and hug her, his chest solid against her cheek.

In fact, she'd been looking forward to today, Wednesday, a Serenity Smiles day for Ben and thus a potentially quiet day for herself; she would chain-smoke in the car and drive up to Forest Glen, stomp around in the woods, stretch out on a big warm rock like a sacrificial offering and just, for a little bit, not have anyone *staring* at her. But now she felt bad, bad for looking forward to being away from their child and bad for not being better at structuring her time, for not filling her free hours with cultural stimuli and age-appropriate acquaintances.

"Are you all right?" Mark asked, pulling back to look at her. "You look tired."

And though it was true, though she'd been awake since 3:10 and if she drank a fourth ineffectual cup of coffee she'd be jittery until sundown but still bone-deep exhausted, she felt slightly wounded.

"Had you wooed me with such agility in our nascent stages I might not have married you," she said, but she forgot to put the lightness in her voice and she heard how it sounded as it came out of her mouth. Mark heard it too; his face—that sweet face!—fell not insignificantly. She wanted to punch him.

"Ouch," he said.

"Whoops," she said. It wasn't his fault; it really wasn't: her turn to touch him gently, barely, like he was coated in something sticky.

"Sorry," she said, just as he was saying, "I love you," and they sort of mashed their cheeks together in a goodbye, and she listened to the front door open and close as he left for work.

Ben's arrival was, as always, a balm; he appeared like a sunbeam in the kitchen doorway, cheek pillow-creased and big eyes still blinking away sleep, his stuffed giraffe dangling from a tiny hand. She felt her heart open, her face relax in a smile, her joy, in such short supply, reserved exclusively for him.

"There's my guy," she said, and his face opened too and she lifted him into her arms, kissing both her son and his giraffe good morning, breathing him in, the sun itself.

Oh God, oh, God, my best friend is three, she thought sometimes. She'd recently tried to explain this to Mark when he'd suggested—using slightly kinder verbiage—that perhaps it would do her some good to find some friends her own age. Of course she knew that Ben was not her friend but her *child*, but the realization somehow had not struck her until Mark pointed it out to her, and the loneliness that followed—loneliness on top of loneliness, loss from what was already such a sparsely populated space—was startlingly powerful; it was so easy lately to kick her when she was down, even unintentionally—and it was never intentional with Mark, the nicest man in the world—because she was always down, not even to be kicked, necessarily, but tripped over, a standing date—a stagnant entity—for emotional casualty.

"Are you sad?" Ben asked, surprising her, and she swallowed the impulse to cry, though surely he was used, by now, to the sight of her tears.

"Of course not," she said into his head. "Mama's so happy." She felt wisps of his hair between her lips. She had the urge sometimes, fierce and instinctual, to eat him. "Sweet, my sweet, you make Mama so, so happy."

. . .

Later they were in the car on the way to Serenity Smiles, Ben recounting a dream he'd had about something he called an "alone Beagle" playing on a playground; the protagonists of Ben's dreams rarely succumbed to anything but the passage of time, moving merrily from one location to another. Most of Ben's dreams were like this, highly imagistic, nontraumatic, things simply *happening*, time going by.

"Our son, Virginia Woolf," she'd joked to Mark not too long ago.

"And Mama?" Ben said. "We wanted to pet him but we did *not* pet him."

"No we didn't!" she agreed, false cheer bordering on mania. She had not been paying attention. She herself was dreaming of ten minutes from now, when she could hightail it onto the freeway, the Replacements so loud on her expensive sound system that it shook the steering wheel—even though she knew that she would miss Ben's presence in the backseat. Parenthood was a persistent cruelty, a constant, simultaneous desire to be together and apart. She dreamed sometimes of violent deaths, her Subaru crushed beneath a semi; a swim in Lake Michigan that ended in slow downward slippage, her feet dusting the cold silty grains of its deepest point. And it comforted her to think about it, about how nothing was forever, how even the monotonous vise grip of her existence could be obliterated by the intervention of nature or circumstance.

She realized, stopped at a light, that she was crying. And it was less the crying itself that scared her—she was crying as often as she wasn't lately, it seemed—than the fact that she hadn't even *noticed*, that she was able to persist, business as usual, this run-of-the-mill sadness just leaking out of her, subtle as breath.

"Are you okay," Ben said. Children confounded her, their baffling mix of acuity and guilelessness.

"Mama's fine, lovey," she said, taking refuge in the parentally sanctioned use of the third person. She'd never had a proper set of tools, but it had mattered less before; now there were others involved.

The loneliness of motherhood; the deadly ennui of the day-in-day-out. So much *life* around her, this electric little person cocreated by her warm industrious husband, a man more comfortably attuned than she to the mundane vagaries of normal life, and all she could think was that she wished she were alone. Life she'd created, living itself, and all she could conjure was how nice it would be if Ben wasn't here, if instead he was elsewhere, one of those few places you were allowed to send your kids, a playdate, perhaps, where he would be fed ants on a log by someone else's mother, a real mother who would flush instead of cringe at his shrieks of delight. The amount of *energy* it took—she thought of her insides sometimes as a slowly leaking battery, an acidic alkaline fizz eating away at her organs—the amount of *effort* it took to bring her voice to a register he'd recognize.

She turned up the stereo, "No Sleep Till Brooklyn," to which she'd taught Ben to head-bang, but he just regarded her gravely in the rearview, stable and still. Her son was not a typical child, not one of the corpulent cherubs she'd imagined during her pregnancy— they'd come to her in dreams, rosters of fat, buoyant children like so many amenable pastries, telling jokes, wearing dungarees, spreading joy. But Ben was tiny, a wisp, and serious, so much so that she worried, often, whether he was enjoying his life as he should be. His gazes were penetrative and mature, his silences meditative and monastic. He was making her nervous; she focused on the road.

When she pulled into the drop-off lane she felt her breathing slow in increments; she was in such proximity, now, to her aloneness, so very close. But when Megan the Serenity Smiles lackey opened the back door to extract Ben from his car seat, he yowled. Ben was not a yowler; Ben was easygoing and soft-spoken; Ben had a good sense, for better or worse, of when his mother needed her alone time, and he almost never put up a fight.

"Sweetheart," she said. His time at preschool tended to fly by for her. She could only be gone so long, only smoke so many cigarettes. She looked up at Megan, an apologetic young brunette in a Patagonia vest, and forced her best weary-mom smile. "Darling, it's time for school."

"No," said Ben.

"Honey, you have to let Megan undo your belt so you can go inside and have tons of fun." It was unbelievable that kids fell for shit like that. The items on Ben's agenda for the day were "TP ghost bowling" and "G is for Going on a Germ Hunt," his midday snack a single organic graham cracker. It would be hard for anyone to rally enthusiasm.

And yet he always did. He always willingly kissed her goodbye and returned to her in the afternoon drowsy and proud, proffering modified toilet paper rolls and unidentifiable creatures made from Q-tips.

"No," Ben said, and he sounded eerily like Mark in the moment, measured and no-nonsense. Julia looked beseechingly at Megan, who was not paid nearly enough to deal with the moneyed unpleasantness of the Serenity Smiles moms, let alone field the emotional unraveling of the school's most reclusive parent. *Please God help me.*

"Maybe you should walk him in today," Megan said, shrugging, and before Julia could reply she had closed the door and moved on to the next car.

Julia drove half a block up to the lot and parked, turned around to look at Ben.

"Do you want Mama to walk you inside today, squirrel?" she asked. It still baffled her that Ben ever fell for *that*, either, the false brightness of her voice, her arbitrary terms of endearment. *Shall we take our bath now, my Popsicle stick?* She never walked him in. She avoided, at all costs, breaching the actual façade of the Serenity Smiles building. She normally fought her way through the carpool lines like a salmon, fighting against the flow to pick up her child with little to no human interaction. She looked with longing at the imposing outline of the building, but she could not, she was certain, handle the inevitable car-accident glee of the other parents when she—the resident hermit mom—came skulking in with her wailing, protesting son. All bets were off when someone else's child was misbehaving or having a tantrum, everyone watching but avoiding eye contact, like when a stranger had a mental breakdown on the subway, a mix of superiority and voyeurism, *thank God that isn't me* plus *ooh, what'll she do next?*

In the rearview, he looked at her sternly. "No."

"Please, Benji," she said desperately. "Mama's got places to be."

Mama's got to be alone today or she might self-immolate.

"No," he said again, and she rested her forehead on the sun-warmed steering wheel.

"Please," she said. "I'm sorry, Ben, honey, please, I'm sorry I'm like this; I just need a little bit of alone time." She started to cry again, and then so did he, the more disturbing because it was such an anomaly, the crying of a very sad adult, not an overtired child.

"Sweetheart," she said. "My sweetheart." And it moved her all the way to the backseat, vaulting the console like a Clydesdale and unbuckling him from his car seat, pulling him into her lap. He wept a big navy blob onto her turquoise T-shirt. She stroked his fine dark hair, her tiny, tiny boy. And she was filled with guilt, base-level guilt over the fact that this impossibly small person was so attuned to her moods, conversant not only in English and beginner Spanish but also in the peaks and valleys of his mother's vacillating emotional state; she'd sworn since before he was born that she would never make him worry about her the way she always worried about her own parents, but it had happened anyway; she had let it happen anyway.

"I'm sorry, sweet," she said, and he tightened his arms around her. "Don't worry about Mama," she said, though she knew it wasn't that simple, and suspected, darkly, that the damage had already been done, that she'd failed at her one job. "Don't ever worry about Mama."

"Can I come with?" he asked, beginning to calm, eyes on the prize, looking up at her equably and blinking away tears from his long lashes.

And she laughed, felt the flat disk of his patella, small as a silver dollar, under the soft grain of his tiny corduroys.

"Should we play hooky, little moose?"

He nodded gravely.

"Let's go somewhere together," she said, and she felt a relief as she said it, because that was what you were supposed to do, wasn't it, put your kids first no matter what, no matter how much you wanted to go rogue? "Let's go on an adventure."

They drove again, slowly over the speed bumps down the alley from Serenity Smiles. How could she ever not want him there behind her in his car seat, her boy with his tiny arms waving to the music? They liked *Summerteeth* and *London Calling* and anything by the Talking Heads. They liked "Debaser" and "Beercan" and "Oh! You Pretty Things." They liked the entirety of *Slanted and Enchanted* because of its alternation between gaiety and screaming. And Ben would lose his shit whenever "Blister in the Sun" came on, demanding she start it over the second it had finished, *again, Mama, again, again, ha ha ha ha ha.*

When she merged onto 290, she pressed the button to change the CD: *Pleased to Meet Me*, another shared favorite. She met his eyes in the rearview again, complicitous now, as "I Don't Know" started to play. It was post–morning rush hour; they zipped by the Medical District, through the Congress Tunnel, a little stop-and-go down Jackson, and then they were on LSD, the lake blurring by. How could she ever have not wanted him back there?

"Are you guys still around?" she sang when it was her turn.

"I don't know!" Ben sang back.

And she had the lurking impression of having spared them both from something—she was not sure what. She met his eyes again in the rearview. She knew how close she was to the edge but not that Helen Russo would appear, in just an hour's time, at the botanic garden, to walk her back from it.

"Whatcha gonna do with your lives?"

"Nothin'!"

3

I n the shower, before Mark's birthday party begins, she revels in the quiet. Their friends will arrive soon, exclaiming dutifully over everything—the crab cakes, the tiger lilies, the little kitschy but tasteful pirate swords that spear the cocktail olives—and this in itself, she acknowledges, is somewhat of a miracle.

Almost none of their friends now knew her then. She and Mark had done everything they possibly could to start over after what happened with Helen Russo, leaving behind as many material vestiges of the life they'd built that had *led* her to Helen Russo, swapping out houses and social ties and school districts. She wonders if they'd even be able to recognize her, if she'd even be able to recognize herself, stagnant and terrified and insomniac, scuttling around the edge of the playground to keep an eye on Ben while avoiding parental conversation, drinking wine alone on the back steps, sleeping in the car in the parking lot of Whole Foods. And those were mild on the weirdness scale, back then; she can't confront the larger transgressions of those days.

Her life had been so different when she knew Helen, so much *paler* and sadder and harder. But it was not Helen who'd almost ruined them. Helen had put certain things in motion, flicked some critical cogs, set them spinning, but it was Julia who'd been the most responsible, Julia who'd erred, enormously and repeatedly, Julia who was beholden to Mark and Ben yet pretended that she wasn't.

She is rattled by the person she became in Helen's presence today, a person who, despite nearly six decades on the planet, proximate respectability, and the benefit of twenty years to absolve her of her indiscretions, suddenly feels guilty again.

She hasn't said anything to Mark; of course she hasn't said anything to Mark, though she has to admit she feels a desire to tell *someone* what has happened, something like the compulsion she remembers feeling as a teenager, when she had a crush on a boy, to bring up his name in even the blandest and most nonstarting conversational circumstances, just so she could say it, and so she could remind whomever she was talking to that his life—to whatever meager degree—brushed against hers, *Oh yeah, Jonathan likes orange juice too.* But there's nobody to tell; almost nobody who is in her life now was in her life then.

She lets the steam out of the bathroom, changes into a gauzy black dress and a string of turquoise beads Mark got her on a business trip to San Francisco. She's drying her hair when she hears, over the motor, the unmistakable tenor of Brady Grimes, and she swears under her breath, because she's supposed to have five more minutes, but she also should have known that Brady and Francine would show up early because they always do, brazen assertion of their closeness with Mark and Julia, maybe, or perhaps some kind of fuck-you power grab, *we're so rich we don't abide by the conventional confines of time.*

She's frantically blinking on her mascara when Ben appears behind her in the mirror like a benevolent murderer.

"Oh!" she says, and rakes a tiny black trail of lines under her left eye. "Shit. Hi, sweet." She yanks a length of toilet paper from the roll, stands on tiptoe to kiss Ben on the cheek before folding it into a wad and, delicately, spitting in it. She dabs at her face, addressing his reflection. "That shirt's nice."

Her children both inherited their father's height—a family of lanks, and she, five foot six and shrinking!—and Ben too has Mark's floppy self-possession, a desire for poise if not quite the knack for it, a dog that's yet to grow into its paws. She turns to straighten his collar. Up close, he looks exhausted, she sees, hollow-eyed, a little stubbly, his jaw turning the bend to right-angled adulthood. He's in the second year of his PhD in geophysics, working as a teaching assistant to undergrads, and she tries, sometimes, to imagine what he must look like holding court over a classroom.

"When's the last time you slept?" she asks, facing the mirror again.

"Do I look that bad?" Surprisingly, he sits on the edge of the bathtub, leaning against the tile wall and smiling tiredly, reminding her so much of Mark she has to force her gaze back to her own reflection.

"Not bad, just a little—peaked."

"*Peaked?*" He lets out a low whistle and picks up one of her little pots of exfoliator, worrying it from hand to hand. It is, upon examination, actually quite weird that he's in here with her; Alma has always been their more dependent child, even in her mean cloistered teendom, but Ben has been fairly autonomous since his toddlerhood. He frequently drops by unbidden to watch basketball or camp out in his old bedroom for a few days when his roommate's girlfriend is visiting, but he doesn't often linger like this, particularly alone with his mother in the bathroom. She sheathes her mascara wand and starts dabbing on her lipstick as she casually—careful, always, this delicate drawing-out dance with the people you've given birth to—asks him, "Everything okay with you, honeybunch?"

She didn't figure out how to be a mom to him—didn't figure out *being*, period, really—until he was, as a person, well under way, so these interactions, lacking a solid foundation, tend to unfold haphazardly, stilted and with only a marginal likelihood of success. It doesn't help, in this case, that she hears the register of other voices joining Brady's downstairs.

"Yeah," Ben says. It comes out weak and halting, the hint of a question. Where Alma is effusive and hyperbolic, Ben has always taken his time articulating his thoughts—be they deep existential revelations or basic preferences—letting them drip out molasses-like, shy and slothful; she recalls so many early-morning moments during his adolescence, everyone running late and rushing to get out the door but frozen on the threshold, like the unassuming victims of a dormant volcano, while they waited for him to decide if he wanted an orange or a banana in his lunch.

She blots her lips, one ear tuned to downstairs—she hears Pari exclaiming dutifully over her cocktail swords—and waits.

"Just a sort of—" He shakes his head.

"A sort of what, sweet?" she asks, and regrets her tone. If you rush Ben, you run the risk of throwing him off his game, doubling his articulation time. "Honey," she begins, but she's cut off by a shrill summoning from Erica, who already sounds drunk: "Julia I'm *trying* to do your job for you but we can't seem to find the Cam*par*i."

In the time it takes her friend to deliver this line, Ben's face has gone back to normal, clear-eyed and eager to please. Their easier child, accommodating and resilient and—well, she doesn't like to throw around the word *perfect*, but he's close, Ben is, and while it used to worry her that his resiliency was born out of necessity, an adaptation to compensate for her own motherly shortcomings, enough time has passed that it now simply seems part of who he is.

"No worries, Mom," Ben says, and then Mark calls up "Jules?" and she shouts, over her shoulder, "Be there in a second," and in the time *that* takes, Ben has gotten up, is leading the way out of the bathroom, down the hallway and then the stairs, where everyone is waiting.

She discovered, sometime in the last fifteen years, that she not only has the capacity to be a formidable hostess but actually *enjoys* it most of the time, sweeping around in her flowy dress like a kind of balletic wombat, refilling glasses and encouraging the consumption of canapes. Tonight's guest list is a roster of couples who follow an unspoken mathematical formula: one half of the pair makes money, the other compensates socially or artistically. Pari works in private equity but her husband, Alan, is an ER doctor at Swedish Covenant; Ted is the head of engineering at Motorola while Carol chairs the social work department at a private college downstate; Tim and Erica are both public defenders, but she's the heiress to a small manufacturing fortune. And Julia and Mark fit snugly in their own slot, she a part-time librarian while he dwells, amply salaried, in the swanky State Street offices of AllAboard Ventures. It's a careful, upstanding balance of doing good and saving face, precisely the right note struck between self-righteousness and hypocrisy. Normally she has easy access to a repository of affection for these people, her friends, but tonight she feels herself beginning to flag earlier than usual.

"May I be excused?" Alma asks, appearing at her elbow with all the prim obsequiousness of a Dickensian governess. "I have to study." She meets Julia's eyes fully, a challenge, because it's a Saturday and she's a second-semester senior.

"Sure," Julia says, because she is afraid of Alma. "Take Suzanne with you."

"I need Ben's help," Alma says, pushing her luck now. "With my AP Enviro."

Ben, behind his sister, looks to her hopefully, the adult she'd seen earlier in the mirror now ten again, eager to go out and play. And because she is so glad her children have each other, that they *like* each other, she assents, and watches them go, taking a detour through the kitchen, where Alma will likely pilfer a glass of champagne.

Someone, apparently trying to drive them all to self-harm, has turned on Joni Mitchell. She refills her own glass of wine.

"Excuse me a minute," she says to nobody in particular, and slips into the yard. It's cold outside, enough that she is surprised to see she's not alone: the silhouette of Brady Grimes, and then Brady in totality, the pinnacle of performative wealth, insufferable edifice of Patek Philippe wristwatch and the overly texturized haircut Alma calls a *bro-flow*. He has a bottle of wine and is, from the looks of it, drinking it without a glass. She had been mistaken, earlier; he has come without his wife and offered no explanation of Francine's whereabouts.

"Am I interrupting?" she asks, and he looks up at her on a few-second delay, smiling sleepily; his gaze, as it always has, lingers on her for an extra beat.

"Am I in trouble?" he asks, and pats the space next to him on the love seat. He's been Mark's best friend since they were toddlers, and yet he still, after nearly thirty years, makes Julia a little uneasy. "Did Mark send you out here to reprimand me?"

"He did not."

"Shouldn't you be in there hostessing?"

"I needed a minute," she said.

"So did I."

"You appear to be drinking wine straight from the bottle."

"I left my scotch inside," he says. "And remembered you keep a cooler out here."

"Please." She rolls her eyes. "Make yourself at home. Where's Francine tonight?"

A darkness passes over his face, a second-long storm. "Out," he says. "Traveling."

"Out traveling?"

"She's in Philly," he says, and then, tacking it on like he's just remembered something, "visiting her parents." He swigs from the bottle. "*Sláinte*," he says. "Here's to Mark."

"Here's to," she says, tapping his bottle with her glass.

Brady starts humming the opening *da-na-na*s of the Beatles birthday song. "Did he tell you I had a masseuse come to the office yesterday? I figured it'd be a nice way to help everyone unwind."

"I'm very surprised that's something you're legally allowed to do," she says. Brady is annoyingly savvy and scarily successful, and also terribly prone to the type of faddishness only attainable by the elite: relaxation retreats in Rio, helicopter drive-bys of sacred ruins, live performances at corporate events by Poi Dog Pondering and Perpetual Groove. He drives a Range Rover Sport with a FREE TIBET bumper sticker.

"Always a good time to celebrate our guy." The *our* bothers her. Brady and Francine are the two other people in the world who know Mark almost as well as she does, and both of them have loved him for longer. But she follows Brady's gaze into the house, through the doorway to the living room. Her handsome husband with his graph-paper shirt and his ardent listening face: she is, in fact, happy for an occasion to be glad that he exists.

"It is," she says.

"Who'd've thought we'd make it here," Brady says, and she gets nervous. Brady and Francine were the only ones of their friends who were around for that time, the Helen time; Brady and Francine were the reason they'd moved to Helen's neighborhood in the first place.

"What?" she says archly, but Brady doesn't notice her tone, just leans back and sighs.

"Just thinking about how *young* we used to be." It's an innocuous statement, if also a trite one; it's not directed at her, she sees, but to some dark internal space, whatever disturbing depths exist beneath Brady's curated façade, his artisanal moccasins—he is currently in a problematically-appropriating-Eastern-cultures-after-spending-two-weeks-at-the-Four-Seasons-in-Bangalore phase—and the disturbingly deep vee of his linen shirt.

"Speak for yourself," she says.

"Sorry," he says, with a sibilant hiss that further betrays his drunkenness. "*You* look the same as the day I met you."

She tries not to feel flattered. "Okay, Casanova."

"The rest of us, though, are getting super fucking old. Facing down the unending forward march of time. The era of obsolescence."

"Did you learn about that in college? Intro to Philosophy at— Where was it? Somewhere in Indiana; I can't quite remember . . ."

How do you know a Notre Dame man when you see one? A joke Helen Russo made once. *He'll tell you.*

Brady sways a little against her, sighs again.

"*Sixty*," he says. "My turn's coming up in May." He pouts, and a lock of his hair falls over his forehead, and he looks for a moment like a petulant female toddler.

"Sounds like someone's having a death crisis," she says. "I'm not unsympathetic. It's just that I had mine when I was about ten."

He smiles at her. "Oh, Julia," he says, leaning his head back. "I'll bet you did."

Later, when they've seen everyone off, loaded the dishwasher and said goodbye to Ben and good night to Alma and to Suzanne, who has fallen deeply asleep beneath Alma's duvet, she trails Mark into their room. He's stretched out on the bed already, eyes closed; she unearths two bright silk scarves from her dresser drawer.

"Hey," he says, "what were you and Brady talking about outside?"

"How great you are."

"I'm a little worried about him."

"You're harshing my mellow," she says, sitting beside him on the edge of the bed and putting a hand on his leg. "And I haven't given you your birthday present yet."

"I thought the party was my present." He opens his eyes and smiles at her. "You also got me new headphones."

She takes his hand, folds the scarves gently into his palm. They've laid so much to rest; Helen Russo has, ostensibly at least, taken a backseat to the daily slog of child rearing and oil changes and high cholesterol, to the preposterous political landscape, to the solicitous reciprocal acknowledgment of aging bodies and lifelong commitment. But she feels unsettled, still, and her desire to connect with him in this way—reaffirming something—is making her edgy.

"What's this?" Mark asks her. He studies the scarves, one geometrically patterned and the other splashily bedecked with a number of small, brightly colored horses.

She offers him both of her wrists, undersides up. "Just something different."

Mark stares at her. "You want me to tie you up?"

She retracts her arms. "Well, when you say it like that."

He dubiously lifts one of the scarves, trailing it in front of him. "Huh."

She sinks back against her pillow, now a little embarrassed. "I thought it might be fun."

He studies her.

"But if you aren't up for it . . ."

"I didn't say that." He leans in and kisses her. "Okay. Sure. Why not."

A moment later, he kneels over her dubiously, tying the knots.

"I don't understand what— It seems like— Is this too tight?"

"Not at all."

"This feels untoward," he says, when her wrists are secured. He loops his thumb and forefinger around one of them and strokes her veins. "What if Ollie were to walk in?"

"She'd be traumatized for life," she says. "But I locked the door."

She lifts her head a little—the angle of her arms, as it turns out, is murder on her back—and she kisses his chest, tilts her chin to meet his face. He kisses her once and she can tell he means it to be perfunctory but she catches his lips between her teeth and impels him down to her.

"Fuck, Jules, that hurt." He swipes at his mouth as though looking for blood.

"Really?"

He lowers his hips gently onto hers, regarding her with a puerile kind of amusement, like they're kids ditching school. "Only a little."

"Good." She enjoys the sensation—splayed out across their bed like some kind of botched crucifixion—though she can't bring herself to imagine how she looks, goose bumps on her pale, naked flesh, half-covered by their hypoallergenic medium-warmth comforter.

"I just don't understand what we're supposed to do," Mark says.

"What we normally do," she says. "Just—have your way with me. Just like normal. Except minus my arms."

"*Have* my *way* with you?"

She closes her eyes, counts a breath in and out. "I know you respect me," she says. "I trust you with every fiber of my being."

"I never knew this interested you."

"Well, look at that. When's the last time I surprised you?"

"You don't need to surprise me," he says. "I like you how you are."

"I like you how you are too." She looks up at him steadily. "Do you trust me?"

It is no longer a loaded question; he no longer has to think about it the way that he used to, and because he wasn't in the grocery with her this afternoon—because he wouldn't recognize Helen Russo even if he had been—he smiles easily.

"Of course I do," he says.

"Then make love to me. Like this."

"Okay," he says. "Okay, just let me— I just need to—*ease* into it a little bit; I'm not used to such—excitement." He kisses her again, cups a hand over her left breast, rubs his thumb along the arch of her right eyebrow. When he lowers himself on top of her, his weight feels different, oddly distributed without the counterbalance of her upper-body strength.

"There you go," she says.

"Don't use your baby voice."

"I wasn't."

"You *were*."

"I don't even *have* a—just—okay—just, like—there you go." She exhales, drops her pitch a few octaves. "*There* you go."

"My wife, Boris Karloff."

It makes her laugh. "Humor me," she says, and he does, deftly, working only with the dexterity of her legs and hips, and eventually she comes, so intensely that he bends to quiet her with his mouth, whispering, winded, laughing, down her esophagus, "You're blowing our cover."

"Happy birthday," she says to him later, when they're falling asleep, the scarves refolded in neat rectangles on her dresser.

"Thank you," he says into her hair, and she curls against him virtuously, like a shrimp.

She doesn't mean to think of Nathaniel; she has never once, since things ended, intentionally thought of Nathaniel, but it happens sometimes anyway. The smell of his sheets in the carriage house, lavender and sweat, and how it felt when he laughed between her legs. His voice is in her head now: *Julia, Julia, Julia.*

"Julia," Mark says, the word warm on her neck.

"Hm?" She presses herself closer to him, and feels sleep in his limbs. It's been so long that he doesn't need to actually say it—that he loves her.

4

Helen Russo had been a volunteer docent at the botanic garden and she had a big, industrious ponytail and she was so breathtakingly nice to Ben—explaining the differences between the cacti, letting him hand-feed spring greens to the rhinoceros iguana—that Julia had started crying a little bit, right in the middle of the herbaceous perennials.

"Sorry," she said when she saw Helen notice. "I'm fine."

"I wonder," Helen said, unearthing a printed silk scarf from her pocket, "about the accuracy of that statement."

She proffered the scarf, and Julia took it, laughing a little, embarrassed, unthinkingly blotting her eyes and realizing, simultaneously, how expensive the fabric felt. Her wrist recoiled instinctively, like she'd just smeared ink all over her face. The scarf was, upon examination, Hermès, probably vintage, bright aqua silk dotted with vaguely offensive-seeming tribal totems.

"Oh, God," she said, but Helen waved her away.

"Should I ask?"

She was unsure of how to answer. *Yes, please, ask; I am a complete fucking head case.* It was probably wise to unearth the truth of this on occasion, expose it to some sun. Ben was in a deep squat before the iguana habitat, tracing the animal's slow path, his tiny finger not quite touching the glass because even at three he somehow knew how to move appropriately through the world; he was somehow autonomously learning to function as a human being despite the fact that his mother was Julia, despite the fact that the botanic garden was the third place they'd visited that day in a demented roster of *motion*, after a hearty climb on the whale fountain at the park and a visit to see Captain and Tennille, the probably incestuous library hamsters, and it was only ten-thirty a.m. and the thought of the day stretching before them made her feel physically sick—despite this he somehow conducted himself with curiosity and grace even though she was so tired that she was tempted to ask Helen, whom she'd met six seconds ago, if she might just lay her head in her lap for a few minutes and rest. *Helen*—with her wide-legged linen trousers and her ergonomic sandals and her big round sunglasses holding back the flyaways of her gray-glinting ponytail—had one of those laps, a mom lap, a whole mom *aura* that just made you want to lean your weight against her, let her hold you up for a little bit.

"Sweetheart?" Helen said. Of course she was one of those women who could easily refer to strangers with terms of maternal endearment. Even around Ben's toddler friends Julia became stunted and awkward, addressing them by their full names—"Good morning, Ava R." "That's a very nice backpack you're carrying, Evangeline; is that new?"—as though they were her employers, or very short visiting dignitaries, waiting to be impressed.

"I'm not normally like this," Julia said, omitting the addendum *in public*. "I'm not—" She laughed a little, tried to adopt a more casual demeanor, whimsically harried instead of just a nutcase. "I haven't slept much lately and it's—just one of those—those . . ."

"One of *those*," Helen said familiarly, perfectly, patting her arm. "I remember them well."

She and Helen were shoulder to shoulder then, watching Ben like an infomercial, the universal stance of unacquainted parents taking in a pee-wee soccer game.

"They're delicious at this age, aren't they?" Helen said, and lowered herself laboriously to one knee beside Ben. "This young lady is almost forty years old," she said to him, gesturing to the iguana, and he blinked at her, nervous, reverent. "Older than your mama, I bet." She glanced up at Julia, winked, and Julia felt something like a stirring, nonsexual but not decidedly so, a *rousing*, of sorts; she couldn't remember the last time anyone had winked at her. It filled her with a kind of complicitous warmth. "Rumor has it their longevity is linked to abstinence and an avoidance of meat. I'd happily abide at least half of that."

She looked again to Julia and Julia laughed, sort of, and then another kid ambled up and shoved his way in, elbowing Ben, hitting the glass with the flat of his hand. Ben, startled, rose, came over to Julia and leaned against her legs, and though she was happy to have him back in her immediate proximity it made her want to cry, her tiny kid who'd already resigned himself to cave to those who talked louder than he did.

"Why's his head so big?" the kid asked, and Helen, not missing a beat, said, "I could ask the same of you."

The kid looked up at her, surprised.

"Don't touch the glass, please," she said. "Someone else was having a turn." She held out a hand to Ben, who glanced up at Julia for the go-ahead before taking a tentative step forward, taking Helen's hand, taking his rightful place before the celibate iguana. "As I was saying," Helen said, lowering her voice to Ben like they were old friends, "they're also an incredibly hearty species—they can lose their whole *tail* and it grows back—though that's no reason for them to be subjected to little Neanderthals if they can avoid it."

Julia watched them—Helen placidly sharing a poetic factoid about how iguanas had also been known to survive falls from great heights—aware of feeling at once self-conscious and soothed; she should have been the one guiding her son around life's roadblocks, teaching him scientific trivia that also had metaphoric self-help resonance pertaining to resilience and personal growth, but she was grateful not to be for that one moment, so very grateful to stand back and watch as somebody else did it for her.

"You're so patient with him," she said as Helen rose from her squat.

"Just practice. I had five of my own," Helen said.

Her purest nightmare. "Oh, wow."

"All grown men now, of course, in name, at least, and difficult to find patience for in entirely different ways. Yours seems like a smart one."

"He is," she said, and then, nervously, "I mean, he's— I didn't mean that in a bragging way, like he's not going to be recruited by Microsoft anytime soon, but he's—yes, developmentally up to—

you know, par." She reddened deeply. She'd simply wanted to distinguish herself from the mothers swanning around Serenity Smiles who pointedly slipped into conversation that their children were deftly navigating cellos twice their size and conversing fluently with the Somali checker at the co-op.

"What are you two doing right now?" Helen asked.

It took Julia a moment to process. What was she *ever* doing? She'd been planning, up until nine seconds ago, a complicated list of ways to fill the rest of the day: Whole Foods, a driving-induced nap for Ben, the single daily allotted thirty-minute rerun of *The Muppet Show.*

"I'm going to go eat some ice cream," Helen said. It was ten-forty-nine a.m. "Why don't you follow me?"

She was about to demur, reflexively, because declining invitations was one of the perks of being tied to small children, and also because it seemed unequivocally weird, all of it. Her ability to interpret the most basic conversational cues was all but dead; her social muscles had atrophied perhaps beyond hope. She was unsure of the etiquette, the first-date rules of friendship as an adult.

"I don't want to impose," she said, but she said it with some reluctance, because she *did* in fact want to impose, she realized; she wanted very much to sit across a table from someone who wasn't a zombie like she was; she wanted to have a warm, easygoing adult friend with social skills and survival instincts and a big happy ponytail. She wanted, specifically, she realized, to sit across a table from Helen, and so she nodded.

They got cups from Flowgurt, the soft-serve place connected to the yoga studio, and then they put Ben in the stroller and headed out on a walk around the park, her second visit that day. By her own rule book, she was not supposed to double up on her weekly destination spots—not just the parks but the arboretum, the pottery painting place, the gymnastics center—both for variety and to avoid leaving too much of a footprint, like an alcoholic spreading patronage across various liquor stores.

"Are you new to town?" Helen asked.

"Sort of. Ben's dad and I moved here when he was—well, still a baby, so I guess not so new."

"Divorced?" Helen asked, and she looked up.

"Pardon?"

"You and Ben's dad aren't together anymore?"

She'd called him "Ben's dad" instead of "my husband."

"Oh, no, we are. We— Almost five years."

Marriage was trying; marriage was burying the hatchet. But they had not buried any of their hatchets; instead she'd covered the hatchets with an assortment of decorative hand towels and they were both pretending that the hatchets didn't exist. She felt Mark's eyes on her sometimes and wondered what he was seeing, if everyone's marriage ended up like theirs had, two people who'd once been mad for each other stranded on opposite sides of the kitchen, dimly aware of excess weight and emotional transgressions, Animaniacs-shaped pasta about to boil over on the stove, trying to remember how it had been before.

"Do I *sound* divorced?" she asked.

Helen laughed. "What does divorced sound like?"

She started crying again, just a little. Helen passed her a wad of paper napkins.

"Boy, someone's having a day, huh," Helen said pleasantly.

"I'm sorry," she said again. One of the primary reasons she so ardently avoided the other preschool moms was because they all, she was certain, regarded her with pity and confusion—*The rest of us got over that in the first few weeks*, they seemed to be thinking. *Why are you still like this over three years out?*

"There's nothing harder," Helen said, "than being someone's mom."

"Oh no it's really not so—" But what was she saying; of *course* it was so bad; being someone's mom was the unequivocal definition of *so bad*.

"The key, I found," Helen said, "is waiting to cry until after they go to bed."

"Yeah, don't worry, I cry then too," Julia said, and Helen laughed again.

She almost couldn't believe it was happening, that she had somehow willed this circumstance into being, recreationally enjoying frozen dessert before noon with an adult woman who probably kept both an EpiPen and Chanel lipstick in her purse. She suddenly remembered Helen's scarf—her snot invisible but undeniably soaked into its sumptuous fibers, stuffed hastily and unthinkingly into the shallow recesses of her own purse—and scrambled to get it. "I'm so sorry, here, thank you," she said, pressing it to Helen, who took it in stride, knotting it around the strap of her bag, dismissive of its attached effluvia, once again emanating the hallmark of her effortless maternity in a way that she clearly took for granted and Julia would eternally envy.

"Is it specific things?" Helen asked. "Or just everything?"

The basic existential facts, the broad strokes: that she was miserable, but that it wasn't entirely surprising. Also, that she was not *allowed* to have the problems she had was another wrench in the system—or she was not, at least, allowed to refer to them as problems.

"It's not—anything really. I'm—" How to complete that sentence, though? *I'm desperately unhappy. Congenitally ungrateful. Awash in constant panic, perpetually worried that maybe it's always going to be this way.* She opened her mouth with the intention of making a joke—*I'll apparently never meet a massive, glaring privilege that I won't figure out how to resent* or *What does Chekhov say about happy families? The moms are always fucking nuts?*—but she couldn't manage to get it out. "Just kind of tired."

She was filled, constantly, with that sick, stale feeling of having been awake too long, trilling in her ears and a sugary ache deep in the roots of her teeth.

"Are you depressed?" Helen asked, and Julia nearly choked on her yogurt but Helen just regarded her, even and calm.

"Oh I'm—" But she had the sudden ability to see herself from a distance, Helen's distance, and the general excuses she made—to her husband, to herself: that she was just having a bad day, just needed a few more hours of sleep—felt comically false.

"I think I could be," she said. "Not that I— I mean, I don't have any real *reason* to be, but nevertheless I guess I—"

"You don't need a reason," Helen said. "That's not always how it works. Has it been going on for long?"

Approximately thirty-six years, she did not say. "Not as long as that iguana's been around," she said, but Helen didn't smile. "I've always been like this to some degree. I mean, not—*this*, not accosting strangers and telling them all of my problems."

"To be fair," Helen said, "I asked. And you haven't actually told me what your problems are."

"I've never been completely sure what they are, to be honest," she said. "I'm not—an especially happy person, generally. It's just kind of—who I am."

Meager a step as it was, she hadn't gotten this far with her ineffectual therapist, and she felt the need to scale back so as not to scare Helen away completely.

"What about you?" she said. "Tell me about—you." She'd lost the knack, since she spent all her time conversing with a child, for making introductory conversation as an adult that didn't sound either predatory or hostile; attempting to compliment one of Mark's colleagues at a cocktail party recently she had accidentally said, "Do you always wear your hair like that?"

But Helen was unfazed, reciting cleanly the roster of her life: she was recently retired, spending her days in the garden; her husband, Pete, was a nontraditional student at the University of Chicago.

"He's been taking one class a semester since I've known him, more or less. By this time in the next millennium he might just about have a completely unmarketable bachelor's degree in classical poetry." Helen stirred her yogurt. "Not especially *lucrative*, his lifestyle, but he's very charming, so I keep him around."

"Wow, how did you—with five kids? Survive?"

"I said my husband didn't make any money," Helen said. "I never said that *I* didn't. Tell me, dear, do you call yourself a feminist?"

She blanched, then saw, blessedly, that the woman was joking. Helen nudged her shoulder against Julia's as they walked, physical contact that startled her, excited her.

"I'm sorry," she said.

"I'm an attorney." Helen smiled at her. "What about you? How do you spend your days?"

This particular phrasing was somehow worse than "What do you do?" She hated those questions, all, really, just dressed-up versions of "Who *are* you?" a query to which she hadn't known the answer possibly ever but especially lately.

"I'm not an attorney," she said.

She leaned over the awning at the top of the stroller. Ben was sucking contemplatively on his green plastic spoon, distracted by a gaggle of geese. The sight of him calmed her, legitimized her; surely it was unethical to use your children for this purpose, but first of all it seemed like everyone did to some degree, and second of all—of this she was certain—it was better than the alternative, using them for nothing at all. Should she tell Helen about her slipshod parenting philosophy, one that could be basically boiled down to *doing better than her own mother*? About Mark's totally elusive but semantically impressive job that allowed them to pay for their dumb suburban house while also keeping him away from said house most of the time? About the minutiae of her days with Ben, serving him sickening circles of hot dog and green beads of edamame, scalding her wrist testing his bathwater, reading him *Snuggle Puppy* for the thirty thousandth time, trying to keep him alive and teach him how to be a good person in spite of the fact that she herself felt neither good nor alive most of the time?

"I *was* working in a library, before I had Ben."

"Do you miss it?"

"Sometimes. I used to miss it more. But now I wonder— I'm not sure I have the energy."

"Different things take different kinds of energy," Helen said generously. "You've got full hands." And it was, of course, precisely true but also entirely not, particularly to someone like Helen, who'd evidently managed to do forty thousand times more than Julia had: Julia's was not remotely an unmanageable life in the logistical sense but she often felt like someone had unrolled a large and debilitatingly heavy rug on top of her. They were back at the entrance of the botanic garden. She brushed away her tears, stopped and squatted down next to the stroller to dab sprinkle smears away from Ben's mouth with a napkin. She felt Helen watching her again.

"Like I said, Pete stayed home with the boys," Helen said, "but the strangest thing I remember about having young children is how interminably the time moves, just these days upon days upon days, and every single one of them feels a million years long, but then suddenly months have gone by, enough time for a new baby to be born or one of the kids to start kindergarten, or *college* for God's sake, and it— The amount of time I've lost *contemplating* that passage of time is—well, really kind of astounding."

"Yeah," Julia said. "I do a fair amount of—contemplation."

"I'd like to ask you a favor, Julia," Helen said. "If your contemplation ever starts feeling like—too much. Would you call me, please?"

"Oh, no," she said, because it was what she was used to doing. "No, I'm—fine, really; you don't have to—"

"I'd *like* to," Helen said. "How about we couch it that way? Forget needing a reason. Would you just do me a favor and call me sometime? I'd *like* for you to call me."

"You really don't have to—"

"I'm a sad, lonely retiree," Helen said, laying it on thick, making Julia laugh. "I am positively *atrophying* and I just sit by the phone, constantly, waiting for anyone at all; would you please do me a favor, Julia, and call me?"

"Yes," she said. "Yes, I'll call you."

How was your date?" Celia asked, bleary-eyed, when she and Mark got home that night. Celia was their savior, the baby-sitter who sang Ben to sleep with Tom Chapin songs and washed his dinner dishes by hand even though they had a dishwasher. Julia had the urge to sit her down and open a bottle of wine and tell it to her straight. *You really want to know, Cargo Pants? I fell asleep in the car before we even got to the restaurant.*

Narcoleptics Anonymous, she called it in her head: she and Mark had a standing dinner date every other Wednesday, a whole stupid rigamarole where she put on lipstick and didn't let herself wear a nursing bra and they went to Randolph Street or Lincoln Park or occasionally some exalted hole-in-the-wall in a distant and ominous suburb, and during the drive they talked about all the regular boring things that regular boring parents talked about while dating under duress, though they'd both rather have been sleeping or masturbating or watching *The Sopranos* on separate televisions:

Ben's achievements and Ben's sleep habits and Ben's moods and oh my God did you notice that he's started using the word *actually* all the time, isn't it hilarious, plus there's an advertisement on the mail table for something called *pirate camp* that she heard about from one of the Serenity Smiles moms and it's supposed to be good for character development, they don't teach the kids actual *piracy* but instead more virtuous traits less often associated with the profession, resiliency and thinking on your feet. This had floated them all the way to the restaurant—tonight an overpriced "Ameri-fusion" place in Andersonville that had dumb cocktails named things like Gravity's Gin-Sloe and Portnoy's Campari—and through a painful recitation of the wine list from the mean hipster who was waiting on them.

"Fun," she said weakly, hanging up her jacket, rummaging around for her wallet.

"Rollicking," Mark said, and he touched her back for just a second with something that felt like tenderness.

After leaving Helen, she and Ben had filled their afternoon in the usual incremental way, lunchtime, Lego time, coloring time, multiple snack breaks, but the whole time she felt high on something, on adult conversation or social stimulation or possibly just Helen herself. She considered how candid she'd been with Helen—it embarrassed her now—and how out of the question that felt where Mark was concerned. She hadn't been truly honest with him in as long as she could remember.

"How was he?" she asked, feeling guilty for not being the one to sing her son to sleep.

"Awesome," Celia said. "We made Colorforms. He ate all his dinner. I'm doing this thing with him before bed where we tell a story together? Back and forth? Sentence by sentence? So he gets to contribute, too? He's so imaginative?"

She was sure that being an imaginative toddler had something to do with having brain-dead parents, some kind of overcompensatory cognitive coping mechanism.

"Thanks for everything," she said. "We're so lucky to have you."

Julia paid Celia—noting, distantly, that the amount of money they now spent on an average night out (dinner plus cocktails plus babysitter plus subscription to premium cable channels that baby-sitter enjoyed watching after kid went to bed plus take-out stipend to keep babysitter decadently fed and unembittered) was almost as much as a plane ticket to Greece.

Later, in bed, she listened to Mark brushing his teeth while she attempted to wrangle her thoughts. Every day her head spouted out a frenetic ticker tape like cable news ranging from the quotidian—*call plumber re: powder room sink, almost out of peanut butter*—to the philosophical—*Ben's new dentist looks like Gorbachev, do other people spend as much time as I do feeling sad about fat animals*—and at night she couldn't figure out how to turn it off.

Another thought she thought frequently, maniacally, indig-nantly: *it wasn't always like this!* She rationalized that of course this could be said for anything, for everything, and she acknowledged as well that *she*, to some degree, had always been the way that she was—dubious, avoidant—but she had not always felt as ill at ease in the world as she did at present.

"What are you thinking about?" Mark asked, coming out of the bathroom.

"Nothing." She swallowed. "I just really wish we could know who killed JonBenét Ramsey."

He studied her for a minute, then climbed into bed, fiddled with his alarm clock before rolling onto his side to face her. The tender-ness of his gaze felt oppressive; she worked hard not to squirm.

"Tonight was fun," he said, such a blatant lie that she couldn't help but smile at him. He'd had a glass and a half of wine, which was pushing it for Mark, and she could see it on his face. "What? It was. I had a good time, at least."

"Me too," she said, and he worked his fingers through her hair, pulled her closer, but then he stopped, moved his head back to look at her. "What?" she asked nervously.

"Did you just—*brace* yourself?"

She swallowed. "Of course I didn't."

"It felt like you were bracing yourself for me to touch you."

"I wasn't," she said. "I was just adjusting my back."

"If you don't want to, you can just tell me."

"It's not that," she said, then: "I—do want to."

He continued to watch her.

"I do, I just think I should probably go to the chiropractor."

"Tonight?"

"Soon."

He paused. "You know, I read this article."

She closed her eyes. "Uh-huh."

"About marriage while parenting young kids."

"Sounds fascinating."

"There were all sorts of statistics about the importance of maintaining intimacy even when—well, even when life may not seem that *conducive* to being intimate, the importance of even very basic forms of intimacy, and the consensus was— I think we should be touching more."

"Like—our bodies?"

"*Yes*, our bodies. What else?"

She didn't reply, stared up at the ceiling, her face burning. She had been content to assume that her sex drive would return eventually, like a nomadic seafaring partner.

"Are you even attracted to me anymore?" he asked.

"I— God, I— Sure I am, I just—"

"*Sure* you are?"

She had never, until after Ben was born, had the impulse to fake it with Mark, never felt the need and also didn't trust herself to be a convincing actress; Mark was many annoying things, but completely oblivious was not one of them, and she had always been attracted to him, always—until they'd waded into the sluggish unsexy ennui that was parenthood—had *fun* with him.

"I'm sorry," she said. "Did your treatise on *touching* mention anything about how not everyone bounces back right away after they have a baby?"

"It's been over three *years* since you had a baby," Mark said. "And I don't think it's fair for you to keep using Ben as some kind of get-out-of-jail-free card, for you to—"

"Are you the jailer in this scenario?"

She watched him hold his breath for a second.

"Forget it," he said, rolling away from her. "Forget I even tried."

Good old agendaless Mark, across the table from her at the restaurant. He wanted another kid. They'd initially discussed three, but that was before they knew was it was like to have one; lately he'd been floating the line *well, maybe just one more*, like he was offering her some sort of prize.

"I've just been thinking about it," he'd said at dinner, like he was talking about trying a new brand of socks—and she'd downed half a glass of wine in one sip. The gist, from Mark's vantage point, was vexing and unsurprising: she was not getting any younger, he really thought Ben would benefit from having a sibling, why else did they buy a three-bedroom house?

She spent a lot of time contemplating a roster of replies: that she had begun to view her advancing age through the opposite lens, one that cared less about taking advantage of her remaining youth and was instead enthusiastic about giving up. That life itself was not some sort of if-you-build-it-they-will-come situation in which empty rooms were required to be filled with children of your own creation.

She struggled, perpetually, to articulate it to him, to his bright optimistic dad-face and his scientific practicality. *I will literally combust if we have another kid. Like oxygen and—* But she could never remember what other elements were involved in the creation of fire.

Let's wait a little bit is what she usually settled on, nice temperate mom-ish in-between, *let's practice being patient; let's use our inside voices; let's try our hardest to avoid another domestic catastrophe.*

But Mark was a good dad. He was hands-on, energetic, constantly delighted to be in Ben's presence. He'd read her Pablo Neruda when she was in labor (even though she one thousand percent did not ask him to), and he went into work late once a week so he could drop Ben off at school. She wasn't exactly sure how any of it worked, but she was fairly certain that you were not allowed to dislike your husband because he was a good dad. You were supposed to want that; she knew this. You were supposed to want everything for your kid and the dregs for yourself.

"Now's not the best time," she'd said to him, ambiguous enough that it could mean *I'm not ovulating at this precise moment* or *Let's wait until I'm not such a fucking nutjob.*

She wished she hadn't bothered with the regular-person bra, the only not-sports-or-nursing bra she owned, which was ridiculous because she'd stopped breastfeeding two years ago and was not remotely athletic, but her nursing bras were just more *comfortable;* she should at least be allowed to be *comfortable* if they were going to persist like this, suffer the indignity of what had become of their dialogue without two sharp smiles of underwire digging into her sides.

"You can be doing whatever you want here, Jules," Mark had said. That had always been their agreement: progressive, free-loving Mark would never force his wife to stay at home with his child. And she knew this, bone-level—that if she woke up one morning and decided to go back to work, take up crocheting or the piano, Mark would support her entirely. He already agreed to Ben's two and a half days a week of preschool even though she mostly used their son's time away to listen to the Bee Gees and stare catatonically out of various windows.

She swore to herself that she'd be better than her own mom. She promised she'd be present and lively; she promised she'd never be the mother whom you missed when she was away but who disappointed you when she actually showed up. But so far those nurturing instincts had only shown themselves in the form of her son's continued existence and in the way she climbed into his bed some nights and held him while he was sleeping, in awe of his autonomy and his sweetness and the way that she could smell the crook of his neck and be transported, instantly, back to those early days when everything seemed like it might work out. She'd been happy when he was born, happier than she could believe; she should have known it wouldn't last.

"It's easier said than done," she'd said, and her husband had inhaled, seemed to be collecting himself, as though being around her required an effortful tolerance. But his voice, when he spoke, was softer than she expected: "I know it is, Jules."

She felt herself soften in turn; this was Mark, elementally: a carer, an empath, her ally.

Mark had taken her to see Pearl Jam on their third date. He had an incredibly full head of hair. He was thoughtful and tidy, and he developed, unbidden, a routine where he made her breakfast on Sunday mornings. He loved her, enthusiastically and with a whole heart, and that was supposed to be enough. Nobody had warned her about all of the loneliness involved, his early mornings and her militant breastfeeding regimen that first year, the weird noises the kitchen floor made at night when she padded across it in search of ill-advised snacks, the way you stopped diving into bed together and started falling, anticlimactically, into unattractive REM sleep where you snored or murmured or conversed, mechanically, about the grocery list. Mark had found it so funny when she conducted an entire unconscious conversation with him about full-fat versus nonfat yogurt but it had scared the shit out of her, how boring she was even when she was cataleptic.

Now, asleep beside her, he exhaled whinnyingly and rolled onto his side. He was long gone, somewhere deep enough that his eyes were flitting beneath the lids. She'd always liked his quiet; it was one of the first things she'd liked about him. He was dorky and self-conscious and kind, and he went about all those things with an admirable quietude. She'd married a nice, humble nerd, and had always struggled to understand it, how they'd come to be together, how she'd fooled him into procreating with a temperamental train-wreck such as herself, how long it would last.

She felt his sudden alertness and stiffened. She closed her eyes and slowed her breathing, feigning sleep. His gaze on her was a physical presence, a weight that sat on her shoulders like a gargoyle.

"Your tongue's touching the roof of your mouth," he said, and she considered for a second that perhaps he *was* still asleep, just in the midst of some troubling psychosexual dream. She opened her eyes, and he was staring at her.

"Excuse me?"

"All your muscles need to be relaxed in order for you to fall asleep. I can tell by your jaw you're pressing your tongue against the roof of your mouth."

Encyclopedia fucking Brown, her husband. He'd shared this irritating whiz-kid factoid with her before, during some earlier time.

She'd probably found it charming then; she used to be endlessly charmed by how different their brains were.

"Go back to sleep," she said. Then: "There's the baby."

It was false for a variety of reasons, because Ben was definitely still asleep and, as Mark had just so bluntly established, hadn't been a baby for quite some time.

"I don't hear anything," he said, but she slipped out of bed anyway, through the cool dark of the house. She inched open Ben's cracked bedroom door and went to sit on his bed, to observe the cathartic rise and fall of his little belly.

Not Encyclopedia Brown: Encyclopedia *Britannica.* That was what she'd meant. Mark was not an endearing, crime-solving pencil sketch from 1970; he was an irritating fountain of useless knowledge who'd just awakened in order to remind his wife to stop *engaging her tongue muscles.*

She angled herself in alongside Ben, her back against the wall. Kids didn't cede to you like adults did; anytime Mark put his arm over her like this she melted helplessly, even if they were fighting, but Ben remained oblivious to her touch, so deep in his own dreamscape that he didn't even notice she was there, which was probably for the best.

She called Helen Russo the next day, when things, once again, as she had known they would, began to feel like too much.

5

Across from them in an armchair, Ben looks like a Jehovah's Witness, clean-cut and wearing a cornflower blue button-down, come to impart news of impending Armageddon. He has arrived on a Thursday evening the week after Mark's birthday asking to speak with them; this is suspicious, as her children have always been expectant rather than beseeching, anticipating their due and their parents' ability to intuit it.

"So," says Ben, "I've been seeing someone for the last couple of months."

And I'm worried she's going to kill me.

And she's turned out to be in Opus Dei.

And I need six thousand dollars because she's extorting me.

Any of these options is as likely as not, because Ben hasn't dated much; it's challenging to imagine any sorts of pitfalls, ludicrous or otherwise. Her son's romantic life is somewhat of a mystery to her, and until this moment she's always more or less assumed it was—well, if not boring then at least free of *mystique*. For all his twenty-four years Ben has been reassuringly prudent, a rule follower. She'd once expressed a fear to Mark that Ben could, owing to his nature, meander inadvertently into celibacy, Boo Radleyism; Mark had demurred, assuring her she was wrong while also tacking on "But Boo Radley ended up being a good guy."

She wonders if other mothers share this creeping curiosity about their sons' sexual lives. She doesn't want details, certainly, but she wonders if and how he's learned to navigate; men, in her experience, just seem to spring forth, ready for action, without all of the hang-ups and trepidation women are prone to, and she wonders if the same is true for her son, who has always taken a little bit longer to find his way than everyone else, who was so tiny until he wasn't anymore.

"Her name is—well, Nora, actually, but she goes by Sunny."

"What does that mean, *goes by Sunny*?" She's agitated already; she's not sure why. Both Ben and Mark look to her with surprise. "I'm sorry, that's just—not something one *goes* by, is it?"

"It's a childhood nickname," Ben says helpfully.

"I wonder if we've gotten off track here?" Mark interjects.

A junior, Ben tells them, studying contemporary Baroque painting. "She's—become really important to me, and she— Well, we're going to have a baby in September."

"Hang on," Julia says. "I'm sorry, *contemporary* Baroque painting?" A *baby*?

"Whoa, whoa, whoa," Mark is saying, but she feels strangely unshocked; because nothing insane had seemed likely, everything had seemed plausible, and this—the fact that her son is *going to have a baby* with a college junior—certainly falls under the *everything* umbrella.

"She's due on Alma's birthday," Ben says, his voice bright, as though this coincidence will excite them.

Alma, the incremental vegan who owns a T-shirt that reads ON THURSDAYS WE SMASH THE PATRIARCHY and still doesn't know how to do laundry, is going to be an aunt. She feels faint and leans a little against Mark.

"Actually," says her husband, "that's statistically likelier than you might think." It isn't until she leans back and stares at him that he withers. "That's not what's—relevant, though."

"Where did you meet this person?" she asks, eyes closed.

"Oh," Ben says, and something about the note it hits spikes her anxiety again, makes her worry about some sort of sex cult or Pentecostal conversion; she decides she'd rather he be Boo Radley than have met a woman at Bible study. He seems uncomfortable. "Around—campus."

"If we continue at this conversational pace," says Julia, "we're going to be here until Sunday."

They met in a class, Ben explains without meeting their eyes, noting with emphasis that she was taking it outside of her major.

"This woman is your *student*?" The sudden edge in Mark's voice snaps her back to attention.

"I'm just a TA," Ben says.

"This isn't like you," Julia thinks to say. It feels maternal and, more important, accurate: Ben being some kind of *predator* has never been one of her concerns.

"We didn't get together until after the semester ended," he says. "And she asked me out, actually. She's twenty-one. It's not like she's— We're both adults."

"That's a questionable choice of word," she says.

Ben seems to shrink. "It just—happened. We didn't *plan* it."

Mark touches her knee to prevent her from saying *Obviously*. Only one of them is allowed to be indignant at a time.

"So, well," Ben says. "We're getting married."

"Oh, you're *kidding* me," she says, at the same time Mark is saying, again, "Whoa whoa whoa, kid." They've finally leveled out, met each other halfway on the continuum of parental umbrage.

"Next month, probably," he says. "Just a little—celebration; nothing too crazy. Sunny's been really tired lately."

He's watching her, a mix on his face of disenchantment and hope that sort of breaks her heart, like he's expecting her disappointment but holding out for the possibility that she'll come at him, instead, with whatever it is he wants, rescue, or joy, full-throated parental acceptance. There has always been a schism, for her, between what she wants to do as a mother and what she actually does; she has never quite trusted her instincts, never quite been able to venture into territory that feels too soft or tender. She has felt, from the moment Mark presented to her the idea of a child, unwieldy, cast in a production for which she hasn't had adequate time to prepare.

"How long have you known about this?" she asks. "How far along is she?"

"She's ten weeks," he says. "We've known for almost a month."

"What I mean to ask, honey, is—"

"*Jules.*" Mark puts a hand on her leg, and she ignores him. She wonders if perhaps nobody else will be brave enough to acknowledge the other options, that maybe the universe is calling upon her to finally, finally say the right thing, not the easiest thing but the thing that needs to be said.

"I don't mean to be indelicate," she says, "but I feel a responsibility to ask you if you've—considered your options."

There's a second-long hitch in the room, collective acknowledgment of the crassness of the question, as though she has just offered to help him dispose of a murder weapon.

"What your mother means," says Mark, but the damage has been done; the hope has left Ben's face and been replaced by something that takes her a minute to identify as anger.

"That's all you have to say? You're suggesting that we—"

"I'm not *suggesting* it," she says. "I'm just asking if you've thought about it."

Ben runs his hands through his hair. "God, I was hoping you'd be *happy* for me."

"Kid, hang on. That's not what your mom's saying."

"Do you really think so little of me?" he asks. "Have I ever— Like, I've never screwed up anything, Mom; I've done everything I'm supposed to do since I was a little kid, and now I've done something that's maybe not expected but it's not *terrible*."

I think the world of you, she can't bring herself to say, and somehow Ben seems to sense this, ceding her, as he always has, more than she deserves.

"We talked about not having it," he says, surprising her. "Okay? We planned on not having it, actually, initially, but we both kept— I kept thinking about it; I couldn't *stop* thinking about it, and then it turned out that Sunny was having all of these weird dreams."

She opens her mouth, closes it. Sunny the contemporary Baroque art scholar. "Dreams about—"

"Dreams where the baby had been born and he was—" He stops, colors.

"He was what?"

"He was— I mean, it sounds kind of ridiculous saying it aloud, but he'd been born and he was still a baby but also like a—tiny man, sort of? And he was riding a bike? In front of this little house, and Sunny and I were sitting on the porch watching him."

She wants to laugh, and weep, and be swept aloft, up through their chimney, into the sky, where surely nobody is making an enormous life decision based on a tiny man riding a bike who came to them in a dream.

"I know how it sounds," Ben says.

"You said *he* several times," she replies, feeling strange and disembodied, incapable of looking the absurdity head-on. "You've found out the sex already?"

Ben's color deepens. "Not yet, we— She's got an appointment later this month and we can technically find out then but we're not going to; we both just have a feeling that it's— Like, it's so bizarre, Mom, I'd stake my life on the fact that he's a boy, and Sunny feels the same way. Did you ever feel that way about me or Ollie? Just a gut thing?"

She'd found the notion of any child at all baffling enough when she'd gotten pregnant; she'd spoken to Mark of the baby in a frightened, abstract way, like the indefinite threat of an impending storm. In her head sometimes, she used to talk to him, the growing being at her center, always in a bizarre royal we: *I think we're in the mood for pancakes; I guess we can't move as fast as we used to; I hope to God we're going to be okay.*

When he'd been born she'd been so astonished by the material fact of him, the sheer inexplicability, that his being a *boy* seemed wholly unimportant; here was a person who had not existed moments prior—half her, half Mark, half cosmos, half divinity, half something all its own; quarters of her own missing father and difficult mother, eighths of Mark's scrappy English grandparents; the math didn't add up, but she'd never been one for numbers. She'd fallen asleep with his warm weightlessness in her arms, awakened at intervals to take inventory of his features. And what followed, eventually: a kind of wholeness that she'd never before experienced and would never again, because too much had happened by the time Alma came along.

"No," she says. "No gut things."

He was born, and then suddenly there was a baby, and she found that she missed the mysterious companionship of his embryonic iteration, missed knowing he was contained inside her, listening. For years after she found herself talking to *the baby* still, in her head—

not Ben but the baby of before, the being confined and ungen-dered and at once self-sustaining and entirely reliant on her; she continued narrating her little banalities and the jokes that only she thought were funny, continued confessing to it after hours, when everyone else was sleeping, *I'm not sure why I'm so sad* or *I don't think I'm cut out for this.* She cannot, now, entirely reconcile that baffling baby with the young man sitting across from her.

"We just want to be sure you've thought this through, kid," Mark says.

"I have. Completely. Sunny and I together. We've got a whole plan; we just signed a lease on a new place. We want to make it work."

"I just don't think you know what this means," she says. "I don't think you have any idea how hard this is going to be."

He smiles at her, a bright peculiar smile.

"Of course I don't," he says. "That's why I'm so lucky to have you guys."

He is lucky, she thinks, to have Mark; having Mark around has almost always made living feel easier, and she has seen it on her children's faces since before they were cognizant of their own emo-tions, a slight slackening when he was nearby, like they knew they could relax.

"Honey," she says, instead of *Are you completely out of your mind?*

"We're doing the responsible thing."

"But I don't think that— I mean, we've never made you feel like you're bound by any kind of arbitrary social norms, have we? You don't *need* to get married."

"I *want* to get married."

"You say that, but I don't think you— It's so much bigger than you can see right now."

"Isn't that part of the fun?"

Another query bordering on delusion, but she isn't sure what to say, because perhaps it *is* part of the fun. Perhaps foresight is over-rated. Perhaps there are a hundred thousand ways to make a deci-sion but those ways lead to only a handful of outcomes.

"But I— Why?" she asks. "What's the—point?"

"The point of what?" Ben, for the first time, sounds a little challenging; there's an unfamiliar angry edge to his voice.

Mark puts a hand on her knee. You aren't allowed to say *what's the point* about a human baby that people have already decided to have. She swallows. "I just mean you're just so *young*. Why get married? You're not— Is she religious?"

"She's irreligiously spiritual," he says, reminding her of Alma, but Julia's unused to this type of rhetoric from Ben.

She stares at him, hard.

"She's not *religious*, no, but we want—we want the baby to feel like it's coming into an actual family, two people who—"

"The *baby*'s not going to care so long as you provide for it," she says, "which you can do without getting married."

"It's not—just that," Ben says, and they wait, but he doesn't elaborate.

"You love her?" Mark asks, and the fact that Ben doesn't answer right away makes her more nervous than if he had.

"I think I was just starting to," he says, "when we found out about the baby."

It's the bluntness that strikes her, the frank lack of rosiness; if the fact of a baby weren't scary enough, this seals the deal for her, terror-wise: he means it, all of it, that he loves this woman and is committing himself to her, to this decision they've made together. And when Ben commits, he, like his father, commits unyieldingly, in full, and occasionally at the expense of things like nuance.

"I would've come to this conclusion eventually," he says. "That I want to be with her forever and—well, things just got—accelerated a little."

The look he's giving her is so too a look of his younger self— vulnerable and imploring, seeking something from her, comfort, assurance—that she nearly rises from the couch, goes to him like she would to lift him wailing from his crib, but she checks the impulse.

In the years after she and Mark married he'd call his parents often—if Ben was running a fever, if there were roadblocks at work—and it had bothered her for reasons she couldn't identify until she realized that she was *jealous*; that she would never call her own mother in a time of crisis not necessarily because her own mother lacked relevant insight but because there was a decent likelihood that she wouldn't answer the phone, and that even if she did answer, her historical reaction to any type of crisis, large or small, was either to laugh or to leave the room in pursuit of a drink.

"I'm—sorry," Ben says. "If I've—disappointed you."

"Sweetheart," she says, and wishes she *had* reached out to him. His face across from her now is not dissimilar to the little one that used to regard her in the rearview mirror, wanting and forgiving at the same time.

"But I've got it under control," he says. "And I hope you can be— happy for us, even if it takes you some time to get used to the idea."

"Of course we can," Mark says, because Mark has never had the same problems that she has; Mark has always loved readily and rightly. "We're here for you, kid; whatever you need."

She takes her husband's hand, squeezes it in thanks.

"I told Ollie this weekend," Ben says. "She's been—a really good listener."

She thinks of them escaping from the party to "finish Alma's homework"; she had assumed they were going off to drink champagne and watch *The Office*, but now she envisions them together in Alma's bedroom, Ben confessing what he'd tried and failed to confess to his distracted mother.

"I know it's a lot," Ben says. He lifts an arm with a little flourish, indicating the three of them, a wry smile on his face. "Look, though," he says, "I turned out okay, didn't I?"

Her son the rule follower, her son who wants everyone to like him, who wants, always, to do the right thing.

"You turned out very okay," she says. *The best person. Better than I ever could have dreamed of.*

"I can't wait for you to meet Sunny, Mom," Ben says, his earnestness painful, and she has to look away. "I think you're really going to like her."

"Great," she says, and then says it again, painfully, "*Great.*"

He smiles radiantly upon her, rewarding her, as he always has, for doing the bare minimum.

elen Russo lived in a gorgeous, massive Spanish Colonial with a garden so verdant that Julia felt embarrassed about ever having had hope for her own tulips. They had arranged to meet around lunchtime when Ben was at preschool; she had tried on four different outfits and, panicking as her arrival time drew closer, drove for six minutes around neighboring blocks so she wouldn't be early. When she pulled up in front she considered simply pulling away again, acceding to the fact that Helen's invitation had been a part of some insomniac hallucination, but then Helen came into view, standing at the side of the house, hands at the small of her back as she craned her neck upward. She appeared to be yelling at the chimney, but she turned when she heard Julia's car door close, smiled brightly and waved her over.

"Julia, you're here. Come over before I implicate myself in a homicide."

She came shyly up the walk. Helen leaned in to kiss her on the cheek, like they'd known each other forever instead of just met randomly last week by an iguana. "Pete, my friend Julia," Helen said, gesturing overhead, and Julia followed her gaze to the roof over the side porch, where a wiry man with work goggles and a dust mask was crouched on an incline, pulling at the shingles. There was an old portable radio balanced precariously behind him, a baseball game blaring tinnily from the speaker. "Julia, my foolhardy soon-to-be-ex-husband, who insists we don't need to hire roofers."

The man waved over his shoulder with one hand and unloosed a shingle with the other. "Good to meet you," he said.

"We're going inside to drink wine," Helen said to him. "We're not calling an ambulance if we hear you fall off of there."

"Just as well," he said, "if you're planning on divorcing me."

Helen suppressed a smile. "Come in for some lunch in a bit, okay, sweet?"

He saluted, and Helen indicated for Julia to follow her inside. "I'll hide the ladder then," she said, sotto voce. Then, in a normal voice: "I'm so glad you're here."

"Me too." She said it on a few-second delay because she was distracted by the interior of the house, which was messy and chaotic and elementally lived-in in the most glamorous way imaginable; she walked in and immediately felt like she was in someone's *home*, a legitimate Capital-H Home, not like her own house, where nothing was charming, because charm didn't just make itself. The *texture* of their life! There was a brass bowl of turning-but-not-rotten clementines in the kitchen and Post-its on the fridge that said things like *defrost chicken!! xxxxx* and pictures of formidable sun-drenched people peppering every free surface, a big one of Helen and Pete— who, in his younger years, looked a bit like James Taylor—the two of them fresh-faced and deliriously happy, kissing on the lips at the Joshua Tree. She was too embarrassed to ask who had taken the photo, was content to just assume that the moment had been captured by God himself. Helen welcomed her with such breathless hospitality that she never wanted to leave, wanted to inquire about vacancies in one of their sons' old bedrooms, wanted to wake up there in the morning and just sit silent at the kitchen table while Pete and Helen drank their coffee together, absorbing them, their love, their compatibility, their *solace*.

Helen waved a bottle of wine. "Will it put you right to sleep? If you have a glass now, you'll have plenty of time to get your wits back about you before you have to go pick up Ben." She smiled. "Clearly I've done this kind of math for myself before."

"Very little puts me to sleep."

"Consider this a silver lining, then," Helen said, prying the cork from the bottle. "I was going to see if you'd let me put you to work helping me plant some bulbs in the front, but then I got lazy, so I thought we'd just sit outside and drink."

"You can put me to work," she said.

"Next time." Helen flinched as a roof shingle fell past one of the kitchen windows. "He's driving me mental with all his projects. That and the garden. He's very worried about his *arugula;* he goes out every night and checks on it and reports back like some kind of persecuted shepherd, as though we can't just go buy some at the grocery." She hitched the bottle of rosé in one hand, nodded for Julia to open the back door. "God grant me the glib industriousness of a man in his golden years. Come out on the deck. Is your husband handy?"

She mistook it at first for *handsy,* colored. "In his most favorable imaginings," she said, but then she felt bad. "Actually, kind of. He's— He has the brain for it, at least. And the interest. Just not the—time, usually, to do much around the house."

"What is it that he does?" Helen poured a splash of wine into her glass and indicated with her chin; Julia, who at restaurants felt distinct homicidal impulses toward anyone she saw going through the motions—the puckering, the swishing, the *horror*—of dime-store sommelierity, self-consciously took a sip.

"Lovely," she said, and it actually was, though she would have said so regardless. "He's a— Well, he trained as a biomedical engineer, but then his best friend got into venture capital and sort of—lured him in." She sipped her wine, felt it go straight to her head, and then she started telling Helen the long version, the distinguished-but-low-paying position at the U of C Mark had held when she met him, how he'd left that in favor of something tangential to his intended career but ultimately much more lucrative. She imagined that this was what it must feel like to be a kid home from college, a kid with functional parents who derived enjoyment from listening to their children. She'd left for Kansas State without a backward glance and forfeited the opportunity to return home, triumphant or belligerent or otherwise.

"You don't like it," Helen said. "What he does."

"I mean, if he's *happy.* And I appreciate the *security,* but— It means he's gone a lot."

"Mm. There must be some perfect medium that neither of us has struck," Helen mused. "Because Pete is *never* gone, and it's driving me to distraction."

Julia leaned her head back against the rattan chair, felt the sun on her face. The Russos' yard smelled like lemongrass and lavender.

"Can I give you a tour?" Helen asked, already getting up, and Julia followed at her heels, listening as she was given a primer on the hydrangeas—whose color, Helen told her, was dictated by the acidity of the soil—and the peonies—who required ants to crawl between their petals to open them up—and the silverleaf nightshade—which was just as allergenic as poison ivy and which she and Pete were paying an arm and a leg to have eradicated. Once they'd made the full lap around the yard, Julia felt almost light-headed, stimulated and relaxed at once.

Helen smiled at her as they took their seats on the deck again.

"You look better than you did last week," she said.

I'm wearing my regular-person bra, Julia did not say.

Helen herself looked like a fancy witch, hair slightly frizzy in her signature ponytail and a wide linen blouse, a strand of huge amber beads around her neck—the product of either a terribly expensive jeweler or a highly uncoordinated grandchild—catching the sunlight like sea glass.

"Not that you looked bad," Helen clarified. "You just seem a little—breezier now."

"Well, this helps." Julia lifted her wineglass. "Plus it's—nice to be out of the house. Nice to talk to another adult."

"It's really a tribulation," Helen said. "When your kids are little. Pete was— Lord, I worried about him. About both of us. Desperate times, those."

"When did it get easier?" Julia asked, and Helen, after a moment, smiled enigmatically.

"Well, I didn't quite say it ever did, did I? Though we had exponentially more *volume* than you do, so I'd bet your prospects are better."

"Yeah, how did you— I mean, *five*, how did you guys do it?"

"That's the question, isn't it," Helen said. "Honestly, looking at it now it's nothing short of a miracle that we're all still alive, that the kids didn't kill each other, that Pete and I didn't kill *ourselves* or each other, that nobody fell down an uncovered well or got abducted from the bus stop. It was complete chaos for— Well, it still crops up now, because some of them have their own kids, or wives I can't stand, or—well, various bouts of arrested development. The crises never fully abate, I'm sorry to say. And God, you're home with yours. I could never do that."

Julia smiled thinly. "Yeah, I'm not sure I can either."

"It's commendable. If I'd stayed home with the boys I'd've been miserable. Pete had jury duty for a week when we had three kids under four and I almost tried to electrocute myself with the Speak & Spell. I must, however, proselytize on the wonders of mothers-in-law, and not only because I am one myself to a handful of ungrateful *daughters*-in-law."

She imagined Helen as her mother-in-law, sweeping in with her beads and her scarves and her easy way with kids, and she couldn't imagine not being transcendentally happy about it.

"Do you hate yours?" Helen asked.

"My— Oh, no, not at all. She's lovely."

"Good," Helen said. "So was Pete's mom; I don't know what we would have done without her. Does yours live here?"

Julia shook her head. "Wisconsin. They don't like to travel."

Helen tsked. "And your actual mom?"

She'd had years of practice explaining away her mother, but her usual *we aren't close* felt inadequate when talking to Helen, who seemed to activate in her some tendency toward the truth.

"Complicated," she settled on eventually, and Helen smiled a little sadly.

"Mine was too. That may be one of the reasons I had so many kids. Compensation. Or possibly overcompensation, in our case. Anyway, yes, whenever I'm feeling lazy"—here she lifted up her wineglass again—"I think back to when we had three toddlers at home and I was pregnant with Natey and still nursing Eric and pumping in a bathroom stall in the office while line-editing briefs and the partners were circling overhead, waiting for me to slip up, and I— Well, this isn't how life works, but I think I've earned a little laziness."

Julia thought of her own quiet house, her tiny, compliant child. "You definitely have."

"Hey," Helen said, looking at her squarely. "It's *all* hard, you know that, right? I chose to have five. I don't get extra points for that."

"Did you always—" But then she realized the intimacy of the question she'd been about to ask.

Helen smiled. "Let's consider this a friendship free of airs, okay? You'd have to go to great lengths to offend me, Julia. Ask me whatever you'd like."

"I just wondered if you always thought you'd have so many kids."

"Cal and Francis were intentional. The others were— Well." She held up her hands in a *what can you do.* "I'm wildly attracted to Pete. Always have been. And we didn't have tons of time for— *talking* back then."

Julia felt her face heat up; Helen clocked it and laughed.

"I don't mean to embarrass you," she said. "Everything about my professional life was so tightly *controlled*, is what I mean. I went back to work when Natey was six weeks old. I was technically in labor with Aaron during a status hearing. There wasn't the slightest margin for me to make a wrong move or accidentally drop the ball, and when I came home at night it was—I'm not sure, *freeing*, somehow, to throw caution to the wind a little bit, or to have a little bit of *fun*, fallout be damned, and that, in turn, increased my accountability, because I was our breadwinner. Vicious cycle, blah blah blah. And Pete never knew what he wanted to do with his professional life. They gave him a sense of purpose." She sipped her wine. "I don't mean to be overly simplistic. I think that drives a lot of parents."

"But not you?"

"The boys weren't my *only* sense of purpose. I always knew I wanted to be a lawyer, and the odds weren't exactly—in my *favor*, back then, to say the least, and that only made me want it more. And then I happened to fall in love with someone who wanted it for me too—or maybe I fell in love with him a little because of that; I'm not sure. In any case, he was a terrific dad, and it brought him joy, so we had the two and then two more, primarily because Pete wanted more. Not that I didn't want them too, but— Well, one person always wants it more, don't you think? Have you and your husband ever been equally thrilled about the same thing at the same time?"

"No," she said. "I don't think we have." She thought of Mark, four years ago beside her on the kitchen floor of their apartment in Rogers Park, hand on her still-flat belly and eyes aglow, ignorant of the emptiness she was feeling, entirely unaware of the fact that she was banking on his happiness to carry them both. She forced her focus back to Helen. "What about your fifth?" she asked.

Helen smiled. "I was scientifically curious. I wanted to see if it was possible for the two of us to produce a female child. But then Natey turned out to be Natey. And so we were seven, and here we are still."

"Mark wants another," she said, feeling somewhat shy.

"And you?"

She shakes her head. "I feel like I've been in this fog since Ben was born and sometimes the only thing that propels me—you know, *on*ward—is the notion that it's going to lift eventually. The thought of inviting it in for a longer stay seems—insane, doesn't it?"

"People seem to find babies exhausting," Helen said thoughtfully. "But I always found high school to be the worst time. Teenagers are far and away the most awful variety of human."

"I barely remember the first year."

"Well, they say that, too." Helen leaned back in her Adirondack chair, drinking her glass of wine at a much more leisurely pace than Julia. "It's partly sleep deprivation, of course, but I wonder if it's not also an extension of the—you know, that Darwinian thing, propagation, maintaining the species. Like how we forget childbirth."

"I remember childbirth," Julia said without thinking, and she felt Helen watching her. Her wine was gone; Ben was waiting; she had to keep her wits about her.

"You know you're allowed to be having a hard time, right?" Helen asked softly. "I don't care if you have one kid or ten. It's very, very hard, what you're doing. What I was doing. And you can't account for it in any mathematical way."

"It's really not so bad," she said, backtracking, guilt riddled, imagining Ben at weather time or in a drum circle. "He's really an easy kid. I don't know why I'm so—"

Helen, accustomed by now to her weird fits of crying, reached over and squeezed Julia's hand. "We want our lives to be better than *not so bad*," she said.

· · ·

Having visited the Russos' house the one time—and then quickly twice, thrice—it felt like she'd been going there for years; it was one of those houses that seemed to have been engineered to entertain a revolving door of people, rosters of children and friends of children and colleagues and craftsmen. She'd sit at the kitchen island feeling suspicious of the ease and also a bit like the homely cousin from a BBC dramedy, swinging her legs in figure eights around the rungs of a barstool and taking in the sweet incongruities of the room, shelves dotted with whimsical little objects, coffee stains etched on the table, notes and phone numbers scrawled on strips of torn-out newsprint.

Helen was endeavoring to teach her how to knit; she had bequeathed on her some angora yarn and a pair of bamboo needles and Julia didn't have the heart to tell her that she didn't find it remotely relaxing. But it provided them with a context, not that they necessarily needed one. Helen, though her life was inarguably fuller and more populated than Julia's, seemed to enjoy Julia's company as much as Julia enjoyed hers.

They were sitting on the back deck one Wednesday drinking tea, Julia doggedly persisting with her soft misshapen red square that would allegedly one day be a scarf, when Pete called from somewhere in the house.

"Jo? Josie, I— Oh, there you are." He appeared in the doorway and gave Julia a shy salute. He was a lanky, soft-spoken man with a hearty energy about him, hippieish but formidable; she could easily envision him erecting a treehouse for their tribe of boys or trekking through the woods with a toddler perched on his shoulders.

"Lower your voice," Helen said, because that seemed to be one of their bits, his constantly annoying her and her exasperatedly pointing it out to him. "What is it?"

"I found the dry rot in the garage," he said.

Helen closed her eyes. "Found it how?"

"I knew there was a problem," he said. "I told you, those big cracks in the—"

"Tell me you didn't take out a wall or something."

"Not an *entire* wall," he said. "I'm going to—"

Helen held up a hand. "Honey, I don't care. Will it be fixed before it gets cold?"

She'd never seen people who talked to each other like this and still liked each other; Helen and Pete seemed to be constantly sparring but with a strong undercurrent of affection, though it was layered on top with Helen's somewhat patronizing exasperation and with Pete's obliviousness, both of which seemed to Julia like affectations.

"*Yes*, Josie. It'll be finished by the end of the month if I can get the lumber."

"Josie?" Julia asked without meaning to. She began to question her own recall; she began to wonder if maybe she'd been imagining all of it all along. The whole arrangement had a rosy, too-good-to-be-true quality, the fact that she'd just *happened* to find an enlightened, magical friend right when she was drifting toward her lowest point.

"This one was a little skeptical of me when we met," said Pete. "So she told me her name was Josephine."

"It's my middle name," Helen said defensively.

"How long did it take you to tell him your real name?" Julia asked. Pete and Helen looked at each other again and she had to turn her head away, the intimacy almost too much to bear. It wasn't even specifically sexual, the charge between them, though that was part of it; it was something more storied and time-tested, the glow of two people who'd chosen to go through life together, who'd figured out how to navigate the shared space of a marriage, the rules of bathroom doors and breathing room and *honey could you take a look I've got this weird thing going on with one of my molars.*

"How many years, darling?" Helen asked. "Thirty-five? Thirty-six?"

"Thirty-*eight*," Pete said mournfully, and Julia wondered which had come first, his meekness or his wife; she suspected he may have shrunk over time, to make room for Helen. "I'll leave you to it. Julia." He made a hat-tipping motion to her and then was gone.

"He'll be the death of me," Helen said. She wondered if Helen couldn't help but resent him sometimes, if she hadn't resented him all those years when she worked all day and came home to him and their children. She'd seen it cross Mark's face more than once when he walked in from the garage and Ben was sleeping and the house was in a state of stasis, Julia at the center watching *Dateline* or shopping online for drawer knobs as though things were always so easy.

"Where did you two meet?"

"College," Helen said. "San Diego. He was majoring in sculpture, very politically active. And a bit of a—well, quite a bit *more* than a player, actually; I think he'd slept with half the girls in my class before he got to me."

"Did that bother you?"

"Maybe for the first month or two. But he was terrific in bed—he still is, as a matter of fact—and he never looked back once we got together." Helen glanced up at her and laughed. "My *God*, it's easy to scandalize you!"

"I'm not scandalized," she said, embarrassed. "It's just not— a huge part of my repertoire at the minute, I guess."

"How often are we talking about?" Helen asked, and Julia looked up from her scarf-in-progress, which she'd knitted so tightly that she could barely work her needle into the stitches.

"What?" She opened and closed her fist, trying to relax; Helen had explained to her that stress could manifest itself in how one knit, that her vise-grip rows suggested she needed to think about meditation or possibly quaaludes.

"How frequently are you and Mark having sex?"

She blanched; they had, prior to Pete's interruption, been talking about an NPR piece Helen had recently listened to about Eritrean refugees.

Helen raised her eyebrows. "Or you and—someone else?"

"No," she said. "God. No, there's no one else."

"I don't judge," Helen said.

"Mark and I—well—it's not an exact . . ."

"Ballpark."

She squirmed, highballed: "Maybe once a—month?"

"And is that sufficient for you?"

"I mean I— Part of me wishes it were more frequent, but I'm

also not exactly, like, raring to go these days." She worked her row of too-tight stitches off the needle, one at a time.

"But it's important to you. Sex. You've implied as much."

"Well, sure, yes, I think it's . . ."

"And there's a time when you had a fulfilling sex life with Mark."

She swallowed. "There—has. But not really since— I mean, it sounds insane to say because it's been so long now, but it hasn't really been normal since Ben was born. And I mean the actual— I think *having* him did something to me."

"Really? For me it was— I really only remember snippets, to tell you the truth."

"What?" she asked, feeling punchy. She gave up on her knitting, handed it over for Helen to fix. "Cat-cow stretches in the gazebo? Cat Stevens during transition? Pete tied off the cord with macramé?"

Helen laughed. "Lord, no. I took every medical assist available."

"I should have," Julia said. "I ended up going completely natural." At one point—hours into it, time having taken on a watery, interminable quality, she'd been in so much pain that she'd actually started laughing.

"Jesus Christ," Helen said. "Look at you."

She'd surprised herself with it, in fact. It was not a decision informed by any kind of research or righteous conviction; it was rooted in petulance, plain and simple.

"It was the most awful nineteen hours of my life." It was a sentence she'd never said aloud. "Mark was horrified," she said. "The noises I was making. The *threats* I was making. By the time I gave in, it was too late for drugs, and by the time Ben was born I was— a shell of myself. An animal. I didn't even ask if he was okay. I just trusted Mark to take care of it."

"Oh, honey," Helen said. "No wonder you're on the fence about another one."

"It's just hard to get—in the *mood*," she said, coloring. "I know it's been a few years, but I just— My body feels different than it used to. Everything feels different."

"It *is* different."

"I guess. But it's that plus—I don't know, just my general baseline, lately."

"Not mood-conducive," Helen said.

"No," she said softly.

"I ask," Helen said, "because Pete's sister is a sex therapist. She's a little—you know, woo-woo for my taste, Santa Barbara, but she was telling me over Christmas how so often what they used to refer to as *hysteria* in women was treated with these incredibly invasive forms of intervention—shock treatment, et cetera."

She had long been amazed by the connectivity of rich people, the elite electric grid of *Oh my father went to Yale with* and *We used to summer next door to* and *My cousin married a man who owned,* an endless fount of free referrals and as-yet-unredeemed favors. And Helen frequently dropped little tells like that, inconspicuous missives that spoke of money, generations of comfort, upper-middle-classicality—"Well Pete had an uncle who was the president of a . . ." "My grandfather once said—he was an endocrinologist—that the most important thing we can do for ourselves is . . ." And Julia sat back and marveled over her ability to talk about her ancestry with such confidence, such ownership. She'd never met her grandparents on either side, knew that her mother had grown up in southern Illinois, but she could trace her own lineage no further, had never bothered trying. There was, as far as she knew, nobody particularly distinguished. And she'd never cared, not really, though she'd always thought it would have been nice to know that there were people, older people, who cared about her existence; always thought it might be fun to possess the knowledge that your great-grandmother came from Sicily or San Jose.

Ben would be able to speak of his parents—or at least of his father—with some degree of possessive authority: "My dad was an engineer." She supposed she wouldn't be spoken of—couldn't be—with any similar ownership. "My mom drove a station wagon." "My mom was a lunatic."

"But in fact," Helen went on, "a lot of problems would never have gotten so bad in the first place if the woman in question had just been orgasming regularly."

"I— *What?*"

Helen laughed. "The look on your *face*, honey, Jesus. Take heart, women don't become utterly agamic when we pass sixty. File that away for the future."

"What are you—suggesting?"

"Do you masturbate?"

"Oh my *God*." She stood up, aware, for the first time, of what it felt like to be conventionally embarrassed by your mother, not because she showed up drunk to parents' night but because she reminded you, in earshot of a dozen classmates, to keep some extra tampons in your backpack.

"I'm not saying it's a cure-all," Helen said, "but it wouldn't hurt to try." Rich people were also, she'd noticed, constantly talking about ways in which they were entitled to bettering themselves.

"That's not the problem," she said.

"Are you sure?"

"I could— I can *come*." She whispered this. "It's more than that." She sat back down. It was embarrassing, almost *insulting*, this proposal of a sexual cure-all to her nonsexual problems, as though she was beneath loftier intervention. "Did you just call me hysterical?"

"Of *course* not; I'm saying that what they used to *call* hysteria was in fact often just—life. That general dissatisfaction with being."

"Mark and I barely talk," she said. "That's the problem, not . . ." She shook her head. "It's such a fucking cliché. I miss him in theory and then I resent him when he's actually around."

She loved him, was the thing. She really, really, really did love him, and was even—despite her sleeplessness, despite the hallucinatory stupor that was being the mother of a toddler—*attracted* to him still, at least conceptually, even if she almost never had the energy to do more than function on a very basic level, let alone *fornicate*. It was larger than that, and murkier, and scarier, and she wasn't sure how to talk about it, even with Helen, who had no qualms about casually discussing masturbatory habits over oolong tea.

"I don't presume to have a cure-all," Helen said. "But I'd love to see you happier."

"Thanks," she said, touched now, her embarrassment not forgotten but already receding.

"Should I intervene? Should I anonymously send Mark a Hitachi Magic Wand and a list of tips? Pete's *very* good with his mouth; I'd be happy to—"

"Stop, stop, stop," Julia said, but she was laughing. "Ben's waiting; I have to get going."

Helen smiled, standing up too. "Never to return," she said.

think I'll go for a run," Mark says after Ben drives away, fiddling with the strap of his pedometer and bouncing a little on the balls of his feet.

She balks. "Right now?"

He presses his palms against the wall, stretching his calves. "Just need to clear my head."

Mark has always preferred to do his hard thinking solo, and while ambulating, but she finds the reaction galling at present, because her impulse, now, is to fix herself to a particular spot—say, for instance, one featuring a Valium drip—and talk about her son's impending nuptials, possibly until the end of time. But there is no happy medium in a marriage when one party wants to be alone and the other doesn't. There is no way to have it both ways; someone always loses, and tonight, apparently, the loser is she.

"Just a few miles," he says, as though he's making a significant concession, and then, as he's jogging upstairs to change, like he's doing her a favor, "We can talk when I get back."

She goes out to the sunporch, where Alma is studying, Suzanne curled next to her. Her daughter declines to look up, out of either genuine immersion or an effort to will away her mother's presence, but Suzanne leaps down to greet her. She lifts the dog into her arms.

"Did I interrupt you being cozy?" she coos into Suzanne's neck.

Her family makes fun of her for the person Suzanne turns her into, one whose voice and general tolerance for just about every-thing Suzanne-related are several registers higher than they are in all other areas of life; the dog has weakened her with her microscopic cuteness and with her intensity. Suzanne looks plaintively up into her eyes.

"Were you being so cozy with your sister, you tiny lady?"

Alma looks at her lethally and she takes a tentative seat a safe distance away on the chaise, because daughters—daughters you nursed, daughters you bathed, daughters whose sleeping teenage hair you now kiss at twilight when you creep into their bedroom just to share the same oxygen at a time when they aren't conscious—are physiologically averse, at seventeen, to touching their mothers.

"So he told you," Alma says, and Julia takes this as permission to look at her directly.

"I could say the same." Beside her in the chaise, Suzanne walks in several tight, determined circles before settling on the perfect coordinates in which to curl up.

"Are you mad?"

"I'm not sure what I am," she says, "to be perfectly honest. What's your take on this?"

"I mean," Alma says, gracefully crossing her legs and sticking a pen in her history book to mark her page. "He's an idiot. And it's personally my nightmare."

She is surprised, frankly, that her son doesn't seem more terrified by this development; since he was a toddler he's had a wild imagination for catastrophe. He used to wake her in the middle of the night to divulge his latest fear: that it was possible for a bat to bite you in your sleep without you waking up and you wouldn't know you'd been bitten until you were dying of rabies; that *okay but Mama what if* an ambulance got into an accident on its way to help someone so they sent out two more ambulances, one to the original accident and one to the new ambulance accident, but *those* ambulances got into accidents too, and so forth, *what then, Mama.*

How warm he was, her boy, those evenings when he'd join her in bed, radiating heat except for his smooth little feet, which always felt cold to the touch. How hard it was to convince him that none of his fears were likely to come true, and how frustrating it was that she couldn't promise him a hundred percent, that there were still plenty of things she couldn't protect him from. *I'm almost posi-*

tive, she'd murmur into his hair, and she could feel herself radiating inadequacy as steadily as her son radiated goodness.

"I guess there are worse things," says Alma, wise, menacing Alma, the ends of her hair newly dyed food-coloring red. Julia wonders whether these sorts of things balance each other out, parentally speaking, if it counts as a wash if one kid is a sagacious tyrant and the other an affable copulator.

"You haven't met the girl yet, have you?" she asks.

"Mom. *The girl?* Are you from 1940? Are you going to kidnap her and bring her to a home for unwed mothers?"

"The—*woman.*"

"No," Alma says, "I haven't met *Sunny* yet. But she sounds nice."

"Does she?"

"I mean," Alma says. "Ben likes literally everyone, so who knows. But it seems like he really, really likes her. It's weird to think of him—like, partnered, isn't it?"

"Yes," she says. "It is." She leans her head back, weaving her fingers deep into Suzanne's fur, rubbing at her skin. When they'd adopted her, the vet had diagnosed the dog with "stress dandruff," a by-product of her previous life, whatever darknesses befell her before she'd joined their family, before she'd become Suzanne. It still settles over her black fur sometimes, a fine dusting of stress-snow, and the sight of it always makes Julia sad. "What did he tell you?"

She's taking a risk by asking, but Alma, surprisingly, shrugs, sets aside her book. "He just said he really needed to tell someone. He was worried you'd be mad, and he's worried Sunny's going to feel like she needs to drop out of school. He said she found them a super cute apartment. He wanted to know if I thought all of it sounded insane and I told him it did but I also— I'm not sure. I think he could be good at it."

"At—?"

"Being a dad? I don't know. I'd trust him to do it over most of the people I know."

It's a lovely thing to say, and Julia finds she agrees with her daughter, despite the worried current running through her veins. Ben has always been capable and openhearted, and those were two of the things that had convinced her, so many years ago, that Mark would be a good father. But it makes her nervous, too, because Ben, despite most outward appearances, still shares half her DNA, and there's a little nugget of misery that's been lodged within her forever, really, since long before he was born, and some days it migrates closer to a dense cluster of nerves, threatening to wreak havoc. Mark is unburdened in this way; Mark is the antidote to her misery, the kindly midwestern bridge that helps to validate her existence. But Mark's capability and openheartedness weren't enough to prevent them from veering dangerously off course; Mark's kind industriousness was no match for what had happened when she met Helen Russo, and she doubts Ben's will be, either, for any similar perils that may arise.

"I do think it's stupid they're having a wedding though," Alma tacks on, and it takes Julia a few seconds to come up for air. "It just seems super antiquated to me. Like, what, their union has to be spiritually recognized by the god of—Restoration Hardware?"

She still derives pleasure from the clumsy self-consciousness with which her daughter throws around sociological terms.

"I value your opinion on this, Ollie," she says. "Very much, for the record."

She thinks she sees her daughter flush; bless her mean, explosive little heart. "Thanks. If you ever accidentally knock someone up, you know where to find me." Alma smiles shyly from behind her book. Julia's spitting image, Mark has always said, from the day she was born, though babies, as they both understood it, were meant to take after their fathers in the beginning, that old evolutionary defense against abandonment. Julia has always wondered if the universe sensed something about her, thought she might benefit from a little extra help in this parental department, or at least more help than Mark would need.

While Ben had been afraid of everything when he was little, Alma had always had a much more open relationship with her fears: once when she was eight, Julia found her sitting in the laundry room with her head in her hands, staring fixedly at the floor, and when Julia asked what she was doing, she explained that she'd written herself a letter pretending to be the Crypt Keeper—*Dear Alma, U R next. From, The Crypt Keeper*—in the hope of scaring herself.

"And now what are you doing?" Julia had asked, and her daughter, furrowing her brow, said, "I'm trying to make myself forget I wrote it. So when I find it, it'll scare me."

"Do you think he's happy?" she asks Alma now.

Alma shrugs, squirms, tucks her legs up underneath her. "He always seems happy. I don't know. He's fine. He's whatever. He's a fucking golden retriever."

Hesitancy, still, when she swears in front of her parents. Her restraint feels to Julia like a form of respect.

She'd been a much different mom to Alma than she'd been to Ben, much more confident, much less terrified. And those things yielded a child who invited fear into her life, sought it out, perhaps taking for granted its unlikelihood.

"I'm trying to forget," Alma had said in the laundry room, such stubborn concentration on her face, and Julia hadn't been sure whether it made her want to laugh or cry. "I'm trying to *make* myself forget."

The good news," Mark says later that night, when they've reconvened in bed, "is that it's not *bad* news."

She glances over at him, incredulous. They're lying side by side, prostrate, like neighboring cadavers. There's a breeze from the open window and the dull sonorous thump of dramatic teen dialogue from Alma's room, TV she's not supposed to be watching on her laptop.

"I'm sorry," she says, "how is this not bad news?"

"I mean—they're healthy. And they have—us."

This is what she feared from him, this infuriating, unnuanced optimism, the belief that they'll be able to make everything okay because they have the resources and because Mark operates with a kind of don't-look-it-head-on logic, warding off unpleasantness by sheer force of will.

"Just a little sooner than we planned," he says, because Mark has always thought about the world this way, in terms of *plans* and *steps*, as though life itself is just an evenly spaced series of mile markers. It is a trait that is convenient only, really, for things like auto maintenance; she finds its application to real life at best annoying and, at worst, disastrous. When she met him, Mark had never considered that other people might not see marriage on their horizon, that other people might be contemplating whether they even *wanted* children instead of when, logistically, would be the best time to have them.

"I wasn't ever *planning* on this, Mark. He's twenty-four years old. He's a student. He's got—what, four more years of his PhD?"

"Three," says Mark.

"In any case. They're both barely older than my mom was when she had me."

"Oh." Now his voice is gentle, sad. "Honey."

"I'm just *saying.* He's young, and he's precarious, and—"

"Since when do you think *Ben* is precarious?"

"We still pay his phone bill. And he's— You know how sensitive he is." She can't reconcile all the versions of her son that exist in her head—Ben as a baby; Ben as a short, solemn middle schooler; Ben as a three-year-old, grinning at her from the stage of his preschool Thanksgiving performance, in which he'd played a yam—with the one at the forefront of her brain now, sitting on their couch and telling them he was about to become a dad.

"I think we have a responsibility to help him understand that he has no idea what he's undertaking."

"He's going to find that out on his own, don't you think? I really don't understand what you're hoping will happen here."

She shakes her head, looks up at the ceiling. Now that this dead animal has been left on the doorstep, her brain can't help but backtrack, unsatisfied with the outcome and unable to compute the steps that have elapsed to get them there. She wishes—desperately, like she once recalls wishing she could undo the experimental haircut she'd given her only Barbie—that she could travel back to those few minutes before Mark's party, looking at Ben in the bathroom mirror. If only she'd heeded that rare moment of maternal sixth sense instead of brushing it aside, brushing *Ben* aside, Ben who was, yes, twenty-four years old but would still always, to some degree, be her baby, her tiny boy in the backseat. She can't help but wonder if she could have stopped it, or at least could have warned him that the things he was about to do were the hardest things she'd ever done, that she'd only very narrowly survived them.

"Jules?" Mark is watching her, and she's saddened by her certainty that he has no idea what she's thinking. *Don't you remember what it was like?* she wants to say. *Don't you remember what happened?*

Someone in Alma's television world screams.

"We should tell her to go to bed," she says.

Don't you remember how hard it was to get past?

Mark takes her hand in his, flips it over, traces the lines on her palm. "I don't know why you always have to immediately default to negativity," he says. "Ben's got a good head on his shoulders. They're renting an apartment *here*, which means they're planning to have the baby here, where we'll be able to help them."

She closes her eyes. Of course Mark has already arrived at this spot, prepared to officiate the wedding or deliver the baby if necessary. "It's a little early for you to have staked out such lush territory in the high ground," she says irritably. All of this is making her feel a merciless roster of feelings, a series of miniature tests of her moral character, most of which she has, judging by the way Mark is looking at her, failed.

But then she feels him take her hand again.

"It's going to be okay," he says softly. "You know that, right?"

She opens her eyes to look at him. "I don't, actually."

"Grand-scheme, Jules, this is— He could've been coming to tell us he was sick, or in real trouble. And the fact that he told us in the first place, God; aren't you relieved about that, that our kid trusts us enough to come to us with something like this? I don't ever want him to feel like he can't trust us. As long as this is happening, I want us to be a part of it."

"So do I," she says.

"It's not ideal, but it's not the end of the world."

"*Unapocalyptic.* Wonderful." She inhales deeply, lifts his hand in hers and holds it to her chest.

"I was thinking," he says, just as her irritation is starting to wear off, "that we should invite them over. For brunch, maybe, this weekend? So we can meet Sunny, and talk through some of this in more detail."

"Oh, *God.*"

Marriage is exhausting in this respect, constant stop-and-start, scrambling to catch up and then wishing you could lag behind again just a little bit.

"She's going to be our daughter-in-law, Jules; we want her to feel welcome." Goodwill: the ammo of the congenial. This has always been a point of contention between them; Mark likes others easily and Julia barely at all.

"Since when do you eat *brunch*? Are you some kind of socialite?"

"As long as it's happening," he says evenly, "we can't pretend it's not happening."

She stays awake long after she hears him fall asleep, resenting the slow deep sounds of his breathing while hers remains shallow, keeping chaotic time with the metronome of her thoughts. It's not an unfamiliar position for her, exactly, but it hasn't felt like this in a very long time, not since before Alma was born, since those days when Ben was several feet shorter than he is now, since that stretch of time when— Here she is again! A bird in a book, a harbinger of something dark—Helen Russo had provided such a welcome diversion.

8

She started doing the thing where you knocked and opened the door at the same time; Helen would call out, "In the laundry room" or "Careful, Pete tracked in water," like Julia lived there too, like they were her floors to slip on or not. Julia had never felt this comfortable—this *brazen*—with any of her friends. She was unpracticed, undersocialized, the most lackluster of guests, but Helen seemed not to notice, or not to care, and she never once appeared anything but happy to see Julia.

"I have *news*," Helen said one morning, turning from the stove, where she was idly stirring something with a wooden spoon. Julia wondered how some people orchestrated their lives to be like that, primed and ready at all times to be walked in on, pots enticingly a-simmer and alluring projects under way, as if they'd never been started and would never end and instead just exist, in perpetuity, in a picturesque in-between.

"Coulis," Helen said, gesturing to the saucepan, and Julia nodded sagely, like she had any idea what that meant. "The fall-bearing raspberries have gone *gangbusters* in the last few days. You should bring Ben by tomorrow and pick some."

"Sure," she said, and then it dawned on her that tomorrow was Saturday.

She had never once spent a non-weekday day with Helen. It wasn't something they'd ever discussed, but weekends seemed to be off-limits, the time when, presumably, Helen's kids came by for cozy family gatherings and her real friends were invited over for fabulous dinner parties. For Julia, the weekends meant Mark, of course, family trips to the aquarium or the arboretum if they were feeling ambitious but usually more small-scale endeavors, Julia and Ben tooling around on the swing set while Mark cut the grass or the three of them walking downtown to get milkshakes. She'd found herself drifting further and further from her husband in the two months since her fateful meeting at the botanic garden, supplanted emotionally as he'd been by Helen Russo, but it had strangely become easier to get along with him, required much less effort on her part to smile at him across the backyard or make small talk at the dinner table. It made her sort of sad if she stopped to think about it, but she was able to rationalize it away: Helen gave her room to breathe, and these things were helping to make her a better mom, a better wife, a better person overall.

And now: a weekend invitation! It would only serve to up her Russoean fluency: *tagine* and *entrelac* and *foliar fertilization* and, presently, *coulis*, which honestly just looked to her, peering over Helen's shoulder, like jam. A Saturday afternoon in the Russos' idyllic berry patch: she pictured Ben in little gingham shorts and a sun hat, neither of which he actually possessed and neither of which would be seasonable against the October chill, but the image nevertheless materialized in her head with ease.

"Sure," she said. "He'd love it."

Just as Julia was beginning to troubleshoot how she would explain this to Mark—*See you later; I'm taking our son berry picking with my new family!*—Helen tapped her spoon once, hard, against the pan.

"Shoot," she said. "Tomorrow's Saturday, isn't it?"

It was almost comical how quickly her heart sank. Like she'd just almost made it out of the store with the stolen goods shoved in her bra, one foot suspended over the threshold when the security guard caught her elbow.

"It is," she said, and stopped herself short—dignity! There it was!—of advertising that she and Ben were free regardless.

"We'll have to make it Tuesday, then," Helen said.

"Sure," she said, willing the weakness out of her voice, trying hard not to feel like a spurned lover. "Doing anything fun?"

"A cookout with some of the kids if the weather holds," Helen said. "Both Eric and Cal have birthdays next week."

It should have relaxed her, because there was no earthly reason for her to be invited to the family birthday celebration of people she had never met. And yet she couldn't quite help but feel a little ashamed anyway, to have her status so clearly demarcated in this way.

"We're anticipating a little *drama*," Helen said, her voice low and conspiratorial, and just like that, Julia was back in, a confidant.

"Right." She perked up. "What's going on?"

Helen turned to face her, lifting her spoon like an orchestral baton. "The prodigal son," she said gravely, "has returned to the nest, if I may mix my metaphors. Natey came flapping in Tuesday night. He went right to the carriage house without even asking us."

"And—*Natey*—"

"Nathaniel."

"He's the youngest, right?" Of course she knew Nathaniel was the youngest; she had committed to memory, without meaning to, the entire roster of Russo children, names and ages and, where applicable, the degree to which Helen hated their wives.

"Our baby," Helen said wistfully. "Natey's a—well, he fancies himself a writer. But as they say, God doesn't give with both hands. You'll see what I mean when you meet him." She smiled a little wickedly. "He's been talking about getting a degree in creative writing, but I swear to you, Julia, if Pete and I have to shell out for an MFA, I will sacrifice myself in a ceremonial pyre in the backyard."

"How long is he staying?"

"*That*," Helen said, "is a question we're apparently not allowed to ask. He seems to be feeling very sensitive, the poor thing."

"Is he your favorite?"

"No, Cal's my favorite." She said it easily, no hesitation.

Julia raised her eyebrows, and Helen, seeing, laughed again.

"I know I'm not supposed to admit that, but he's the clear winner. Natey, though— I don't know. He tugs at something in me. He just seems so lost lately."

She'd felt a similar tug earlier, watching Ben toddling into Serenity Smiles with his tiny knapsack, something grown-up in his posture, a resignedness. Helen was staring out the window over the sink now, in the direction of the carriage house. Julia had admired it before, a perfect little cottage shrouded by two dense towering pine trees, iron spiral staircase, ivy creeping up the brick like something out of an elite British school where the faculty were covering up a decades-old murder.

Perhaps sensing Julia's gaze, Helen turned back to her, smiled a little sadly.

"We do this to ourselves, don't we?"

"I suppose so," she said, but it was in fact Helen who did this to her: for just a second she felt sage and maternal, a fellow martyr who'd chosen to take on all that excruciating love.

I t was early December when Julia shyly trotted out to Helen the topic of her career. She mentioned it while sitting on the living room floor with her back against the Russos' sectional—the notion of her *maybe doing something else, getting out of the house*, putting her skills to use again—and Helen took it and ran, as Julia supposed she'd known—had she hoped?—would happen.

"Yes, Julia," Helen had said gravely, taking her hands and looking deep into her eyes. "Good Lord, yes."

They were sitting amid a sea of boxes, wrapping paper carpeting the floor. Julia was helping Helen wrap Christmas presents for what appeared to be seventeen million different people and Ben was battling himself in a very noisy game of Hungry Hungry Hippos. There were four sourdough baguettes baking aromatically in the oven and a gentle, unsticky snow fell outside; Julia was not sure she had ever experienced such ambient festivity in her life and she was beginning to grasp, for the first time, why people got excited about the holidays.

"Just something I've been thinking about," she said. "I think I—miss it, kind of. And Ben's going to be starting kindergarten before long, and then I'll just be . . ." She waved a hand in front of her face.

"You want to be back in a library? I'm thinking of an old friend of mine who's a librarian in Lincoln Park. She hasn't been on my radar because she thought for a while that I was sleeping with her husband, but it occurs to me now that she might be a resource for you."

"What kind of resource?" Julia asked, then: "Wait, were you sleeping with her husband?"

"Of course I wasn't," Helen said, then: "For a job."

"Oh. I mean— I'm not sure I'm ready to— But that would be . . ." There they were, as she had known they would be, zero to sixty in a few seconds flat. "It just seems so—I'm not sure—*different*, from my life now."

"Isn't that the point, though?"

Coming from Helen, somehow, these statements never sounded judgmental. They came across as basic troubleshooting, problem solving, even if you had yet to identify things as troublesome or problematic.

"I guess so."

"Can I ask you," Helen said, unloosing a strip of Scotch tape, "why you decided to stop working in the first place? Was it just the numbers of it?"

"Not—exactly," she said. Then, surprising herself: "My mother was— I mean, she . . ."

Helen glanced over at her, eyebrows raised.

"I mean, it wasn't *because* of her that I decided to, or not completely, but I— She wasn't around all that much when I was a kid, and when she *was* it was . . ."

It was less that she was blocking anything out and more that she simply couldn't remember, childhood amnesia; she'd read about it in a magazine at the dentist's office. It was common, not always linked to trauma, and hers hadn't been traumatic, not exactly; that's what was hard to explain to someone like Mark, that nothing had been gravely wrong, per se, but very little had been right, either.

"I'm not sure why I said that," she said. "I decided to stay home because I thought it would be the best thing for Ben."

"Is she in his life?" Helen asked. "Your mom?"

Julia shook her head, watching her tiny son scramble around the board from one hippo to the next, so good at being his own playmate. "She stopped by after he was born," she said. "Literally. For about ten minutes. Even that much surprised me, honestly, but when she showed up I couldn't help but think that maybe— I don't know. Things might change. That she might see him and—be inclined to stick around."

"Being away from that cuteness," Helen said. "She must have a good reason."

Julia looked up at her, surprised, and felt a little barb of anxiety, that perhaps Helen's clairvoyance, God forbid, extended beyond her current situation, that she could somehow telescope deep into the past and see everything that had happened there, too. "Do you think so?"

"It may not be an *actual* reason," Helen said, and Julia relaxed slightly, "but I'd be willing to bet she's convinced herself of whatever it is."

"Was yours around? Or—*is* she around?"

Helen shook her head. "No, she died about ten years ago. And she wasn't around much before then. She was a very—withholding woman. She liked things a certain way. She married my father because he could give her those certain things, and she had me because she was—well, supposed to, I guess, back then. And I was supposed to do the same, marry an investment banker, have excellent taste in tableware. And I— Well, I think I *do* have excellent taste in tableware, as a matter of fact." She smiled. "But I married Pete, and for the first few years of my career I was with the ACLU and it didn't matter to her that I was happy because the things I was doing weren't the things she wanted me to be doing. And then for several decades we engaged in that kind of passive-aggressive civility that people call *family*, checks on birthdays and—well." Helen indicated the spread of gifts around them. "Big to-dos at Christmas. But at least I take *pleasure* in it. My mother was more concerned with going through the motions."

Julia was drinking in the details, envisioning a young, rebellious Helen and her prim, domineering mother, a far more vibrant scene than her own, which had been characterized primarily by distance and need. Rich people, too, had a knack for making romance out of historic hardship; she supposed it was easier to cinematize the past when you had the right set dressing.

"Better to go through the motions than not, though, maybe,"

Helen said. "Did your mother work? Or— She must have, if your dad wasn't around."

She noticed that Helen assumed—albeit correctly—that there hadn't been any family money, and Julia wondered what it was specifically that had tipped her off, what unconscious ways Julia was displaying her lack of pedigree just as Helen emanated her abundance of it.

"She did," she said, and she was ashamed to feel a split second of embarrassment before she said, "She worked in a bakery."

Helen nodded contemplatively. "Good leftovers, I bet."

It annoyed her at first, but then she realized Helen was simply doing to the story what she'd done with her own, colorizing it, making it palatable for human consumption. Perhaps this had less to do with wealth and more with perspective, the ability to take your own narrative and polish it up, make it more digestible. She almost never let herself think about the nice parts, but there *had* been—between the drinking, and the shitty boyfriends, and the constant state of having just less than enough—good leftovers, day-old pastries in waxy bags and once, two days after her ninth birthday, a cake that a customer had failed to claim; Anita had carefully chiseled off the frostinged name of the intended recipient and piped *Julia* in a happy, looping script that Julia hadn't known her to be capable of, script very different than the cramped hand with which she wrote checks and signed school forms.

"She did her best," she said. She wasn't sure she believed it, but something about discussing Anita with another mother felt a little traitorous. "She had me at twenty. I don't think she wanted to have me, and she never really got over that. I— Part of that's why I decided to stay home with Ben, because I think I— I can't exactly— explain it. But I've always been worried that I could be screwing him up without even knowing it because it's never been clear to me exactly what I'm supposed to be doing, like everyone else has this skill set but I got passed over, so everything takes—more work. Like, sometimes just to *feel* things I have to work at it, things that I think normal people feel innately." She'd never said it aloud. She glanced up quickly at Helen. "Do you think I'm a sociopath?" She tried to make her voice light, but it didn't work; the words came out frank and wobbly.

"No, honey," Helen said. "You feel a great deal, that's obvious. You just have a harder time making sense of it."

"I just want him to know I love him," she said softly, watching Ben, who, across the room, had moved on to a miniature garbage truck that scooped up binfuls of sparkly puffballs.

"That is very much a child who knows he's loved," Helen said gently. "But don't you think he deserves to have a mom who isn't miserable?"

"Doesn't he deserve a mom who's happy enough just being with him?"

"You can't bank all of your happiness on a single person. That's a recipe for insanity on all fronts."

"I guess so," she said.

Helen watched her for a long minute, and then pushed herself up from the couch. "The bread," she said. "I'll be back in a second."

Alone in the living room, she watched Ben, who, after a minute, sensed her watching him and came sidling over, dropping himself contentedly into her lap.

"Can we take the truck home with us?" he asked in a conspiratorial whisper.

"No, sweet, sorry," she said. "That's Helen's."

"Oh, take it," Helen said, coming back into the room wielding a browned baguette wrapped in a towel. "Its intended recipient lives in Florida and finds joy primarily in destruction. Better it find a home where it'll be appreciated."

"Oh, Helen, no, you—"

"It's all yours, mister," Helen said to Ben, whose eyes were now enormous with disbelief. "And you'd better take some of this home; I did the trick with the pan of water in the oven and it seems to have turned out perfectly, if I may say." She wagged the baguette at Julia like a lightsaber.

"Can you say thank you, sweet?" she whispered to Ben, and he nodded vigorously, looking up adoringly at Helen, this mystical dispensary of surprise garbage trucks.

"My pleasure, my pleasure," Helen said, drifting back into the kitchen. Over her shoulder, she said, "It also freezes beautifully."

"Pardon?"

"The *bread*," Helen called from the kitchen.

"Oh." Julia felt, as she often did with Helen, blindsided by the journey they'd just taken, existential despair to the science of baking.

"You've done archival work in the past, haven't you?" Helen asked, returning to the room with what looked like a Rolodex.

She nodded. "For years. But I never went to grad school."

Helen waved this away, flipping through the business cards, and when she finally found what she was looking for she pulled it from its slot. She handed it over and Julia took it, feeling the raised edges of the printing, a professional connection, like Ben's truck, now in her possession simply because someone who had more than she did had decided to give it to her.

S he met him the following week, one afternoon when Helen was seeing her off.

"Hold on, don't forget the dieffenbachia." Helen claimed she was running out of room for it. "It's in a huge pot; let me see if Natey can— Darling? Nathaniel?" She cupped her hands around her mouth, directed her voice toward the carriage house. "We require your brawn."

One of the upper windows jerked open and a messy-haired head appeared. "What?"

"Go pull your car up to the door," Helen said to Julia. To the head, she said, "Come on down and earn your keep, would you?"

Julia did as she was told, backing the station wagon up the Russos' long driveway. The head was waiting for her, revealing itself to belong to a man in his late twenties, carob-haired and unshaven. He was vibrantly green-eyed, wearing a faded Sublime T-shirt and hugging an enormous ceramic pot.

"You're Nathaniel," she said, getting out of the car. She wished, absurdly, that she'd put as much thought into her appearance as she had during her first visit to Helen's house, but she'd defaulted to her tried-and-true combo of smashed bun and nursing bra.

"Thank you," he said, "for clearing that up." He had the sort of body, slender but muscled, that seemed a little bit wild, *rangy*, like he'd be able to scale brick walls at will.

"I'm sorry about this," she said. "For interrupting you from—"

"No problem. I wasn't doing anything."

She tried to think of something else to say, something beyond *You have extremely well-sculpted cheekbones* or *Are your pecs just like that on their own?*

"You want this in the back?" he asked.

"Oh," she said. "Yeah, yes, please; thanks so much."

Helen appeared in the front doorway to oversee them; she leaned against the jamb and shrugged, as if to say, *Lo and behold, in addition to being beneficent and wise, I also just happen to have a maladjusted and unfathomably handsome man-child living in my garage.*

Julia popped open the hatch and he angled in the pot alongside an industrial-size box of Pull-Ups.

"My son's," she said inanely, as though he may have thought they were hers.

"What?"

God, as Helen had said, evidently did not give with both hands.

"Nothing. Thank you, really."

"Sure thing," he said, and then was gone as quickly as he'd come.

9

Alma's applying to college has occupied the better part of their last two years, an athletic family-wide participation in what strikes Julia—privately—as a frankly ludicrous rat race populated by an abjectly shifty-seeming cast of SAT tutors and admissions counselors and precocious college sophomores—safely to the other side—who were paid to read Alma's personal statements and make comments like "Something more inspirational here?????" Her daughter is a very good student, unremarkable only in that she has failed to cultivate eccentric hobbies—one of her classmates is an avid player of something called a *clarsach*, in celebration of generations-removed Scottish lineage—or attract media attention for self-serving philanthropic ventures, like the sixteen-year-old recently featured in the local paper after raising money for childhood obesity from her "therapeutic pole dancing" TikTok videos. Everyone is scrambling to distinguish themselves, but Alma has simply kept her head down and worked hard, which Julia admires both for its virtue and because it has not required her to buy her daughter a large medieval instrument or to applaud her twerking for change. Her daughter occasionally wants to skip gym class and get smoothies with her friends; her daughter does not, at seventeen, have a ten-year plan; her daughter is observant and interesting and wholly, confidently herself, and Julia refuses to acknowledge the validity of a system that deems this *not enough* while also praying, to some overhead nondenominational blob, that things will work out as Alma wants them to.

It has not been until recently—now that the applications are submitted, all seventeen of them fired off into the universe like space shuttles, each with its own outrageous fee—that she's begun to see the anxiety wearing on her daughter: Alma's picked-over cuticles and hand-raked hair, circles under her eyes and toast left at the breakfast table. There has been, for months, nothing to do but wait, something at which her daughter has never been particularly skilled. They have now officially entered the time in the semester when it's plausible that Alma will start hearing back—"Larson got early acceptance to Duke," she'd announced yesterday over dinner, gravely, as though passing along whispered word of a planned declaration of war—and she has become somewhat feral, pacing around like a panther, even quicker than usual to bite off their heads if they so much as look at her the wrong way.

Other, better mothers may have encouraged exercise, or productive bonding activities like closet organization or the collaborative study of a foreign language, but Julia has never had a great deal of creative stamina when it comes to her children, and so when she and Alma pass the time together, they do so whilst watching television. Their favorite is *Gold Beach*, an hourlong drama that chronicles the exorbitantly wealthy and dramatically afflicted populace of an idyllic town on the Oregon coast. The show follows a handful of high schoolers who are constantly finding themselves in romantic entanglements and also a disproportionate amount of physical peril, surfing accidents and rogue vintage pistols.

Mindless television is not a bonding activity you are supposed to have with your child, and yet it is her only mainstay with Alma of late besides mealtimes and verbal abuse. Her daughter has made brownies; they're sitting on the couch close enough so that either end of the pan is on their respective laps and they're eating from it with soup spoons, Suzanne sniffing ostentatiously from where she's perched behind them on the back of the couch.

She is almost never happier than when she's sitting with Alma like this, close enough to smell the distinct medicinal perfume of her T/Gel shampoo, close enough to feel the warmth of her skin and her exhalations, close enough to reach out and touch her, though she rarely does. A calm comes over her daughter; she sheds her huffy affectations and her tightly wound teenage façade and allows herself to speak easily to her mother. To acknowledge any of this would be to ruin everything, so Julia sits, sometimes, in complete stillness, trilling, like a rock absorbing sunlight: the marvelous fact that, for an hour, her daughter is her friend.

"She's too smart for him," Alma says, indicating one of the characters with her spoon. "But I bet they'll hook up at least."

Julia glances over at her, always looking for clues in their exchanges, details that will color in the gray shapes of Alma's time not spent at home. She is reasonably certain—as certain as one can be when cohabiting with a hostile and terrifying sniper—that her daughter is a virgin, but she doesn't know for sure. She also doesn't know what *hooking up* means, if it's sex or some lesser variant; to ask would violate the rules of their *Gold Beach* evenings.

On-screen, two characters make their way to the couch, losing both of their shirts en route. Is this hooking up? The romance on this show is always so *athletic*, people constantly shoving their partners against walls or assailing them, chimplike, from across rooms.

"That woman's awfully thin," she says primly.

"Mom," Alma says, teasing but with a hint of a real question: "God, why are you so weird about sex?"

She stills. "I'm not."

She's talked to Alma about it, at least once a calendar year since she turned eleven, explaining the basics and trying to provide opportunities for her daughter to ask questions, and she bought her a graphic nonfiction title that featured an entire instructive chapter— hotly contested among the middle school moms—on various forms of masturbation. She has *tried*, at least. She gamely answered her daughter's tentative sixth-grade questions about whether you could get herpes from a drinking fountain ("It's unlikely," she'd said, though she looked it up online afterward to confirm) and how old she was when she'd lost her virginity ("Twenty-two," she'd said, rounding up generously and remaining otherwise tight-lipped). But at a certain point Alma had taken the reins herself, turned inward, surfacing only long enough to introduce them, a few months ago, to Margo Singh.

Her own mother never said a word to her about sex, but it was a more ubiquitous part of their life together: Anita almost always had a boyfriend, and so sex was just a thing that happened, a lot; it wasn't until Julia was fourteen or fifteen that she became aware of it as anything besides white noise from behind Anita's bedroom door, and by then it seemed too late to ask.

"Honey," she says, as a commercial begins, "how are things going with Margo?"

It is dangerous territory. She always wanted her mother to ask her things like this until she actually did ask. So she has always treaded lightly with Alma, tried to make herself available but unobtrusive, like a laundry hamper. Neither she nor Mark had given it a second thought when their daughter told them she was dating a girl; they both liked Margo and it had also made a bone-level sense to Julia, who had of course, technically, known her daughter since before she was born, and while this did not necessarily mean she knew her better than anyone, it meant she knew Alma better than most, and she was utterly unsurprised to see her fall for Margo, *Ollie's Margo*, she and Mark call her, because the mailwoman is also named Margo.

"Fine." Alma remembers to roll her eyes. "Ew, what? Why are you asking me that?"

"Is it getting—serious?"

"*Mom*," Alma says. But then, surprisingly, she goes on: "I'm not sure. I guess it depends on where we both end up next year?"

Their girl! Once so tiny, and born into such fraught circumstances, during a time when she wondered if they were going to make it. The way she is so intently avoiding eye contact, the restraint she is keeping over her own voice—this stab at measured maturity—is making Julia's insides hurt.

Her daughter seems to weigh something in her head, then says, "We've been fighting kind of a lot about it lately."

"Have you?" She's never seen Margo be anything but mild-mannered, her voice at the dinner table almost comically soft, like someone trying not to wake a sleeping child. "Well. Fighting can be an important part of a relationship. Airing things out."

"You and Dad never fight."

"Of course we do."

"You *argue*," Alma says, "about things like whether or not Boz Skaggs is white, or when the dog's birthday is. You don't *fight*-fight."

"Of course we *fight*-fight." Aren't there implications about couples who get along too well? Is there not some implied darkness lurking beneath the surface for those people, buried bodies or betrayals so massive that they can't ever be unearthed again without causing some terrible seismic shift?

"Like when?"

"There are elements of my life that you aren't privy to, Ollie."

"Gross."

How horrified her daughter would be—scarred for life, no question—to think of her mother's birthday gift to her father, those merry silk scarves. She'd walked in on them having sex once when she was a toddler—please, God, let her not remember—and Julia had tried to turn it into a game, calling out for her daughter to retreat into the hall and count to ten, which Alma did, in German, which they were learning at her Montessori school, Mark and Julia clothing themselves, stifling laughter to the soundtrack of Alma's tiny, cooperative *vier, fünf, sechs.*

"Dad and I fight plenty," she says.

Alma holds up her hands. "Whatever you say."

On the television, a woman effuses over a particularly absorbent mop.

"If you want to talk about it," she says. "Any of it. Margo, whatever, sweetheart. You know you can— You know I'm here, right?"

Her girl, straight-necked and equable: "Sure, Mom."

And it's said with such confidence that Julia almost believes her, focuses on the pleasure of the moment instead of all that is to come for her daughter, all of the moments beyond her control; she focuses on the fact that, for this moment, her girl is close enough to smell, to feel: she brushes some of Alma's damp hair back from her shoulder, and Alma lets her.

10

The Russos, now that their kids were grown, spent the first six weeks of the year at a cousin's house on Sanibel Island, and Julia found herself preemptively mourning Helen's absence, wondering how she would survive without her only social outlet.

"I want you to finish your scarf when I'm gone," Helen said on the phone the day before she left. "And I want you to stop over tomorrow after we leave. I made Ben a little birthday treat."

"You— Really?" Ben loved the Russos too, Pete especially. He'd often amble off to wherever he heard banging sounds coming from in the house; it had initially made Julia nervous, but Helen assured her Pete was excellent at turning toddlers into low-risk tradesmen and Ben would chatter on the way home about how he'd sorted washers into blue plastic bowls and helped push globs of spackle into holes in the walls. That Helen had not only remembered he was turning four but made something for him touched Julia deeply.

"Of course," Helen said. "I baked him a galette."

Julia blinked. "Oh, wow, that's—"

"Apricot. I know he likes fruit."

Ben did like fruit, or at least the limited array of fruits that most kids favored, the sweetest ones, apples and strawberries and the occasional tiny clementine. In his hierarchy of preferred foods, fruit landed somewhere well beneath white bread, Goldfish, and the obscenely named Gushers.

"I'm sure he'll love it, Helen; thank you."

"It'll be in the fridge," Helen said. "Middle shelf. Let yourself in tomorrow and get it— Pete and I are leaving at the crack of dawn so use the key in the geranium pot—and when you're ready to serve, heat it up at 375 for ten minutes."

"Okay," Julia said. "I will."

"All right, honey. We're— Just a second, sweet; I'm on the phone— God, he's driving me up the wall. Okay. I've got to go repack Pete's suitcase because *he never remembers to roll*." This last bit inflected, clearly directed at Pete; Julia pictured them in their bedroom, filling two Samsonites with linen beachwear, Helen undoubtedly ticking items off a list.

"I'm going to miss you, Julia!" The line came out so easily, and with such frank sincerity. Julia was touched anew. "You've become a fixture."

"So have you," Julia said, though it felt like a wild understatement.

"Next year you should join us for a week. Has Ben been to the ocean?"

"Not yet," she said.

"It's a date," Helen said. "All right, so we'll— Pete, would you leave that *alone*; I told you I'll do it— We'll see you when we get back, okay? Love to you, sweetie. Don't have too much fun without us."

And with that she was gone, leaving Julia to ponder the *love*, undoubtedly thrown out sans thought, amiable as an air kiss, but it popped into her head several more times throughout the day, and it kept making her smile even when all she was doing was the dinner dishes.

"Someone looks happy," Mark said, coming up behind her at the sink. She startled, and he kissed her hair. "I'm glad to see it," he said. "It suits you, Jules."

The next day, after she dropped Ben off at Serenity Smiles and stopped at the dentist's office, she drove to the Russos' house, and the sight of their empty driveway depressed her profoundly; she felt, for one of the first times since she'd started spending time with Helen, the familiar gaping hollow in her gut, *dread*, left once again alone with nothing but expanses of time and her own dull thoughts to entertain her. And she couldn't believe it, how instantaneously paler her life became without Helen and how *pathetic* that was. Helen was probably in the sky right now, drinking plane wine with her husband, glad to be free of the long roster of people who needed her, which most likely included Julia.

She trudged up the walk and fished the key out of the geranium pot, half-hoping all the while that Helen's head would come popping out of an upstairs window and call her inside.

But the house was quiet, vacant. On the mail table next to the door, there was a stack of twenty-dollar bills with a note paperclipped to the front that read *Please don't forget the orchid! Thanks, Marta!* and Julia pondered, not unjealously, the heart drawn beneath the woman's name.

She turned away, proceeded to the kitchen. There was another note on the counter, a pink Post-it that read *Ben's cake!!!* in Helen's looping scrawl; it was unclear whether it had been a reminder for Helen herself or a note directly to Julia, but she took it, regardless, as a point of pride—her son's name on a note in the Russos' kitchen, joining the family clutter, proof of their existence—and tucked the paper into her purse.

In the refrigerator, the galette was on the middle shelf as Helen had told her it would be, on a blue glass plate, and Helen had arranged scraps of leftover pastry on the top to spell out Ben's name. Julia herself had made Ben a sheet cake frosted with the characters from *Blue's Clues*, though Blue had turned out looking not like an affable puppy but a pharma advertisement's cartoonish rendering of a germ. She found herself wondering from whence Helen's conception of four-year-old palates had come, but on the heels of that she found herself wondering if perhaps her own conceptions were the problem, if she was raising her child to be dull and unadventurous.

"Are you a robber?"

She yelped audibly and very nearly dropped the plate. Nathaniel was standing in the kitchen doorway, the sole of one bare foot pressed against the jeans-clad indentation of his opposite knee.

"Jesus Christ," she said.

"Are you?" he asked.

"*No.* I— Of course I'm not. We met a few weeks ago; I'm a friend of your mom's. I was just—"

"I'm kidding," he said. "You know she's out of town, right?"

"She told me to come pick this up." She lifted the plate, feeling, ludicrously, like perhaps he *had* just caught her stealing it.

"What did you think of Natey?" Helen had asked her after the dieffenbachia encounter, and she'd simply said *he's nice,* because what else was she supposed to say, that he had the biceps of a Renaissance equestrian?

He cocked his head, studying her. He was wearing a Black Watch plaid flannel whose soft napped knit she could almost smell before she saw it. She was sure she imagined, as well, his eyes tracing the swoop of her sweater neck.

"You don't look like one of the Unitarian rummage sale ladies," he said after a minute. "They tend to be pretty intense busybodies. And you're too pale to be from her hiking group; all of those women are just asking for melanoma."

"No, I'm—"

"Planned Parenthood," he said suddenly. "Do you guys escort together? You seem like you could take on some right-to-lifers."

"Thank you," she said uncertainly. "No, I met her at the botanic garden a few months ago and she—"

"Took you in?"

"I guess so."

"She has a tendency to do that. Are you an arborist?"

"What? No, I take my son there."

"The one with the Ultratrim Training Pants? Let me guess: *Ben?*"

He gestured to the galette. He had remembered the Pull-Ups.

She opened her mouth, closed it. She had the sense, somewhere at the back of her neck, of wishing he hadn't said Ben's name, that her son was meant to be kept separate from whatever this interaction was. His eye contact unnerved her.

"What's *your* name?" he asked her.

"Julia."

"Pretty," he said.

Her cheeks warmed. "Thank you."

"Your kid can't be older than, what, five? If we're judging by the Pull-Ups, which I guess I shouldn't, because one of my brothers wet the bed until he was thirteen."

"He's turning four tomorrow," she said.

"Who the fuck makes a galette for a four-year-old?"

She smiled grudgingly. "She said your brother Eric used to love—"

"Yeah, I know; Eric has been outclassing us all since he was two." He rolled his eyes. "How the fuck do *I* even know what a galette is? That's the real question."

"Refined palates in this family," she said.

"And yet still a few bed wetters," he said. "Self excluded."

"You must be very proud."

He smiled at her; he had a very nice smile, the kind that filled every corner of the face.

"I should go," she said. "Sorry your mom didn't tell you I was coming by."

"You want a beer?" he asked.

"I— Sorry?"

It was barely ten in the morning. Nathaniel studied her steadily, waiting, something of his mother's canniness in his face beneath the sleepiness around his eyes.

"Okay," she said, and he moved past her to get to the fridge; the flannel smelled just the way she knew it would, damp and dry at the same time. She watched him pull the caps off of two bottles.

He gestured to the stool behind her. "Can I take your coat?"

"Oh," she said. "I— Sure." She shrugged it off. She'd had to pick up Mark's special toothpaste at the dentist's, so she was dressed presentably, and wearing mascara, and she caught herself feeling grateful for that. Nathaniel folded the coat over a kitchen chair. He was one of those men who made a lot of eye contact, and who always seemed to be on the verge of smiling, like he was thinking of something funny he wasn't going to share with you.

"What did you eat for breakfast?" he asked.

She had eaten the remnants of Ben's Honey Nut Cheerios, and several slices of banana that he had abandoned on his Clifford the

Big Red Dog plate, and an old piece of Halloween candy she'd found in the cup holder of her car.

"Cereal," she said, with dignity.

He nodded contemplatively. "I was considering the same," he said. "However." He opened a drawer, brandished a knife. "Is your son good at sharing?"

"He is, actually."

Nathaniel nodded again, and without further ado, sliced cleanly into the galette.

"Your mom said to heat it up," she said, remembering. "Three seventy-five."

"I won't tell if you won't."

She sipped her beer and watched as he pulled two dessert plates from a cabinet, extracted two forks and, an oddly thoughtful gesture, folded two napkins into neat triangles. He started to eat his leaning against the island, a series of large, efficient bites. She felt only slightly bad as she took a bite of her own.

"This is very, very good," she said.

He was already almost done with his. "You're over here, like, all the time."

It took her aback, that somebody else had noticed, that *he* had noticed.

"Just an observation," he said. "My mom must really like you."

"I really like your mom. It's possible I've—come to rely on her a little bit too much."

"Oh yeah, so have I," he said easily. "So has everyone."

"Does she have a lot of friends?" She steeled herself.

"They cycle," he said, making a circular motion with his hands. He cut another slice of galette. "You're definitely the most popular at the moment."

She glowed, watching him decimate his second piece.

"She says you're funny," he said.

"I'm glad someone thinks so."

"You seem more sad to me," he said.

"Oh." She wasn't sure how to feel about this, wasn't sure whether or not to be offended.

"But my radar isn't always very accurate."

"That's not—inaccurate, I guess." She studied him. "You seem a little sad too."

He pushed his crumbs around his plate, trying to collect a mass of them on his fork like he was shoveling snow. "Yeah," he said vaguely.

She slid the remains of hers across the counter and he finished it off in two bites.

"Are you here—indefinitely?" she asked.

He shrugged. "Maybe. I'm working on some things."

"Yeah," she said, "so am I, I guess." She stood up from the stool. He was close enough that she could smell the apricot on his breath, and a kind of sweet, hibernatory odor, like he'd just woken up, which he probably had. "I should let you get back to it," she said, and she wondered what she smelled like, if she'd become one of those mothers who always gave off the scent of sour milk. They stood like that for a moment, inches apart, and then he moved to get her coat.

"Come back sometime if you want," he said. "They'll be gone till Valentine's Day."

He held the coat out to help her into it; she slipped her arms in self-consciously, and when she turned to face him, he leaned in and kissed her, very gently, on the lips.

"Oh," she said, and before she knew what she was doing she was kissing him back, and she couldn't believe—when she pulled away a minute later, ten minutes later, she had no idea how much time had passed, or where her mind had gone while it had—how very, very, very good she'd felt, kissing him, light-headed but alive, so alive that she'd forgotten, while it was happening, how used she'd grown to being half-dead.

11

The version of Sunny that has been assembled in her head is blond and cunning and, frankly, homicidal; the one who actually arrives on their doorstep is blondish but otherwise unlike her imaginings, anatomically microscopic but lustrously horse-haired, barely five feet, freckled with very symmetrical features and huge blue eyes, a little snub-nosed, alt-preppy J. Crew getup.

Mark goes to hug her—one of life's great mysteries, that she'd married a *hugger*—and Sunny startles, laughs, waves tiny tree-nymph hands in front of her face before throwing her arms around him.

"I'm so sorry," she says. "I wasn't expecting you to be so *nice*."

"Yes, well," says Julia. "Water torture begins at sundown."

"My mom," says Ben, and Sunny pulls back from Mark, hands in front of her face again, laughing, a high tinkly sound like a windup toy; her hair has been French-braided away from either side of her face like an elfin queen. She seems to be trying to assess whether or not the hugging rules apply to all members of the family, and Julia, though she feels a little bad, clasps her own hands in front of her, nixing the prospect of any sort of embrace.

"It's so nice to meet you, Mrs. Ames," Sunny says, and though this is normally where she would fall over herself insisting *please call me Julia*, she just nods.

"Ditto," she says, a word she hates, borrowed from Alma, and everyone stalls for a few seconds. Mark puts an arm around her waist, tugging her close to him, not overtly coming out and saying *be nice* but not quite convivial in his embrace, either.

She doesn't mean to be this way, or she doesn't *usually* mean to be this way; she is, in fact, usually not like this, but she's feeling at once disembodied and emboldened, everyone but she apparently content to pretend that everything's okay, and there's something about her family's anticipating her bad behavior that makes her want to behave badly.

She has prepared well culinarily, at least, for their ragtag brunch, French toast and fruit salad and a potted array of artisanal jams. Alma is sitting up on the lip of the sink, and though she's a good six inches taller than Sunny, they could otherwise be contemporaries.

"Wait," Sunny says to Alma. "Your hair is *amazing.*"

It's such a frank, unadorned compliment—and true, too! Alma's hair *is* amazing!—and to hear another person so baldly appreciating her daughter is a balm.

"Oh," Alma says, and her face shines with the particular pride that comes from a magnetic older person openly admiring you. "I mean—thanks. Yours too."

"No," Sunny says, as though she finds this statement genuinely objectionable. "The color is like— I'd kill for it. Oh my God, you have it too." And Sunny is suddenly reaching toward Julia like a kid at an art museum, lifting her hand past the invisible personal space barrier to touch her hair.

She doesn't mean to flinch—does anyone ever *mean* to flinch?— but Sunny clocks it, recoils, and Julia sees the twinge of hurt in her expression, before Sunny speaks again: "Well. Let's hope the baby gets *those* genes."

It's as though there's been some collective order for everyone to freeze. Sunny has been impregnated by Ben, who shares genetic material with his sister, Alma, because they have the same parents, Mark and Julia, in whose kitchen they are all arranged like the cast of some low-budget absurdist matinee: inarguable truths! Just *facts*, so why are they all reacting like this? Sunny, more than any of them, gets to decide what information is revealed, and when; so why does Julia, normally fond of straight shooting, suddenly want to crawl out of her own skin? Even Suzanne seems wary, though Julia posits privately that this may be because she'd overheard Ben telling them on the phone last night that Sunny was "not super comfortable with dogs."

"You all have good hair," Sunny goes on. "Your dad must not have been bald, Julia."

"I— Sorry?"

"It's a maternally inherited trait. If you have a bald dad, you'll probably end up with a bald son."

"Oh, I—" She glances quickly at Mark. This is the problem with having a family history like hers. The honest answer to this question is even less palatable brunch-time fare than what Sunny has just presented them with. "No," she says instead. "No bald dads."

"I think we'll be set in that department regardless," Ben says, putting his arm around Sunny, gently taking a fistful of her hair and—even as she watches it happen she can't quite believe it's happening—nibbling playfully on the ends of it. Now they all look away not from the truth but from the weirdness of the gesture, the performative intimacy that is, nonetheless, intimate, this girl's hair in Ben's mouth, both of them laughing. She has the impulse to walk out, down the driveway Ben and Sunny have just come up and all the way to some distant horizon, but Mark's hand steadies her, pressing into her lower back, *let it go, Jules,* and also she becomes aware of a smell, suddenly, and goes to the oven door to release a cloud of smoke: the plate of French toast she'd intended only to warm is now charred a dark brown.

"Something's burning," says Alma, helpfully.

She'd returned earlier that morning, in pursuit of lox, to the same grocery at which she'd encountered Helen Russo, making the argument in her head that its seafood distributor, judging by the feedback on her crab cakes, was superior to the one closer to home. She'd been, the entire time she was there, envisioning a scenario in which Helen had found herself seized by a need for some early-morning pine nuts.

But she hadn't run into Helen, and when she brings out the lox at brunch, Sunny lurches to her feet and staggers from the room.

"She's really sensitive to smell lately," Ben says with apology, relocating the lox to the opposite end of the table, and Julia—who'd been sick for months when she was pregnant with Alma, vomiting unbidden left and right and triggered by stimuli far less offensive than a pink pile of brined flesh—feels momentarily shamed for not having considered this, and, regarding the glistening folds of fish, a bit nauseated herself.

Sunny returns a moment later looking sweaty and wan, apologizing profusely.

"It's like I'm a *child*," she says, commandeering a bagel, biting into it, unsliced, like it's an apple. "Like, I just completely lose control of my whole body for the foreseeable future? Okay. And the only thing that *doesn't* make me want to puke is eating, so I'm pretty much doing *this* all day—" She takes another bite of bagel, chews theatrically—"or I'm doing the opposite. I'm super fun at parties!"

"It's an undignified time," Julia says, and she means it in a commiserating way, but it comes out—of *course* it does; who *says* something like that—sounding like she's calling Sunny's dignity into question. Mark raises his eyebrows at her, and she scrambles mentally—trying to recall some embarrassment of her own, a gravidinal instance of incontinence—but she comes up blank, or at least, sifting through a card catalog of the spurting horrors of childbirth, comes up devoid of brunch-appropriate examples.

"Ben tells us you're from Connecticut." Mark takes over, proffering this bland nonquestion like a wilting bouquet.

"Born and raised," Sunny affirms.

The conversation stalls again. Julia and Mark are both bad at chitchat for different reasons; if she became slightly more boring and he slightly less, they might find some fruitful middle ground.

"What brought you to Chicago?" Mark asks.

"My parents are narcissists," Sunny says, as though this is a logical response.

The common denominator Julia has noticed among people who brazenly claim their parents are narcissists is the claimants themselves, who also usually seem like narcissists. Julia, whose mother actually probably is a narcissist, and who has never met Sunny's parents, has the impulse to defend them, to say *takes one to know one*.

"My family's toxic," Sunny continues. "I wanted to get as far away from them as I could."

She sees Ben's hand disappear under the table, presumably to cover Sunny's knee; she has noticed, too, throughout the meal, the way Sunny cocks her head imperceptibly in Ben's direction when he speaks, attuned to the pitch of his voice. It should please her, the evident fact of their closeness. She knows she, too, once had scientific radar for Ben's voice, even the most infinitesimal warble; she would awaken from the depths if he so much as coughed when he was a baby.

"Sorry to hear that," Mark says.

"No, it's fine," Sunny says, smiling up at Ben. "It worked out."

"Lucky me," Ben says, and Julia marvels momentarily over how it's possible that she has raised a schmuck without noticing it until now, but then she sees the look on Ben's face, one that's less of dumb infatuation than something deeper and genuine: he's proud of Sunny; he cares for Sunny. This, for just a second, touches her.

"Jules made a couple of moves like that herself, didn't you, honey?" Mark says, and she feels Ben looking at her. It became part of the stories she'd tell him before bed—it was so easy to run out of topics with children, the mathematical mundanity of fairy tales and morality plays; she found herself dipping into the repositories of her own story, cross-country road trips and the cinematic seconds you could only experience when in a new place for the first time.

Chicago, before she'd returned to it, had simply been *home*, existing to her as a series of syllables: *the lake, the Vic, the El;* she knew nothing, then, of the more complex monikers awaiting her: *AllAboard, Serenity Smiles, unspecified perinatal mood and anxiety disorders, Helen Russo.* Chicago in metaphor had stood for something much larger, murkier: the little bungalow on Washtenaw where they lived until she was seven, the squeaky swing on the playground at Nightingale Elementary, where her father sometimes took her, the winter night she'd sat in her mother's lap after her father had left, tires on the street outside pressing the snow to reveal dark wet asphalt.

"I moved a few times," she says, because she is bad at this game, and irritated, and wishing she had opted to serve mimosas, which she had nixed in deference to Sunny. "Nothing out of the ordinary."

Mark and Ben both regard her with that same beseeching intensity.

"How long have you two been married?" Sunny asks.

"Longer than you've been alive," she replies, and Mark knees her under the table. She tries to smile. "But who's counting?"

"Ben told me you have gorgeous wedding photos," Sunny says, which seems categorically odd; she hadn't ever known Ben to even be aware that they *had* wedding photos, let alone have an opinion on them. "I'd love to see them sometime."

"You two should go look at them," Mark says pointedly, like he's trying to reunite an estranged couple, and this time when he knees her, she kicks him back. "Ollie's got homework, right, sweetie?" he says, rising from the table. "And Benj and I can do the dishes."

Ben rises too, touching a palm to the top of Sunny's head before going into the kitchen.

"If we end up having a photographer I'd love to have some pictures done in sepia," Sunny says.

"Well, we're not *that* old. We didn't get married during the Gold Rush."

Alma snorts.

"Oh, no, I know that," Sunny says, as though she actually has to clarify that she knows it.

"I'm not sure where our pictures are. I'll see if I can find them the next time you're—" She pauses. "Give me some notice next time."

Her life has been full of moments like this one, when she shuts things down without trying, and every single time it happens she experiences the twofold sensation she's feeling right now: shame, first of all, for her humanistic inadequacy, but also the nagging remorse over failing to learn from your mistakes. She feels this way with Alma constantly, her embarrassment reflected in her daughter's implacable face: *Why aren't you better at this?*

"A dead body was found," Alma supplies brightly, "after their wedding."

Sunny frowns.

"It was *not*," Julia says. "A body washed up on the beach a few *miles* from where our wedding was. Last year. More than twenty years *after* our wedding."

She and Mark had married quietly and inexpensively, to little fanfare, a party in a park. And it had been *fun*, a certifiably good day, though she'd been conceptually resistant to weddings in general, to say nothing of marriage—the hugeness of the decision rendering it somehow hollow and playful, easy to commit to because it didn't seem real. She had allowed herself to focus on the minutiae— the park permit, a recycling bin filled with ice and bottles of cheap white wine, a vintage cream slip dress from Way Back on Division that had cost thirteen dollars, pleasing Mark's conventional parents by inviting distant relations Mark had never even met—instead of the gaping expanse of a *marriage*, and what it actually meant to be tethering one life to another. She'd been wearing too much makeup; Mark had too many cousins; they'd spent too much money on the food; she had experienced the whole day from a point of remove, not even like a guest at the wedding but a bird perched above it, ready to swoop in and pick up the crumbs after the real participants left.

"I'm losing my mind trying to get our logistics sorted out," Sunny says. "We have it narrowed down to three dates and two venues, but I can't finalize the venue until the wedding planner gets back from vacation, and we're working around the move, and the end of the semester, and my roommate is spending her summer abroad in *Greece* and she keeps changing the day she's leaving but she's supposed to be my maid of honor, plus Noah's moving to New York, and he keeps saying he's going *whenever's good*, as if that's helpful information for anyone, as if we haven't put down deposits at both venues just in case and it's *kind of important* to know if we'll have an equal number of bridesmaids and groomsmen. But we'll let you know as soon as we can. I know there's a lot of maneuvering with these things."

Julia experiences a strange disembodying moment where she wonders what possible maneuvering she could have to do and realizes, a second later, that it's her son getting married, her attendance and participation required.

"Noah?" she asks on a delay.

"Ben's Noah?" Sunny says, with the tiniest hint of *duh*, and it dawns on her—*Noah*, of course; Noah has been a household name for nearly twenty years, but it's Sunny's offhand mention of him that has thrown her for a loop.

"Noah's moving to New York?" Ben and Noah on the swing set, sword-fighting with sticks; Ben and Noah studying for chemistry at the kitchen table, their legs too long for their bodies, fingers orange with Cheeto dust. Ben's first friend, both of them on the quiet side, cautious except when they were together. She'd been so happy when they'd found each other but also, shamefully, just the tiniest bit jealous, the first death knell of her baby growing up, finding company other than her own.

"He's been hired by the *Times*," Sunny says importantly, like she's the one taking the job.

Julia has always wondered if Ben might move away, New York or maybe somewhere slightly less overwhelming, Denver or Berkeley; she has always hoped that he might venture out for a bit, even if only to return home again. She has always hoped—a little selfishly, perhaps—that he might try the things that she hadn't been able to try herself, or that she hadn't allowed herself to try; that kind of experimentation had always felt just beyond her grasp, unaffordable both monetarily and mentally.

"Is anything off-limits for you?" Sunny asks.

"Pardon?"

The girl blinks at her. "Weekends? In the next two months?"

"Oh. No, I— Mark may be traveling for work, but that's usually negotiable."

"Mom?" Alma says, affronted. "My *graduation*?"

"Right," she says. "Sorry, honey; I'm in denial." She slips an arm around Alma's shoulders, taking advantage of the odds that her daughter won't shrug her off in the presence of an intimidatingly cool twentysomething. "Except for that," she says to Sunny. "The last weekend in May."

Sunny pulls a little face. "Okay, that was one of our finalists. So I guess that narrows it down!" She pulls out her phone, taps in a note. Then she looks up at Julia and smiles a big white smile. "Don't worry," she says. "I'm type A; we'll figure it all out."

"I'm *not* type A," Julia says, approximating a smile of her own. "So no worries over here."

"Yeah," Sunny says, frowning down at her phone again. She's distracted by something else, some part of this new venture she's undertaking, this new family, one that seems, at present, to only tangentially feature Julia and Mark and Alma. "Ben said that."

12

B en's fourth birthday was a small family affair, a frigid trip to Brookfield Zoo, home for presents and the garish blue birthday cake. Her eyes welled up as they sang to him, her and Mark's reedy, unpracticed voices, their son's face candlelit and burstingly happy: what an incandescent little person he was. Four. Four years of all this, somehow.

Mark caught the break in her voice and smiled at her across the table as Ben blew out his candles; his eyes looked a little shiny, too, and she remembered that wild otherworldly morning Ben had been born, silence, suddenly, after hours of a rising, rising roar, two that were suddenly three, and neither she nor Mark had said a word for what felt like hours, both of them transfixed, passing the baby back and forth, touching his cheeks, his creased wrists, his inexplicable eyebrows. You couldn't not be filled with wonder in a moment like that; it was how the universe hooked you and reeled you in to parenthood, having fattened you up with all that *promise*, the miraculous fact that your baby had eyebrows.

Mark kissed the top of her head when he got up to help Ben pull his four candles from the cake. She wondered what her son had wished for, if he was yet capable of conceptually grasping the notion of wishes; she hoped, if so, that he had asked for something material, something fun and easy and gettable. She wasn't sure when the darker, more existential kind of wishing started—on her own tenth birthday she'd wished for her mom to like her more—but she hoped very dearly that it wasn't starting yet, in her son's case.

He requested that they both read to him before bed, so they squeezed in on either side and took turns with a tall stack of books. She watched Ben watching his dad, Mark doing Welsh possum accents for his son, and it made her gut pulse with love for them both.

Ben drifted off halfway through her comparatively lackluster rendition of *The Rainbow Fish*; she became suddenly self-conscious when she realized only Mark was listening.

"Sorry," she said. "Can you live without knowing how it ends?"

He smiled at her over Ben's head.

"I'd like to just *preserve* him like this," she said, looking down at their son. She didn't particularly love the current swatch of time in her own life, but for Ben it was extraordinary, so many synapses firing beneath the surface, cells growing and shape-shifting. A perfect person, progressing. That was motherhood: she would stay here forever, mired in her own unhappiness, if it meant his sweet sleeping head didn't move from where it rested on her stomach.

"Let's look into it," said Mark. "Must be some kind of experimental trial happening."

She shifted beneath Ben's weight, settled herself more deeply against his pillows, sighed. Mark reached for the throw blanket on the rocking chair and covered their legs with it.

"Thanks," she said, and he put his arm around her, pulling her closer to him.

She was almost never alone with him anymore, and now that she was she felt the shame of what had happened with Nathaniel begin to bubble up, filling her chest like reflux, Mark beside her, none the wiser, running his fingers through the ends of her hair. It occurred to her that today had been a perfect day, one of the most perfect days she could remember them having since the day they'd inventoried Ben's eyebrows together. She should have felt so content, lying there with the two of them, her little family, nothing but love, exhalations and radiator clanks, but instead, suddenly, she felt very alone, a cold and somehow inevitable inadequacy, these two upstanding people alongside her and she the deviant, the one whose heart wasn't in it, the one who'd yesterday, with someone else's son, eaten her own son's birthday galette.

"You feel like doing something tonight?" Mark asked. "Watch a movie?" It was a completely reasonable segue, an utterly normal expectation: they were best friends, weren't they, partners, who'd become that way because they enjoyed being together. And she *wanted* to, she realized upon reflection. She would have *liked* to do something nice and mindless with her husband, open a bottle of wine, doze off side by side in front of *The Wire*.

"I'm—" She stopped, swallowed. Mark's fingers stilled in her hair.

"Or something else," he said, and there was a kind of desperation in his voice that she wasn't used to hearing lately, the same kind of nervous uncertainty she remembered from when they'd first met, when he thought he had to work hard to win her over, which wasn't nearly as true as he believed it to be.

"I'm—pretty tired," she said, and she felt him wilt. "I'm sorry."

"No," he said. "It's fine."

She couldn't bear the thought of sitting beside him without the buffer of Ben between them, couldn't stand thinking how it would feel, the silence no longer easy because she'd ruined it.

"Maybe we could—just stay here for a little bit, though," she said, and he seemed to come to life again; the muscles of his arm relaxed behind her and he rested the back of his hand, for a second, tenderly against her neck.

"Sure," he said. "Yeah, sure we can, Jules."

Ben was snoring just the tiniest bit, and Mark continued combing, rhythmically, through her hair, everyone but she doing what they were supposed to be doing, everyone but she, who had kissed another man yesterday.

And yet there she ended up again, a morning the week after her encounter with Nathaniel Russo, having dropped Ben at school, wanting so much to be going to a routine Wednesday at Helen's, the fireplace roaring and homemade chai along with the warmth of Helen's close, companionable chatter. That was inaccessible to her at present, of course, but she couldn't, despite how hard she tried, stop thinking about how she'd felt in the kitchen with him, the way her brain seemed to turn off when he kissed her. Being a woman was frequently humiliating, but single womanhood carried its own particularly terrible set of shames, and she knew she'd be crazy to open herself up to that when she didn't have to, when she'd made decisions that propelled her beyond the place of needing to show up in the middle of a weekday morning at the door of an underemployed twenty-nine-year-old who lived with his parents.

And *yet.* There she was, lurking around the perimeter of the Russo property like a pervert, wondering if perhaps Nathaniel was still sleeping, or if—God help her—he might have company already. Just as she was about to scuttle back to her car, the front door swung open.

"Dude," he said. "It's two degrees outside; what are you doing?"

She had come so far, really, past the point of having to suffer the indignity of being called *dude.* And yet.

"Come in if you're coming in," he said, which was not the most inviting invitation she had ever received. And yet, and yet, *and yet,* she followed him into the house.

"I'm sorry to just—stop by," she said.

"I'm glad you did."

"Really?" she asked. *Because I am a depressed mother of a toddler. Because I'm not entirely sure that whatever happened between us actually happened.* Because even if it had in fact happened—*especially* if it had in fact happened—*here* was the last place she should be.

"Just looking through some of my dad's records. You want something to drink?"

"I— No, thanks, I'm fine." She wasn't sure what she was expecting, but now that he'd invited her in, she had the impulse to head right back out through the door.

He went over to the record player. "You like music?"

"I do," she breathed, and watched him flip through a stack of Pete's albums. He was wearing his dumb, irresistible flannel shirt with the sleeves pushed up to the sexiest degree possible—just below the elbows, cuffs at the widest part of what was called—she remembered it from a college anatomy course—the *brachioradialis.* He selected one and she prayed, perched on the couch, that it wasn't jazz or classical or anything experimental, nothing that required her to nod meaningfully while he quietly explained its brilliance to her. She had done enough of that in her teens, in her twenties.

"Second Hand News" began to play, and he came and sat next to her.

"I realized I was an adult," he said, "like, a full, legit adult, the day I finally admitted I love Fleetwood Mac."

"A seminal day in anyone's life," she said.

"My mom used to play this for us when we were little. When we were driving her insane, that was, like, the code. We knew we were supposed to go in the living room and—I don't know, work out our energy, I guess. She called it a *good galloping song*. We were just supposed to—like—freak out or run around or dance or whatever, to give her a few minutes to herself."

She felt a pang in her sternum, and she couldn't fully identify why: glee, from this unexpected glimpse of Helen from another perspective? Or jealousy, for the same reason? Neither seemed quite spot-on; there was something else there, tessellation at the edges of her memory—the kitchen of her childhood, her own mother's arms waving over her head—but before it crystallized, Nathaniel's knee touched hers.

"Cool bracelet," he said.

"Hm?" It came out as a squeak.

A twisted clump of plastic lanyard string that Ben had "woven" for her during a Serenity Smiles demonstration of "native handi-crafts." There was, empirically, nothing sexy in Nathaniel invoking imagery of his mother and she of her preschool-age son, and yet she felt her breath growing shallow, the same puerile, exciting, tentative bodily awareness she remembered from carpeted teenage basements and gross collegiate dorm rooms, worlds away from the storied comfort of marital proximity.

"Thank you," she breathed, as he threaded his finger beneath the bracelet.

"Is this okay?" he asked.

"Is what okay?"

And then he kissed her again, his hand suddenly on her thigh, and she felt herself weaken, emit a little moan that sounded fake but wasn't. She let herself melt backward, into the buttery linen weave of the Russos' expensive sofa, the warmth of Nathaniel's weight against her, his mouth on hers, and then time seemed to blur again; the song changed to "Don't Stop," which made her think very unpleasantly of Bill Clinton, and then her eyes landed on an image over Nathaniel's shoulder, a large framed photograph of a young Helen and Pete on the beach, one baby—Cal, it had to be—in Helen's lap and Pete's arms wrapped around them, predictably perfect tableau of new parenthood, Pete looking adoringly at his wife, Helen laughing her throat-baring laugh, and she stiffened.

"What?" asked Nathaniel.

"I should—go," she said.

Helen seemed to be staring at her.

"You just got here," Nathaniel said, and kissed her again, and she shifted so Helen was just outside her peripheral vision.

"All right," she said. She would insist, next time—because of course she would come again, on Friday, the next Serenity Smiles day—that they meet away from Helen's line of sight, out in the carriage house.

At first it was just kissing. Hungry, unwieldy kissing, and what she supposed could be classified as the folkloric heavy petting that got so much airtime during high school health lectures. He put his hand up her shirt a few times but she stopped it before it could weasel its way beneath the cups of her bra, mumbled *not yet* like a prudish sixteen-year-old. She wanted to *take it slow*, she told him; she wasn't *ready yet*, though she was glad that he did not ask *ready for what*, because she didn't know the answer.

Clothed, cumbersome congress. That was what she told herself: that it didn't matter, that it didn't *count*, that it didn't mean anything, that it was just *a thing that was happening*. It was unfolding nonsensically, and now she and Nathaniel were on the furry rug on the floor by the bed while he drew lines with his fingers up and down the soft underside of her forearm, each one-way of his touch leaving a chilly trail of gooseflesh in its wake.

It felt sort of like being in a play, or possibly a fugue state. Sometimes he'd stop kissing her and talk to her instead, and she would watch his mouth, only half-listening. Nathaniel worked part-time at a used bookstore and was "working on a collection of essays" and

"thinking about an MFA" and "interested in the fluidity of specula-
tive storytelling." If she'd been his classmate, she would have found
him insufferable; if she'd been his mother, she would have worried
about him. But she wasn't his peer or his parent, so she felt both of
those things, and also, when she was kissing him, neither of them.
Happiness seemed to come to him either easily or not at all. He
sighed a lot, and succumbed to meditative silences and sad, faraway
looks, and in between those things he came impishly to life, making
her laugh, telling her stories about nothing. He seemed, at times,
like just a normal guy, and she would wonder, in those moments,
what in the hell he was doing with her, but then he would tell her
something weird, like the fact that he'd read *Jesus' Son* nine times
or hadn't spoken to one of his brothers in eleven years because of a
fight they'd had at Thanksgiving about capital punishment, and it
would start to make a little more sense. He'd *had a hard time in high
school*, he told her, and at some point he'd *fallen in love with the wrong
person* and *made some bad decisions*, and she sort of wanted to say *who
hasn't*, but she didn't, and she also didn't ask for details, because she
didn't want to know and because he had the courtesy to not ask her
anything, either.

It seemed to her they were both missing something that most
people had. Different somethings but nevertheless; neither of them
ever walked outside feeling completely prepared to be one with the
world.

"I have a Doors song stuck in my head," she said, "but I'm not
sure which one."

Around him she felt weightless and untethered, and she pretended that she didn't know full well she was neither of those things.

He rested his head on her stomach just below her breasts, warming her. "Sing it to me."

"I don't know the words; it's the one about—*beer, Southern California, flowing hairstyles* . . ." She adopted her Jim Morrison voice.

Nathaniel cracked up, laughter she could feel through the material of her shirt. He had a nice laugh, though to his discredit he was
also clearly aware of having a nice laugh. "Not any Doors song I've
ever heard," he said.

"And yet it is also *every* Doors song ever recorded," she replied, "because every Doors song ever recorded is exactly the same." She could flirt when she wanted to; she was capable, she was remembering, of charm, so long as she didn't have to sustain it. "They just made one, and then they rereleased it, with slight modifications, four hundred and twenty-six times."

It was her fifth visit to the carriage house and she was still not quite at ease. Nathaniel was clearly comfortable kissing women; Julia, conversely, had not kissed a man who wasn't Mark in over six years. She focused on the unusual warmth of Nathaniel's body and on the nuances of the room—macramé planters and cheerful Chindi rugs, surely Helen's selections—because if she allowed herself to focus on the breadth of what she was doing, she'd be blinded by the sweeping magnitude of her betrayal, the sheer badness of her bad behavior; it was unconscionable to think that she was doing this to Mark, who was, objectively, even though she often wanted to strangle him in his sleep, the best man she'd ever been with.

"Your philodendron needs some water," she said.

"I think *your* philodendron needs some water," he replied, kissing her stomach over her shirt. Then he lifted it, trailed his kisses downward, over her belly button to the fly of her jeans. She stiffened, remembered to think of her stretch marks. He was trying to convince her that it still counted as taking it slow if she let him do all the work.

"You have a terrific body," he said. "I don't know why you're so self-conscious."

She put a hand on his head. "How often do you do it?"

"Do what?" His breath was warm through her jeans.

She inhaled. "Water your plant."

He pressed his lips into her skin, spoke: "My philodendron? I don't know." He put his hand on her pubis, rubbed at her fly. She sat up and scooched away from him.

He flopped back. "You're killing me, man."

"I'll water it for you," she said. She rose, felt him watching her, slowed her movements, tickled by the fact of someone besides her son—who found butts funnier than anything on the entire planet—being captivated by her ass.

Ben in the room suddenly. She shuddered, shrank into herself, rubbed one of the leaves between a thumb and forefinger. There was an empty Cabernet bottle—Helen's sanctioned cheap brand—on the counter, silt at the bottom, and she rinsed it under the tap. A black-and-white photo postcard was taped over the sink, Fiona Apple wearing very little clothing and looking aggrieved. It was such a strange, self-conscious teenage-boy detail that she stalled for a moment, studying it, before returning to the plant. "You should do it every three days or so. Not too much. Half a wine bottle."

"Of wine?"

"Are you of compromised human genes?"

"Half a wine bottle. Got it." He rolled onto his stomach. "Plants are actually more my mom's territory, to be honest."

And then Helen was there too, along with Ben, the two of them side by side and staring; suddenly the room was too peopled, too hot. "How often does she come in here when she's home?"

"Maybe every day or so."

"Seriously?"

"She puts stuff in the fridge."

Helen slipping in at off-hours, bagfuls of groceries, warm piles of Nathaniel's folded laundry. "Well, then water it once a week. She'll be suspicious if she gets back and it's suddenly thriving." Helen would return in three weeks; she was acutely aware of this, a pulsing red heart looming on the calendar.

"I doubt she'll notice."

She wondered, idly, if she *wanted* Helen to notice, to be proud of her arboreal conscientiousness and her sexual audacity. "She'll notice," she said.

"Come back here, would you?"

She floated back over, let him pull her down beside him. He slid his hand down her waistband. Her bodily self-consciousness had been obliterated entirely when Ben was born, only to be replaced shortly thereafter with something akin to the way she'd been in adolescence—clumsy, unsure, feeling often like she had too many limbs, some too large and some too small. She shaved her armpits when she remembered, neglected her pubic hair entirely. Mark had never cared, or at least never mentioned it, but of course someone else would, someone who wasn't beholden to her in that way. And yet—*and yet*—Nathaniel seemed undeterred by what he encountered beyond her underpants, finding his way easily through the forest.

"Okay?" he asked her, and after a second she nodded.

He was stroking her in that gentle, thoughtful, slightly-too-slow way adopted by men who liked to talk about how they were feminists. She squinted in the sun, resisted asking him, this unlikely gift horse, to speed it up a little, use some more pressure.

"You want me to close the blinds?" he asked, and she shook her head. He slipped his hand from her pants, started playing with the fly of her jeans, and after a beat she squirmed to help him get them over her thighs. She kept two inarguable thoughts at the forefront of her psyche, scientific truths: first, that things had been creeping downhill for her for a couple of years, and so it wasn't *so* terribly unexpected, her need for comfort, for friendship, and the fact that she'd sought it out elsewhere. But second, that she was a terrible person, that what she was doing was unequivocally wrong: that there was, despite the platitudes and nuance contained in Truth #1, no excuse for it whatsoever.

He pulled her jeans off inside-out.

"'*Light of my life,*'" he said, starting to burrow, nosing her legs apart with his hands. "'*Fire of my loins.*'" He slipped her underpants down over her thighs; she'd been wearing her most boring underwear on purpose, thinking it might dissuade her from letting him take off her clothes. She leaned back, tried to relax. "'*The tip of the tongue taking a trip.*' Joo—*lee*—"

"Ugh," she said. "Stop it. Be serious."

He pushed himself up with his palms and looked at her, brows furrowed, reminding her of Ben just a few seconds before a tantrum. Nathaniel could be childish and unpredictable, little barbs of bratty impertinence. This was wholly unsurprising and yet somehow still disappointing: of course this transient man-child going down on her in his parents' outbuilding wasn't going to solve her problems—any of them, whatever they were.

"I'm bad at this," she said. She covered her eyes with her forearm. "I'm sorry."

"You've got a lot going on." He surprised her, leaning to kiss her more tenderly. "Let me take the edge off." He began to forage downward again, as Fiona Apple stared at her from over the sink. "Julia, Julia, Julia," he said, enunciating.

She put a hand on his head, steadying them both. "Doesn't this feel—"

He kissed the inside of her thigh and she inhaled sharply. His breath was warm between her legs. "Doesn't this feel *what?*"

"Well, I—" She tried to compose herself, tried not to squirm. "Well, I don't know. Doesn't it feel kind of—"

"You're overthinking this."

"Doesn't it feel kind of *untoward?*"

He laughed and the sensation made her reach instinctively for the ballast of his shoulders.

"Totally," he said. "It is the least toward."

She wondered if Mark sensed the change in her, because to her it felt fluorescent. That she could be doing something so awful without any kind of outward physical manifestation seemed unbelievable; she looked in the mirror sometimes expecting her hair to have turned white or her ears tripled in size, but her same traitorous self kept looking back at her, and Mark, it seemed, continued to look through her.

They had become colleagues, really, cordial occupants of the same elevator. This was, she supposed, what happened when two relatively undramatic people married each other and things went south: the marriage didn't fall into aesthetic disrepair; all of the detritus and carnage simply settled beneath the surface while both parties adjusted their weight around it, kissed each other good morning and delivered civil accounts of logistical banalities. Mark stayed late at work many nights and she filled her days with a mystically agreeable friend and, now, the proxy that was Nathaniel. It seemed both inconceivable and inevitable.

She was suspicious about how unguilty she felt, though. She expected—not that she expected any of this—to be racked with it, kept awake by the weight of her transgressions, the ghosts of another man's hands on her body. But surprisingly, her insomnia had abated. She slept kinetic, dream-filled sleep with meandering schoolgirl narratives featuring both Helen and Nathaniel: Helen, beside her in a yoga class, patiently critiqued her puppy pose; Nathaniel drove her in Helen's Volvo to the Indiana Dunes and fucked her standing up in a public shower, the walls gritty with sand. She dreamed so vibrantly of orgasm that she awakened alive between the legs, unsure of whether she'd actually come or not.

It was following one of those dreams that she was half-awake with a hand in her waistband, her husband asleep beside her. Coming in a dream did not, mercifully, preempt her from being able to come again, in real life, shortly thereafter. Carefully, she rolled onto her stomach, lifted her hips, angled her wrist. She was thinking now of almost nothing; there was a warm alkaline whiteness where fantasy usually resided, and the very faint, close feel—she could not distinguish dream from memory, in the moment—of Nathaniel's mouth on her skin. She pressed her face into her pillow, bucked against her own hand. She lifted her face to breathe, whimpering involuntarily.

And the mattress moved. A declension to her left, Mark's side, and she froze; he rustled the blankets, cleared his throat, *la-di-dah, let me just fluff my pillow and pretend my wife isn't zealously masturbating beside me.* She pressed her body into the mattress, slipped her hand out. She was holding her breath but short of breath as well; when she opened her mouth to inhale she gasped instead. She wanted to die. She could feel Mark's alertness, the way he'd arranged himself, on his back with the covers tucked neatly under his armpits like the father in an old-timey cartoon about the night before Christmas. Her fingers were wet; beneath the blankets, she tucked them, surreptitiously, under her shirt, and wiped them on her stomach.

She was so used to being awake beside him, but for him to be awake too—and under these circumstances—made her suddenly, unimaginably sad.

She opened her mouth to speak—to say what, exactly? That she was sorry? Sorry for masturbating six inches away from him, sorry for letting another man eat her out, sorry, sorry, *sorry*, Mark, for being—how could either of them be surprised, really?—who she'd been all along.

It stood to reason, given how tenuously human she'd been feeling for the past few years, that her behavior might veer into unrecognizable territory. She tried, as she was driving the familiar route from Serenity Smiles to the Russos' house, having shaved her legs *just in case*, to consider her behavior objectively—*how* she was doing what she was doing, and why, and whether there would be any coming back from it. Something about the specific set of circumstances—Helen was gone, it was the most unbearably frigid part of the winter, Nathaniel had the odd transitory air of a historical ghost—made the whole thing feel misty and unreal. And she was almost giddy about the prospect of Helen coming home, a giddiness that rivaled the climactic satisfaction she'd found being with Nathaniel while being considerably less morally reprehensible. She hoped, delusionally, that perhaps Helen's return would erase some of the impact of what she'd done while Helen was away. And obviously she and Nathaniel both understood that things would end when Helen and Pete returned; surely Nathaniel wanted his mother to catch him sleeping with one of her friends as much as Julia wanted Helen to catch her sleeping with one of her sons.

But Helen wasn't home yet, and when he would start kissing her with his untethered-guy verve, she found herself succumbing to it easily, in the way that she used to, in her early days with her husband but primarily in the days before she'd met her husband, days of slapdash, wherever's-convenient sex, stale dorm mattresses and damp peat moss.

"You smell really good today," he said into her neck, and she did not tell him that she'd bought her new L'Occitane bodywash on his mother's recommendation.

"So do you," she said, and they were on his bed, and she'd been thinking all morning about the fact that Ben seemed to be coming down with a cold, and the weird noise the dryer had started making, and the stupid fight she'd had with Mark last night about whether they had to go to Brady and Francine's Valentine's Day party, and the big flashing red heart that was Valentine's Day, a week from now, when Helen and Pete would return, but then suddenly she wasn't thinking about those things, and it felt *good* to not think about those things. She might be morally bankrupt and borderline insane, but for a few moments, when she was with him, it felt like none of it mattered. And the less you looked at yourself, she found, the harder it became to start doing it again. For the first time, she unzipped her own jeans, and then she started in on his.

"You sure?" Nathaniel asked, already opening his bedside table drawer, fishing through the contents for a condom. She wondered if Helen knew he kept them there; she wondered what the Russo stance on sex-in-the-carriage-house had been when Helen and Pete had five teenage boys at the same time, and what it might be now, if Helen could see her, splayed before her son in—she'd upped her game, bought some lace—strategically fetching underwear. She closed her eyes against all of it, and against the little collection of dried sea anemones Helen had arranged on the windowsill.

Only a week left; one more week to get through until Helen came back.

"Yes," she said. "I'm sure."

When she got home, her body felt terribly, electrically alive; she still had forty-five minutes until she needed to pick up Ben again and she knew she'd be better off if she at least lay down for a few minutes, assumed the illusory position of sleep. She went to her bed, got under the covers, which smelled—that strange scent of sleep in the day—like Mark, like herself; she set Mark's alarm clock for half an hour, just in case, and then she pulled the duvet up over her face, tightly closed her eyes. She ran her tongue over her teeth, over the shingled roof of her mouth, and then she remembered her muscles, pressed it lower, into the well of her bottom teeth, willing, willing, willing herself to fall asleep.

She imagined Mark telling her, wistfully, like she was a child, that that wasn't how it worked.

13

She finds the shabby inside of Ben's apartment building comforting. It is a building where a twenty-four-year-old boy is supposed to live; the setting suggests such an obvious lack of permanency, is so clearly a transitional space. There is a pile of what appears to be garbage outside the door, or the remnants of an erstwhile scavenger hunt, a single running shoe and a battered copy of *The Red Badge of Courage* and several mixing spoons. On the back of an old envelope, Ben has made a sign that reads FREE.

Ben, when he opens the door, is dressed for teaching, wrinkled khakis and a graph-paper shirt, looking so much like his father that she forgets her pleasantries and says, "I can't imagine there's going to be a lot of foot traffic here. For your—wares."

He glances down at the pile. "You'd be surprised. Dal left out the blade from his Magic Bullet a few weeks ago—literally just the blade—and it was gone in half an hour." He opens the front door wider to let her in.

"Comforting," she says. "I brought you some boxes." She uses her most nonthreatening voice. Ben and Sunny are moving in together in two weeks' time. She is trying, trying, trying, the nice, box-wielding clown mom in her capacious linen pants. "Dad said you needed them, and the restaurant down the street from the library was getting rid of a bunch."

"Oh, terrific, thanks." He sounds almost proud as he adds: "I'm halfway packed."

She realizes he is pointing to a cluster of garbage bags, piled in the corner of the living room like an art installation, stuffed indiscriminately with clothes and more angular objects and, for all she knows, actual refuse.

"Is the rest of your stuff—in your bedroom?" She regards, with some suspicion, a large turquoise erection, something in the furniture family—a plush, curved banana of a seat atop a round swiveling base—that would fit nicely in the flamboyant lobby of a Latvian hostel.

"Dal's gaming chair," Ben says.

"*Gaming* chair? You need a special chair just to—"

"He's gotten really into the old Sega games from the nineties."

"Well," she says. "Who can blame him." Beside the chair is the sagging futon that predates Ben himself; it had been in Mark's apartment when they first started dating and was later moved into Ben's nursery. She used to nap on this futon, the baby asleep on her chest and the sun warming them weakly from the window that faced Paulina, flashes of traffic lights across Ben's sleeping face if he awakened in the middle of the night wanting her company. She looks up at him now, his shirt wrinkled and his face drawn, this impossibly tall, tired person she's produced. She is reminded, again, so much of Mark—Mark at thirty-two, Mark the disheveled researcher he'd been when they met.

"Are you okay?" he asks.

"Yes. Sure. Fine." *Remember when you used to nap on top of me.* There is never any context for saying things like that, which feels at once merciful and very unfair.

Instead she wanders idly down the hallway. "Has Dal found a new roommate?"

"Emma's moving in, actually."

A tiny version of Mark appears on her shoulder like an angel, reminding her not to say something snide about everyone playing house, about how Emma's going to have her work cut out for her, cohabiting with someone who has a *gaming chair.*

Ben's bedroom door is open and she's surprised by its neatness. Mark's old apartment had been similarly, monastically sparse, an unforgiving reading chair and a huge beige desktop computer beneath a complicated Magritte print—the lovers with the sacks over their heads; she hadn't been sure, at the time, whether it seemed cultured or menacing. Ben has the Pavement poster she'd had framed for his fifteenth birthday, a windowsill lined with fat softcover textbooks, *Parameter Estimation and Inverse Problems, Rel-*

ativistic Geodesy. She skates her gaze over the bra looped around the doorknob of his closet, seafoam lace, the cups unfathomably small. She pulls the covers up on his bed, and a supercluster of detritus is set aloft, hair and string and dryer fuzz, the Flemish giant of dust bunnies.

"Does Sunny have a regular-size bed?" she asks.

"What do you mean?"

She gestures to his, a full. "Bigger than this. Big enough for two adults."

"Oh, no, this is fine; we both fit."

She resists the visual, nods once, slips past him out of the room. She pokes her head into the bathroom, which is in fact a great deal cleaner than Alma's bathroom at home—girls tend to be more slovenly in this respect, gummy facial potions and knots of hair the size of hamsters, tissue-mummified tampons in or near the trash like pigs in a blanket—but she turns, anyway, and heads back down the hall to the living room.

"Everything okay?" Ben asks, and she can't say *Nothing is,* because she is trying, trying, trying; because she has to try.

"Let me take you shopping," she says.

They drive to a chaotic big-box hellscape in the South Loop, and she wonders how many times she has showcased her love for her son in this way, by procuring for him school supplies, enormous tureens of snacks to last him through cold collegiate winters, a hundred thousand pairs of boxers and athletic socks. She's better at this than she is at other things, better at anticipating need, owing in part to the abundance of need she'd had until she and Mark married.

"When I first met your father he was using an empty toilet paper roll as a toothbrush holder," she says, and Ben blinks at her uncomprehendingly.

"I have cups," he says.

"This is a toothbrush cup."

He studies it. "I can just use a normal cup. You don't have to buy me a special cup."

The superiority in his voice annoys her, coupled with the fact that he's allowing her to lead him around Target in pursuit of basic human trappings that he should have anyway because he's twenty-fucking-four years old; but this, of course—his evident failure to launch—is kind of her fault in the first place, isn't it? She surveys their cart, overflowing: bath towels and hand towels and various kitchen instruments and cases of seltzer water and a pallet of paper towel rolls, all of which she's thrown in like some kind of maniacal game show contestant.

"Do you have a towel rack?" she asks, and, at his blank look, she assesses the wall-mounted options, then: "Do you have an electric screwdriver?"

"Hey, Mom?"

She glances over at him. "What?"

"I have sort of a strange—favor to ask you."

Trying, trying, trying, the nicest mom in the world: "Of course, honey."

"Sunny and I were— We're putting together a guest list." The wedding—it has finally been decreed—will take place a week before Alma graduates. She wonders at the sadism of whoever is governing the universe, making her endure these two milestones in such close proximity. "And I was— Well, so, we don't *know* that many people. Sunny's mom and stepdad are coming, but other than that she—doesn't have much of a—showing." It's a sad way to phrase it, and one that she relates to, having been severely underrepresented at her own nuptials. There had been no bride side or groom side, or if there were sides, they belonged almost exclusively to Mark, his big hearty Wisconsinite clan and his friends from grad school and work and Brady and Francine Grimes. Julia had invited a few of her coworkers mostly because she was embarrassed not to have more friends, and she'd suspected they'd come out of pity, or possibly just curiosity. Major events could have the effect of throwing your loneliness into stark relief.

"I was wondering if maybe we could invite Grandma," Ben says, and she stalls.

Grandma. The word calls to mind merriment, a bustling storybook figure, bosomed and comforting. And it doesn't applicably refer to anyone in their actual family: not only had Mark's mom gone by Nana, but she's also been dead since Alma was a baby. This leaves, of course, only Julia's mother, who's never really gone by anything at all, not even *Julia's mom* or *Anita*, because she's only met Ben twice—only once when he was a sentient being, and both times by accident—and almost never comes up anecdotally, so far has she receded to the outer rings of their familial stratosphere.

She should understand, *does* understand, that these two young people, light on blood relatives, are suddenly desperate for bodies in the room, bodies who will love their baby. She and Mark just pretended it was normal on the occasion of their own wedding, borrowed the chipper comfort of Mark's parents and ignored the fact that Julia's own mother, defying all biological logic, didn't seem to care one way or the other.

"I just thought maybe she'd like to be included," Ben says, the confidence in his voice flagging a little.

"She's never been *excluded*," Julia says. "It's not like she's been standing outside of the gates trying to gain entry; she hasn't—" She can't say *wanted to see us* here, true as it may be; the impulse exists, still, will always exist, to safeguard her children from other people, their cruelty, their disinterest. "She hasn't been here in almost eighteen years," she says. "You haven't even talked to her since you were—"

"We've talked a couple of times," he says, and it stops her in her tracks, as she supposes he knew it would. "I did an oral history project on her when I was in college."

She refuses him the upper hand. "I wasn't aware of that," she says evenly.

"I thought you might get mad." It took his voice forever to change. There's a hoarseness to it, still, that sometimes seems like it might give way to the reediness of his boyhood.

"Oral history of *what*?" Arrested development? Gin?

"Just—life, I don't know; you don't have to freak out."

"I'm not *freaking out*. You'll have to forgive me for being a little surprised by this, though, honey. Did you—*see* her?"

"No, we talked on the phone."

"How did you get her number?"

"It's on the fridge."

She takes a mental inventory of the space, so familiar she's ceased to notice it, settles on a blue Post-it, faded with age to a pale sea green, her own handwriting, mocking, ANITA and ten numbers. It's still there, if she's not mistaken, though she assumed it had, along with expired restaurant gift certificates and seasonal Ace Hardware coupons, been rendered obsolete by the passage of time.

What has transpired between her and her mother over the last eighteen years is not unlike a prolonged game of chicken, neither of them wanting to be the one who drops the ball completely on their communication, neither of them wanting to be the one to blame—though Julia suspects they are both strong in their convictions that the other party is guiltier. Every few years her mother calls during the middle of the day, when nobody is likely to be home, and leaves a terse message with an updated address or phone number. And every few years Julia will feel nostalgic and dash off a Christmas card—a generic message, the scrawl of her name and a photo of the kids tucked inside—and every time she does, she regrets it the irrevocable second she slips it into the mail slot.

"Was she happy to hear from you?"

He looks over at her with something like suspicion. "Yeah, she was."

"And you called her with the specific intention of—what?"

"Seeing if she'd let me interview her," he says. "It was a stupid project for one of my freshman requirements, Braiding the Personal Narrative."

He's drawing her back into his confidence, using his awareness of her disdain for his touchy-feely undergraduate institution as a point of commonality, and she appreciates it.

"But you didn't tell me," she says, grabbing a dish brush and leading them onward. "Your—*grandmother* and I have never been especially close but it's not like I ever *kept* her from you intentionally."

You're excessively inflecting, Mark says to her when she gets like this, Nice Guy for *Calm the fuck down, Julia*. She steadies her breathing and begins perusing the laundry baskets.

"We just talked a few times. She told me about her life."

"What *about* her life?"

"All of it," he says, and she hopes ardently that this isn't true, cannot imagine what Anita would see fit to disclose about Julia herself. "Or not— I mean, it was really pretty basic stuff, all things considered. Did you know she dated one of the Temptations?"

"Not one of the original ones," she says, and relaxes at the prospect of Anita giving Ben the same highlight reel she's been giving Julia her entire life, pithy sound bites only, darkness lurking at the edges but never quite encroaching.

"She didn't say much about your dad," Ben says quietly, and Julia, palming a dryer ball, replies, "Not a whole lot to say."

There's a strange silence, something fetid and uncertain, on the precipice of hostility.

"Look, Mom, we can—talk more about this, if you want, but I wasn't trying to dig anything up. I'd just like to invite her and see if she'll come. This is all a little—overwhelming? For Sunny especially. And we'd just like to know that there's more than just—us. I'd like for my kid to know it's got—people."

It does a mix of things to her, this line, her kid saying *my kid*, and the sudden awareness that she herself doesn't exactly fill the bustling shoes of a *grandma*. Myriad new ways to let down her kid and, now, his.

"It's just," she says carefully. "Honey. It's just that she's a bit of a wild card. I'd hate to see you be disappointed."

"But isn't it worth a try?"

No, she cannot say. *No, my darling, it's not.*

"My instinct is that it isn't a good idea."

He seems to deflate. "Oh. Okay."

"I don't want to see you get hurt."

He opens his mouth, seems to reconsider, closes it. "Fine," he says. But she senses a shift in the air between them, the fizz of something acidic, her stomach primed for a fight, though she never fights with Ben.

"One less thing to worry about," she says, and she means it lightly, but it doesn't quite come out that way. "I'm sorry, honey."

"Are you?" he asks, and she stops to look at him. "I just— Like, this is the hill you want to die on? Really? Not letting me invite my grandmother to my own wedding?"

"I'm not not *letting* you, Ben," she says. "You can do whatever you want. I'm just saying that I don't think it's a good idea."

"You're saying no without actually saying no," he says. "Which is emotionally manipulative, for the record."

"Honey, you asked for my opinion. My opinion is that I wouldn't do it if I were you. My opinion, on this subject, is that someone always gets hurt when my mom is around."

"But shouldn't it be my choice, whether I want to risk that or not?"

"You *asked* me," she says again, but Ben's flustered now, angry.

"You're constantly worrying about things that aren't your business, but they're never the things you actually *want* your mom to worry about; it's always—like, things we're perfectly capable of taking care of ourselves. You assert yourself *then*, when we don't need you; and then when we *actually* need you you're too busy worrying about the stupid other stuff to be there for us."

She stills, for a moment, in the strangeness, how prepared he seemed to mount this argument, how odd it is for him to raise his voice at her. *When we actually need you you're too busy.*

She's not sure how to respond. There are various Mom Approaches that could theoretically be taken in an instance like this, Wounded Mom or Don't-Take-That-Tone Mom or, a page torn from her own mother's playbook, Mocking Mom. It's how she, lacking instincts, navigated her life when he was a baby, a toddler, stopping and taking stock: *How would a normal mom handle this?* And she'd borrow whatever seemed to make the most sense and if that one didn't work she'd try another, substitutions in a recipe.

"I'm trying to protect you," she says mildly.

"I can protect myself. I'm an adult, Mom." Now he rubs his forehead. "I didn't want to get into this now."

"Get into what?"

"Forget it," he says. "I'm sorry."

"I'm sorry too," she says. *Sorry for singing you to sleep every night until you were five. Sorry for helping you build a scale model of Hogwarts out of Legos. Sorry for sneaking you in to see Andrew Bird at the Hideout for your seventeenth birthday, you unbelievable ingrate.* Ridiculously, she selects a toilet plunger, sets it delicately into the cart. *I love you this much because I was so afraid I wasn't going to be able to love you, but that doesn't make it count any less.*

"Should we just go?"

She suddenly wants to cry. "Sure," she says. "I've got to get home; Ollie's waiting."

Ollie is not waiting. Nobody is wholly reliant on her anymore, and this is supposed to be a good thing.

They stand silent in line, Ben's gaze directed at his shoes and Julia's straight ahead, waiting together like they're any other mother and son out shopping for a toothbrush cup, like what has just happened hasn't just happened.

S he hasn't been here in twenty years, and she can recall, vividly, the last time. She'd walked over late at night, when she knew Helen would be sleeping, to retrieve her car, which she'd left parked at the curb when she climbed into Pete's pickup truck. An embarrassing thought, a *painful* thought, one she hasn't allowed herself to dredge up for a very long time.

There is no plausible reason for her to be here, idling on the curb; Helen's street is a cul-de-sac. And yet she's here, wondering, *wondering* what a universe would look like in which she just walked up the front path; what a universe would look like in which she pressed the doorbell—grimy white with a dim orange glow in the middle; she remembers it all so well; what would happen if she just *did* it, popped by and said *It was just so nice to see you that day by the organic lettuces.* There's a vibration in her veins, something akin to panic. She feels frayed, unraveling: sad about what has just happened with Ben, nervous about his invocation of her mother, and lonely in a way that she hasn't felt in years.

The Russos' house is not exactly how she remembers it, now muted by its surroundings, the houses on either side having gone toward behemoth expansion and understated homogeny, additions jutting out like tumors. She's avoiding looking at the carriage house, staring instead at the old elm tree, the side yard full of birdbaths, the rounded front door like the gateway to a fairy compound. She'd never had a childhood home to return to, never felt attached to a place in the way she did to this one. There's a shiny little hybrid in the driveway instead of Helen's old Volvo. The Russos were some of the first people in her life who were rich enough to be allowed to casually make a statement like that, rich enough that they didn't care what other people thought of their cars and also rich enough to have developed cultish loyalty to certain brands that they would cling to with a proud, desperate fervor, *Audi people* or *Aldi people.*

When she was growing up, a car was some rattling, screaming collection of parts that her mother acquired at the tail end of its life from a transient acquaintance, usually paid for in small bills and discarded shortly thereafter when it bottomed out on the highway or, once, when the engine caught fire in the parking lot of the White Hen, where, mercifully, Julia and her mother were inside buying groceries. They had zero brand loyalty; they went wherever things were cheapest and got only what they needed. But Helen and Pete were Volvo people, and also Charles Shaw people (you were allowed, she discovered, to drink cheap wine so long as you *mindfully* drank cheap wine, and if you threw a Domaine Leflaive into the mix every once in a while), and also do-your-own-gardening people, which is apparently still the case; the border of the lawn teems jauntily with perennials.

She can see it now, immersed as she is in her own suburban life, more cynically: the smug flag planting in territories considered beneath yours simply because you *could*, the snobbish cultivation of down-home hobbies by people with too much money. But at the time she'd found it intoxicating, Helen's commitment to Jewel-brand vanilla ice cream (which she swore was better than any gourmet varietal) and her beat-up weeding clogs and the fact that, though they had an antique hutch full of crystal, she always served drinks in decades-old Tupperware bell tumblers.

But she remembers riding in Helen's Volvo, en route to the farmers market or to Flowgurt, and she remembers feeling so comfortable and proud in the passenger seat, a normal person voyaging normally around town with her fancy but still somehow normal friend, a friend who was old enough to be her mother and so lent an extra level of intrigue to Julia, whose actual mother had never gone anywhere with her *just for fun.*

It was manic, sometimes, how much she enjoyed Helen's company, embarrassing in its spilling-over uncontrollability. There were times when she'd find herself, among the obsessive ticker-tape thoughts that unspooled regardless—lying awake next to Mark, one ear tuned to Ben—just *thinking* about Helen, in the way that she used to think about her husband when she first met him, obsessive cataloging of recent visits and imaginative anticipation of future ones. It felt like a sickness, until it turned into something else and then violently exploded, but seeing Helen at the grocery had reminded her of the fact that she's always felt her most important internalizations—fear, or jealousy, or love—like a fist around her gut.

She shifts slightly toward the house; she can still conjure the shape of her son in her periphery, behind her in his car seat, the son who is now six-two and sovereign and mad at her. There were, all things considered, far worse places she could have taken him.

It occurs to her for the first time that Helen may not even live here anymore, that it's likely, in fact, that Helen has moved elsewhere. It's absurd for her to be here, behavior unbefitting the person she's supposed to be. Then again, she is a *middle-aged woman*, an unobtrusive mom in a late-model Subaru; she could sit here all evening and nobody would give her a second look, and her family might not even notice, either, the absence of its ineffectual matriarch. Regardless, her children will continue slipping away, and her mother will continue floating dangerously in the periphery. She could fall asleep here, like she used to do in the Whole Foods parking lot; she could do anything, really, and it wouldn't matter one way or another.

But then her phone rings and it's Alma.

"Mom," Alma says when she answers, with such vigor that Julia feels immediately frightened. "Mom, Mom, Mom, Mom, oh my God, Mom."

And it pulls her from a ledge she didn't quite know she was standing on: her daughter's voice, imploring her, needing her.

"Honey? What is it?"

"Mama," Alma says, and with these two syllables Julia registers her daughter's joy; she can't help but catch it herself, like a yawn. Happiness never came easily to her until she had children; on their behalf it has always sprung forth readily, and she is proud of herself for that, if not for many other facets of her mothering. "I got in, I got in, I got in," Alma says.

She feels a bit like she's been tasered.

"No," she says, but then, remembering herself, her daughter, "Oh, sweet thing, of *course* you did."

She puts her hands firmly on the steering wheel, rubbing in an arch from noon to nine and three, then back up, listening as Alma breathlessly delivers the details: Herzog College, *ohmyGodI'msore*lieved, just one of her safeties, not like she'd actually *go* there because the governor of Iowa is a homicidal clown but it's nice to know she officially has an *option*, right, Mama, right?

"Right," she says, blinking away the tears that have formed in her eyes. "Right, little girl, I am so proud of you, right, right, right."

"Where are you?" Alma asks, like she can tell something's amiss, like she knows her mother is parked outside of this swanky house like some kind of white-van predator.

"I'm close by," she says. "I'm on my way."

But then Helen's front door is opening and suddenly Helen herself is standing on the threshold with a watering can, and Julia's field of vision narrows, her awareness of Alma's voice decreases. Helen is talking to someone inside the house. She's still long-legged and spry, having not yet, in her mid-eighties, resorted to the camouflaging clown pants Julia has been wearing for years; her ponytail doesn't bounce, exactly, but it bobs, like the tail of a shy but healthy dog. And she can see it, instantly, can't she, what their lives may have looked like if everything hadn't gone as wrong as it had? They could still be friends; they could try to pick up where they'd left off, because it doesn't feel all that different from how things are now; Helen could counsel Julia on how the fuck she is supposed to prepare herself for grandchildren of her own; Helen could counsel her on everything, because everything was Helen's specialty; Helen had a way of making everything feel less terrible.

Helen turns to call something over her shoulder, and Julia swears she feels her heart stop as a man comes out through the front door, a rangy man in a baseball hat and a black T-shirt.

"Mom?" says Alma.

He seems to be headed straight for her. But then, no: there's a small gray pickup parked in front of her. It's insane that she's here; she promised Mark, all those years ago, that she would not ever, again, be here.

"Here," she says to Alma, as though it isn't taking her enormous effort just to form syllables, let alone lift her voice to a recognizable register. "Yup, coming, practically home."

She starts her car and executes the required three-point turn to navigate away from the Russos' house—she still remembers how to do it; she must have done it a hundred times back then—and by the time she's turned around she can see in the rearview that the man has stopped, is watching her, and so is Helen Russo, a hand held up to shield her eyes from the sun, but she's driving away, astounded by the abilities of her body, by the fact that it's possible for her to feel the way she does and still have the presence of mind, dutiful suburbanite, to flick on her blinker before she turns the corner.

14

Helen returned from her trip deeply tanned and effusively happy to see Julia and Ben, whom she'd invited over to bake cookies.

"I deserve *barrels* of credit for not m-u-r-d-e-r-i-n-g Pete's cousin," Helen said, spelling over Ben's head as she helped him roll out the dough. "She's one of those women who tells you *every single thing she's doing* as she's doing it, like she's narrating a *bus* tour; it's excruciating."

She'd been apprehensive, walking up the driveway holding Ben's hand; she felt not unlike she had the first time she'd visited the Russos' house, conspicuous and uncertain and worried she had the wrong address. She had not looked in the direction of the carriage house.

"This has been really fun," she'd said, ominously, after the last time they were together, prelude to a goodbye, and Nathaniel, thumbing through a copy of *Confederacy of Dunces* he'd brought home from the bookstore, had said, "What?" and then, distractedly, "Oh, yeah," and she, watching him, took his lack of interest as permission to forgo formally ending things; they'd never formally started them, really, and he'd be easily able to fill any gap she left.

"I also discovered she has some kind of ocular tic," Helen went on, getting flour on her forehead as she brushed her hair from her eyes, "not quite a *lazy* eye but a sort of—*roving*. What do you think, sweetheart, did we get it thin enough?"

Ben examined the cookie dough and, after a beat, nodded. Helen smiled down at him, rested a hand on his head.

"Gosh, I *missed* the two of you," she said.

Julia, who had contented herself with sitting back at the kitchen table to watch them, was thinking the same thing, and she smiled at Helen, was so glad to be back in the main house and for it to be filled, again, with Helen.

"We missed you too."

"Did you like your birthday cake, sweetie?" Helen asked Ben, and Julia panicked for a second, but her son, none the wiser, nodded heartily, undoubtedly thinking of his abstract rendering of Blue the dog.

"Say thank you, honey," Julia softly prompted him, and though he looked at her quizzically, he complied, and she only felt marginally guilty; she worked so hard to keep the bad parts of her life separate from him, and this was, as far as they went, a very minor form of abetting.

"So tell me," Helen said, eyes bright, "what you've been up to when I was gone. Is something different about your hair?"

She'd had it cut a few weeks ago, one of her small efforts toward making herself seem more like someone worthy of sleeping with a hot twenty-nine-year-old and less like Emily Dickinson.

"How are we feeling?" the stylist had asked her, pulling it back from her face in the mirror. "Are we wanting sexy, Victoria's Secret, I-just-woke-up-this-way layers, or do you like something blunt and simple?"

"I think we'd like—the former," she'd said.

"Just a trim," she said to Helen.

"Natey said he ran into you when you were here," Helen said suddenly.

Like being smacked with a baseball bat. "He— Did he?"

But Helen's expression was easy and unaccusing. "He likes you, I think. Who can blame him?" She handed a cookie cutter to Ben. "Right, darling? Everyone loves your mama."

Ben nodded, frowning in concentration.

"I don't know what you two talked about," Helen said, turning her attention back to Julia, "but I wanted to thank you, in any case."

"Thank me?"

"He seems— I'm not sure. Slightly less adrift than he did when we left him. I won't pry too much, but can I ask if he talked to you at all about what's been going on with him?"

She swallowed with difficulty, her throat suddenly dry. "He did a little bit," she said. "We didn't talk all that much." *The least toward.*

Helen nodded thoughtfully. "Things have always been a little harder for him than they are for most people."

"Yeah," Julia said. "I—understand that."

Helen smiled at her. "Whatever you said to him," she said, "I'm sure it helped."

There was nothing on the earth so tedious as a child's playdate at which the parents were required to be present; Julia resisted such horrors with a vengeance, but she couldn't ignore Francine Grimes, and, after Francine had invited Ben to come swimming in her heated infinity pool, it was Julia's turn to reciprocate. Francine arrived with another mom, one who was new to the neighborhood, and as Julia saw them coming up the walk she allowed herself a few-second fantasy about sneaking out the back door with Ben and heading to Helen's house instead, no mommy posturing or social one-upmanship, just Matchbox cars and mimosas.

Francine's twin daughters swept in with an intense, jubilant energy, cooing over Ben, at that age—six, now? God, she remembered when they'd been born—where anyone younger than they were was a novelty, and Ben was happy to indulge them; it astounded her, watching, how easily play came to him, how readily sweet he was.

"They've been *beside* themselves about this," Francine said, kissing Julia on both cheeks. "Julia, this is Monica, Monica, Julia."

Monica was exactly who she expected Monica to be, Serenity Smiles through and through, pure Ativanned Stepford brahmin, luxuriously sweatpanted and improbably gaunt, a ponytail that looked like it would whisper about you when you left the room. She was wearing one of those vague, faux-vintage BROOKLYN '79 shirts, a baby on her hip and a stroller leading the way. She appraised Julia with a flat, bored smile.

"Pleasure," she said, and Julia blinked—was it a greeting? A command? "This is Nash," she said, gesturing with her chin to the baby in her arms. She nodded downward to the stroller, where another baby rested, potatolike. "And that's Cure."

Cure. *Cure!* She wanted to call Mark. The impulse to tell him ludicrous things still existed; there was a comfort in that.

"Welcome," she said, and instantly felt lame and inadequate, like an unpopular child ushering in classmates who'd been coerced into attending her birthday party. It was less that she'd never been comfortable in the company of women than she'd never been specifically comfortable in the social company of *anyone*, but there was something about the moneyed, fine-tuned firing squad of preschool moms that set her particularly on edge. Around them she instantly felt three inches shorter, thirty pounds heavier; they limpened her hair and delegitimized her actuality. Francine was one of those elegantly plump, sun-kissed women whose cloud of pale hair didn't move when the rest of her did. Julia had never completely trusted her, a condition that was not ameliorated whatsoever by the fact that she was peering around the foyer like someone doing a radon inspection.

"This house is so *cute*," said Francine, who lived in a hideous modernized *Wuthering Heights* manor more befitting an entire prep school populace than a family of four.

"Let me get you some wine," she said, and both women hummed agreeably, following her into the kitchen. She regarded Cure—she refused to ask Monica *boy or girl*; history had trained her the answer she'd receive would be smug, laced either with progressive self-righteousness or the affectedly weary isn't it *ob*viousness of a person who has knowingly given their child a stupid and confusing name—in the stroller, the fat legs, the unsparing eyes.

"Twins," she said dopily, struggling with the cork. *Helen wine*, a barrel-aged Sancerre said to have "generous character," whatever the fuck that meant. She'd purchased it from a pretentious "open cellar," made her selection with the aid of a man wearing an ascot who seemed forcefully like he didn't want to help her. "I don't know how you guys do it."

"It actually worked out perfectly for us," said Monica, brazenly beginning to nurse Nash at the table. "I just got to knock out both in one go. Didn't you *hate* being pregnant? I hated it."

Julia hadn't, in fact, hated being pregnant; it was in some ways the time she felt the most whole, justified, on the precipice of something and constantly accompanied by someone whom she never felt to be judging her, someone whose needs her body knew innately how to fulfill, someone who almost never made her feel like she was meant to be doing anything else, and she'd felt close to Mark during that time too, united in waiting for something, bonded—for once, most of their fears pitched to the same tune—in their collective anxieties. All of her emotions had been there, for once where they were supposed to be, just beneath the surface and ready to spring forth whether she wanted them to or not.

"I feel sort of—nostalgic about it, actually." She hadn't meant to say it.

"Are you and Mark talking about having another?" Francine asked.

Another thing she hated about feminine socialization: the fact that such intimacies got thrown into the mix with complete ease, that you were just expected to talk about your sex practices and your reproductive choices while someone was sitting across from you with her entire left breast on pallid, blue-veined display.

"Another baby?" She wondered how fluid the lines of communication were in Brady and Francine's marriage. "No, we're not." It felt like a betrayal of Mark.

"Nash," Monica said firmly, jostling the baby, whose large pale eyes were beginning to wander around the kitchen, his mouth hanging slackly open. "Nash, Mama needs you to *focus*."

Julia met Francine's eye for just a second, and in that second she registered a hint of amusement in the woman's face, and Francine gave her—unbelievably—a tiny apologetic shrug.

"We are *focusing now*, Nashie," Monica said, and Julia looked away, because she worried that if she didn't, she and Francine might—just imagine!—make each other laugh.

When the doorbell rang, she thought nothing of it. That was living in the suburbs: people could just walk right up to your door, and for some reason you were expected to answer it. She left Francine and Monica in the kitchen, and she was feeling relatively okay—proud of her wine and her cute house, proud of herself for not letting Monica's dumb ponytail make her feel bad about her own hair—until she pulled open the door and found Nathaniel Russo on the front step, hands in the pockets of a red parka.

"Hey, there." He smiled at her, pure underemployed-handsome-guy oblivion, the young dad in the L.L.Bean catalog who was probably cheating on his taxes and sleeping with a call girl but it didn't matter because it was Christmas morning, Goddamnit, and he looked the part with his wife and golden retriever.

"Be right back," she called over her shoulder, and hoped she didn't sound as unhinged as she felt. To Nathaniel, she hissed, "Outside, now."

She slipped out the front door, pulled him over to the side of the house. It was March; things were just beginning to thaw, and the sun, today, was melting the snow and ice that had frozen on the roof, and the water dripped forcefully from the gutters; a fat drop landed on her head and slipped down her forehead.

"Nathaniel," she said, brushing it away. She almost never used his name, addressed him with *hey* or occasionally, if she was feeling coy, *hey, you.* "What the *hell* are you doing here?"

His face didn't quite fall but morphed into something confused and offended. She suspected he was unused to people not being happy to see him.

"Whoa," he said. "Um, okay."

"What are you *doing* here?"

"I was just taking a walk," he said. "I was just in the neighborhood."

"You're always in the neighborhood. You *live* in the neighborhood."

"Good to see you too."

"How did you know where I live?"

"You told me," he said. "Superior Street, blue door."

Had she told him that? *Why* had she told him that? Had they ever exchanged anything beyond self-conscious recitations of pop culture references and saliva? Perhaps she'd dredged it up during some dull fact-finding search; she was constantly, despite how little time they actually spent talking, running out of things to say to him, pulling banalities from a boring interior satchel. *Did you know that "borrow or rob" is a palindrome? Did you know a group of owls is called a* parliament? *Did you know "I Will Always Love You" was actually written by Dolly Parton?*

"Can you stop acting like I'm, like, Michael Myers? I just came to say hi. I hadn't seen you in a while."

"What if my husband were home?"

He blinked. "You're married?"

"Of course I'm *married*, I— You didn't think I was married? I have a child."

What does divorced sound like?

"Plenty of people are single mothers, Julia," he said, and she heard, in his voice, strains of the sanctimonious student he must have been. "I guess I just assumed you were one."

"Why did you assume that?"

"I'm not *sure*," he said. "I guess you just didn't seem like a married person who cared that she was fucking someone else."

She flinched.

"I really don't think it's fair that you're mad," he said.

Oh, God, this coddled youngest child; she didn't have time to suss out Nathaniel's *feelings*, this twenty-nine-year-old boy whose mother still did his laundry and had probably bought his expensive coat, this comfortable, comfortable *kid* who had probably never not gotten what he wanted.

"This isn't mad. You haven't seen mad." She'd suddenly become her mother; it almost never happened to her but there it was, Anita's voice coming out of her mouth. "Jesus *Christ*."

"Calm down," Nathaniel said. "I'll go."

"Thank you," she said. "Good, great, thank you."

"I just didn't realize— That's just a little bit cold, like were you just waiting for my parents to come back so you could hang out with them instead?"

"Of course I wasn't," she lied, because of course that was exactly what she had been doing, and of course it was, inarguably, very, very cold. She took a step closer to the house. "I just— Nathaniel, I'm sorry; my life is maybe more complicated than I let on."

He stared at her in his way, and then, after a minute, he nodded. "Okay," he said, like it was a negotiation. "I accept that."

She could feel the pulsing proximity of Francine Grimes. "I have people inside," she said.

"Fine," said Nathaniel, and then, after a painfully long beat, "Okay."

"*Thank* you," she said.

"I had fun with you, Julia," he said, and leaned in, awkwardly, to kiss her on the mouth, and for years after she would associate the damp, thawing smell of early spring with this moment, the moment she pulled away from Nathaniel and saw Ben watching her, her little son at the front door and, behind him, Francine Grimes.

"Is that your kid?" Nathaniel asked.

"Yes," she said, and reflexively lifted her hand and waved at him, smiling in a way that hurt her cheeks, the lunatic last-ditch smile of an adulteress. She made her way over to him, praying that Nathaniel wouldn't follow her, that he would know to flee—he seemed like the type who'd be adept at scurrying out of girls' bedroom windows. "Everything okay, pumpkin?"

He stared evenly up at her. He was a precocious boy intellectually, but emotionally he'd always been a puff of cotton candy, trusting to the core.

"Who's that, Mama?" His expression remained neutral as he regarded Nathaniel behind her, Nathaniel, who was still just standing there. She wondered if this was what it would look like, the moment she fucked everything up, ruined her life, destroyed her marriage: dead leaves and melting snow, the squeak of a nearby squirrel, and her little boy, sullied by her carelessness. She wondered if the memory would surface in Ben years later, her son catching a whiff of that loosening spring damp and being transported back to this moment, this horrible day when he was four.

"That's Nathaniel," she said, squatting down next to him. "That's Helen's son, honey. He was just bringing me my—something I left at their house." And then she looked at Francine, the woman's face a knowing moon overhead, and said, like she owed it to her, "Helen's a friend of mine."

"Okay," Ben said to her, and, to Nathaniel, "Hi," and then, to Julia again, "Mama, can you come see my dogs?" Her secret now theirs, her failure absorbed and dismissed at once. A tiny kindness from this tiny person, whether he was aware of it or not, and later, tucking him in, she would tell him how grateful she was for him, how wildly lucky she felt that he was hers.

"Yes," she breathed. "Yes, sweet, of course, I'll be in in just a minute."

"I'll just—go keep an eye on him," Francine said, looking away.

"I'm sorry," she said to no one in particular, to everyone, and she was left alone on the stoop with Nathaniel.

"Right," he said. "Back to the salt mines. Good luck with everything."

"You too." She watched him walk across the lawn. The water from the gutters was snaking its way down the driveway toward the street, a tiny river of melt, and Nathaniel did an unself-conscious little leap over it before continuing on his way, walking down the middle of Superior Street like he was the last person alive.

She took three deep breaths before she went back inside, and when she did, Francine was still standing in the foyer.

"Are you all right?" she asked softly.

Monica was still in the kitchen, now sternly nursing the other potato, lecturing it about the importance of finishing what it started.

She realized she was shaking. "Fine," she said. "I'm—fine. That wasn't— Francine, that really wasn't what it—looked like, whatever it looked like; it was— I don't know what he was doing here." She realized, as well, that she was crying, desperate crying that crept up her throat and came out in short, sharp breaths. "Jesus Christ," she said, and buried her face in her hands. "I know you don't know me very well; but I have to ask if you could please—"

"Julia." Francine put a hand on her shoulder, rubbed it up and down a few times; the gesture was unpracticed but not unkind. "It's between us, okay?"

She uncovered her face, looked into Francine's round blue eyes with their perfect swoops of brown mascara.

"Thank you," she said, almost dizzy with relief. She was so relieved that she didn't, in the moment, question it; she would not question it until later, when she was alone with her thoughts, replaying the scene over and over again in her head and distrusting every single second of it.

15

She couldn't tell if she was imagining it, but there seemed to be a shift in the air the next time she went to Helen's house. She was holding out hope, though, that the universe might just take care of her, allow the one nice part of her life to remain that way even though she'd shown it such gross disregard, put everything so gravely at risk.

She walked the familiar steps to the side door and, seeing Helen through the kitchen window, rapped three times on the glass. She saw a second too late that Helen had the phone wedged between her ear and her shoulder; she glanced up, pointed to the receiver and pulled a face that suggested she wasn't crazy about whatever conversation she was having, then waved Julia in.

"Well, no, honey, I can't imagine they *do* appreciate just how much you've— But listen, Frankie, I still think it would be smart for you to—"

She paused, interrupted, and rolled her eyes at Julia and made a yap-yap-yapping puppet with her hand, a conspiratorial gesture—cahoots!—that would've sent Julia over the edge a few months ago. Now it felt to be increasing the odds of her throwing up; the air in the room felt warmer than usual and it smelled like someone had burned the coffee.

"Sweetheart, Dad already wired over the— No, honey, I *know* that but there's a—"

She waited again, letting him talk, and covered the receiver with her hand to whisper: "Make yourself at home. I might be a while."

She sat on the same stool at the island where she'd been sitting before Nathaniel kissed her for the first time and tried not to listen as Helen talked to one of her sons who, from the sound of it, was having a problem at work about which most grown men would not call their mothers. She found herself wondering if all the Russo boys were this helpless, if Pete and Helen used a payroll service to systematize all the ways they assisted their adult children.

It was a snarky thought, and she was surprised to be thinking it.

"God help me," Helen said, slamming down the phone after a few more minutes. "Let me at that wine. I need ten glasses."

Julia had brought a bottle. Helen reached for it gleefully, but then, upon reading the label, said "Huh." Julia watched nervously as she did her routine with the cork, poured a splash into a glass, sipped it and made a little face. Julia tensed. She had purchased it at the same time she'd bought her ill-fated playdate Sancerre.

"It's Italian," she said feebly, and Helen nodded, swallowed.

"It's a little sweet for my taste. Let's open the Muscadet and we'll save this for Pete."

She said it so brightly that not only did it not immediately register as insulting but Julia very nearly forgot to be embarrassed. It wasn't until a moment later that she felt the flush of something hurt warming her cheeks. It had cost forty-seven dollars. If someone had brought her a forty-seven-dollar bottle of wine—if someone had brought her a *seven*-dollar bottle of wine—she would have drunk it, courteously, no questions asked. But the Russos had many areas like this, areas from which they wouldn't budge; Helen didn't like to be inconvenienced, and she didn't like to incur any kind of unpleasantness just to make other people happy. And Julia could see the logic—why *should* you drink something you didn't like, especially after you'd spent more than sixty years working to arrange your life precisely how you wanted it—but there was another part of her that couldn't get the impoliteness out of her head, how *rude* it seemed that Helen had rejected the wine, and how infantilizing too; if Julia had been someone more formidable, more esteemed, she was sure Helen would have sucked it up, literally, but she had asserted herself, from day one—with the weeping and the band T-shirt and the congenital confusion—as a child, and Helen was content to treat her as such, because Helen, too, liked when people fit neatly into boxes, and she liked to keep them inside of those boxes whether they remained the right boxes or not. Her daughter-in-law, even though she'd been twenty-two at the time in question and several election cycles had elapsed since, was *the Libertarian* because she'd once professed at Christmas dinner that she didn't think Harry Browne was so bad; Nathaniel was *the writer* even though he currently worked ten hours per week hawking used copies of *Old Yeller.* Julia felt alarmed, suddenly, as she considered how Helen might view her: the trainwreck; the lost cause; the peddler of too-sweet Italian wine.

She realized she'd been quiet for an uncomfortably long time, but Helen was none the wiser, blithely uncorking her Muscadet.

"Grab the door for me, would you," she said. "Come on out."

She held the door for Helen and then followed her out into the yard, trailed at her heels like a puppy.

"Have you called Melinda yet?" Helen asked.

"Who?"

Helen turned to her, smiled. "My librarian friend."

"Oh. I— No, not yet, I've—been busy, I guess."

"Have you? Doing what?"

This was one of the problems with getting close to someone: it became much harder to lie.

"I—just—family stuff." It was the first time she had ever, with Helen, used Mark and Ben as an excuse.

"Mm," Helen said, and Julia heard something in her voice she didn't recognize, but when she looked over, Helen was still smiling, a knowingness in her eyes that, after a second, abated. "Did you see the crocuses starting to peek out underneath the redbud?"

"No," she said, and then, when Helen pointed them out to her, "Oh."

"I'm sure they'll be dead upon arrival," Helen said. "There's more snow coming. But it's nice to labor a bit under delusion for the means of enjoyment, don't you think?"

She felt another prickle at the back of her neck.

"Are you all right, Julia?" Helen asked. "Something seems off."

It also became much harder to lie when you got close to someone and then had an affair with their transient son. She wanted to tell Helen about the incident at the playdate, about Ben and Francine in the doorway, but she couldn't; those things couldn't happen because she had fucked up, shot everything to hell for the sake of a few instances of oblivious pleasure. She understood, for a moment, why her mother drank the way she did, and as she watched Helen—able to enjoy a midday glass of wine without veering into uncontrolled territory, able, because she had both the fiscal and the intellectual means, to justify the enjoyment thereof as a hobby—she felt an intense under-the-skin current of anger that was replaced almost as quickly with sadness. Because Helen hadn't done anything wrong, or Helen hadn't done anything that she hadn't been doing for the entire time Julia had known her; Helen was just being herself. And Julia, it seemed, was being herself too, stumbling through life incapable of not hurting the people who cared for her.

"Honey?" Helen now looked concerned, and Julia wished she could confess to her again, as she had the day they'd met: *I'm a child, I'm a mess, I need your help.* But it seemed too late for that.

"I'm fine," she said, and smiled. She'd heard, before, the death knell of a relationship—or rather it was something feelable, like a storm in the air—and in her experience it began in this way, with small lies of propriety that amassed into little towers, lulls in conversation or split seconds of strange eye contact or a line or two spoken by the other person that made you think *huh, that's not what I expected you to say.* Of course she always *hoped* her relationships, as they were beginning, wouldn't meet their ends, but the fact was that she'd always *expected* them to. She hadn't expected it with Helen, though, until that moment.

She sipped her wine. She had, by then, almost entirely forgotten about her own offering, languishing alone as it was in the Russos' kitchen; Helen's Muscadet was, as she should have known it would be, exquisite.

16

Alma resists being woken but is also chronically prone to sleeping through her alarm—a clip from "Blitzkrieg Bop" that blares, startlingly, on a violent loop, almost fatally scaring Mark and Julia no matter how far they happen to be from their daughter's room and yet somehow failing to wake Alma—so she runs late almost every day, which means Julia, who drives her to school when she runs late, also runs late almost every day.

"Ollie, come *on*," she calls up the stairs, unconsciously rattling her keys like she sometimes does for the dog; Suzanne appears in the doorway, regarding her expectantly.

There is, not necessarily in response, a collection of thumps overhead, then silence.

"I'm sorry," she says to Suzanne. "That was misleading."

Julia would prefer to take the train to work, would happily be halfway downtown right now, trying her hand at the crossword while someone else handled the navigation, were it not for her daughter, or perhaps more accurately were it not for her own weakness, her own failure to rear a pleasant, punctual child who can make it to homeroom every day without the aid of an eleventh-hour parental rescue.

She has a ten o'clock meeting, will undoubtedly hit traffic, and she's just opening her mouth to call up again when Alma breezes past her, stirring an actual gust of wind in the air, wearing one of her inexplicable outfits, cutoffs and black nylons and an incongruous floral blouse unbuttoned over a familiar turquoise shirt and, hooked on her shoulder, an old AllAboard tote. She does a lap around the kitchen island, collecting a banana, a Clif bar, and her aluminum water bottle, dutifully awaiting her in the dish drainer, hand-washed last night by her mother/hostage, whom she does not acknowledge before disappearing out the side door.

Julia stands for a minute in the stillness, feeling—as she often does after encounters with Alma, even silent ones—like she's just been smacked asunder by a wave. She hears the car door slam and, in her head, counts to six before she bids Suzanne a good day and then follows her daughter outside.

"Good morning," she says when she joins Alma in the car, aggressively jovial.

Alma's head is resting against the window; she's staring wistfully through the glass as though at a departing lover. "Hi."

She's not *always* unpleasant, and it's in moments like this— moments when her daughter seems beleaguered instead of belligerent, just plain *tired*—that Julia can most readily access love for her; it's in moments like this that their problematic cycle of coddling and enabling gets renewed; Julia would be late to work for the rest of her life for just a few quiet moments like this in the car with her daughter, who isn't *elementally* an asshole, not on an *atomic* level, just—with her chewed-down nails and her ridiculous shorts—*seventeen*.

She backs out of the driveway. "Anything of note going on today?"

"No," Alma says, then, "Calc test."

She leaps at them, two tepid syllables that are nevertheless better than smoldering silence or abject verbal abuse. "Oh? Calc. Nervous?" She finds herself unconsciously rationing her own syllables in Alma's presence, aware that each time she adds one she increases the margin of error that she's going to say something inadvertently offensive to her daughter's hair-trigger sensibilities. She isn't sure what else to ask; she certainly never took *calc*, certainly never faced down a math test with anything but indigestion and formulas inked, in tiny, cheating script, on the palm of her hand.

"*No*," Alma says.

She waits, pathetically, for elaboration.

"The light's green," Alma says.

She eases off the brake and into the intersection.

"Did you get Sunny's email?"

Julia glances over at her. "What email?"

"Did it not make it to you," Alma asks, "all the way back in 1702?"

Alma for some reason finds it endlessly amusing that Julia's email address ends in *SBCGlobal.net*.

"I haven't checked it yet. What is it?"

Alma shrugs. "Long. I just sort of skimmed it. About the wedding." She is still staring out the window, her knees pushed up against her chest, her feet pressed to the dash, and Julia notices a puffiness around her eyes.

"Did you not sleep well, honey?"

"No."

"How come?"

"I don't *know*, Mom. Maybe I should get a stupid watch like Dad's so I can analyze every second I'm alive."

"I could actually," Julia says, "do without the attitude, okay? I just asked a question."

"And I *answered* you." Alma lets her hair fall in front of her face, hugs her knees, and Julia catches, again, a familiar glimpse of turquoise: there it is, her Jesus and Mary Chain shirt from the show at the Aragon, an early date with Mark, one of her favorite shirts of all time—if she, like Mark, had the time or energy to create a ranking system for her material possessions—and a bedtime mainstay, washed to the perfect level of wear and a private emblem of their life before any of the grout was laid, before any of *this*, the Subaru and the sullen seventeen-year-old and the nonexistent next-day residuals of decades-married sex. None of the things she used to think were cool about her life—Beck shows and brogue boots, the tripping offhandedness of her endeavors—have proven to actually remain cool, especially not to her children, but because nothing belongs to her anymore, her daughter will still steal her favorite T-shirts and wear them defiantly beneath hideous thrift store Lilly Pulitzer *just because she can*.

She'd like to make a thing out of this, would like to point out that she has given *quite literally everything in her entire life* to her daughter and would in fact have been happy to loan the shirt *if only Alma had asked*, that one day Alma, too, will cling to stupid things like T-shirts to remember earlier, easier iterations of herself.

"Honey," she says. "Is that my—"

"Is *what* your?" Alma snaps.

She breathes, clenches her teeth. "Nothing," she says. "Never mind. Is Margo coming over after school?"

Her daughter doesn't respond, and when Julia glances over to assess whether she is still being punished, she is surprised to see that Alma's face has clouded over.

"Honey?"

"No," says Alma. "She's not." She opens the door practically before Julia pulls up in front of the school.

"Bye, Ollie," says Julia, and stops short of telling her daughter to have a good day, because she worries it might lead to homicide. She notices, as Alma waves a little at her, the sharp angles of her daughter's shoulders, the red tips of her hair faded to a bruised maroon. "I love you," she says, because she can't help it, but Alma has already disappeared inside.

47 days to go!!! reads the subject line of Sunny's alarming wedding missive, and Julia clicks on the email with some distrust, as though it might contain a virus. It's her afternoon in special collections— quiet days, her favorite kind of day, usually—which affords her the time to peruse the message in detail.

There are—she counts—seventeen people copied on the email, including Mark and Ben and Alma. She scrolls through it, dazed; the message is color-coded and seemingly endless: *Thank you so much for being part of our special day!! We are so excited to celebrate with you!!!* And a bulleted list, bolded in some areas, declarative statements— *JORDAN WILL HANDLE CUPCAKES*—reinforced with illustrative emojis: a slice of cake, a tiny pink bouquet, a needle and thread so small she needs her cheaters to decipher what it is. *LETTUCE PRAY: MARK* reads one line, highlighted in hunter green, and then, concerningly, *JULIA: PEONIES!* It's like a ransom note, something that should have been flagged by the library's firewall. Before she realizes what she's doing she is going over to the corner of the basement where cell service is strongest and pulling up Ben's name.

"Hey, sweetheart," she says when he picks up. Her voice is over-compensatory, saccharine.

"What's up, Mom?" His voice isn't quite unfriendly, but there's a chilliness she doesn't recognize.

"I just got Sunny's email," she says.

"Which email?"

"There were—multiple?"

"I don't know what email you're talking about," he says slowly, his voice obstinate.

"About the wedding," she says, then, "You're copied on it too."

"I'm at my office hours," he says.

"Well," she says, and feels foolish, disturbing him at work with this nonproblem, a bored child calling to tell its mother the sun's out. "It's very—elaborate. And I just wanted to—clarify a few things."

There's a beat, then, "Sunny's the one who sent it, Mom. You'll have to ask Sunny."

"I— Sure, I'm happy to ask Sunny, but I just thought I'd call you first because—" Why? *Because you're my son?* "I don't have her number," she says lamely.

"I'll text it to you."

"Thank you," she says. "That would be—helpful."

There's a lag, then, quiet uncharacteristic of their interactions.

"Was there something else?" he asks, just as she asks, "How are you?"

"Good," he says. "Really good."

"And Sunny?"

"Good too."

"Good," she says.

She has not been able to stop thinking about her last interaction with him, his unprecedented anger and how readily he seemed able to access it. *Emotionally manipulative* reeks of buzzy self-help books and/or a coercive psychotherapist; she has now envisioned an entire scenario in her head, Ben and Sunny side by side on a chaise longue, he talking about his uncaring mother and she her narcissistic parents, both of them vowing to do it better on their own go-round. This was quite literally the tack she'd taken—*anything but Anita*—in regards to her own mothering, but surely she's done better, surely she can't be a catalyst, given how hard she's tried, for an anything-but-Julia approach to child rearing.

"Just getting ready for the weekend," he says.

"What's the weekend?"

A beat, then, testily, "We're moving?"

"Oh, God, right. Sorry. Of course. Is there anything Dad and I can do?"

"No, thanks, we're all set."

"Good," she says. "Great."

"Was there something else, Mom? I've got a student coming in in a minute."

"No," she says. "Sorry, no, sorry to bother you, honey."

There is a grumpy-looking patron standing at her desk when she returns, awaiting assistance with the microfiche, and she gets back to work, grateful for the distraction and pleased, for the moment, to be useful to someone.

t should have made her nervous when, a week or so after the play-date, Mark came down into the kitchen at five a.m., her designated time to be awake and alone.

"There's coffee," she said.

"Thanks." He took the Reiman Aquarium mug from the cupboard.

"You going in early today?"

He shook his head. "Just couldn't sleep." He sat down across from her, flat-haired in his yellowed-white Stanford T-shirt and flannel pajama bottoms. She couldn't remember the last time they'd been alone together, awake, but still she was surprised by how strange it felt, to be sitting six feet away from him and not have a single conversational impulse.

"I've been feeling like we should talk," he said. "Could we? Talk?"

"Sure." She swallowed. "Of course. About what?"

"I'm worried about you," he said.

"That's okay," she said, like he'd just offered to get her car washed. "I'm okay."

"Jules." He hung his head, looked down into his coffee cup as though it might contain a premonition. "I don't know what to do anymore."

"I'm not asking you to do anything."

"But you *can*. If there's a problem, you should be asking me to do something. That's what we're supposed to do for each other."

She stood up from the table, floated over to the sink. She leaned against the counter, observing the kitchen, observing Mark, trying to remember how they'd ended up here and trying to itemize all the other places she could potentially be: Whole Foods, a yurt, the United Kingdom, Forest Glen, Frank's Nursery & Crafts, San Diego, Ben's bed, Helen's house.

"Julia?"

"There's no—point," she said. And she meant it; there weren't enough hours in the day. It was like looking closely at the construction of an old house: once you started looking, *really* looking, you saw that almost everything needed fixing, and that many of the fixings were contingent on the fixing of other things first, so you had to get the order right: ergo, if the house was still standing, and not actively on fire, it probably made the most sense to just look away.

"What does that mean? Of course there's a point. That's the *whole* point, Julia, is being honest with each other, otherwise I don't see how we can keep . . ." He trailed off and stopped making eye contact, and she watched him curiously.

"Keep what?"

He shook his head.

"You don't see how we can keep what?"

"Keep on like we are, the way that we're— I've been putting off bringing it up because I thought you might be turning a corner, but you seem—God, Jules—so unhappy."

"Are you happy?"

"No," he said frankly. "I love you, and I love Ben, and I love— a lot of things about our life, actually, but I'm not happy because you're not happy, and I feel like it's my fault."

"It's not your fault."

"I know it's not. Rationally, I know that. But I— Honey, would you sit?"

She did, on the kitchen floor, cross-legged, and Mark looked down at her like she'd just done something a whole lot weirder, started crocheting a vest or sprouting a tail, but then he got up and came over to her, knelt across from her, took her hands.

"I love you, Julia," he said. And it *bothered* her, that he was being so nice to her when she'd worked so hard to blow their life apart, that he was being so nice to her when he should have known, from day one, that she would probably blow their life apart.

"I love you too," she said. "But I don't think that's—" She hadn't thought beforehand about how to finish the sentence. *Enough.* "I don't think that's specifically the problem, that we don't love each other; I've never been worried that you don't *love* me."

He softened, smiled a little at her. "Have you been worried *you* don't love *me*?"

"Not—exactly," she said, and watched his face fall.

"What the fuck." He let go of her hands.

"That didn't come out how I wanted," she said.

He stared at her expectantly, allowing her a do-over, but she didn't know what to do with it.

"It's not personal," she said.

Mark laughed dryly, pushed himself up from the floor. She heard his left knee crack and winced. "It's not personal that you don't love me?"

"I *do* love you. We can love each other and there can still be problems, Mark; that doesn't mean that everything else can't still be wrong."

"Everything else? You think everything else with your life is wrong?"

"*No*," she said. "God, it's not—"

"Not *what*? For Christ's sake, Julia."

She felt suddenly very tired. "It's me that's wrong, all right?"

"What does that mean?"

"I don't *fit*; that's what's the problem."

"Fit where?" But when she didn't answer, the anger drained from Mark's face, was replaced by something distinctly sad. "Julia," he said. "Look, this is why I think you should . . ." He sank back down into a kitchen chair, and he wasn't looking at her when he spoke again. "Listen," he said. "Don't get mad, all right? Can you just listen to me first before you get mad?"

She raised her eyebrows. Perhaps this would be her out: an unforeseen plot twist, that Mark had been carrying out a betrayal of his own.

"I was talking to Francine," he said.

Surely she deserved it, the actual, physical pain that arrowed through her ribs when he said her name. And surely she couldn't have been surprised to hear it, *Francine*, given what the woman had seen, despite her promise not to say anything. Brady and Francine had been Mark's friends first; they had never, really, been her friends; why had she ever thought Francine would keep a secret for her?

"Mark," she said. "Let me— Wait."

But he plowed on. "A friend of hers from Philly just started up a practice here," he said. "She's supposed to be really terrific."

She looked up at him on a delay.

"A therapist," he clarified, and she struggled to make sense of the gentleness in his voice when she'd just begun to prepare herself for accusation. "Just something to consider," Mark said.

"I—what?"

"It could be good to talk to someone."

"I saw," she said, finally catching up, "a therapist. Last year."

"Well, sure," he said. "But he wasn't— I mean, he couldn't have been all that good, Julia, if you're doing how you're doing right now."

"You talked to Francine about us," she said, trying out the sentence, listening as it came out of her mouth. "About me."

"I told— I mean, I talk to Brady about everything, Jules, and I guess he mentioned it to Franny, and she just *suggested* this friend of hers; she meant it to be helpful."

"What did you tell her? What do you mean *everything*?"

This was, of course, different from her talking to Helen about Mark. Wasn't it? Mark didn't even know Helen existed, didn't have to sit across the table from Helen at tiresome dinner parties, knowing she knew all about his shortcomings. She felt like she was floating a few measures above the kitchen, anchored only by a pulsing, embarrassed anger.

"Just how down you've seemed, honey. That's not a secret. I wasn't going behind your back, I just— I'm at a loss here, Julia, okay? I don't know what to do anymore."

"Have you considered," she said, "that this may be one possible cause of our problems? That every time something crops up you run to fucking Dave Matthews and the PTA Queen instead of just talking to me about it?"

Mark's face hardened. "When am I supposed to do that? Whenever I'm home you're sleeping, though all I hear about is how you *never* sleep."

"I'm fake-sleeping," she said, "to avoid having to be around you."

"I *know* that. We're married, Julia; do you really think I'm such a fucking idiot that I don't notice what you're doing next to me in bed?"

She met his eyes, her newfound enemy; the bitterness in them was unfamiliar and unnerving.

"Of course not," she said. "We both know you're the smart one."

"Oh for Christ's sake."

"You knew I never wanted any of this."

"Any of what? What the hell does that mean? And who the hell *cares* what you wanted, Julia; we're here now, we've already *done* it, you can't just decide after the fact that you don't want to do it anymore."

"And you can't just decide," she said, "that you made the wrong choice."

She carefully, quietly got up from the floor, dusting crumbs from her pajama pants. He should have chosen someone who'd be better at keeping their house clean; he should have chosen someone who'd be better at everything than she was.

"I don't know what you want from me." His voice was exhausted, and free, now, of malice. "I don't know what's supposed to happen next."

"Ask her," she said, though she knew it wasn't fair. "Why don't you go ask fucking Francine, Mark, because I don't have any idea."

18

She was already crying when she walked up the Russos' driveway. Despair had a way of multiplying, rabbit DNA: suddenly everything seemed sad, the already-sad things exponentially sadder. Mark had left without saying goodbye to her. Ben had solicitously allowed her to drop him off at Serenity Smiles, though she knew her quietude made him anxious. She wiped her eyes with the sleeve of her coat and pressed on the doorbell.

She had never before gone to see Helen without an invitation, and as she waited, she began to worry that she'd overstepped; she thought of Helen rejecting her wine and imagined her huddled behind the living room curtains, peering out the windows and waiting for Julia to leave.

But then the door opened, and there was Helen, ushering her in. "Darling. Well, don't you look like you're having a day." The same phrase she'd used the first time they'd met—though if Julia wasn't mistaken, there was something wilted about Helen today, as though whatever had just transpired in the kitchen on Superior Street had settled heavily over the entire region. "What is it, honey? Come sit."

The weariness in Helen's voice put her on alert; Helen had never sounded weary around her before except when talking about reproductive legislation or her daughters-in-law.

"Sorry," she said. "Is it a bad time?"

"Oh." Helen's face cleared; she smiled. "Of course not. *I'm* having a bit of a day, is all."

She was embarrassed by how much it surprised her, the notion that Helen, too, could have had a bad morning. "I'm sorry," she said again. "Is it— Do you want to talk about it?"

Helen flicked on the burner underneath the teakettle. "No, no, no," she said. "It's nothing catastrophic. Eric tore his ACL falling off a *powder* board, whatever the hell that is. Francis is having money troubles. And Natey, well." Helen met her eyes for just a second before turning away, and Julia felt something cool wash over her. "Would you like some coffee? I'd prefer a martini, but." She made a little flowery gesture and started scooping grounds into the French press. "What's ailing you today? Is the universe conspiring against us?"

"I— Mark and I got into a fight." Her throat filled again, but now she felt embarrassed. There it was, the thing she'd been afraid of: that carefulness, the change in their dynamic. The inevitable death.

"Fighting's healthy," Helen said. "Honestly, honey, maybe that's what the two of you need, just some good airing out. What'd you fight about?"

"He's been talking about me to his friends," she said. "The rich ones. About our—stuff, our personal—problems. His friend Francine suggested I see a therapist." When Helen didn't immediately respond, she prodded: "Doesn't that seem like a—breach?"

Helen paused. "Not an extraordinary one," she said, "as far as they go."

She worried she might start to cry again.

"I mean, of all the— Lord, out of all the possible ways there are to hurt each other in a marriage, that one seems rooted in *care*, at least, even if it's misguided. Mark cares for you. You have a family who *loves* you, Julia. If I were you I'd count my blessings. Or absent that—at least try to will yourself to want it."

"I do want it." Did she? "I'm—*trying* to want it."

"Are you?"

"I— Of course I am; what do you mean?"

"You just seem," Helen said carefully, "pretty hell-bent on destruction, from what I can see."

She stilled. "What?"

Helen sighed, rested her forehead briefly into the hammock between her thumb and forefinger. "You know I hate pretense, Julia."

Her heart, pounding, figured it out before she did.

"I know about you and Natey, honey. You— Surely you can't be surprised to hear that."

Surely she couldn't, but also *of course* she could. Because Helen had always had the ability to catch her unawares like this, from day one: *Are you depressed?*

"You— How?"

"He told me," Helen said, easily, like it was normal, like Julia should have expected this, too, the same way she threw out the names of obscure international destinations and the complicated cuisines therefrom, assuming Julia would have any idea what she was talking about. "Though I knew before he told me. Or I *suspected.* You wear your emotions very clearly on your face, Julia, do you know that? So does Natey. It's one of the reasons I thought you two might hit it off."

"Hit it off," she said, feeling hollow.

"It does feel like a bit of a—*perplexing* choice on your end. But to some degree it makes sense to me, the two of you. You're both so lost. And I didn't hate the idea of his confiding in you."

"Helen, I'm not— He wasn't *confiding* in me."

"You're both at similar stations in life. Wonderful people trussed to these dead-end situations."

She had only ever heard Helen speak this way about other people, and it hurt much more than she could have imagined.

"I have—a little boy," she said haltingly. "I'm—still *married;* Mark isn't a dead end."

"Did you not tell me, when we first met, that you'd been unhappy for most of your life?"

"I don't think I said that exactly," she said. "And that's not— It isn't Mark's fault; that's never been Mark's fault."

"And it's not my fault that Natey's so lost," Helen said. "But that doesn't mean I'm not allowed to want better things for him."

"I don't think that's a fair comparison." Julia felt her anger rising; she'd never been angry at Helen before, but the entitlement in her voice was evoking something akin to fury. "And maybe it *is* sort of your fault, for coddling him."

"Come see me in twenty years," Helen said. "We'll talk about how easy it is to stop *coddling.*" There was a flicker of self-satisfaction on Helen's face, and it soured Julia's stomach. She would never be as proud of her life as Helen was of hers, as readily defensive of her positions. She would never feel as simplistically satisfied with her own existence.

"Helen, were you—" She wasn't sure how to say it. "Did you intend for this to happen?"

"Oh, for Christ's *sake*, Julia, I'm not some kind of criminal mastermind. Of course not. I'm just saying that it makes a certain amount of sense to me. Two people who seemed like they could use a friend."

"My marriage might be ending."

"Surely you aren't *blaming* me for this, honey," Helen said.

She shook her head numbly. "No. It's my fault."

"Does Mark know?"

Julia stared deep into a knot of wood on the table. "I'm not sure."

"Did you want him to find out?" Helen asked. "Didn't you assume that he might?"

"I didn't get that far," she said. "In my head. I haven't really let myself—think about that." How stupid it sounded out loud; how stupid *she* sounded, stupid, selfish Julia.

"That's the part I don't understand," Helen said more gently than Julia would have expected. "This type of thing is— Well, no offense, but it's pretty much par for the course for Natey. But you, darling, you've got such a good head on your shoulders, and yet you seem . . ."

"What?" Julia asked. "What do I seem?"

"So intent," Helen said carefully, "on setting fire to it all."

She didn't bother denying it; she allowed Helen the satisfaction of, yet again, hitting the nail on the head.

"Why is that, do you think?" Helen asked.

What might her life have looked like if she hadn't met Mark? A solitary, footprintless life. She couldn't imagine a world without Ben, but she had a strong suspicion that he would have come to exist in any case, with or without her, a tiny life force, a vital element for the continuation of the universe.

Mark without her was much easier to imagine. He would be fine. He would keep being a good dad, find someone new, someone whose pitch better matched his own. Had she simply been trying to help this process along? Had she, in fact, been trying to force his hand, to hasten the inevitable?

"I know I don't deserve them," she said. "I know I don't deserve to have—any of this."

"Oh, Julia, any of what? Comfort? Happiness? People who love you? What makes you any less deserving of those things than anyone else?"

"I ruin things," she said. "I'm not—cut out for this." To her own ears it sounded pathetic, and the pity on Helen's face was so frank that she felt sick.

"Oh, honey," Helen said, and her voice was all compassion; her hand, cupping Julia's now, had nothing in it but kindness. And yet it made her feel laid bare and flayed, Helen's pity radiating hotly down on her, pity that had—why hadn't she let herself see it?— been there all along.

"I should go," she said.

Helen's face furrowed. "Julia."

Helen would be fine without her, of course, her load lightened by one bushel of crises.

"Helen," she said. "I don't—" She'd never been good at saying goodbye to people; nobody had ever really taught her how. How to tell Helen she'd miss her terribly? How to thank her for saving her life, even if she'd only done it out of a sense of moral obligation, the way one might splint the wing of an injured bird?

"Julia, please."

Helen, I love you, she could not say. *There have been days, Helen Russo, when I loved you more than I love my own husband.*

She felt Helen's eyes on her as she put on her coat. All these things she could have said, but instead she said nothing, which seemed somehow fitting too.

I t stood to reason, given how the universe seemed to be pitched for her that day, that she would run into Nathaniel Russo on the way to her car. He was at the end of the driveway, tripping down the stairs of the carriage house with a pair of cross-country skis.

"Whoa," he said, seeing her, and she realized she was crying, that she'd started crying before she'd made it out Helen's front door. "Are you all right?"

She pressed the heels of her hands into her eyes. "I'm fine."

"You seem—not great," Nathaniel said.

She noticed Pete's pickup truck, then, backed up to the carriage house, the cargo bed packed with a couple of duffel bags, a neat stack of firewood.

He saw her looking. "Big snow predicted this weekend. I'm heading up to our lake house for a while."

"I didn't know you had a lake house," she said distractedly, though—yet another Russoean inevitability—of *course* they had a lake house. She glanced skyward, seeing only an expanse of blue. "There's snow coming?"

"Starting this afternoon. Are you sure you're okay?"

She nodded, not trusting herself to speak. She wasn't sure she trusted herself to drive, either, in fact; she did not trust herself to do anything at the moment.

"What are you doing up there?" she asked finally. It came out too fast, nearly hysterical. "At the lake?"

"Just getting out of town for a little bit. I just need a—" He waved his hand to indicate the driveway, the carriage house, and, if she wasn't mistaken, she herself. "Break," he said.

"Yeah," she said. "I hear you."

He studied her for a minute, then turned to rearrange the cargo bed.

"Where's your lake house?" she asked.

"Outside of Sheboygan," Nathaniel said, and she nodded as though she knew what that meant. Mark always drove when they went to his parents' house in Wisconsin.

"It sounds nice," she said.

"It is nice," said Nathaniel, slamming closed the hatch. He glanced up at her. "Why, you want to come?"

"Really?"

This seemed to give him pause. "I was joking. But— I mean— You'd want to? Come with me?"

She envisioned it in the way she made lists as she tried to fall asleep: matter-of-factly, one item at a time. She could leave her car here, get in his. They could make some headway, then stop for some throwaway clothes, contact solution. The thoughts came to her with an ease that surprised her; she felt at once proud and afraid of her brain for its quick ingenuity. *Ben would be better off, Ben would be better off, Ben would be better off:* that in her head, incantatory. She wondered if this was what it meant to hit rock bottom; she felt, instead, free-falling, and like there was still a lot of depth beneath her.

"Okay," she said.

Nathaniel cocked his head at her. "Seriously?"

"Seriously," she said. She turned to look at the Russos' house; the sun glinted hard against the kitchen window, so there wasn't any way to tell if Helen was looking back at her.

19

They got stopped by a funeral procession on their way out of town and she found herself getting antsy, looking around, wondering if someone might catch them, a Serenity Smiles mom or one of her neighbors—*what on earth is the disaffected shut-in from the Craftsman on Superior doing in a pickup truck with that gorgeous man-boy?*

Nathaniel started singing from the driver's seat, "I see a line of cars and they're all painted black . . ." Long ago, she and Mark had gone, on an ill-advised lark, to see a "Stones tribute bluegrass band" in the basement of a bar; they made it through three songs before she dragged him out the back door and onto the street, clutching her chest.

"What is it?" he'd asked, panicked, and she'd fumbled for her cigarettes.

"That," she said, gesturing back at the bar, "was the worst thing that has ever happened to me."

And they'd both dissolved into laughter, and for months afterward, Mark would come up behind her, his arms around her middle, gruffly warbling "She's a *rayn*-bow," and she would laugh until she was breathless.

Nathaniel was tapping at the steering wheel, humming the chorus, and after a few seconds he glanced over at her.

"What?" he said, then: "Oh, shit, that's, like, sacrilege, isn't it? Mocking the dead?"

"Well, kind of," she said. "But I—"

She felt suddenly silly. One wasn't allowed to say *That's my thing, my thing with my husband* about Rolling Stones lyrics, not any more than one was allowed to say *But that's* my *grocery store*, especially not when one was actively running away from said husband. Her stomach clenched.

"Forget it," she said. The procession ended; Nathaniel gunned the engine through the light and then suddenly they were on the highway; suddenly, without her son, she was on the highway, and she began to feel a little light-headed. The quiet in the car had an unpleasant humming quality.

"Tell me about your book," she said, though she could think of very few things that she wanted to hear about less. She suddenly felt like his teacher, or someone she was trapped with on a stalled transatlantic flight. She had never felt the need to fill their space with conversation; there had always been other things to fill it with.

"Well," he said furtively. "It's still in conceptual stages."

She closed her eyes, pressed her head against the seat back. A memoir about his teenage years going illegally to Chicago clubs, he said, an unbelievably wearisome topic that propelled them, as she had known it would, up the shoreline of Lake Michigan, past the Wisconsin border, the same route they took when visiting Mark's parents in La Crosse. Nathaniel started telling her about the time he'd tried to sneak into the Empty Bottle to see Built to Spill when he was in high school and had to run away from the cops.

"I think I was at that show," she said dimly.

"Shit, seriously?"

She nodded, digging her fingers into her thigh. She couldn't remember who she'd gone with; it had been before she'd met Mark, that sad, sparse expanse of her twenties when she could have been anywhere, doing anything, and nobody would have known or cared. But she remembered every show she'd seen with Mark: the last time had been before Ben was born, Paul Simon at the Auditorium, fifth-row seats; she'd been six months pregnant and "Still Crazy After All These Years" had made her cry.

Nathaniel had moved on, was now talking about the pros and cons of graduate school without any regard for the fact that she was about to lose her shit in the passenger seat beside him. And why should he care? It wasn't his fault she was doing what she was doing; it wasn't his responsibility to comprehend the magnitude of the fact that she was in another state and nobody knew. She wondered how it felt to be so unencumbered, a cocky, handsome young man with rich parents who loved you madly and the belief that everyone wanted to hear what you had to say.

"My mom thinks it's a bad idea," he said, and she forced herself to focus.

"Well," she said, recalling what Helen had said about his writing abilities. In solidarity, she straightened in her seat, adopted the confident suburban mom authority she pulled out at parent-teacher conferences and Build-A-Bear. "It *is* a huge investment."

"God, did she tell you to say that?" he asked.

"She didn't," she said, and, because she'd just become aware of the fact that he was driving awfully fast, wrapped her fingers around the handle that Mark called the *oh-shit strap*, christened thusly by a friend he had in high school who didn't believe in red lights. Mark never drove over the speed limit, not even when she asked him to, when they were going to miss the movie trailers or she really had to pee.

"Precious cargo," he said sometimes, and it was usually a nice enough sentiment to distract her from her bladder, from her affinity for previews.

"Would you mind slowing down a little?" she asked Nathaniel.

She watched the truck's speedometer drift down to eighty.

"Thank you," she breathed.

"My mom's completely out of touch with what people are actually doing," he said. "She thinks we're all supposed to do exactly what she did, climb the corporate ladder or whatever, even though the options that were available to her aren't even there anymore."

She bristled, thinking of Helen, who so fiercely loved her sons, who'd worked so hard to do what she'd done for them.

"I'd argue there have *always* been quite a few more options available to you than there ever were to her."

"Oh my God," he said. "Please don't start with me. I know, okay? I'm just saying she doesn't really get it anymore."

But still her feelings were hurt on Helen's behalf, Helen, who'd been so good to her, who was trying to help her get a job and taught her how to make paella, stylish Helen with her wide-legged trousers and her West African statement necklaces, kind, generous Helen who'd smelled the desperation on her and taken her out for frozen yogurt. It was, she supposed, easier to have compassion for someone else's mom than it was to have it for your own.

She noticed that the vibe in the car had shifted; the fact that he'd seen her naked was now irrelevant, and replaced by the fact that while she wasn't anywhere near old enough to be his mother, she was expected, both societally and apparently by he himself, to act like it. She wondered a little depressingly if this had anything to do with Nathaniel's attraction to her in the first place. She became tangibly aware of herself in a way that she hadn't been in ages, the materiality of her body, its autonomy and actuality, its pathetic transgression. She wanted to erase whatever imagery Nathaniel had retained, the hair between her legs, the pallor, the excess. She crossed her arms over her breasts.

"Moms understand more than they're given credit for." A sickly bulge bloomed in her throat. Loyally she said, a toast to Helen: "It's the hardest thing in the world."

Nathaniel snorted. "Where the fuck did you hear that?"

She pressed her cheek to the cool glass of the window.

"This little place by the botanic garden."

"What?"

She shook her head. "Can you let me out?"

"*What?*"

"Can you pull over and let me out?"

"Are you going to puke?"

She wept in the shower some mornings and shuffled through the Trader Joe's checkout line like a refugee purchasing organic mini peanut butter cups and she had no idea who she was, ever, not for a single minute of a single day, but Mark was right that it was too late to change her mind. That she'd signed up for this whether she wanted it or not, signed up for Ben, who of course she wanted, the tiny person who relied on her. And she had been reliable; until today, she had been.

"Are you being serious?" Nathaniel asked.

"Yes."

"What the fuck," he said.

"Nathaniel." She touched his comely shoulder, this person whose mother she'd fallen in love with. It wasn't his fault. "Please."

She tried to imagine what Helen would say if she found out that her son had abandoned her surrogate daughter at a rural gas station. She had never, since Ben, spent this much time physically unaccounted for; she had not, since she was seventeen, since she'd left for college, felt this untethered. She washed her hands with hot pink soap whose nauseous sugary perfume would stick around for hours, for years; she exited the bathroom, perused a rack of car fresheners, another of Wisconsin license plates with names spelled out on them, DENNIS, MALLORY, RICK: *America's Dairyland*, and then another full of bumper stickers that simply read FORWARD.

"State motto," said the teenage cashier.

"Ominous!" she squeaked. "Is there any chance I could use your phone?"

She dialed Mark's number, and his voice, when he answered, sounded tired, but still so blessedly familiar that it made her throat hurt. It was astonishing that it had only been a few hours since they'd fought, that he had no idea she was gone. That it was still only eleven-twenty a.m. on a Friday, that not everything was entirely ruined, at least not yet.

"It's me," she said.

He must have heard something in her voice, because his own sharpened. "Are you okay?"

"I need you to pick up Ben."

"What?"

"At school," she said, and felt a kind of panic bubbling up into her chest. "Mark, I need— He's at school, and I'm not going to be there." She regarded the cashier, the bumper stickers, the rotisserie box full of spinning hot dogs; she pictured Ben, at Serenity Smiles, falsely reassured that he had a mom who was there for him, waiting, and she started to cry.

"Why not?" Mark asked. "Julia, what the hell is—"

"By twelve-fifteen," she said, the panic rising in her chest. "You'll need to— You should leave your office now. Like, right this second. He'll flip if we're late; you know how nervous he gets; I don't want him to just be *waiting* there." With his little backpack, and today's craft, her boy. "I'm sorry," she said to Mark's silent side of the call. "Mark, I know this is my fault and I shouldn't be telling you what to do but you know how he gets, he'll panic, and I—"

"I was just getting my stuff together. I'm walking to the elevator. Tell me what the hell is going on."

"I'm not—exactly sure."

"What does that— Where *are* you? Are you safe?"

"I'm— Yes." She swallowed. "I'm not sure how to—say it."

"Say what?"

"I fucked up," she said. "I don't know how else to . . ."

"Julia." His voice was quiet, cool. "What are you talking about."

"I need you to come get me, too," she said softly. This was where she had arrived: she was a grown woman who still needed to call the dad to pick her up.

"Where are you?"

"I'm at a gas station. I'm— Christ, Mark, I don't know; I'm in the ass-fuck middle of—"

"Kneeland," the cashier supplied, and she blinked.

"I am in the ass-fuck middle of Kneeland," she said. Her heartbeat sounded in her ears, bumped in the hollow of her throat, a kind of violence.

"Off of forty-three," offered her new friend.

She relayed the information to Mark.

"In Wisconsin?" he asked. "What the hell are you doing in Wisconsin?" There was a long beat, one that filled her with dread, but then he said, "Okay. Fine. I'm on my way."

"Thank you. It's called Budny's Ultramart."

"Bundy? Like the—murderer Bundy, or—?"

"*Bud*ny," she said, and suddenly she was laughing, some blurry slip from despair to hysteria. "Sorry," she said. "I'm fine. I'm waiting with—" She looked up at the boy's name tag. "With Stefan here. Just come. If you—don't mind."

"For fuck's sake, Jules," he said. She heard him exhale. "No, I don't mind." All Mark had ever wanted was a normal life, but instead he met her. Her laughing morphed disturbingly back into crying and Stefan regarded her with unease.

There was a long pause where either or both of them should have said *I love you*.

"Thanks," she said. "I'm sorry."

"We'll be there as soon as we can."

"But will you know how to—"

"I'll find you," he said.

20

Mark, Alma and Suzanne—perched on a kitchen chair like a person—all look at her soberly from the table when she gets home from work. She wonders if they have been discussing Sunny's wedding email.

"I'm thinking stir-fry tonight," she is saying, depositing her stuff on the empty chair beside Suzanne, scratching the dog behind her cocked ears, "unless either of you is feeling more ambitious."

"Honey," says Mark, and it's then she pauses to take them in, the fact that Alma appears to have been crying: her daughter's face is red, scrunched, like the baby she'd been at the beginning, except now it's streaked with mascara and much, much sadder, or if not that—Alma had felt her infant discontent deeply, and expressed it with gusto—at least a more complex sadness, because sadness got more confusing as you got older, accreted and layered and camouflaged itself until the source was buried beyond discovery.

"What is it?" She feels the unique guttural panic, an instantaneous splenetic throb that starts up right away whenever she sees them hurting, and she remembers to be terrified for her daughter, terrified in all the usual ways one must be terrified when raising a young woman, all the ways the world will try to make her vulnerable, try to stymie her and slight her, to take away what's hers. Of course she should have seen this coming, but she's been distracted. It is entirely plausible, given the ridiculous logic that has governed the rest of Julia's life, that her daughter is pregnant, that she's addicted to cocaine, that she's contracted herpes from a drinking fountain. There is no clause anywhere that prevents one of these things befalling Alma simply because Ben's life has been upended too.

"It's okay," says Mark, intuiting her panic, touching her wrist. "It's going to be fine."

She looks to her daughter. "What is it?"

Alma shakes her head, swipes a wrist across her eyes, says something inaudible and then begins to cry again; her chin palsies with a sob and she is both child and not in the moment, a grotesque suspension between the two. Julia sinks down across from her at the table.

"Ollie heard back about her other applications," Mark says gently, his hand on their daughter's back. "Not good news, Jules."

And her first thought is to be relieved, a sweeping sense of *That's all?* But then she observes her daughter, how utterly defeated she looks, like she's just staggered through some terrible journey only to find that her intended destination doesn't exist, her shoulders impossibly narrow in the Jesus and Mary Chain shirt.

"Oh, sweetheart," she says. "Ollie, when?"

"I got a bunch of rejection emails a few days ago."

"Why didn't you tell us?" It comes out sounding more critical than she means it to; she sees the indignation flash across Alma's face. "I just mean, honey—"

"I was *embarrassed*," Alma says. "It's fucking *mortifying* that I— God, I did everything I was supposed to do. And it's just like—there must be something wrong with me."

"Kid," says Mark. "There's nothing wrong with you."

"And you're already in at Herzog," she says. "You didn't not get in *anywhere*, honey."

Alma glares at her. "Great," she says. "So I can move to fucking *Iowa*."

"It's a good school, sweetheart."

"That's not the *point*," says Alma, getting up so quickly that she startles Suzanne, who begins to bark, the fur on her back raised in a line. "The point is why did I even *bother* with any of this? Why have I been working so hard if none of it was going to matter anyway?"

She wants, very much, to take Alma into her arms, but there's the table between them, and Mark has his arm around her already, and she knows that short of reabsorbing her daughter into her own body there is no way at all to protect her, especially now that she's on the precipice, about to leave home. She shushes Suzanne, policing her emotions before lifting her up into her lap. She meets Mark's eyes and sees her own helplessness mirrored in them. Something that has always astounded her, particularly since her children were born, is how truly, consistently bad the universe is at time management; instead of meting out crises at manageable intervals it seems to deposit them in erratically spaced piles, like the salt trucks in the winter, each pile containing a rainbow of miscellaneous emergencies.

She reaches across the table to take one of Alma's hands.

But her daughter jerks away from her. "I took Margo's Adderall a bunch of times second semester last year," Alma says, her tone defiant. "I tried it before the SAT and it worked so well that I did it for, like, all of my AP Bio tests."

"Oh, honey," she says.

"Ollie, that's incredibly dangerous," says Mark.

"I did really well," Alma says defiantly. "And neither of you noticed. And it doesn't count for anything? This is all just so *stupid*, and everyone just acts like it's important but nobody talks about what it actually means, or what you're supposed to do if it doesn't work."

Julia and Mark have never acted like it's particularly important, but she sees now that they have done nothing to discourage their daughter from getting so wrapped up in it, which is itself an infraction.

"It's going to be okay, Alma," she says. "Honey, I know it feels— Right now, I know it feels terrible, but it's going to be all right."

"Oh my *God*, Mom, you can't just— This has been four years of my *life*. And you *let* me care so much about it. And now all you can do is quote stupid wisdom from, like, a tea bag and think it's going to mean literally anything?"

"Hey, Ollie," says Mark. "Watch your mouth."

"It's fine," she says, even though her face feels numb. They both listen to Alma stomp up the stairs, and Julia flinches when her bedroom door slams.

"I'll go," says Mark, but he comes over and squeezes her shoulders. "She didn't mean that."

"It's fine," she says again. "Go ahead."

He turns to go; Suzanne dismounts her chair and begins to follow but stops when she sees Julia isn't joining them. She looks longingly at Mark, headed up the stairs, and then casts another glance in Julia's direction, as though she might change her mind and make it a parade.

"You go too," she says, taking pity, and the dog, mollified, scampers up the stairs behind Mark. Julia rises and goes to the landing to listen; she hears her husband knock on their daughter's door and then, a moment later, the low tones of his voice, a few short punctuative replies from Alma. After a minute, the rhythm settles into something more normal, a steady back-and-forth, and she goes into the living room and drops onto the couch.

It is without question that Ben is her child and Alma is Mark's; she had known it would be this way before Alma even existed; she knew, from those first early hours of Ben's life, that he was unparalleled, that nobody would ever mean the precise amount to her that he did. And her love for Alma was overflowing too—a countless, shimmering quantity—but she could tell, in the moments after Alma was born, blunted by exhaustion and already telescoping into the future to enumerate all the ways her daughter's heart would break, that her daughter would break her heart, that Mark would love her more than he loved Ben, and that this wasn't a transgression because it was the kind of love that was incalculable in the first place, that was impervious to quantification, that didn't know *more* or *less* but simply *was*. She watched him with his shoulders hunched protectively over the tiny bean of their daughter and she was torn in three, part of her breathing easier knowing that equity was being restored and part of her already guilty over her awareness of the subsequent inequality and part of her—the tiredest part—envious of the unyielding, solid love that she knew Alma would grow to know, to count on, to take inevitably for granted. Mark would wander around with her when she was a baby, a sweet sleepy look on his face as he sang her modified lullabies—"I've been to Ollie-wood; I've been to Redwood"; "I'm so happy 'cause today I found my friend; she's going to bed"—and Julia would stand by, watching, feeling extraneous and knowing it was only fair.

There's a feeling she tries not to feel when she sees Mark and Alma together—not jealousy, of course not, or not exactly; she wants Alma to know an abundance of love, all the love in the world. But there are days she wishes that her daughter better understood the tenuousness of it, wishes she could conceptualize the possibility of losing it; she sometimes wants to take Alma by the shoulders and warn her to appreciate Mark's steadfastness—his presence, the constancy of it, as careworn and certain as a kitchen towel—and to contemplate, if even for a moment, what it might feel like to wake up and find it gone, as Julia had. She herself has the baseline, and this feels like an especially cruel twist; she has a frame of reference; she knew acutely, once, what it felt like to have a dad, to love a dad and to feel his love in return, the bald simplicity of it, the blunt fierceness, a reciprocal circuit that's as natural as an air current, and she knows, too, how it feels to lose it.

Mark is better at these things than she is, though; Mark is better at pragmatic advice, and he's better at delivering it with confidence and delicacy. She has no doubt that her husband, upstairs, has not only dried their daughter's tears but started a bulleted list about what they'll do next, how he'll make it okay.

She has comparatively little to offer Alma. She can impart to her the obsolete nuances of the Dewey decimal system; advise her to never schedule a dermatological procedure in the days before her period or trust a dry cleaner with a cashmere sweater. But nothing of substance, nothing about how to *actually live*, about how to move easily through the world or fall in love or have confidence in her abilities, nothing about how to stay upright, when there are so many forces conspiring to knock her down.

"Are you sleeping?" Mark appears in the entryway, and she seems to have lost time, sitting there.

She straightens. "Is she okay?"

He slumps down beside her. "She's going to be. But God, I want to kill someone. She's so disappointed. And exhausted; have you noticed how worn out she looks? How have I not noticed that until now?"

"Did she say anything else about the Adderall?"

"She said it was short-lived. A few months. She hasn't done it since last year."

She chews the insides of her cheeks.

"I believe her," he says, putting a hand on her thigh. He closes his eyes, dips his head back. "We'll keep an eye on it."

"Yeah."

"I convinced her to go to the admitted students thing at Herzog," he says. "It's in a couple of weeks. And then she started talking about ways to prevent contracting glyphosate poisoning from nearby Monsanto plants, which I actually think could be a good sign."

"How?"

"Proactive thinking," he says. "It means at least she's imagining herself there."

She finds herself laughing, and Mark starts too, the delirious laughter they've defaulted to repeatedly over the years, parental crises put at least to bed if not behind them, tucked away so tenuously that all there is left to do is laugh, *ha ha ha what the fuck is going to happen next*—and it's okay, now, for the tears to spring to her eyes; she won't let them fall, but the momentary sting of them is a comfort. She leans her head against him.

"Hey, Mark?"

"Hmm."

"What the fuck," she asks, turning her face inward, feeling her breath warm his shirt, "is Lettuce Pray?"

She feels him start to laugh again. "Oh, God, that email."

"I figured we should get back to what's really important."

"I told them we'd take care of the food. Sunny found this place in Wicker Park that's—paleo, I think? I had to call and give the credit card info to someone named *Blessing* today."

She lets herself laugh at this instead of telling him about her conversation with Ben this afternoon. She'd given him the abridged version of what had happened at Target, the bare-bones fact that Ben wanted to invite Anita and she'd discouraged him. She'd known he would support her on this, at least; she knew that even if he found her behavior wanting elsewhere, he would agree with her when it came to saying no to her mother. She has not told him what else their son had said to her; she has not, subsequently, told him how much the entire thing has thrown her for a loop, or how much time she has spent—alone, awake, in the middle of the night—turning it over and over in her head.

"Jules?" He's looking down at her, his chin resting on the top of her head.

"What am I doing with peonies?" she asks, with more levity than she feels. "Can you shed some light on that?"

"You'll have to ask Sunny," says Mark, and she thinks of Ben's voice on the phone, the unfamiliar coldness of it.

She lifts her head from his chest. "I should make Alma some dinner. Something comforting."

Her whole family makes fun of her efforts to ameliorate problems with carbohydrates and togetherness; she has always wondered if the tendencies come from some lingering vestige of her father, her latent Italian genes within, or if they came from Helen Russo, the woman who taught her that everything could be solved, or at least made momentarily better, by a glass of wine or the smell of baking bread.

"Something *vegan* and comforting," she amends, remembering.

"She's off that," says Mark. "She's eating cheese again."

So she makes neon orange macaroni from the box, which Alma had been devoted to, in young childhood, with a ferocity that they used to find concerning. She holds her breath as she knocks on her daughter's door, bowl in hand.

"Yeah," says Alma, and she enters to find her curled around her laptop in bed, Suzanne in a tight cinnamon roll on her pillow, nose tucked beneath the extravagant plume of her tail.

"Are you hungry?" she asks. "I thought you might be." She edges in sideways, like a crab, and assesses the electricity in the air, finds it neutral enough that she ventures to sit on her daughter's bed. She sets the bowl on the nightstand.

"Sorry for being a bitch," says Alma.

"You never are," Julia says, an abject lie that she's sure would nevertheless be sanctioned by the iron-fisted gods of parenting teenagers. "I'm sorry this happened, honey."

"Thanks," her daughter says tonelessly.

"We'll figure it out," she says. "All right, sweetheart? It's going to work out."

"I know," says Alma, and then, not unkindly, "Mom? I'm watching this stupid show about regular people making busts of famous people out of cake and I just kind of—want to do that? Instead of talking about this? Is that okay?"

"Of course it is," she says, and she waits, pathetically, for an invitation, but when it does not present itself she rises. "Space out, Ollie. Is that still what they call it?"

Her daughter deigns to roll her eyes.

"I'm here," she says before she leaves. "Anytime; you know that, right?"

Alma and Suzanne give her twin parting glances in the doorway, vaguely placatory expressions on their faces, like she's a waitress and they're all set on water, thanks.

Well past midnight she creeps into the yard, bringing a blanket with her to the love seat where she'd caught Brady Grimes drinking a bottle of wine what feels like nine centuries ago but was allegedly only last month. Suzanne insists on accompanying her; Julia has dressed the dog in her tiny blue polar fleece.

Her family makes fun of how she is with Suzanne, yes, but she feels they don't fully understand the complexities of their relationship, all of the various points on the map that draw them together. Suzanne—her name at the shelter had been, condescendingly, *Sneakers*—had presumably been born with the instincts to love and trust, but experience had taken them away from her. Suzanne had come from mysterious origins, origins that made her fearful of everyone, especially vacuums and lurching toddlers and those giant inflatable decorations people put on their lawns at Christmastime, origins that made her slow to trust but fierce when she finally did.

Sometimes Julia marvels at the dog's seeming relief to be living with them. *Really?* she thinks. *Us?* But she understands it too, completely. The dog had worked hard to make their family hers; she was subsequently resistant to change. Julia strokes Suzanne's back, curved into a comma.

"You're a good friend, tiny lady," she says, and the dog opens one eye, sighs with her whole body at being interrupted in sleep but scoots just a fraction of an inch closer, so her butt is touching Julia's leg. "You are the best, tiniest friend," she says in her Suzanne voice, and watches the dog fall back asleep.

She studies her own house, then, its signs of life: the dim glow from the light over the kitchen sink, the haloes of the solar lanterns Mark has stuck at mathematically precise intervals along the walkway to the garage. The darkness of a house when all of its inhabitants are expected to be asleep, the darkness you can only experience when you aren't asleep yourself, when you are supposed to be sleeping, when you are supposed to not have seventy-five thousand things keeping you awake; she hasn't spent time with it in so long but she knows this particular darkness, really, so very well.

21

Mark, as she had known he would—known, to some degree, since she met him—found her. When she saw his car pull into the vacant gas station lot she felt a distinct dizziness. She and Stefan had been playing rummy, but she laid down her hand and stood up.

"That him?"

There was the outline of his head in the driver's seat. "That's him."

The snow started a few minutes into their drive home, as Nathaniel had predicted, and the ride was, at first, the quietest of her life, a cavernous rural silence punctuated only by the sleeping exhalations of Ben and an odd occasional inhale from Mark, who hadn't looked at her since they left the parking lot; a public radio jazz retrospective played softly from the speakers and Mark reached, just as they passed the sign welcoming them to Illinois, to turn it off.

"Are we going to talk about this?" he asked. "Or should we wait until we get home? Am I even *taking* you home?"

"Are— Yes, of course you are."

He glanced over at her. "I don't think it's a crazy question."

"As long as you— I mean, yes, of course, as long as it's all right with you. And we can— Whenever you want, Mark. We can talk about it anytime."

He just kept driving, impassive, his thumbs threaded through the triangles at the sides of the steering wheel. "I don't want to upset Ben," he said finally.

"Me either," she said, and recoiled at the look he gave her, though she knew she deserved it. All of this meanness, all of this being driven around in other people's cars. "I— Mark, I'm—not entirely sure what to say, but I want to be as honest with you as I can about—anything. I want us to— I want *you* to feel free to ask me whatever you—"

"Lest there was ever any ambiguity about whether or not everything ends up being about what *you* want."

"I didn't mean—"

"I don't want to ask you anything," he said.

She looked over at him, surprised.

"I know, Julia." He looked back at her for just a dark, portentous second. "You know?"

"You know—what?" she asked. "How?"

"I *surmise*. I know enough. And I've decided I don't want to know anything more."

Her breathing felt shallow, the air between them crackling and opaque. She'd braced herself for the fallout, for the painful disclosure of everything that had happened in the last few months, the last few *years*, all her uncertainties and darknesses and doubts and, most recently, her betrayal, which, funnily enough, had come to feel like the least serious thing overall, simply a stupid manifestation of less tangible things, everything that was wrong projected cartoonishly on a tiny screen. She'd been so ready for an explosion that the stillness scared her.

"I only want to ask you one thing," he said.

"Of course," she said. "Anything."

"You don't—" He drew in a small, sharp breath. "God, you don't love this guy, do you?"

She wanted to hug him; she knew he wouldn't let her even if he weren't driving. "Of course not. It wasn't—anything, Mark."

But this seemed to make him even sadder. "What do you mean *of course not?*"

Watching a face like Mark's darken was so much worse than watching a regular person get upset; the impulse, in her husband, was still unpracticed after so many years of living, and his hurt, his anger, his confusion all appeared with a childlike candor. The snow had begun to fall densely, heavily, and she straightened in her seat as she felt the car skid a little, felt Mark steer into the skid like he'd taught her to do, a staple of midwestern driver's ed; he was white-knuckling the wheel, his shoulders hunched around his ears.

"If it wasn't—" he started to say. "Then what was the— Why? What was the point?"

"I'm not sure," she said. "I'm not sure it was—about a point, exactly; it was more complicated than that. I'm—friends with his mom."

"His *mom*?"

"I'm sure I've mentioned her, the woman I met at the botanic garden?"

Mark glanced over at her like she'd spontaneously started speaking Arabic. "What does that have to— Like you sought her out? To get to him?"

"*No*, of course not; she and I became friends and then—things just happened."

"That old story," he said flatly.

"I know it doesn't make sense," she said, though it did, to her.

"Did he ever meet Ben?"

The slightest pause, an eighth of a second, that melting day in early March and their little boy at the door, watching Nathaniel kiss her. She swallowed it down. "No."

"And it's over? It's— Your whole going off the grid like this, it's—"

"It's over. Mark, I— You can't know how sorry I am. And I know—there's nothing I can say here that doesn't sound like a cliché, but it truly didn't mean anything, it was just a—"

"I don't want to know."

"But I—" She wanted to absolve herself, vocalize it and in doing so make it theirs. She wanted to stop being alone with it; she wanted it to become Mark's too, something they discussed at length, however painfully, because once they did that they'd get further and further away from it, turn it into something anecdotal like they'd done with everything else from their pasts. Was that not the point of being married, having to carry less?

"You don't get to unload this on me," he said. "It's not fair, Julia, and it's cruel, and you— God, you have to have some fucking accountability. You don't deserve to feel vindicated, okay? Because I'm never going to stop being hurt by it."

"I know," she said. "I'm sorry. I— Mark, I want to— I want this to work." She colored, again, at the *wants*.

"So do I." His voice broke; he wouldn't look at her. "But I never want to talk about him again. Whatever happened, I don't want to know. All right? You kept it from me for however fucking long, you can keep keeping it from me forever."

She didn't notice he was crying until she saw him swipe angrily at his cheek with the back of his wrist.

"Honey," she said, but before it left her mouth she could tell the rules had changed.

"Don't," he said.

"Okay."

"I stopped being worried something like this would happen," he said. "I was worried it would when I first met you; for *months* I was worried I wouldn't—that I *wasn't*—that you'd need something different, or convince yourself that you needed something different, or do something just for the sake of doing something without thinking about how it would affect me."

"I didn't—"

"I *stopped* worrying about it," he said. "I thought—once I really got to know you, I thought— I stopped being worried because it seemed like all of your—whatever it was, that *thing* you'd always do—it seemed like it was just some kind of defense mechanism, and I decided I could stop worrying because you knew I loved you and you could trust me and because I thought you loved *me* and I—"

"I *do* love you."

"It never occurred to me that you wouldn't grow out of it," he said. "I just— I feel so *stupid* because it never occurred to me that you'd be capable of being so fucking mean."

It was then that she realized his insisting she not tell him was the meanest thing he could think to do back to her, forcing her to be alone with it, and it wasn't until that moment—that flicker of cruelty from the nicest man on the earth—that she realized the magnitude of what she'd done, and the miracle of his still sitting beside her like this, of his not steering her into a snowdrift.

"I didn't mean to hurt you," she said. "Or I didn't—*entirely* mean to hurt you."

He glanced over at her with something like interest.

"I think part of me was trying to give you an out." It suddenly made sense to her, that of course this had been her intention, and it seemed so wildly pathetic now, so childish and transparent. She'd been trying to push him away, doing whatever she could to make him unable to forgive her.

"What the hell does that mean?"

"You didn't sign up for this. For—whatever's been going on with me, it's not what you— It isn't what we agreed on."

It would be easier for him to leave her—she had always known this, even if she hadn't known she knew it—if he knew she'd been cheating on him. And it would be less painful for her, too, to know that he wasn't leaving her just because of who she was by default.

"You're saying you want me to leave you?"

"No," she said. "I'm saying it's bound to happen. Or—with anyone else on the earth, it would be bound to happen, but you'd never do that to me unless you had a good reason."

This was what she'd been waiting for all along, the inevitable door closing, and she wondered if she hadn't perhaps been trying to accelerate the process by doing what she'd done.

"So you were doing me a favor."

"You deserve better than this. All of this. You've deserved better from the get-go."

"I decide what I deserve. Okay? You aren't some kind of vigilante here, Julia. I signed up for this. So did you. If you've decided you want out, you're doing that of your own volition."

The desperation rose in her throat suddenly, like bile. "I never— I wish I could— I'd take it back, if I could." It sounded feeble and silly; of course it did.

"I'm sure you would," he said, less bitingly than she would have expected. "But I'm not sure that changes anything."

"I know that."

"You aren't planning on leaving?"

"No," she said. "Mark, I can't." *Please don't make me.* It was a brazen thing, she thought, to disappear, much bolder than she was capable of. Her mother had always couched her father's leaving as cowardice, but actually leaving—Julia didn't begin to look at it this way until her mother left her too—had to take something like gumption; going away and staying away forever must have required a not insignificant amount of tenacity. How many times had she wanted to leave in the last few years? But she lacked the follow-through, the strength. She was not tenacious in the least.

"Mark," she said.

"*What?*"

"I'm sorry," she said. "Mark, I'm sorry; tell me what I can—"

"I don't ever want you to see him again," he said. "Okay? Or his—God, his *mom*, whoever the hell you've been— I want you to stay away from them. All right?"

"All right," she said. "I'll stay away. I won't see them."

"They're out of our lives. I never want to talk about it; I never want them anywhere near us."

"Okay," she said.

Ben's voice from the back startled them both. "Hi," he said, and Julia's vision cleared to reveal a field of cows fixed to the left as they whizzed by. "Hi," Ben said again, his sweet voice, aware only of cows, unaware entirely, she hoped, of how close his mother had come to complete annihilation of everything he knew. She reached behind her, took his small foot in her hand.

22

She is moved to call her mother, perhaps, by the kind of retroactive sympathy you can only feel when you become a parent yourself, when you realize how terrible it is possible for your own children to make you feel whether they mean to or not. And she wonders, too, if Ben has been right, if she has misjudged, if perhaps she has spent all these years worrying about her mother when she should have been worrying about any number of other things.

She doesn't tell Mark she's doing it; she waits until Friday, her day off, when she's out walking Suzanne. As she listens to the ringing, it occurs to her that she can't remember the last time she actually picked up the phone and *called* Anita.

After four rings, at precisely the moment she begins to relax, the line clicks on and someone says, "Whoops—hello?"

She stops walking. "Hello?"

"Yep, who's calling?" The voice sounds young, not unpleasant but distracted; it brings to mind the image of someone with a rotary-dial receiver clamped under her chin to free her hands.

"I'm sorry, I must have— I'm looking for Anita Greene."

"Sure, sorry, she just ran outside for a second to get the— Anita, your phone."

"Who is it?" It's unmistakably her mother's voice in the background, and Julia is surprised to feel something like sadness in her chest to hear it for the first time in so long, her mother living her life, talking to somebody else.

"Sorry, who's this?"

"Her— Julia," she says. "Daughter."

"*Oh.*" Now she is imagining the woman's facial expression, dramatic wowing eyebrows and a mouthed *Your daughter?*

There's a scuffle, and then her mother's voice is closer to the receiver. "*Who's* this?"

"Hi, Mom," she says.

"Christ, I— Hold on one second."

She hears a hinge creak, a door close.

"You still there?" her mother asks.

"I am. Who answered your phone?"

"That's Lydia."

"Who's Lydia?"

She knows she does not imagine the second's hesitation before her mother replies, "Girl I work with. Is everything okay?"

"Yes," she says. "Fine. Sorry, I didn't realize you were at work."

"It's one in the afternoon."

"It's when you always call our house," she says archly. "And also you always used to work the early shift."

"Well, I don't anymore."

"If now's a bad time—"

"No, it's fine. I've got a few minutes."

She watches Suzanne forensically inspect a cluster of sprouting peonies. For the first time in probably a decade, she wishes she still smoked, and just as she has the thought she hears the flick of a lighter and her mother's deep inhale.

"How are you?" she asks.

"Good," Anita says, exhaling. "You?"

"Well," she says. "Fine."

"You sound different. Do you have a cold?"

"No."

"Is something the matter?"

"No," she says again, though it doesn't exactly feel true. "I was actually calling because—well, Ben's getting married."

There's an odd beat of silence, and she wonders for a second if her mother remembers who Ben is.

"Well," Anita says then. "Good for him."

"Sort of last minute," she says. "Next month, actually. His— He and his girlfriend are having a baby." It's the first time she's told anyone, and she feels a woozy few seconds of déjà vu. Suzanne tugs on the leash, looks back at her sternly.

"God," Anita says. "What is he, eighteen?"

"He's twenty-four."

"Really?"

She clenches her teeth. "Yes, really," she says. "He'd like to invite you. To the wedding."

"*Would* he?"

"It's the third weekend in May," Julia says. "Only about six weeks away. Soon, I realize, but it would mean a lot to him if—"

"I can't," Anita says.

"You— Are you sure?"

Her mother is quiet again, then: "Yeah. I'm sure. I'm working."

She hasn't been expecting this curt a rejection. "I realize it's a big ask," she says, "both the short notice and the travel." This is something she can do, isn't it? Even if there's little else, even if all the other things she does don't matter as much as she hoped they did, even if she has, as Ben suggested, been doing the wrong things all along. "If there's any way I can make any logistical things less of an issue, I'd be happy to."

She feels a bit like she is offering to have someone killed on her mother's behalf.

"Are you offering me money, Julia?"

"Just—if we can help, we'd—"

"What, push back the date for me?"

"Well, no, I can't do that, but if I could— Mark has tons of airline miles from work; or—"

Anita snorts.

It's true: that Mark, who likes almost everyone, has never liked Anita. He's absorbed the bulk of Anita's blows on her behalf, blunted her resulting resentment or frustration or hurt feelings by experiencing them himself, tenfold. She'd learned early that reacting too strongly to her mother was futile, but Mark—who'd only had to deal with her retroactively, and in a handful of real-time instances—finds fresh upset every time, and it is a generosity for which she has always been grateful.

"God, I'm not *destitute*. Do you just assume anyone who's not living like you do must be in the poorhouse? I've never once asked you for money."

"I *know* that; I just thought it would be a nice gesture to—"

"I can't come because I'm working. Not all of us can just take off whenever we want."

"I work part-time," she says. "And I didn't expect you to—"

"Forget it," her mother says. "Forget it, forget it, I'm blowing this out of proportion."

Julia startles. "You—are, kind of, yes."

"Thank you for offering," her mom says. "I will not be accepting."

"It would mean a lot to Ben," she says. "He really likes you." She does not say *for whatever reason*; she does not say *even though he has only talked to you about four times in his entire life*. He'd slept with the giraffe Anita had given him when he was a baby until he was nine.

"*Ben*," her mother says, "barely knows me."

"Maybe that's why he likes you," she says, because it is her mother's kind of joke.

To her relief, Anita laughs, but then: "It's just not a good idea, Julia."

"Why not? And it— What, it's not a good idea, or you're busy?"

"Both," Anita says, sounding unfamiliarly sad.

"Okay." She isn't sure what other tacks she can try, and is even less sure that she will be able to stomach being rejected from a third angle. "Fine, forget it."

"It was nice of you to call," Anita says, then, after a beat, "Are you doing okay?"

This catches her off guard as well. "Me?" she asks, then: "Sure." *I'm obsolete*, she does not say. *My kids don't need me anymore; my life feels, once again, like it might be unraveling; I think I might actually, at fifty-seven years old, need a mom, Mom.* "I'm fine."

"Good," Anita says.

"Are—you?"

"Yeah," her mom says. "I am."

There's a silence that she swims around in, trying to imagine where her mother is, what she's doing with her hands, if her hair's still the dark blond it used to be and if she, like Helen Russo, moves as confidently through the world as an older woman as she had when she was a young one.

"I'd better go," Anita says. "Tell Ben congratulations."

"You could tell him yourself. I'm sure he'd love to hear from you."

Anita pauses. "Tell him for me in the meantime," she says.

"All right."

"Take care, Julia."

"Bye, Mom." She's glad to be walking, because she's worried how it might feel to hang up and still be standing in the same place.

23

Everyone told you not to put too much stock in due dates, but she remained hopeful when hers rolled around. It was early September, more than two years since the day at the gas station, and unseasonably hot. Her maternity leave from the library had begun at the start of the week, and after she'd dispatched Ben to school in the morning, she had spent the day lying in the air-conditioning, unable to get around the fact that she was very, very pregnant with a baby who was, it seemed, not at all concerned about being born.

She considered not answering the doorbell when it rang, but it was almost time to pick up Ben anyway, so she heaved herself out of bed and went downstairs, hoping that the comically long time it took her to do everything lately might act as a deterrent for whomever had rung the bell in the first place.

But the person had waited, and was standing on the front porch, and was, undeniably, her mother, though she was thinner than Julia remembered, and her skin was deeply bronzed in a way that didn't specifically seem healthy. She was wearing jeans and carrying a familiar, cartoonish duffel bag, and Julia had the unpleasant sensation of having traveled back in time.

Her mother looked her up and down, and the corners of her mouth twisted indecipherably. "I knew it," she said, and Julia thought of an earlier time, when she'd called to tell Anita she was pregnant with Ben: the hope she'd held out that there was a universe in which your mother, even if she didn't care about you, still *knew* things about you.

"Really?" she asked, and it felt like someone had just pulled a chair out from under her when her mother laughed and said,

"Christ, of course not. How could I have known? But boy, are you *kidding* me? What are the odds? When's it due?"

"Today," she said, touching her stomach, feeling a strange sense of remove, and her mother laughed, a tinkling, easy laugh that she recognized but not well. "What are you doing here?" Considering how her mother's last visit had gone, shortly after Ben was born, Julia had been certain that she would never make another.

"Getting some things out of storage."

"I didn't know you had a storage space."

"Since we left the house on Washtenaw," her mom said. "Where did you think all our extra stuff went? Lawrence's records, the encyclopedias?"

"I didn't think about it, I guess. There are things of Dad's in it?"

Anita gave her a hard look. "It's good to see you too, Julia."

She blinked. "Sorry, I—just didn't realize he'd left anything behind." She'd kept his shaving kit, moved it in a box of miscellaneous tchotchkes from one apartment to the next; the box was now, she was pretty sure, in their basement, though she hadn't thought about it in years.

"Nice place. Nicer than the last one."

"The one you saw was two places ago, actually." They'd found a new house in a new suburb, one that ranked higher in her hierarchy of suburbs and had the added benefit of being fifteen minutes away from Helen Russo and thirty from Brady and Francine Grimes. "I sent you a change of address."

"How do you think I found you?"

It seemed, somehow, that she had lost the upper hand.

"Where are you coming from?" she asked.

"New York," Anita said.

"City or state?"

"Oh"— she waved a hand vaguely above her head—"you know."

"Listen," Julia said. "I have to go pick up Ben from school."

Anita looked at her, waiting. She didn't want to invite her mother along, but she also didn't want to leave her alone in the house, not because she thought she'd *do* anything but because she simply couldn't envision it.

"It's just a few blocks away," she said. "If you want to come."

She pulled the front door shut behind her and started down the front path.

Anita gawked behind her. "We're *walking*? Jesus. It's eighty degrees and you're enormous. Do you want me to just go get him?"

She stiffened. "It's not 1970 anymore, Mom. They don't just let strangers pick up your kids from school."

Too late she realized what she'd said. But, of course, it was true; Ben would never recognize Anita as his grandmother.

"You should come with," she said, and then—a lie of consolation; she couldn't help it, the little glimmer of irrational optimism that always wobbled just offstage for her when her mother was around: "He'll be happy to see you."

What happened after they picked up Ben she couldn't quite say. It felt chemical, or possibly cosmic; sometime between arriving at the school and reintroducing her mother to her son, between a few rounds of Candy Land during which Anita interrogated Ben about his enemies and favorite colors, between the three of them ordering enough Greek food for sixty-five people— somehow, in little pockets between all of those things, Julia began to find herself relaxing. She found herself laughing at Anita's jokes and admiring the way she spoke to Ben, as though he were a tiny adult she'd befriended in a bar. She found herself recognizing a side of her mother she'd forgotten she'd ever known, a side that was lighthearted and amusing and easy to be around, though of course there was always an edge; there would always remain, in Julia, that familiar fear that everything was about to go wrong.

"Your wife," Anita said to Mark when he arrived home, "is quite a bit more *pregnant* than when I last saw her."

And Mark replied, flatly, "Yes, what a difference six years make."

But even that Anita just laughed off, the same flirtatious laugh that used to drive Julia mad when any of her mother's dubious string of boyfriends visited the apartment on Fifty-Fourth Street, but that night it rolled easily off her back, and she found herself, as they all ate Popsicles after dinner, asking her mother if she had a place to stay that night.

Mark looked at her hard across the table.

"Of course I do," Anita said.

"Oh," she said, a little deflated. "Okay, good."

"But if you're offering," her mother said after a minute.

"We are," Julia said, avoiding Mark's eyes, embarrassed by her own excitement. "If you're— I mean, as long as you're here, this bizarre stroke of timing, you should—stay."

There was a suspended, awkward quiet before Anita said, "All right."

"We could think of something fun to do tomorrow," she said.

For the first time in a month, she had the thought that it was fine for the baby to take its time, that if it did so it might buy *her* some time, some rare, rare time with this person who looked very much like her mother but who she actually—could it be?—*liked*. She'd be content to be pregnant for another week if it meant enjoying whatever this alternate reality was.

"Maybe we could go to the Shedd? Benj, you feel like skipping a day of school?"

Ben cheered, and Mark watched them all like they'd metamorphosed into giraffes.

"Let me just call my friend and let him know I'm not coming," Anita said, and set her Popsicle right on the kitchen table. Mark and Julia both watched, instead of looking at each other, as it melted a wet red ghost into the wood grain.

He waited until later, when they were in bed, to ask her.

"Jules," he said. "What's—happening here?"

"What do you mean?"

"Julia."

She finally turned to look at him. "I'm not sure. She's not usually like this."

"Is she on something? Some kind of uppers?"

"*What?*"

"She seems—a little imbalanced."

"I meant like *nice*, not like she's on *drugs*. She's never used drugs. Jesus."

They settled into an unsettling quiet. There were still plenty of moments like this between them, moments that hitched and snagged and left them hyperaware of themselves, of each other, of the fact that they were sharing a bed. She hefted herself self-consciously onto her side, her back to him. It was drizzling out, the rain lightly drumming the screens and a dim, distant bolt of lightning rendering the sky occasionally sickly. She inhaled the smell of damp dirt.

"She used to love storms," she said, and she could hear the delusion in her own voice.

She had a nice memory of sitting on the balcony of their apartment on Fifty-Fourth Street when everyone else was huddled inside, scary until it wasn't anymore, watching the sky grow green, her mother's cigarette smoke being lifted away in efficient clouds and Anita's utter lack of fear. How it seemed like that may have been the only time she ever relaxed, loosened her shoulders: when there was a front coming in.

"Maybe it wouldn't be so bad," she said. "To have someone else around. For Ben's sake, even. To— You know, so you won't have to be scurrying back and forth from the hospital; she could pick him up from school if need be . . ."

Had she not, just a few hours earlier, scoffed at the idea?

"This is what happens," she said, beginning to feel a little desperate. "So much time passes that I forget—she's a human being. I forget I can trust her."

Mark was quiet for a minute. "*Can* you trust her, though?"

"I—think so." She had a hand on her belly, the baby rippling beneath. She'd never really gotten to be the kid with a parent who showed up and was suddenly, at thirty-nine—better late than never—imagining how nice that would be, picturing how nice it would be to have your mom around when you gave birth, to have a new baby and be surrounded by people who loved it and loved you, drowsy afternoons and extra pairs of arms. You could get used to not having someone in your life but you could never completely stop wanting them there.

"I can't explain this," she said, feeling herself starting to cry a little. "I can't— It's like I don't want to look at it too closely because it's just been so *nice*."

"Okay," Mark said carefully. "Honey, it's okay." There was a time he would have taken her into his arms, but they weren't there yet; they may not, it seemed, ever be there again.

"I just can't help but think, like— God, what if it could be like it is for normal people whose moms actually want to be around when their grandkids are born; I can't help but think how *nice* that would be, even if it's unexpected, even if it's not how things have ever been."

"That would be nice," Mark said evenly.

"I know I'm hormonal," she said.

"That's okay," he murmured, and put a hand tentatively on her shoulder.

"I wasn't a*pol*ogizing," she snapped, and, then, hearing herself: "Sorry." She shifted onto her back, covered her eyes with an arm. "Am I not allowed to just—enjoy this time?"

"You're allowed to do whatever you want, Jules. I just want to make sure that you're not setting yourself up to be disappointed."

"Do you think I am?"

"I don't know. I'm not quite as sold as you are on whatever's happening here."

"I just wonder if maybe it's seeing Ben, seeing what she's missed with him and how—God—how great he is, how could you *not* want to be around him?" And for just a split second she thought of Helen Russo, taking Ben in as her own—taking *Julia* in as her own—despite her abundant roster of biological relations, and her eyes filled again.

"Maybe," Mark said.

"Do you think that's possible? How insane do I sound, on a scale of one to ten?"

"You don't sound insane, Jules. It's—generous, really, but I wonder— I just don't want to see you get hurt."

Mark: the truly generous one, the reason she was still here, beside him, a new baby awake inside her and their son sleeping down the hall.

"Come on," he said. "You need to get some sleep."

She tried to relax, closed her eyes and slowed her breathing.

"She has your voice," Mark said as they were drifting off. "It's the strangest thing. She opens her mouth and you come out."

She had seen Helen Russo about six months ago. She had been working part-time at the library and now, newly pregnant for the second time, was perpetually suffused with sleepiness. She was so foggy, in fact, that when she saw Helen, both her brain and her body reacted on a delay, taking several seconds to register the familiar ponytail, the bucket bag, and the fact that she was accompanied by a woman in her mid-thirties and a little boy who looked to be about three. If she hadn't been covering for a colleague that day, she would have been safely downstairs in the archives. If she weren't, instead, on a step stool, reshelving some new fiction, she wouldn't have seen them headed to the children's section, wouldn't have been filled with the eerie sensation that she and Ben had been efficiently replaced, two for two. Even still, she couldn't believe how easily the feeling returned to her, that intense, familiar pull to Helen, the desire Julia had felt not only to know the woman's life but her own placement in it, where she ranked among the rest. It extended beyond simple jealousy and was not quite obsession, and she discovered, that day in the stacks, that the feeling had stayed inside her all this time.

"Helen." She couldn't believe she was doing it, and she couldn't believe, when Helen stopped and turned to face her, how nice it was to see her.

"Oh." Even Helen, with her impeccable social graces, couldn't stop an initial reaction of what appeared to be genuine surprise. Then her face softened, but her smile didn't quite meet her eyes, and Julia registered this in the form of a deep abdominal twinge. "Gosh, look who it is."

The woman and child stopped to see who she was talking to, and Helen waved them on.

"You two go ahead; I have to stop and say hello."

I have to, not *I want to*. How could she be surprised?

"Melinda told me she hired you," Helen said. "How could it be that I haven't seen you here before now?"

"I'm usually downstairs," Julia said. "In the archives, I mean, not—"

"Hiding?" Helen smirked.

When Julia had decided to call Melinda Wolcott a few months after she'd severed her ties with Helen, she worried, briefly, that her hard-won business card could no longer be called upon, that perhaps there was some sexual transgression clause in the rich-people-favor nexus that rendered networking opportunities inutile. But then she'd asked herself whether it was likely that Helen had ever let a personal matter get in the way of her professional ascent, and she'd picked up the phone.

"I'm so happy to hear from you," Melinda had said. "Helen was singing your praises just the other day. Tell me about yourself."

It had stirred her to think of Helen talking about her, and it touched her, deeply, to think that Helen was still willing to speak well of her, despite everything.

She'd been about to point out to Melinda that she did not specifically have the qualifications required for this particular kind of work, but she felt the spectral weight of Helen's gaze urging her to be confident, to fake it if she had to. She would come to realize that this was how many people had gotten what they had in life: by lying a little bit, and pretending to be better than they were. By the end of the phone call, she had an interview, at which she was offered the job on the spot.

"We were just at the zoo," Helen said. "I thought we'd stop in and say hi to Melinda. And we saw the sign for the two o'clock story hour."

"On the second floor," Julia said, dismounting the step stool. "Miss Amanda's reading today. She puts on a good show; I didn't mean to—derail you."

"Oh." Helen waved over her shoulder. "My daughter-in-law and my grandson. They're visiting from Boston this week. They can fend for themselves for a few minutes."

"I thought you didn't like your daughters-in-law," she said, attempting levity.

Helen laughed, and then she leaned in, and with her nearness Julia felt a childish excitement, a familiar firing of synapses.

"I don't," she whispered, close enough that Julia could smell her perfume. "Slim pickings around here." Now Helen seemed to be studying her. "When are you due?"

She was gobsmacked into silence. She was far enough along to just be showing but it was still, by her own paranoid specifications— she was astronomically old according to everyone who weighed in on the subject, tempting fate right at the start—too early to be telling people. The baby was her secret with Mark, the secret that was replacing her old secret, the secret that they were sharing: the secret upon which they, together, were building a new foundation. She'd been concealing it—artfully, she thought—with Mark's clothing; she looked down at herself appraisingly, the geography of her body from that angle on the verge of change.

"I have a sense about these things," Helen said.

Helen was the first person to formally acknowledge it, the first person besides Julia and her husband and her doctor who knew there was anything to acknowledge. For a spell she felt naked, like the woman could see through her, all her secrets unveiled, the shameful late-night fights with Mark and the number of times already she'd second-guessed her own decision making.

But that was followed by something much warmer, a sensation so profound that she almost wanted to cry, that of being recognized, of having someone know her well enough, even after all the time that had passed, to sense a change. And in that moment she realized how much she *wanted* to tell Helen; she'd *been* wanting to tell Helen, all along.

"September," she said.

"A *baby*," Helen said. "What news." And suddenly she leaned forward and took Julia into her arms. They stood for a moment, pressed together, and Julia realized that this, too, was what she'd been seeking the whole time: Helen herself, the comforting, steadying proximity of her. "It's a girl," Helen whispered into her ear. "I'd bet my life on it."

Her voice sent a shower of sparks down Julia's neck.

"That glow's a real thing; you look—Lord—really so well," she said, pulling back and appraising, and then: "I worried about you, you know. Quite a bit."

Somehow, among all the possible reactions she'd envisioned—and she had envisioned plenty, lying awake at night, mentally trying to rebuild her life—Julia had not foreseen relief. She thought Helen would probably be mad at her, but that she may have been worried had not crossed her mind, and she saw now, of course, what a great oversight that was, a gross underestimation of Helen's compassion. She had a tendency, she knew, to turn people into her enemies before they'd actually had a chance to wrong her, just for the sake of cleanliness. Until her conversation with Mark on the way back from Wisconsin, she hadn't realized how insane it was to do that to your partner, and seeing Helen's expression now, she realized she'd done it twice: shut out someone she loved, someone who—could it be?—had loved her back, in anticipation of what only she saw as an inevitable ending.

"You two really got the hell out of Dodge, didn't you? I walked by your house one day and saw it was empty inside."

She colored. They'd bought their new place before even putting the old one on the market.

"I called you several times," Helen said.

She looked down again. "I know. Helen, I'm sorry, I— Things got—complicated."

"I assumed so," Helen said. "Are you happier, at least? Now?"

How to answer the question? She was, still, fucking lonely, and scared, and she wanted, even after all that had transpired, now that the prospect had suddenly materialized before her, Helen's counsel. Standing a foot away from her, she allowed herself to acknowledge how much she'd missed Helen over the last two years, how many times she'd wanted to pick up the phone and call her. Her eyes had filled with tears.

"Difficult days, those," Helen mused. "Early stages. Is your husband happy?"

Her pregnancy—incited to bring them back together—seemed sometimes to be pushing them further apart. She had imagined he'd be like he'd been when she was pregnant with Ben, always wanting to *touch* her, calibrating the shifting nuances of her body, ingratiatingly eager to understand how it felt to be her: how are you *feeling*, what is it *like*, let me *in*, Jules. But this time around he was less interested, cool and removed.

"Hard to say," she whispered.

"Well, he stayed," Helen said. "So his heart must be at least partially in it."

She took a step back. "I— Sorry?"

But Helen's expression was unchanged, bright and blithe as ever. "I'm happy for you."

"Thanks," she said weakly.

"Good luck, okay?" She heard in Helen's voice—felt it in her gut—the shellacked pleasantness she knew the woman used for exchanges with cashiers and telemarketers.

"You too," she said quietly, but before she could turn away, Helen spoke again.

"Julia."

She looked up at Helen's face, softer than it had been a second before.

"You know, honey, you're always in my heart."

And she knew, at least in the moment, that it was true.

24

Those days with her mother passed dreamlike, time moving languidly. They took Ben to the aquarium; Anita—always an incongruous clean freak—scoured their kitchen and the inside of their washing machine and the cobwebby stairs to the basement; they sat in the sunroom drinking iced tea and folding laundry and talking about their neighbors on Fifty-Fourth Street. It did not exactly feel like spending time with her mother as she'd always known it, but it felt like spending time with *a* mother, and Julia went with it, needed no convincing to go with it.

Her third night there Mark was working late and Ben was in bed; they were sitting on the sunporch, playing rummy.

"I thought we could go to the old neighborhood tomorrow, assuming the kid doesn't show up," her mom said. "I bet she has a big head. That's genetic, you know."

"Is it?" There was a gentle tightening in her abdomen, as though the baby were listening.

"Absolutely. From your father's side. Almost wrecked me."

"Terrific," Julia breathed, but then, considering the statement, more detail than she'd ever been given about her own birth, "Was it difficult? When I was born?"

"We survived," her mother said.

"Was I on time?" Julia asked.

"You were a couple days late. And you took your time, my God. But no, no complications or anything. You were a little bruiser. I don't think I heard you cry until you were about three days old."

"Really?"

"The nurses called you Charlie Chaplin. I thought there was

something wrong with you, but you were just—how you've always been. Watching. *Plotting*, maybe."

She wondered if this was another dig, but there was a faint smile on her mother's face.

"It would be nice," she said after a minute, because it suddenly *did* sound nice, "to go back to Hyde Park."

"Want to make a bet on whether Mrs. Richardson is still alive?" her mom asked. "I'm betting she is, and that she still has a glass eye."

"Why wouldn't she? It's not like the real ones grow back."

Her mother laughed, her same wicked laugh, picked up Julia's discarded jack. "I'll bet you five bucks."

It was so much easier to be this way—had always been easier to be this way—than it was to look at anything directly.

"You're on," said Julia. "Just don't tell Mark we went without him; he's still very nostalgic about grad school."

"I don't think he likes me very much," Anita said, surprising her.

"No, he does," she said unconvincingly. Then: "Mark likes everyone."

Anita laughed. "There's a hell of a compliment."

"He doesn't dislike you," she said. "He's just protective."

"You need protection from me?"

She swallowed. "In general."

"You've never needed protecting from anything," her mother said, "in my experience."

She looked up, trying to assess this comment, but found no combat on her mother's face.

"Hope he's not underestimating you," Anita said.

"He's not. Over, if anything."

"Oh? How do you figure?"

She'd found herself, in the last two days, telling her mother more about her life than she possibly ever had, but she'd been keeping it all fairly pedestrian: little stories of workplace innuendos and weird elementary school parents, the great unending drama that was other people. She hadn't said much about her interior life, or about Mark, but there was something about her mother's tone now that she found inviting, and though she couldn't tell if it was a menacing invitation—a siren on the rocks—she felt suddenly eager to talk.

"We've—been going through some things," she said. "These last couple of years."

"Clearly," her mother said, gesturing to her belly.

"No, I mean—we hit a pretty rough patch. Things got— I'm not sure, they got kind of bad for me, and I did something I—shouldn't have done."

Her mother arched her eyebrows, waiting for more.

"There was a—" How to describe it? *A massive and multilayered betrayal. The meanest thing I could do to the nicest man on the planet. A monthlong lapse in sanity.* "I let him down," she said finally, and looked away.

"Well, sure," Anita said. "You got that from your father, too."

It hit her sideways, a hard tap on an exposed nerve. She vowed, to whomever was inside her, that she would try never to make them feel that specific kind of pain.

"What does *that* mean?" she asked. She'd wanted, since it happened, to talk to Helen about what she'd done, but of course she couldn't, and of course her mother was not a logical alternative, as evidenced by the happy little downturn at the corners of Anita's mouth, that same old prurient interest in the misfortune of others, even if the others were her daughter.

"Oh, don't get like that," her mother said. "My God, you're so *sensitive.*"

And her anger flared, anger she wasn't supposed to be feeling now, with the baby on its way. She hadn't been a bratty kid—she hadn't been given the opportunity, really—but she found herself prone to *meanness* as a child in a way that always struck her as slightly unnatural, a knee-jerk distaste for most of those around her and a tendency—like a stewing, necromantically afflicted child from a movie—to silently wish for misfortune to befall classmates who had wronged her, or who had things she wanted. And she felt a very familiar feeling now, a kind of sweeping, generalized jealousy for lives that weren't her own. She had never been good at imagining what normal people did, but that didn't stop her from trying: other people awaiting their tardy unborn children were getting manicures with their moms and baking banana bread and listening to inspiring stories about their own arrivals into the world. They certainly weren't fanning away cigarette smoke while their mothers made cruel jokes at their expense.

"That isn't funny," she said.

"I wasn't kidding," her mother said evenly, taking her time as she laid out her hand, four threes and three jacks. And then Anita looked hard at her, a deep, unyielding look that made Julia feel very unloved. Normal people's mothers didn't look at them like that.

"Are we talking about this?" Julia asked. "We can talk about it, if you're trying to talk about it."

"No." Anita blew out another stream of smoke, still looking at her squarely. "We can't."

Julia broke her gaze, watching, instead, her mother's hands as they gathered up the cards, began to shuffle the deck, a neat fan followed by an even neater bridge, like an optical illusion; it used to mesmerize her when she was a kid, how easily her mother made this particular magic happen, but she'd never been able to do it herself.

"Don't ruin this, please, okay, Julia?" Anita said. "God. We're having a nice time, aren't we?"

Because of course it was her fault; of course she was, as always, the one to ruin things.

"We are."

"Great," said Anita stiffly. "Your deal." She handed over the cards, freshly shuffled, and Julia obediently began to dole them out onto the table.

Anita rested her head back against her chair, inhaled deeply on her cigarette as she picked up her hand, fanned the cards out and studied them. "Oh, Julia," she said, exhaling, and Julia waited, waited some more, but that was, apparently, all her mother had to say.

After she found the note the next morning, she got in the shower, which was the safest place to cry in the suburbs, and she stayed there until the water grew cool. When she came out of the bathroom, Mark was waiting for her, sitting on the edge of their bed, and she could tell that he'd seen it too, the torn piece of paper Scotch-taped to the coffeepot.

"For the record," she said, "I'm mad at you because you're right."

"You're mad at me?" Mark asked.

She sat next to him on the bed. "No."

"I really, really wish I hadn't been right, Jules."

Change of plans, had to run, the note had read. In the shower, she'd critiqued it from all angles, noting the comma splice, the hurried alternation between print and cursive. *Good luck w/ everything.*

"I feel so—" It was something like grief, sprinkled with stupidity. "Let down."

"She did let you down."

"But I shouldn't have *let* her let me."

"Jules, stop." He reached up and began to stroke her damp hair, and she felt the kindness of the gesture radiating down her neck.

"You're going to be late for work," she said, and Mark shook his head.

"I called Brady. I'm starting my leave today. All yours, Jules, whatever you want to do."

It made her start to cry again, this glimpse of him—Mark! Back, after such a long time, when he knew she needed him.

"Did something happen last night?"

"I thought something had," she said. "But then I thought it hadn't. She seemed fine when we went to bed." She paused. "Mark? I have to tell you something."

And though it was a sentence that had, since that day in Wisconsin, taken on new meaning, and had the power to evoke real fear, Mark said, calmly, "All right."

She'd never told anyone before. It seemed unbelievable that with all the chatter, all the white noise that came along with being a person, there was still something she had never told anyone; that with all the time they'd spent together, all they'd said to each other, there was still something she had never told Mark.

So she told him the whole thing, matter-of-factly, beginning to end.

"Oh, Jules," Mark said when she finished. And then—unbelievable, really, this, too, that there was another thing that nobody had ever said to her—"Julia, you were a child."

"I knew what I was doing."

"You couldn't have known, though. Not really."

"I was seventeen."

"That's a *child*, Julia. That's— Oh, honey." And she thought she had never seen Mark look so sad, even when he'd picked her up at the gas station.

"I'm sorry I never told you."

"That's okay, Jules; that's— God, I *wish* she were still here; I'd—"

"Don't," she said. Hatred wasn't in his nature the way it was in hers; to hear it in his voice made her feel like her mother hadn't left, or like she'd left something noxious behind, particles in the air like a cold you could catch.

"It was her job to protect you. Things are the way they are with her because she chose to have them be that way. None of this is your fault."

"I pushed her away."

"But she's your family. You don't let your family push you away, not like that."

She looked up at him, her family, the man now holding both her hands, the man who had chosen not to let her push him away, despite how hard she'd tried.

"I'm so sorry that happened," he told her, and she wasn't sure which part he was referring to but supposed it was applicable to a lot, where Anita was concerned. She felt suddenly exhausted, listed back into her pillow, and he came with her, pulling her head to his chest.

"You're so much better than she is," he said, and though she knew it wasn't completely true, she knew too that it wasn't completely false.

She said "Thank you," which was also applicable to a lot.

Ben tiptoed in a minute later, sleepy-eyed, and they made room for him between them, and she stayed awake while the two of them drifted off again, contented by the sounds of their breathing, her whole family in her bed, everyone who mattered.

Alma was born, huge-headed and leisurely, late that night.

PART II

∽∾

Via Chicago

25

The hallway outside Ben and Sunny's new apartment is pristine, no orphaned running shoes or dismantled blender attachments, and Ben receives his father and sister far more warmly than he does his mother, hugging Alma—who has bucked up for the occasion of this dinner but still, to Julia, seems quite fragile—and ironically fist-bumping Mark but seeming to take Julia's full hands—they have picked up Thai on the way—as an excuse to greet her with only a gruff, eyes-down hello, like she is a neighbor he's not especially happy to have run into. There seems now to be a film between them that gives their interactions an unsteady, wavering quality.

"We're so glad you could make it," says Sunny, ushering them in with a great deal more enthusiasm. "It was a good motivator for me to get unpacked."

The apartment is nice, wood floors and a defunct fireplace, and despite the fact that they just moved in last weekend, the space already looks like a Pottery Barn showroom: a cream sectional that makes Julia think immediately of the messiness of babies, curtains on the windows and tasteful rugs on the floors. The shelves are filled sparsely with books and richly with objects, squat candles and chunks of quartz.

"My mom," Sunny says, seeming a little embarrassed. "She sent over—some things."

Julia is apparently not the only one compensating materially for her lack of prenuptial enthusiasm. There's an awkward beat before Mark says, "Well, it looks great."

"Beautiful," she echoes—trying, really, and Sunny smiles at her, but Ben just looks at her skeptically before turning his attention to his father.

"Dad, do you think you could take a look at the Wi-Fi router with me?"

"Yes, go," Sunny says, and then, to Julia and Alma, "and I'll show you ladies Baby's room."

They follow her down the hallway, Julia bolstered by the presence of her daughter, who seems a lot more comfortable around Sunny than she herself.

"Here," Sunny says portentously, stopped in a doorway, "is where Baby's going to live."

Julia knows she's meant to feel something sentimental here, to be conjuring heartwarming images of her impending grandchild, but it just looks like a *bedroom* to her, the umbilicus of an old phone cord poking from one outlet, several pale gray lines etched diagonally into the hardwood from someone moving something heavy without a rug underneath.

"Obviously it's the only space we haven't set up yet; the bassinet's on back order."

She searches for something to say, but then, from beside her, Alma pipes up with a bright female-bonding voice that Julia didn't know she had in her. "*Super* cute."

"Right?" Sunny says.

"Great light," says her daughter, who has never in her life noticed light quality, and Julia feels, for a second, betrayed.

"It's lovely," she says, and her voice, again, sounds hollow in comparison. She feels a kind of inadequacy that she hasn't felt in a long time, the kind that started cropping up when people in her life started having babies and she couldn't think of anything to say about them beyond *She seems nice!* or *I like his hair!* or, later, when she had a baby of her own and she'd stall when people asked her absurd-seeming questions; she could never remember precisely how many weeks old Ben was—twenty-one, twenty-three, who knew, who *cared*—nor did she have much to say, upon presenting him to others, beyond *Here he is!* with a sad, desperate exclamation point tacked to the end, overcompensating for the internal lack of enthusiasm that she was sure had been visibly branded on her.

Sunny goes to stand by Alma. "We're going to put a glider over here, so he'll get used to the street sounds when we're night feeding."

Julia has a strange memory, sitting in a beanbag chair across from a very pregnant and very smug Francine Grimes, and it occurs to her that Francine would probably be Sunny's ideal mother-in-law, a fellow blond, bustling bassinet enthusiast who would always say the right thing.

"We're doing a tree theme," Sunny says. "Very woodsy color palette, a big stencil on this west wall."

It seems comically broad, like declaring something house-themed or life-themed, but she simply nods, a little startled by the realization that preparations are already under way, or at least extant, spectrally, in some dark corner of Sunny's Pinterest account.

"Let me know if you want help," Alma says—the perfect thing to say; she is proud of her daughter and resentful at once, that Alma got to it first.

Julia rests a hand on Alma's back. "That's a great idea, sweet," she says, and she can tell almost immediately that she sounds too enthusiastic; Alma looks witheringly at her over her shoulder, making clear that she's well aware of Julia's motives to get her out of the house, to stop brooding in her room watching old episodes of *Meerkat Manor.*

"I'd love that," Sunny says, but Alma is already skulking out of the room, down the hall, presumably to assist with the wireless router.

"She's extremely fond of me at the moment, clearly," Julia says, embarrassed.

"How's she doing?" Sunny asks.

"She's—working through it," Julia says. "She's really disappointed. It's hard to watch."

"Ben said the same thing when he got off the phone with her the other night. That he wishes there was something he could do."

"They talked on the phone?" It surprises her, for once a pleasant surprise.

"They were texting, and Ben was—like, laboring over these incredibly long replies, and I was like just *call* her, so he did, and they talked for over an hour." Sunny leads the way to the kitchen, lowering her voice a little. "And I totally get it; I went through all this—I mean, really recently, even more recently than Ben, so I know what a nightmare it is, how it feels like your entire *world* is riding on where you get in."

"Did it work out for you?" Julia asks. "I mean—did you end up where you wanted to?"

"I did," she says. "It was far away, and it's also one of the few places in the country that offers my concentration, so it was—two birds with one stone, I guess."

Julia starts taking the Thai containers from their bags and resists asking about contemporary Baroque painting; she does not feel, at the moment, emotionally equipped to handle the answer, and she is still enjoying the visual—tugging hard on heartstrings she had forgotten she possessed—of her monosyllabically texting children talking to each other on the phone.

"But I wasn't anything like the kind of student Alma is," Sunny goes on.

Julia smiles faintly. "Yeah, I wasn't either." And then, with a little surging of confidence, she asks, "Did they— Do you know what they talked about? Ben and Alma?"

"Oh," Sunny says.

"I mean— Sorry. It's not my business, I just— I wondered if he'd said anything about where her head was at; it's been a little hard to get a read on her at home, so . . ." But she feels like she's overstepped, somehow, inquiring after these two people who are composed of half her stock, and it becomes clear, too, amid Sunny's discomfort, that she has not—of course she hasn't—imagined her son's frostiness toward her. "Forget I asked," Julia says.

"I like those pants," Sunny says after a minute.

She'd fallen down a rabbit hole at work last week, filling a virtual cart with a closet's worth of new clothes, no clown pants to be seen; she isn't allowing herself to think too closely about what motivated her to buy these pants—wide-legged, high-waisted, trendy—or to wear them today specifically. It's not because of Sunny, or not *specifically* because of Sunny, though the girl—what with her braids and her defensible bralessness and her ballet flats in bold-toned suede—

does have a tendency to make her aware of her own matronliness, make her feel—well, old, and soft, and suburban.

Last night she'd ordered a dress for the wedding; furtively, after Mark and Alma had gone to bed, she'd snuck downstairs with her laptop, clicking self-consciously through satin and florals like a person watching bestial porn. The consensus seems to be that mothers of the groom are supposed to look like old-timey stewardesses or the funereally coiffed corpses of Victorian children, lots of fussy little suits with square shoulders, stiff gauze and Peter Pan collars. She'd gone in under the guise of sheer curiosity—of course nobody cared what she wore to the wedding—but the more horrors she unearthed (The scalloping! The inch-high pumps!) the more determined she became to find something normal, something flattering and inconspicuous and God forbid *pretty*. She can't quite put her finger on what has caused it, this sudden inclination to care about how she looks around her family, a newfound awareness of herself as someone cumbersomely three-dimensional.

Sunny is shoving an entire spring roll into her mouth. She leans against the counter, hand at her throat, as she chews and swallows. "God, I'm starving. I'm literally fighting the urge to hurl all over the floor, and I still—" She lifts the box of remaining spring rolls. "Were you sick a lot with Ben?"

A new initiate into the club of maternal woes, Sunny seems to enjoy this kind of commiseration—another thing Julia herself had never been able to do naturally. She was pondering genetic predisposition toward insanity when others wanted to talk about cloth diapers and their pelvic floors.

"Oh, gosh, a lifetime ago," she says, but she realizes, halfway through the sentence, that it's an inadvertent death knell for the beginnings of their banter, and she supposes it would behoove her to make an effort at conversation, even if the conversation is about vomit. "Actually," she says brightly, remembering, "I once threw up on the Sheridan Red Line platform."

"I forget you lived in the city when he was born," Sunny says.

"Until Mark dragged us away."

"Ben's never told me how you two met."

"At random," she says. Some of Alma's green curry leaks sauce onto her hand. "He loaned me some change. You should ask him; he's got a whole bit."

It annoyed her a little when Mark told this story, because it was so *clean*, a carefully arranged narrative brimming with memorable sound bites. He'd woven a story that was fun to tell at parties, based in fact but buffed around the edges, shined to a sharp gleam: a Korean restaurant, a parking meter, his future wife sans quarters, Mark displaying none of the bumbling discomfort that she would later admit endeared him to her. But nothing about their inception had been clean, and it bothered her that he was able to so easily compartmentalize it, whitewash his own memory. He always reminded her a little of Brady Grimes when he told the story, like he was selling it to the room.

"Do you have a paper towel?" she asks, sauce dripping down her wrist.

Sunny reaches past her for a dishcloth, hanging from one of the little hooks she'd chosen for Ben during their shopping spree, before he'd told her she was a bad mother.

"Aren't they cute?" Sunny asks.

I bought them, she resists saying.

"They're a little—I mean, not exactly my taste," Sunny goes on, "but I just thought it was so adorable to think of him picking them out."

A little what? she wants to ask, offended.

"Ben's so funny," Sunny says, getting down a stack of plates.

"How's that?"

"He's just—so in his head sometimes, but then he thinks of things that would never have crossed my mind, like towel hooks or a silverware divider."

I bought that too. Wasn't this what she'd intended, stocking him up as she had? Why does she feel mildly defensive?

"A few weeks ago I saw him literally walk into a door because he was distracted, but then I go to use his computer and see that he's been googling the child safety ratings of his car. Isn't that sweet? Was he super sweet as a kid, too?"

"Yes," she says simply, because it's the truth, her tiny boy who said hello to cows and took whatever she could offer him, never suggesting that it wasn't enough. "The sweetest."

The sweetest boy is avoiding her eye contact over dinner, while Alma and Mark listen raptly to Sunny talking about the car seat that her mother has just ordered them. She used to revel in their family dinners when Ben still lived at home, not only the nice geometric breakdown at the table—a person per chair and a kid per parent—but also, privately, the sheer unbelievability of it, that she and Mark had made it through, made amends, made *Alma*, the universe improbably rewarding her with a second perfect person despite all she'd done not to deserve it.

Now she feels simply extraneous. A literal fifth wheel: the table is a square, so she's scooched back a little from everyone else, sitting at one of the corners. She'd lived about ten blocks from here with three other girls from KSU her first year out of college, a lost year, really, one of many in her twenties; the hole it left in her life was infinitesimal enough to have closed up almost immediately, like a lobe around the absence of an earring. She worked at a coffee shop in the mornings and, in the evenings, listened to her roommates whispering about how they thought she was depressed, which, to be fair, she was. Her mother had left Chicago earlier that year, before Julia returned to it, without telling her, relocated to Columbus— a move that seemed as random and implausible as her going to Atlantis—so that when Julia came home, nostalgic for her city, she found it almost unrecognizable. There had been a lot of alcohol, and a lot of sad novels, and a lot of bland, indistinguishable boys, boys with pilled jersey-knit sheets and too-tight Hüsker Dü T-shirts and an utter lack of regard for her as anything beyond a little bit of fun. Not until Mark came along had she felt extant, and it had been mutual, hadn't it, the two of them finding each other? One of the greatest gifts of her life, finding him. It's a miracle, really, that they found each other, that together they strike the balance that they do, that they've made it through so much together without—what was it Helen had said, so long ago? Killing themselves, or each other.

He catches her eyes on him, her husband, and smiles at her across the table.

26

The actual story of how they met: a chilly Thursday evening, a parking meter in the South Loop and she with no pocket change to be found. She felt beset, at that time, by similar problems: a sluggish bathtub drain that forced her to shower in a rising inch of water, milk that quickly soured, the swollen wood in the front door that prevented its closing without a struggle. Surmountable things, problems that with the slightest exertion of energy could be solved, but problems too that aggregately amounted to a low-level current of mild despair.

She'd soon be turning thirty, having watched a decade pass in a way that had felt at once interminable and terribly brisk, and so she'd paused to take stock, tidy up, do a little inventory. She went through those phases sometimes, possibly cyclically, phases where she stopped and tried to assess objectively: she had curiosities and interests and reasons to get up in the morning; check check check. She had her health. She had an outwardly normal-seeming life, obligations and silverware and an alarm clock and, until recently, a man who went down on her at least twice a month.

But it was easy for her to poke holes in all of that, to lay bare everything that was wrong. She had done everything she was supposed to do and yet her life had a hollow, flimsy quality to it. She had no real friends. She was working three jobs and still somehow drowning in student loan debt. Despite her best efforts, she had managed, over three decades, to leave almost no footprint on the earth whatsoever.

Her job at Harold Washington Library paid so little she had to supplement; she spent her mornings at a coffee shop in the basement of the Hancock Building and both weekend evenings tending bar at a douchey Irish pub in the Loop. And now her twenties were ending, and the guy she was sleeping with had started, unbeknownst to her, sleeping with their shift supervisor, who was named *Kristin* and whose face was too small for her head, and she couldn't get over how mercilessly unkind the world had turned out to be—though really, how could she be surprised?

She could not assess where she was on the lostness scale, nor could she determine to what degree she had fallen, because she wasn't sure how upstanding she'd been to begin with, if she was wasting her potential or had simply never had any. So she had decided, at the very least—she could not quit her job, nor travel through time, nor, really, travel anywhere beyond, like, Walgreens—to take a little break. She was currently on day three of what she'd been referring to as a *sexual sabbatical*, which sounded loftier than being cheated on by a dirtbag who she hadn't even liked that much in the first place.

She'd done everything she was supposed to do, and yet here she was, alone—and she *liked* being alone, and was *good* at being alone, but she'd started to feel *too* alone, like everyone else had figured out something she hadn't and begun to leave her behind.

And that night was Thursday indulgence night, her ritual: Korean food and a book at the perfectly lit corner table of Saenggang, where Yong-rae, the son of the owner, had a crush on her and allowed her to hole up until closing time. Thursday nights were her nights to eat sticky rice and not talk to anyone while her roommate, Ann, got the apartment to herself so she could hook up with praying mantis printmakers from SAIC while Ralph the Irish setter—*Ralph*, as in *Fiennes*—looked on in silent judgment. It was one of the few fixed things in her schedule that she had fixed there herself—a fixed thing that wasn't sleep or work or Sunday basement laundry—and she wanted it to go as planned, hitch-free.

But there it was, a hitch—the parking meter, her empty pockets—and she was *hurt*, she realized, and the sensation was so stupid, so outsize that tears sprung to her eyes.

"*Fuck*," she said.

He appeared to her left as though conjured by a spell, leaping into her periphery and then away again before she could make sense of him: "Oh wait, let me!"

A boy—*man* seemed generous—bounding a few paces down the sidewalk to his own car, a two-door Civic. He was gangly, too tall for his body; his corduroys, as he bent into the backseat, hung loosely from his hips. She noted a Soundgarden sticker on the bumper of his car and frowned just as he emerged. He came back with something in his hand; there was no telltale jingling of change and she stiffened, relaxing only fractionally when he thrust a roll of quarters in her direction.

"Oh," she said, "wow—thank you but it's—"

"My pleasure." He tore the paper, freeing the coins from their tight column; one slipped from his palm and landed on the sidewalk, an icy pinging sound that chilled her, in the quiet, because who the fuck knew who this guy was; he had the unkempt hair of a potentially crazy person and he didn't seem particularly good at maintaining any reliable kind of eye contact and he was *quite* tall, upon examination, and while he was not exhibiting any kind of grifting characteristics she wasn't sure if she'd recognize them to begin with. The quarters were suspect, their abundance and their receptacle; maybe he was some kind of thief.

"Laundry day," he said as if reading her mind. "Be glad you're seeing me today instead of yesterday, because I really played it fast and loose this week."

"What?"

"I normally go every Saturday, but I've been really busy, so by the time yesterday rolled around, I was down to the dregs."

"Oh." She didn't mean to ask: "What were you—wearing?"

"I mean, nothing crazy," he said. "Just not—you know—up to my usual standards. Nothing as fancy as this." He gestured elaborately to his outfit and she heard herself laugh; he smiled as though she'd just given him wonderful news.

"Well, lucky me," she said. Then, remembering the sabbatical: "Anyway."

"Here," he said, holding out the quarters again. "So you don't get a ticket."

"You don't have to—"

"Please; I don't mind at all."

"Really," she said. "I'll risk it. But thank you."

"You'll *risk* it?" He was incredulous. "It'll be at least thirty bucks. And the meter readers in this neighborhood have God complexes like you wouldn't believe." Then: "Oh, you think I'm— Look, I'm not some kind of weirdo, I just saw you and I figured you could maybe stand to catch a—break." At that he met her eyes, just once, quickly, and she felt a flash of something—something chaste, friendly, a little nonsexual surging of oneness with fellow man— but she was also cold and, she remembered, still annoyed on a very broad existential level, and so she shouldered her bag—wallet and *Blood Meridian*, ChapStick and tampons and a cassette tape of *Surfer Rosa* accidentally stolen from her stupid ex-boyfriend and several binder clips intentionally stolen from the library but not, from the sounds of it, any coins.

She paused. "Well, it's my roommate's car. Thirty bucks, huh?"

"Give Dennis the lowest level of municipal clearance and suddenly he thinks he's the mayor."

"You know the meter reader by name?"

"It was a guess." He held out the quarters again and this time she took them.

"Sounds like you've gotten quite a few tickets," she said.

"One more and they'll have me arrested." He glanced down, then quickly back up at her. "Actually, no, I've never gotten one."

"A ticket? Never?"

"I'm kind of a stickler," he said, then reddened. "Or not a— Boy, Mark, nothing like painting yourself in a flattering light. Not a *stickler*. I'm just—"

"Law-abiding."

"There you go," he said. "That sounds a little better."

"Is Mark another fictitious city employee?"

"No, Mark's me."

"Mark's *I*."

"Your name's Mark too?"

She suppressed a smile as she fed the quarters into her meter and

turned the crank, the red TIME EXPIRED flag tucking itself away and
the needle jumping to two hours. "Well," she said. "Thanks." She
reminded herself of the sabbatical; she reminded herself that things
like this never ended well for people like her.

"Of course," he said. "You're welcome."

"Take care." The midwestern equivalent of a door, gently closed
on a traveling salesman.

He seemed a little surprised. "I— Yeah, you too."

She moved past him and it wasn't until her hand was on the restaurant's door handle that she stopped—compelled by something—
and turned back to him. He was standing there like he'd just been
mugged.

"Have a good night," she said, then, again—the curse of contemporary womanhood: this effusive tendency toward both guilt and
gratitude—"Thanks, Mark."

She was good, she had learned in the last decade, at blowing
people off. It was surprising how easy it was to let other people
forget about you, and how hard it was to stop being by yourself
once you started, and so she'd just begun to accept it as a fact: some
people were investment bankers, and other people were serial kill-
ers, and she, Julia, was alone.

In her booth, she ordered dumplings, fried tofu; Yong-rae, sensing her existential unrest, brought her oxtail soup with an extra side
of rice. When a shadow darkened her table again—too soon to be
another course—she glanced up to see the man from outside, tall
and apologetic and not quite recognizable; she had only registered
him in a rudimentary way. She hadn't taken in any of the intricacies
of his face, the specific gradient of his hair, whether he had a nice
voice. She would notice those things later, begin to flex them, like
a muscle. It wasn't quite as cinematic as igniting at the first glimpse
of someone, but it was no less potent, as far as she could tell; and
she wondered sometimes too if their love was more formidable,
heartier, because it had been so carefully cultivated, tended like a
plant until it took on a life of its own.

Before her, he stood: gangly, floppy-haired, very clearly paralytically nervous, with extremities that seemed to be awaiting the arrival of a larger body.

"This is the boldest I've ever been," he said, "but . . ."

And he trailed off, half-smiling at her in that goofy expectant way of men, like *look at this bare-minimum thing I just did; look, look! acknowledge it!* And for a split second he met her eyes, and she looked him up and down, those corduroys, allegedly freshly laundered but still saggy, like they belonged to one of the fucking Boxcar Children.

She put a finger in her book. "But what?"

He opened his mouth, closed it.

"*What's* the boldest you've ever been? What did you do?"

He extended his hand toward her; it was so weirdly formal that she reached out, impelled by some latent notion of propriety, to shake. The gesture intrigued her, as did the fact that she could see, so close to him now, the nervous quickness of his breathing. She took off her glasses and peered up at him curiously.

"Sorry," he said, "what did you say your name was?"

"I didn't."

He waited, but she waited longer, and he finally dropped her hand. "I just was wondering if maybe you wanted to . . ." He shifted his weight. "I was wondering if maybe you were free to— I guess I wanted to know if . . ."

She reminded herself for a third time of her sabbatical; she reminded herself of the statistical unlikelihood, given her track records both recent and historical, of anything coming of this beyond a few good weeks, beyond some inevitable disappointment.

"Mark," she said. "Hear me out. You paid for my parking. That was really nice of you. Honestly. But—"

"I'd do that for anyone." He shrugged. "I carry a lot of change."

"Dime fetish?" She hadn't meant to say it.

A beat, then: "I've always had a thing for Thomas Jefferson, actually." Reddening, he said, "He's—on the nickel; that wasn't funny, sorry. Listen, could you throw me a bone, here? I'm humiliating myself in a public place. You think I've ever done this before? You think I just habitually wander into shady restaurants and ask the patrons out?"

"I don't have any idea what you habitually do," she said. "And it's not *shady*; there's a very positive Zagat review framed right up there by the door. Also, you didn't actually ask me—"

"I made an impulsive decision. You don't *know* this about me, but I very rarely make impulsive decisions."

"So the onus is on me to give you a prize?"

"Are you referring to yourself as a prize?"

"I'm busy," she said, but she was deeply flushed. "Very busy. For the foreseeable future."

"Me too," he said.

"I'm reading."

"I'm not asking you out for right *now*."

She squirmed. "I've given up men."

"Like—for Lent?"

She closed her eyes. "It's less of a—more that I don't *believe* in men."

He blinked. "It's not like we're leprechauns."

"A leprechaun can't admit to being a leprechaun. I think it's some sort of rule."

He studied her. "If you're going to say no, can you just say no?"

"To be fair, you haven't actually asked me anything yet."

He took a deep breath. He had already cemented himself as kind and earnest—there were similarly kind, earnest, floppy-haired boys all over the Midwest—but this visible anxiety advanced him to a higher plane on which men took risks and feared the outcomes. She saw his trepidation, the amount of nerve it must have taken for him to come into the restaurant at all.

"Could I join you?" he asked.

She observed the landscape of his face; there was something about it that she found at once disarming and alarming, its openness, its bald green candor; it was nothing she'd ever seen before and she'd never know if it was attraction or exhaustion—the two began then, and would continue, to bleed together—that caused her to give in. She nodded in a way that did not feel entirely voluntary to the seat across from her, and Mark sat down.

27

They have to coax their daughter out of the house for an awards ceremony the high school is calling The Celebration of Promise and Alma herself is referring to as A Rite of Bullshit. Every single member of the student body, it seems, is being honored for something—their athleticism, their strength in each letter of the STEM acronym, their kindness to fellow humans, and animals, and inanimate recyclables—and though it sounds to Julia like, well, bullshit, Mark—who admits to having read an article in the *Trib* about teenagers and the stress of overachieving—insists it's important for all of them to go, for Alma to get out of her room and stop moping and for her parents to showcase how proud they are of her, even if she isn't feeling proud of herself.

"It'll be fun," she says, and, withering beneath Alma's glare, "You might regret not going," and then, losing steam, "Your hair looks really good today." It's actually true, and scientifically perplexing, given that she's barely seen Alma, languishing in her bed with the celebrity-cake-bust show as she has been almost ceaselessly for the last two weeks, lift her head from her pillow, let alone run a brush through her hair.

"It is literally just going to be Sara Carmody bragging to everyone about how she got into RISD, even though we all know she forged her rec letters to say she was a creative visionary," Alma says. "And Laurent's mom, like, orgasming about how he's a fourth-generation legacy at Yale, which, yeah, you've already kind of told us that by naming him *Laurent*. And I'm supposed to say—what? *OMG congrats, I literally didn't get in anywhere.*"

Julia is also not looking forward to socializing with fellow parents, not because she could care less about what Laurent's mom thinks about Herzog College but because the thought of conversing with anyone outside of her immediate family, lately, exhausts her; she's worried she won't remember how to do it, even with the people she likes, Tim and Erica and Pari and Alan, the people she'd very recently enjoyed having in her house. She has yet to tell any of them about Alma, let alone about Ben and Sunny.

"You tell them you're still deciding," Julia says. It is technically true; the three of them are making a pilgrimage, next weekend, to Iowa, for the admitted students weekend. "Or don't tell them anything. Tell them to mind their own business."

She's worried about Alma, to tell the truth; she isn't sure how long to allow her daughter's descent into melancholy, how many cake busts and meerkats are too many. She doesn't want to go tonight, but she does think it would benefit her daughter to get a little recognition, acknowledgment of her greatness from someone other than her parents.

"Dad already bought you flowers," she says, her trump card, because nobody in their family can resist the congenital kindness of its patriarch.

"God, you guys are so *dramatic*," says Alma, but she is dragging herself from her bed. "I am *not* driving with you," she says, banging into her closet, and her voice is muffled when she adds, "I'll meet you there."

An hour later, the aged velour slipcover of the auditorium seat itchy through the material of her shirt, Mark beside her with a bouquet of Stargazer lilies in his lap, Julia is more than a little worried that Alma will fail to show up. She and Mark watch an untalented flutist play a barely recognizable rendition of "Candle in the Wind"; they watch a very nervous boy named Sebastian, upon being recognized for his contributions to the badminton team, trip over an extension cord and face-plant on his way off the stage; they watch three surprisingly dour-looking teens be awarded for their formation of the school's first comedy troupe. And then she hears her daughter's name—Alma Ames is being recognized for her successful campaign, in the fall, for the cafeteria to switch to biodegradable silverware—and suddenly there she is, onstage, in black cutoffs and fishnets and a flowered blazer over a T-shirt that reads OUAIS. Julia breathes a sigh of relief, and Mark takes her hand. The principal gives Alma her certificate, and their daughter turns for a second to scan the audience; she breaks into a tiny smile when she spots them, and it's enough to crack Julia's heart wide open.

Afterward Alma appears at the end of the hallway, flushed and bright-eyed, a far more animate version of herself than Julia's seen in weeks.

"Can we take you to dinner?" Mark asks, his arm around her.

"Okay, so," Alma says, hugging the Stargazer lilies. "There's actually a party? At Farina's? Emmy's mom rented out the rooftop for us, but a lot of the parents are going to be in the restaurant part downstairs, if you wanted . . . ?"

It's as close to an invitation as they'll get from their daughter—*come stand silently at a distance from me in the same building while I pretend we are not related*—so they accept; Alma says she's getting a ride and she'll see them there, but before she scurries off she comes within kissing distance of Julia.

"Mom? Can I borrow some lipstick?"

"Oh." It's so unexpected that she almost drops her purse. It's her last tube of Power Raisin, which was discontinued seven years ago, after which she bought the six remaining tubes she could find at three different drugstores; she has been rationing this final tube like someone meting out the last drops of a life-saving elixir, but as soon as she finds it at the bottom of her bag, she hands it over to Alma.

"Thanks!" And then her daughter bounds away with it and all she can do is watch, as though Alma is a dog who's just made off with one of her dismembered limbs.

Mark, unaware of the loss she's just endured, puts a hand between her shoulder blades.

"Off she goes," he says. "Into the wide blue."

"I think it's *wild* blue," she says, and she leans back into his hand, still following with her eyes the floral, feral blur that is Alma: their daughter who had not so long ago been small enough to nap in the ninety-degree crooks between their wrists and their elbows.

. . .

The restaurant is packed, with the kind of collective vocal din that makes the floor vibrate; the second Mark opens the door for her she wants to leave.

"Forty-five to an hour," the hostess says tonelessly, not meeting their eyes. Normally Mark would comment that there isn't an entrée in the world worth that kind of wait, but they're here for their daughter, so he just shrugs.

Julia puts their name on the list and allows Mark to guide her over to the bar, where he stakes out the last vacant seat and stands beside her. She orders drinks just as another couple shows up, edging in alongside the bar, the woman pithy with perfume.

"Let me guess," the man says. "You're here for the convention."

Julia looks at him blankly and his wife laughs.

"He's kidding," she says. "He's never met a joke that liked him."

"Celebration of Promise?" the man asks, smiling sheepishly.

"How could you tell?" Mark says. There's something about his face that seems to act as a magnet for the desperate and maligned, for the people who have been unsuccessful finding kindness elsewhere. Privately, Julia stews, knowing this will open the floodgates to a roster of other insufferably boring questions: *Son or daughter? Junior or senior? Any other children?* Knowing Mark, they'll trickle through blood types and zodiac signs and opinions on the legalization of marijuana before she finishes her glass of wine.

The seat next to her opens up and the woman sits down and they all do a cat's cradle of handshakes. They are Nick and Elise Mooney and their son is Sebastian, undoubtedly the kid who had face-planted during the ceremony. Julia subtly kicks Mark's shin; he, smiling, artfully avoids her eye contact.

"We felt a little slighted that he didn't want to have dinner with us," Elise says. "But I guess we have to start practicing letting him go since he's off to college in the fall."

"Ours too," says Mark, and she feels suddenly nervous, both because she is trapped in a restaurant with a hundred suburban parents and because their daughter's leaving has become a conversational point of fact, a trading card available for barside commiseration.

"So are you beside yourselves?" Elise asks. "Or is it just us?"

"Good beside or bad beside?" Julia replies, smiling weakly.

"Well, both, I guess," Elise says. "Of course it's wonderful that they're—making their way. But God, thinking of the house without Baz." She reaches for her husband's arm.

Julia sips her wine and wills Nick to not make a sexual joke. "Yes, we're on the hunt for a stray little one," she says, "so we can continue to be distracted from each other."

And though the expressions of both their new companions are troubled, Mark smiles, leans his shoulder a little into hers.

"Jules has never met a joke she didn't make uncomfortable," he says.

"And Mark has never met a joke, period." Her wineglass is nearly empty.

"Actually," Mark says, "we've got a grandchild on the way. So the nest won't be totally vacated."

Nick and Elise are suddenly fawning—how could you *possibly*, you're so *young*—but Julia feels cold, wondering what possessed Mark to share this news with two complete strangers, *a grandchild on the way*, like they're a couple of kindly septuagenarians living in the Welsh countryside.

"Boy or girl?" ask Nick and Elise. "When's the due date? Is this your first? It *must* be your first."

He's right, though, she supposes, leaving him to field the questions. They're not only losing their daughter but simultaneously, like it or not, attaining grandparental status, aging rapid-fire. The next time they see these people—please, God, let them never see these people again—Mark will probably have one of those foldable photo sleeves in his wallet, showing baby pictures to anyone who asks, or doesn't. She'd noticed an irritating tic last weekend, Sunny slipping mention of the child into every available crevice—"We'll have to take Baby to that next year"; "Baby's going to need a good humidifier"— not *the baby* but *Baby*, as though that was its given name; there was something affected about it, Sunny saying it every fifth word—"Just in time for Baby!" and "We'll read that to Baby!" That was what she'd been fixating on—how annoying she found her daughter-in-law—when everyone else in her family was behaving according to the rules, not even needing to *reference* the rules to know what they were supposed to be doing, feeling *excited* about the baby's arrival, feeling *happy* about a new life. What was *wrong* with her?

Mark gives her a little earth-to-Julia touch on the back and she surfaces, tries to smile at him, orders another glass of Cabernet. Mark will make an excellent countryside septuagenarian, a wonderful grandparent. She has trouble envisioning herself in anything resembling that role, can only imagine being in some dark periphery, the bog witch who will show up at the baby's christening to bestow a curse upon it.

"Cheers," say Nick and Elise Mooney. "Mazel tov."

"Cheers to Sebastian," Julia says and then, knowing it will steer the conversation in a less fraught direction: "What's he planning to major in?"

She allows herself to zone out but snaps back a few minutes later to hear Elise say the phrase *recharge my needs battery.*

"Your what now?" she asks.

"My needs battery," Elise repeats.

"The book they're reading, sweetheart," Mark says pointedly, touching the small of her back again. "One of the Eight Small Acts of Love."

"Only eight?" Julia says.

"Well, each one has a bunch of bullet points," Elise says. "Like—being a good listener is one, but that encompasses not only active listening but also mindfulness in speech. Listening to yourself as though you're the other person."

"And sharing everything," Nick chimes in. He takes a theatrical sip of Elise's martini.

"So you only have to recharge one needs battery, then," Julia says, unable to stop herself.

"I know it sounds a little silly," Elise says. "Such a cliché, couples counseling when your kid goes off to college, but we've just been focusing on Baz for so long that we—well. Just thought it wouldn't hurt to get a refresher on how to be alone together."

The easiness of this line strikes her, *how to be alone together;* Julia pictures herself and Mark wafting around their empty house like drafts of cold air, the quietude of dinners without the indignant interruptions of their incremental vegan.

"I don't think it's silly at all," she says softly. "I think we all need all the help we can get." She tries to smile at Elise to show her she is being sincere but nothing, lately, seems to be coming out the way she means it to.

"Jerry!" the hostess yells, and she meets Mark's eyes, and they make a decision; this silent complicity in the face of annoying strangers is one of the greatest parts of being married.

"There's our cue," Mark says.

"Oh, I thought they said—"

"Great to meet you guys," Julia says, and she allows herself to be led up past the hostess stand and out of the restaurant, into the mild spring evening. They bustle down the block, past an inflow of other parents and their promising children. When they turn in to the entrance of a nearby park, she looks back toward the restaurant with some amount of complicated longing, feeling like she's left her handbag there, or forgotten to pay the bill, though Mark left cash at the bar. "We can't just leave Ollie."

"Text her. She won't mind."

She unearths her phone, uneasy, and pulls up her messages with Alma.

Dad and I couldn't get a table, so we're going to head home. Alma used to cling disturbingly to the chain-link fence surrounding the playground when they'd leave her at kindergarten, a barnacle or some deeply afflicted howler monkey, red-faced and utterly betrayed. *Unless you'd like us to stay; we're also happy to just sit at the bar.* "God, it's like being texted by Herman Melville," Alma had said recently, waving her phone at Julia, displaying one of her admittedly novelistic messages. *Also happy to come back to pick you up anytime.* Happy, happy, happy. She frowns, presses send, then worries she's sounded too cold. She starts typing again, begins *You look beautifu*—and then *We're so proud of y*—and then *I can't believe how much I'm going to mis*—but then the little gray dots pop up; Alma is already responding.

no prob! The exclamation point is unusual, kindness induced either by her participation in social merriment or, hopefully not, by the imbibement of alcohol, which is surely present on the restaurant rooftop regardless of how vigilant Emmy's mom has been.

will get a ride with m
11???
Then a series of emoji hands, praying.

Receiving messages from Alma, conversely, is like being texted by William Carlos Williams; her daughter's texts always arrive in three- or four-word clusters, little hailstorms of intel delivered in real time.

"She wants an extra hour on her curfew," she tells Mark, who is wandering a few yards away, hands clasped behind his back and bent slightly at the waist as he reads the memorial placards settled at the bases of the trees.

"Why not," he says.

She writes back *Not a minute later*, leaning a little into her Melvillian affectation because it's one of the rare things she does that seems to amuse her daughter more than annoy her.

tx!!!!!
She worries again about alcohol.
and tx for coming
love u
We love you too, she writes, *and we're so proud of you.*

Bedtime with Alma used to be an unbelievably tedious production, hours of reading and singing followed by a breathtakingly slow creep backward through her bedroom door, an interminable back-and-forth of *I love you*. Alma never wanted to be the last one to say it, *always* wanted to be the last one to say it; she was afraid, she admitted once, of death, of one of them dying in their sleep and she just wanted to be sure that whoever it was *knew*. Though her daughter had been intrigued, as a child, by more fantastical unfoldings—the Crypt Keeper, and the endless series of books she'd read about vampires and time travel and time-traveling vampires—she was terrified of the more run-of-the-mill horrors that could befall a person: tragedy, illness, death. Seismic monitoring thereof would have revealed a bell curve of increasing desperation, the pitch rising, rising, rising, until her daughter simply couldn't keep her eyes open anymore and it petered out on her end, sometimes in midsentence.

Julia herself hadn't been prone to this kind of thinking as a kid—she'd just assumed that ties were fleeting, that misfortune would inevitably befall her, no sense in worrying about it before it happened—but she'd come to it belatedly, inherited it in reverse from her daughter, perhaps in some unconscious attempt to shoulder some of her burden, this tiny girl with her outsized fears.

"Just shut the *door*," Mark used to say, watching from the hallway, baffled and not a little annoyed too—because it wasn't terribly *quiet*, this production; Alma wanted each declaration audible and on the record. But Julia could never make herself shut the door. Julia would stand there for what felt like an eternity in this deranged metronomic chorus with her daughter, varying cadence and inflection, *I love *you* I *love* you I *love you*, while her husband and son moved on with their lives behind her, keeping a wide berth as they passed her.

Because it broke her heart to think of her daughter thinking like this, dreaming of dying. And because she, too, couldn't choose which was worse, being the leaver or being left.

"There's a red oak over there dedicated to someone named *Bacon Daniels*." Mark has circled back to her.

She glances down at her phone screen again, waits a few seconds for any sign of reply, those billowing gray dots, but nothing comes.

"Hopefully a dog," her husband says.

"Hmm?"

He wraps an arm around her shoulders. "Should we get some dinner?"

"Sure." She leans against him. "How did you start talking about couples counseling with those people?"

"How can *you* just completely drop off the face of the earth like you do?"

"Survival instinct," she says. "Whatever part of the brain knows to make us black out when we see our own broken bones."

"You've never broken a bone," he says.

"That I can *remember*."

"Do people really need *therapy* to prepare to be alone with their spouses?"

"Do you think we do?" She eyes him sideways.

"I don't—think so, no. Do we?"

"I didn't *think* we did," she says.

"I didn't either."

"But now you do?"

"No," he says. Then: "Do you?"

"*No*, Dr. Seuss," she says. "For fuck's sake."

Mark laughs, pulls her against him. They walk in silence for half a block, Julia thinking about Alma on the rooftop.

"It's funny," she says. "There have been so many times that I've dreamed of the prospect of—I don't know—getting some part of myself back, or just little things like spending less time ferrying her places in the car, but now it— God, it just seems like it's gone by so fast."

"I'm not worried about being alone with you," he says. "For the record. I think it's going to be fun. Like when we first started dating. Except we have a bed frame now. And we can afford dental insurance."

"And we like to go to bed at nine p.m."

"We *get* to go to bed at nine p.m.," says Mark. "See? I can't wait."

He smiles at her, kisses the side of her head, then stops to look at a glassed-in menu for a Mediterranean place, doing that long-necked squinting maneuver they've both started to do when trying to read things on their phone screens; Alma enjoys pointing it out—"You're making your phone face"—every time she sees them doing it. It moves her, this old-man expression on her husband's face.

"*Couples share everything*," he says, glancing over at her. "We share everything, don't we?"

It makes her nervous. "Is this your way of telling me you have chlamydia?"

He laughs. "Just a little flare-up."

She leans in to read alongside him, takes his elbow. "Happens to the best of us."

28

An incomplete list of things Julia Marini did not believe in when she was twenty-nine years old: raisins, Libertarians, scented candles, white people with dreadlocks, any people with degrees in communications, Chardonnay, toothpicks, the Royal Family, people who referred to children as *kiddos*, flavored coffee, astrology, Americans who got too excited about distant Irish heritage.

But she did, she found, believe in Mark Ames.

Mark, who was a researcher at the University of Chicago, could not get over the coincidence of her having grown up just blocks from the campus where he spent his days.

"It's a big city," she said inflexibly.

"Small world, though," he said.

"Not so small."

"You lived on Fifty-Fourth?"

"I lived a lot of places."

They were having cocktails at a little patio bar on Van Buren by the library. He smiled at her across the table and she softened. Meeting Mark had been like finding a beloved old sweatshirt she hadn't realized she'd lost. He smelled right; their bodies fit peaceably together. Like he'd been there all along.

Mark took her to see Wilco at the Auditorium, and he opened doors for her (which she knew she wasn't supposed to care about but still did), and as far as she knew he didn't have any dumb affected hobbies except for jogging and he was punctual to a fault and he always, always seemed genuinely happy to see her; she had never been with someone who lit up the way that he did when he caught sight of her coming up the stairs to his apartment. She had a sense that he would never forget her birthday, even if they broke up.

The strange ease of their relationship seemed to startle them both. Their lives were suddenly intertwined, their rapport complex and codified. They went on three dates, then four; then suddenly they'd gone on ten and stopped identifying them as such; they were simply together, *a lot*, of course they were, why wouldn't they be? There was a manic quality to that time, awash in the blind, dumb admiration of another person, admiration untarnished by the inevitabilities of commitment, betrayals and meannesses and misunderstanding. She'd never been sentimental, but his hand in hers moved her. She couldn't believe how much more livable the world seemed with him around. Suddenly she wasn't alone anymore; he'd arrived in her life with a strength of presence that she truly found baffling. And she liked—a lot—having him across from her at a table.

"Tell me about your mom," he said, his ankle twined with hers under her chair. He didn't say it in a drawn-out ironic way—"tell me about your *mother*"—but just inquisitively, casually.

"She's a force," she said obstinately. She and Anita had spoken on the phone a handful of times since she'd left for college, short, stilted conversations—nothing more than wellness checks, really— but the last one had been at least a year ago.

"That bloodline flows strong." He rubbed her knee under the table. He was a little tipsy. He was a surprise to her in all ways, a handsome, accomplished man with very kind eyes. The universe finally lobbing her a softball.

"Yeah, apples and trees," she said, willing it away. She was versed already in Mark's nuanced biographical rundown: he was born and raised in La Crosse, Wisconsin; his parents were named, like living renditions of PlaySkool farmers, *Bonnie* and *Skip*. His father was a mechanic and his mother an elementary school secretary; he had an older brother named Drew. His departure to Stanford, for college, had been a source of both pride and pain for the family, his subsequent move to Chicago continued fuel for their bafflement.

She, conversely, hadn't told him much, or there just wasn't that much to tell: that her father was dead and her mother lived in Colorado so he wouldn't be meeting her parents anytime soon. It was all technically true, and until recently he hadn't worked that hard to know more. But things were beginning to accelerate—their lives, without her noticing, had become something close to contingent, and it made her nervous.

"If she were a tree," Mark said, getting uncharacteristically silly, "what kind of tree would she be?"

She smiled at him. "You should eat something."

"A birch? An elm? A weeping willow?"

"Look at Mr. Whimsical," she said with more of an edge in her voice than she intended.

He wilted. "Why are you in a mood?"

"I'm not in a *mood*."

He reached across the table and squeezed her hand; the tenderness, as ever, was startling.

"What's going on in there, Jules?" he asked, pure, kind inquisition—*I just want to know you*, he'd said to her recently—and she shrugged, swallowing down the fullness in her throat, the acidic surge of something distasteful. "Throw me a bone," he said. "You're shrouded in mystery."

"Fine, go ahead." She waved a hand. "Ask me whatever you want."

"What's your earliest memory?"

"I don't know, Oprah."

"Best vacation you ever took."

"Are you reading these from a script?" she asked. "Jesus, I'm not in a mood, but I'm not in the mood for *this*." She'd never taken a vacation, not really, unless you counted—she hadn't thought about this in years; the memory startled her—the day trip she'd been on as a very young child to the Indiana Dunes, a rare outing with both of her parents. She could suddenly recall the warm air blowing into the open windows of the car, the way her dad drove fast on the empty stretches of highway, leaning theatrically left and right like they were on a roller coaster, making Julia lift her hands over her head and squeal with delight, *again again again*.

"Hey, Jules?" he said quietly. "You can tell me anything, you know."

And she wondered if perhaps she could, if the twinge she felt—sharp, abdominal, halfway between excruciating and enlivening—had anything to do with *love;* she wanted him suddenly, terribly, and she pressed her knees together, hugging his hand between them.

"My mother is a phone tree," she said, and lifted his palm to her lips, and the moment passed without incident.

They were huddled together against the cold, her arm twined through his. He'd come to the Loop for a meeting and was walking her to the bar for her Friday night shift. She was animatedly telling him a story about one of her colleagues, a sallow young woman she referred to as Squeaky Fromme, lifting her voice to be heard over the wind and slyly studying Mark as he laughed at her jokes.

It was a knack you had to pick up, letting someone adore you. She hadn't had any practice, before Mark. And when you fell for someone, she realized—she had never fallen like this before—you started to fall for yourself a little bit too. Everything became funnier and more interesting once she vocalized it to him.

"She told Maya she couldn't work today because she's getting an abortion."

"*Oh,*" he said.

Mark was measured, not unjudgmental, but he was slower to strike than she was; Mark gave nearly everything a few minutes to steep before he settled on a verdict, which slowed things down in a way that was not unpleasant.

"But if that's the case," she said, "it's her third one this month."

Admittedly sometimes she found herself trying a little bit to scandalize him, this bright-eyed, sheltered Wisconsinite who'd been a student his entire life. He was easy to shock, and nine times out of ten she found it sweet and refreshing, though it made her even less inclined to get into the nitty-gritty of her comparatively colorful formative years. She had begun to mete out details, slowly releasing air from the balloon instead of blasting him in the face. She had yet to tell him anything that seemed to give him pause, though she'd watched him swallow his surprise a few times when she'd parroted certain sound bites from her mother.

They stopped a few storefronts down from the bar, in front of the dubious place that sold discount luggage, and he put his arms around her. "You coming over after?"

She nodded against him. "I'll be late though."

She wondered, in more cynical moods, if one of the reasons these salad days were so intensely rosy was how little time they had to actually spend together, their limited interactions leaving them hungry for each other, their ample time apart allowing them room for romanticization.

"I can come pick you up."

She smiled, shook her head; it was a familiar exchange, and one she hadn't tired of, rooted in someone being concerned for her well-being, even if she was completely capable of maintaining it on her own.

"Take a cab, then."

"I promise," she said, and finally stepped out of his embrace. "I'll see you."

The wind blew fiercely from the lake. He wrapped his coat more tightly around him, bouncing on his toes, and kissed her again, ready to take off, solo, to his meeting.

"Have a good shift," he said, and then it happened—delivered offhandedly, unthinkingly, like a handshake: "I love you."

They both froze as though he'd done something reckless or disgusting, called her a horrible name or wet his pants. She watched the widening of his eyes; his cheeks were red already, from the wind.

"I mean," he said, then, "Wait."

She smiled a little, bemused. "Wait for what?"

He looked so much like a boy sometimes; his face had a way of softening when he was nervous or tired, and he was so frequently either or both of those things around her.

"I didn't want it to—be like that," he said.

"You didn't want what to be like—what?" She felt a sudden, familiar nervousness, one she hadn't felt since the most nascent stages of their being together—that creeping fear that he'd realize his error in being with her, scramble to take it back.

"I wanted it to be more—seminal," he said, and she laughed, couldn't help it.

She cupped a hand to his face. Her heart was racing, but she didn't want him to know that, was glad for the protective layers of their coats. "You must know by now that if you made some big public declaration I'd be *horrified*."

"No, I know, but I didn't mean to—I don't know, blow my wad like that."

"*There's* an expression."

He blinked. "It's from the Civil War," he said. "It refers to the premature detonation of cannons."

"Okay," she said. "You are the only person on the earth who thinks that, but okay."

"Will you let me do it again?"

"Blow your wad?"

After a beat, his eyes crinkled up at the corners, and it dawned on her that the feeling she was feeling was possibly love too. She'd never been prone to sentimentality; never until she met him had she felt that warm liquidity in her chest, something about to spill over. But she didn't *know*; she'd always heard that you just *knew*, and she'd as yet, in her lifetime, only experienced gut reactions of the dread variety.

Mark loving her: she wasn't sure what to do with that. She found *love*, too, too intangible a notion, one of those catchalls—like exercising—that people used to outwardly assure the world of their smug ascendance. If love in fact was an *actual thing*, she wasn't sure she would recognize it, and this seemed sad and scary for its own whole set of reasons.

And yet she wasn't, standing there across from him in the wind, completely convinced that she didn't feel it back.

"Will you let me—say it again? Not right now. Sometime that's—better."

Up until then she had always foreseen eventual—inevitable!—endings, taperings-off or knock-down, drag-outs, depending, but she couldn't seem to quite conjure them with Mark, couldn't picture what it would look like for him to stop being around. She'd begun to find herself missing him when they weren't together, nothing crazy—it was dim and distant, a dull missing, interspersed with moments of panic—Mark!—like she'd left the house without dressing or forgotten to turn off the oven. She didn't like it, didn't quite trust the sensation of feeling linked to another human being. She was distrustful, generally, of happiness, any amount, any sort. And she was suspicious of anyone who told her she'd know something when she saw it. She had not ever experienced certitude when it came to inarticulable feelings: love, for instance, or orgasms. She had known decent sex; she had known affection. But she had always been convinced that there must be a higher level of ascendancy. It was not something she gave a great deal of thought to; she avoided the pursuit thereof for the same reasons that she'd never tried hard drugs, because she didn't want to be disappointed or get addicted.

She stepped closer to him, put her arms around him. He held her, a hand in her hair, and waited. "Hey Mark?" She hugged him harder, hoping it was conveying everything she wanted it to, even if she wasn't entirely sure what that was. Her voice was muffled against him. "Me too."

29

She has been regarding Alma's admitted students weekend at Herzog with the removed optimism of a person refusing to think too hard about what's to come, the same deluded maybe-it-won't-be-so-bad attitude with which she has previously approached dental procedures and childbirth, and Alma does nothing to get them off to an auspicious beginning, standing imposingly in front of the driver's side door like a carjacker.

"Can I drive?" her daughter asks.

She should have known this was coming. Her own mother—she had to hand this to Anita—had taught her how to drive, early mornings in Oak Woods Cemetery, but she has left the entirety of her children's vehicular instruction up to their father; for all the driving she has done in her adult life she could not bear to shepherd her children through this particular rite of passage, a rite that would literally take them even further away from her than they already were.

"Maybe on the way home," she says, and Alma, radiating rage, curls up into the passenger seat and pulls the hood of her sweatshirt tight over her head.

Her daughter is angry already that Mark has bailed on their trip at the last minute, citing a trip to New York that his assistant forgot to put in his calendar.

"I'm sorry," he'd said last night, rolling moisture-wicking T-shirts into his stupid ergonomic backpack. "But these students at Columbia are— God, they all look like they're about twelve but if you could see what they're doing, Jules; it's a robot the size of a sperm cell that accelerates the body's recovery from major surgery."

"And they'll—what? Scrap it if you don't meet them for coffee tomorrow morning?"

"They're graduating in a few weeks," he says. "This is my chance to meet with them before they get snatched up by someone bigger."

"Ollie's graduating too," she said, but all he'd said was "It'll be good for you two to have some time alone."

But being alone, now, in the car with Alma does not feel particularly good.

"Oh my *God*, Mom," Alma says, when Julia waves in her rearview at the car who has let her merge onto the expressway. She makes herself even smaller in her seat. "Do you *know* that person?"

Herzog College boasts its status as an almost-but-not-quite venue for one of the Lincoln-Douglas debates. This fact seems hard to prove and Julia finds herself wondering why, as long as they were going to brag about a hypothetical, they hadn't made up something sexier, more exciting, the fact that Patti Smith had almost donated a darkroom or that it had once been considered as a site by the Olympics host committee.

Their tour kicks off in the lushly furnished sitting room of the college's president.

"I'm aware of how hard this can be," he is saying. "Thinking about saying goodbye to your babies." It's an awkward line, delivered with a self-conscious affectation, and she pictures the president's wife writing it for him.

"We give birth to them," he continues, and she bristles at the *we*. "And we raise them, and we keep them safe, and we help them make good choices. And then we have to let them go." She's newly, viscerally aware of her daughter's presence beside her. "I'm here to promise you," the president says, gaining momentum, like a dictator, "that we'll provide your children with everything they need to thrive."

Another parent raises her hand to inquire about the dining hall meal plan, prefacing her question with a novelistic paragraph about her daughter's gluten intolerance; the next thing she knows the tour has begun, a mass, meandering stroll across campus, into the old bell tower, through an impressively glassy art building (*Paul Newman almost donated this*, they could have said) and into a requisite cinder block dorm room, stale carpet and a twin bed in the corner.

Her heart begins to race. She inhales slowly, so Alma won't notice her breathing. There's a judgmental little iteration of her psyche who stands on her shoulder sometimes and assigns designations: *The Kind of Mother Who* (fill in the blank): *Reeks of Cigarettes at Preschool Pickup, Is Not Good at Drawing Hearts, Lets Her Kid Eat Funyuns.* Today she is, apparently, the kind who almost has a panic attack at admitted students weekend.

"I need a minute," she whispers to Alma, louder than she intends. A couple of fellow parents turn to look. She wants to tough it out for the sake of her daughter not dying of embarrassment, but her vision is darkening a little at the edges, so she ducks out of the crowd and makes her way down a narrow, institutionally lit hallway past a vending machine that appears, disturbingly, only to dispense plastic pint bottles of milk, up a gummy flight of stairs. The air, when she pushes out the heavy door, is oppressively warm, musky; out in the country the atmosphere is arid, reminiscent of somewhere far more exotic than Iowa. Alma will unequivocally murder her if she necessitates an ambulance being called, so she sinks down onto a bench, breathes as deeply as she can. She dips her head toward her knees.

A shadow covers her feet. She doesn't miss smoking, usually, but she misses the instantaneous relief it afforded, and also the toxic clouds it produced that kept strangers at bay.

But the shadow does not belong to a stranger; Julia makes out its familiar shape and looks up to see Alma, her daughter sun-squinting and square-shouldered.

"Sorry, sweet," she says. "Just got a little warm in there."

"Corn *sweats*," Alma says. "Did you know that? That's why it gets so humid here."

"I didn't know that, no."

Alma sits down beside her. "Are you okay?"

She puts a hand on her daughter's knee. "I'm fine. You should go back in."

Alma leans a little against her and it's so nice, despite the heat; she would sit here forever if she could, her mildly sweaty daughter stuck to her side.

"What do you think so far?" she ventures to ask, and she feels Alma shrug.

"It's sort of pretty."

"It is." She envisions her daughter traipsing across campus to her dorm late at night, pockets full of dining hall cookies and a laid-back sense of purpose; she pictures her going to sleep in that drably belinened XL twin bed, and suddenly there are tears in her eyes.

"We put you in this daycare when you were a baby," she says, remembering. "It was supposed to be one of the best in the area but they— I remember I brought you there for the first day and they showed me the room where they had all of the kids take naps and it didn't have any windows and there were these tiny cots lined up along the walls, like a little doll prison, and I pictured you sleeping in one and I started crying right there; I ended up taking you home. I couldn't stand to think of you taking a nap in a place like that."

Alma eyes her askance. "Are you having a stroke?"

"Just pining. Don't worry about me, Ollie."

"Want me to get you a milk?" Alma asks. "From that gross vending machine?"

She feels such extraordinary love for her daughter that for a second she gets woozy again.

"Everyone's going to the dining hall after this," Alma says. "The tour guide keeps talking about a *frozen yogurt buffet*."

"What is it with these people and *dairy*?" She can think of nothing that sounds less appealing, but she remembers they're supposed to be encouraging, nudging their recalcitrant daughter into the deeper waters of independent living. "Should we—"

"That's my nightmare," Alma says. "Like—all of this is my nightmare, this *tour*, the food-allergies mom, for fuck's sake, like just raise your kid in a *cage* if you're so worried about her coming into contact with flaxseed. Could we—just go somewhere else? Instead? For a little bit?"

The primary reason it had been so hard to find her a daycare was how much Alma hated to be left, how forcefully she would weep every time Julia dropped her off, clinging tearfully to whatever part of her mother's body was grabbable, tiny fingers digging bruises into thighs and forearms. Her daughter's capacity for feeling things was almost a little scary; every joy and heartbreak burst from her with force, tantrums giving way to radiant happiness in a matter of seconds. But she had been what Julia always wanted: a child who felt secure enough in the world to tell it how she was doing. The guilt she felt for how things were when Ben was small was a physical object, something attached to her body that bumped burdensomely against her like a shoulder bag, but she made room for it around the constant kinetics of her daughter. Alma hurtled; she foisted and barnacled; she began breathless tales in midsentence, too excited to give any sort of preamble.

"And Yurtle ate a *lettuce* and then we thought we saw a *lepre-chaun*, but Sadie says it wasn't and she knows because her mom's been to *Ire*land; Mama can we bake this weekend not for any special *casion* just because or maybe for *autumn*; have you ever been to *Ire-*land; I missed you Mama *so much*."

And Julia drank her in, marinated in her.

"Could we?" Alma asks her now. *I'll be so good if we do, Mama.* She has never been able to say no.

They find a café close to campus, a place that likely banks on the transitory presence of parents and occasional faculty trysts to keep itself afloat. She tries to picture her daughter in this small town, growing familiar with the stretch of downtown, accruing ownership of a new place, its idiosyncrasies and local charms; she imagines—her gut clenches—returning to this restaurant in August for freshman move-in, she and Mark sitting across from their daughter, preparing to say goodbye. She pictures Alma coming home for Thanksgiving subtly changed, maybe some physical manifestation—a haircut, a piercing through her ear cartilage—but the bulk of the transformation elemental, defamiliarization of her movements and her posture, her gaze off-center, still affixed to the private life she'll resent having to leave in order to come home. And she and Mark will surely be different too, months dwelt together in an empty nest; all anyone seems to be talking about lately is the departure of children wrecking or rekindling marriages, and it's not clear to her if her own marriage is a candidate for either.

She stopped going home when she went away to college; she'd pick up house-sitting gigs over Christmas and whatever she could find in the summers, waiting tables or tending bar, camping out in short-term rentals on the edge of campus like a specter. She identified her own shortcomings before anyone else could, designated herself the Weird Scholarship Girl so as to own it rather than fall victim to it. College hadn't for her been the door-opening that it's likely to be for Alma, who will be leaving the comfort of one world for the slightly different comfort of another, a well-woven parental safety net beneath her.

She orders a carafe of Chianti and pours a few sips into her daughter's empty water glass.

"So," she says, "any thoughts?"

Alma—swirling the wine around at the bottom of her glass, sniffing the rim, an affectation she must've picked up from television—shrugs.

"I'm a little nervous about how—*small* it seems? Like what if I hate everyone? And then I'm just trapped here in, like, a boxcar, with a thousand terrible people." Alma is swishing her wine around in the back of her mouth, once again approximating sophistication but looking, instead, exactly like she had as a toddler, blowing bubbles in her milk.

Julia struggles, most of the time, to find traces of herself in her daughter; when they emerge like this—almost always little darknesses, flashes of misanthropy or fatalism—she's never sure whether to feel proud or ashamed. Other mothers must not have this problem, must joyfully recognize their own generosity or glee within the fibers of their offspring.

"I think the odds of your hating *everyone* are slim," she says. "It's also very possible that being at a huge school could make you feel— well, even more alone." She'd remained on the periphery of her collegiate life because it seemed less risky, because you couldn't lose what you didn't have in the first place.

"Yeah, if you can't find a single friend out of fifty thousand people, you're kind of fucked, I guess," Alma says.

She wishes now that she had spent all the years she worried about other people thinking she was weird actually *being* weird. There is a decent chance, in hindsight, that nobody would have batted an eye if she'd stayed still long enough to let anybody notice her. She'd done the same thing after college, immediately filling her hours with work, sparse, dead sleep in between, the occasional company of men. And she'd done it again a few years later, baby Ben strapped to her chest, skirting the Serenity Smiles moms at preschool pickup like a fugitive.

"What happens," Alma says suddenly, "if I hate it here?"

Julia studies her, this girl she's been studying her entire life, watching her daughter grow from shy pigeon-toed preschooler to surly adolescent, the years passing merciless and blinklike.

"Nothing happens," she says. "Dad and I will be just a couple of hours away." She finds comfort herself in considering this, the fact that Alma won't be across the country at Stanford or Vassar. It is also, she acknowledges, the thing she wished her own mother would have said to her, ever. *I'm here if you need me.* She wonders how much of a difference something like that makes, the mere awareness that there are people nearby thinking about you, not hoping you'll break down but ready to help if you do.

"Margo thinks I should try," Alma says.

"I agree with Margo," says Julia. "I think you can make something really good out of this if you want to, Ollie. But if not? That's fine too. Almost nothing ends up being as big of a deal as you think it's going to be. Very few things."

"But what if this is one that—does end up being a big deal?"

"I just have a feeling," Julia says, "that it isn't."

"I know I'm being bratty," Alma says. "I just—really thought something different would happen. I guess I wanted to be able to *say* I was going somewhere impressive, because it seems like everyone else is."

She shifts to face her daughter more squarely, steels herself. "I got a scholarship when I was your age," she says. "To Northwestern. A pretty significant one."

Alma furrows her brow. *"What?"*

She has, unconsciously or otherwise, neglected to share much about her early life with her children, as though she'd only really begun to exist when they were born. And though this feels true sometimes—her days before Ben and Alma, before Mark, have taken on a wobbly, psychedelic quality, a series of poorly dubbed short films—she has also always suspected that she has insufficiently let go of those days, keeping them stowed away for easy access when she needs to make sense of things, blame or forgive herself.

"I didn't take it, obviously," she says.

"Why?" her daughter asks. "I mean, like, *how?*"

"It wasn't the right thing for me at the time."

"And your mom let you?"

And it guts her, that this comes as a surprise to Alma, her own maternal supervision apparently such a given that she assumes all mothers must do it, but also the simplicity of the question. Her mother had let her go. Her mother had practically pushed her out the door.

"My mom wasn't as—interested in all of my stuff as I am in yours." Then, feeling, as she always does when speaking ill of Anita, a little traitorous: "It was a different time."

"But it's a really good school."

"It is," she says. "I needed to move away more than I needed a really good school."

Alma, her father's daughter, looks at her like she has just confessed to a federal crime.

Julia reaches out to touch her wrist. "I'm telling you this to say that it wasn't the end of the world for me. Kansas wasn't my dream. Not what I was envisioning, not what I'd planned on, but it worked out. Things usually *do* work out, Ollie. They're almost never as huge as we think they're going to be." She takes her daughter's hand now, risking that Alma will pull away, but she doesn't. "And, Alma, my God. How much *better* you are at things than I was. How *lovely* you are. How funny and brilliant and openhearted. You're going to be that way whatever you do." Her voice catches in her throat.

You weren't going to exist, darling girl, she does not say. *You almost didn't.* She thinks of herself scuttling across campus at KSU, existing on the fringe. She'd been in such a hurry, but she can no longer entirely remember why. Had she known then what she does now—that it would all come to matter so little; and also that she wasn't as weird as she'd thought, that there had surely been potential there for friendship, for community, for something other than utilitarian loneliness—she may have lingered longer, enjoyed her schooling instead of simply trying to get through it unnoticed. But of course if she hadn't, everything would be different; if she'd had a more socially fruitful time in college, she may not have moved back to Chicago, almost certainly wouldn't have met Mark. It's an enormous, dizzying thought, walls collapsing easily to reveal further fallout—if she hadn't met Mark she wouldn't have had Ben; if she hadn't had Ben she likely wouldn't have met Helen Russo; if she hadn't met Helen Russo—well, Alma wouldn't be here, would she? It makes her nervous, a fluttery feeling at the base of her throat.

Alma squirms, embarrassed. "Thanks."

Julia smiles at her. "It's just true."

Where did you come from, little one, she does not say, because she knows all too well.

She lets Alma drive them home the next day; her daughter is a conscientious if lead-footed driver, and Julia has to repeatedly stop herself from reaching up to grab the oh-shit strap. After they pull into the driveway, Alma is looking at her phone almost before she puts the car in park; she stumbles inside furiously typing, their buds of mother-daughter friendship, so promisingly cultivated on the trip, already frosting over to their death. Julia takes her time unloading the car because she can see it from the corner of her eye: the box on the front porch, her dress for the wedding, wrapped like a bomb, ignored by her daughter once Alma saw the address label didn't concern her.

She tucks it under her arm but is forced to immediately set it down in favor of Suzanne, who has emerged from her twenty-four hours with the dog sitter like someone who has been trapped for weeks in a collapsed mine. She stands on her back legs, flailing with her forepaws in the air, waiting for Julia to pick her up so she can immediately leap from her arms again and begin the procession anew.

"It is so hard; I know," says Julia, and "Life is a struggle for us all, Suzanne," and "You were incredibly brave," and the dog goes about one of her favorite reconciliatory pastimes, trying to lick the inside of Julia's mouth. "Come on, my darling," Julia says, "let's go face our fears."

She and Suzanne trek upstairs to open the box.

She hangs the dress on her bathroom door and appraises it, Suzanne studiously sniffing at the hem for what seems like several hours before bestowing upon it a single, grave lick. The dress is viridian Leavers lace—Mark's always liked her in green—and she is afraid to try it on. One perk of having money is the disguises it allows you to buy, big shapeless alpaca capes and artisanal yeti boots and three-hundred-dollar mother-of-the-groom dresses that cover your abdominal paunch and cap silk crescents over your drooping shoulders.

"I need your counsel," she says to Alma a few minutes later, and her daughter looks up at her lazily, hunched over her laptop at the kitchen table. She has, since the Celebration of Promise, finally begun to migrate from her bed, sprawling insouciantly on the living room couch and occasionally leaving the house to get acai bowls with Margo Singh. "In my bedroom."

"Gross," Alma says, but she rolls her eyes and rises to follow her upstairs.

"Your father's going to say I look beautiful no matter what," Julia says, removing the dress from its gunmetal garment bag. The implication being, though she won't articulate this fully: *I need someone who hates me enough to be honest with me.* Alma twists herself into a complicated lotus position on the bed and regards her expectantly. "I've lost four pounds in the last month."

"You know people have done studies about how girls inherit body-image issues from their mothers, right?"

"Are those people fifty-seven years old? Have they given birth to two inexplicably enormous babies? Are they currently experiencing postmenopausal metabolic deceleration and water retention?"

"God, Mom." In their hotel last night, Alma had borrowed her favorite black pullover, and Julia watched her daughter traipsing barefoot across the room, the sweater transformed from a matronly magician's cloak into something glamorous, hanging long to expose the tops of her comely white knees.

"I'd just like your honest opinion."

"Fine. Jesus. Just put it on."

"Isn't this lovely, us bonding?"

"*Mom*."

She stops pushing her luck and goes into the bathroom to change. When she undresses, she regards her body in contrast with that of the kinetic pretzel verbally abusing her from her bed. She knows Mark still finds her attractive—or at least cares for her enough to lie convincingly—but what they say about breasts deflating has proven to be true, and since Alma was born she's had ten to fifteen viscous pounds around her waist that she can't seem to lose.

Aging has turned Julia not into her mother but instead into another kind of stranger entirely, one who drapes herself in shapeless pieces of gray cashmere, one whose eyes crinkle leaflike at the corners whether she's frowning or smiling, one whose frown is subsequently difficult to distinguish from her smile. She weighs 152 pounds. Her forearms are toned but the skin around her armpits wobbles infuriatingly. Her hair has not lost its chestnut luster and sometimes Mark buries his face in it and tells her it feels like corn silk.

She shimmies the dress up over her hips, swan-dives her arms into the sleeves. She looks at her reflection, squares her shoulders, makes what Alma calls her *weird mirror face.*

"Mom, I was *legitimately* doing homework."

"Coming." She wrenches the zipper as far up her back as she can manage and emerges from the bathroom. She feels suddenly bashful. "Can you zip me?"

Alma rises dexterously from the bed and comes over to her. "It's pretty," she says. "The color's nice."

Julia turns her back to her daughter, imagining the stubborn wings of flesh below her rib cage, the constellation of sun damage at the nape of her neck. She sucks in her stomach. Alma's fingers are nimble and efficient.

"All set," Alma says. "Let's see."

She turns shyly to face her daughter, and Alma gives her a thumbs-up.

"Really nice," she says. "Super cute."

"Really?" She feels a little disappointed. Was she expecting that they'd hug? That they'd suddenly morph into a much more amicable pair of people, flop onto the bed together and discuss male entitlement and reproductive rights and the difficulty of finding flattering formal wear?

"Mom, yes. I really do have a lot of homework."

"Sure," she says to Alma, ashamed. "Of course. Thanks. I just wanted a second opinion."

Alma heads for the door but stops just before the hallway. "You look really pretty, Mom. Good call. Dad's right."

When Mark gets home from the airport and finds her asleep in her half-unzipped wedding regalia, he rouses her teasingly, kisses in the hollows of her clavicles.

"Hang on," she says, startling awake. She leaps from the bed. "Don't look at me." She'd realized too late that she couldn't reach the clasp halfway up her back, and she'd been too embarrassed to interrupt Alma again, preferring instead to wait for Mark to come home and save her. "Unzip me, but squint, okay?"

"Are you serious?"

"Come on," she says. "I think I might actually like how I look in this."

"I can see why," he says, and she folds her body behind the closet door.

"When else in this lifetime will I get to feel excited about presenting myself to you?"

"I can't undo a zipper with my eyes closed, Jules."

"Come over here. I'll help." She reaches behind her back to guide his hands down her spine, and she feels the dress fall to her feet. "Now go away so I can hang it up."

She returns the dress to its garment bag but neglects to get dressed again, studying herself dubiously in the mirror, her disappointed-

looking breasts—two beanbags left on a playground during a storm—
and the shiny lines that fleece her hips. When Mark appears behind
her in the mirror, she realizes that she can't recall the last time he
saw her body on such complete display, and in such unforgiving
light. She moves to grab a towel.

"Do I have jowls?" she asks.

Mark presses himself to her back. He bends his neck around
hers, gently, crane-like, and kisses her jaw.

"Are you placating me?" she asks.

He loops his arms around her waist, slipping one of his hands
into the folds of the towel. She shivers.

"You don't," he says. "And I'm not." His hand has found her
right breast and he rolls her nipple between his fingers. Her grip
on the towel loosens and it falls; Mark trails his hand between her
legs, his wrist tenting the unsexy blue nylon of enduring marriages
and his fingers working their way through her brittle thatch of hair,
finding the spot that weakens her, catching her gaze in the mirror.

"You're beautiful, Jules," he says.

"Oh, stop," she says, turning to face him. She puts a hand to his
chest; he touches her face, tilts it to him, and kisses her in the way
that had made her fall for him in the first place, at once effortless
and full of studied deliberation.

"Come here," she says.

They make love with reciprocal consideration, she thoughtfully
turning onto her stomach as he prefers for angular precision and he
working earnestly at her clit until she finally reaches back for him
and breathes *okay, now.*

When he's holding her afterward, his chin hooked over her
shoulder and a hand kneading idly, lovingly, at one of her breasts,
she asks him how New York was.

"Good," he says sleepily. "Uneventful. How'd it go with Ollie?"

"She's going to go," she says, and though she forces her voice to
sound optimistic, saying the words makes her unimaginably sad.

"Good," he says, and she can hear the sadness in his voice, too.
He pulls her even closer, fits his knee between her legs; it has always
surprised her, his need for closeness and how baldly he makes it
known.

"I'm sorry," she says.

"What for?"

"All the— With my dress. With everything. All the—folderol. I'm being silly. I'm feeling a little insecure."

He presses his face into her neck and she can feel him smile. "Get your folderol over here," he says.

30

M ark's parents had a woven mat on the front porch that said EVERY BUNNY WELCOME, and his mom looked at Julia as though she were a confounding illustration in a picture book, one that she couldn't tell whether or not was appropriate for children. But Julia could see, instantly, where Mark's good nature had come from—they were miraculously all like him. Chicago was exempt from the trend of midwestern niceness, but the Ameses of La Crosse were peak Wisconsin geniality, two-armed hugs and samplers on the walls, a flattering kind of rapt attention regardless of how boring whatever you were saying was, a bustling, fresh-aired hospitality that made her feel instantly welcome, if also a little edgy.

"It's so beautiful here," she said to Mark's mom, because it *was*, wide open space and the lush green humility of the country. And she fell in love, a little bit, with Wisconsin, the Land of the Nice, but it made her nervous as well, in the same way it had made her nervous to go to other people's houses as a kid, everyone conversant in a language she didn't speak, a normal, household language, affectionate shorthand and shared history, somebody pass the salt.

"Tell that to Mark," Bonnie said, nudging her conspiratorially. "We've been trying to lure him back since he left."

It struck her strangely, and to a degree she would have preferred not to be struck while making the initial acquaintance of her boyfriend's parents, this firsthand exposure to a mother who actively wanted to live in the same city as her child, a mother who nearly vibrated with pleasure upon being reunited with her adult son, even though she saw him regularly.

"We're here now, aren't we?" Mark said, putting an arm around his mother's shoulders, and that gesture, too, struck her in the stomach.

Mark regressed instantly upon crossing the threshold of the cute green farmhouse where he'd spent his formative years. His older brother called him *Teddy* for reasons that had not been explained to her and his father immediately started talking to him about the Bears and she was surprised when Mark responded with an enthusiasm and an athletic lexicon she hadn't known he possessed. He seemed at once smaller and larger in his parents' house, and to see him this way felt like both a privilege and an invasion of privacy.

They'd been invited up for Easter weekend, an occasion Julia had never in her life even acknowledged but for the few times her father came by when she was small bearing Cadbury eggs, whose thick, grainy yolks always made her queasy. But the Ameses had decorative wreaths on the doors and woven plastic baskets for Mark's two nephews and a dinner headlined by a fake-looking and thoroughly disquieting ham that held court in the center of the dining room table like a magistrate.

The Ameses were keen and easygoing, inquisitive and quick to laugh, chattering ceaselessly about a palatable roster of apolitical current events both regional and personal, the Cubs and the children, one of whom, after dinner, sidled up alongside Julia with his upturned Easter basket on his head like a soldier's helmet and asked if she wanted to hear a joke.

"Absolutely," she said. She was trying hard to convince the people at the table that she was as nice as they were, that she was a blithe, tenderhearted soul worthy of their ham, even though she was surreptitiously feeding it to the dog under the table.

"What do you call an alligator in a vest?"

"An— Oh! An investigator?"

The kid's face darkened and she realized her error.

"Oh, no, I meant— I'm sorry." She did not have a natural way with children, never had, and contact with kids in her day-to-day life was nil as they tended not to frequent bars or archival rooms.

"Tell her another one," said the kid's dad, Mark's brother, Drew. To Julia he said, kindly, "This is a pastime of ours; there's no shortage," and she loved him, too; it was astonishing that there was so much niceness in one family.

"What do you call cheese that isn't yours?" the kid asked, and though Julia also knew the punch line of this one, she feigned ignorance as well as the enthusiasm of her amusement as the kid bellowed "*Nacho cheese!*" and then galloped away.

"He's darling," she said, because it seemed like the thing she was supposed to say, and Drew smiled at her, and Bonnie smiled at her, and Mark, beside her, rubbed his palm a few times over the space between her shoulder blades. They seemed to *actually like her*; it seemed somehow that this visit was *actually going well*; she couldn't believe it and it was her instinct not to trust it, but that seemed like the instinct of someone who didn't belong, so she brushed it aside, smiled back at them and petted Pippen the rotund dachshund, sitting at her feet awaiting more clandestine ham.

"Do you have siblings, Julia?" Bonnie asked her.

There was not an honest answer befitting this audience. "I don't," she said.

"And are your parents still in Chicago?"

A simple *no* would be the easy answer, but that was not something a normal person would say.

"My dad passed away," she said. "My mom lives in Colorado." She was not entirely sure the latter was true, in fact; she was never sure that her information was current, but this was the most recent update she'd gotten the last time they spoke on the phone, her mother having at some point relocated from Columbus to Fort Collins, once again because of a man, though the new relationship had ended by the time she'd spoken to Julia.

"I'm sorry to hear that," Bonnie said, and she wished, not for the first time, that she had a better story to tell or, in this particular case, two loving retirees who did still live in Chicago but had started spending the winters in Scottsdale, a matched set of parents who she'd be happy to trot out for a meet-and-greet with the benevolent Ameses.

"No need to be," she said, trying to sound chipper. "It was a long time ago."

"I've heard Colorado's beautiful," Mark's dad said, because these were the nicest people in America, and because it would have seemed too sad to admit that she'd never been there, the place her mother had been living now for several years, she agreed.

The rest of the evening seemed to progress with the same unbelievable smoothness, Julia watching raptly from the sidelines like an urchin outside a lit window. They ate a cake that Bonnie had made, lamb-shaped with shredded coconut for wool; everyone settled in for a familial round of Scattergories; they were all in bed by nine. Bonnie had pointedly showed them to separate rooms upon arrival, so Julia found herself lying alone in a twin bed in Drew's childhood bedroom, trying not to have a panic attack beneath a poster of Wayne Gretzky.

It had gone well. By any calculation, it had gone swimmingly; Julia had nailed her very first ceremonial meeting of the boyfriend's parents. And she *liked* them, felt incontrovertible fondness for inquisitive Bonnie with her Easter egg sweater and her maternal goodness, and for Skip, who'd patiently explained to her the difference between fir trees and pine trees, and for Drew, the brother, who was only thirty-six but already had the affable weariness of a grandfather. She had a renewed fondness for Mark as well, Mark who had fallen asleep for eighteen years in a bed like this one. But it was now tinged with an overall distrust about how he could have lived through a childhood like that and still want to be with someone like her.

There was a raindrop tapping, fingers drumming on the door, and she scrambled half-upright and grabbed a book from the nightstand and started paging through it, feigning occupation.

But it was Mark. "Are you awake?" he asked, slipping in through the cracked door, then: "Are you reading *The Guinness Book of World Records?*"

"What do you think this is," she said, relaxing, scooting to make room for him, "some kind of brothel?"

He lay down beside her. "Hi."

"The world's tallest teenager was two-point-four-five meters," she said. "Good luck fitting in here, Robert Wadlow."

"Sorry about this," he said, gesturing to the bed.

"Is it some kind of hazing ritual?"

"God, no," he said. "She really likes you."

And though it made her glow a little inside, she asked, nervously, "Not your dad?"

"Him too," Mark said, putting a hand on her knee. "Everyone does. Are you okay?"

She nodded, leaning back against the pillow. They lay in silence for a few minutes, Mark meditatively rubbing her leg while Julia studied the poster of Wayne Gretzky, whose eyes she suspected would follow her movements were she to leave the room.

"I'm sorry," Mark said finally. "If that was—if it didn't go okay."

She stiffened. "What?"

"If it wasn't—if it didn't go how you hoped it would go, I'm sorry."

"I thought it went great," she said. "I thought— Did it not?"

He pushed himself up on an elbow. "No, I thought it went *great*."

"Then what are you apologizing for?"

"I don't know, you seem sad. Did something happen?"

"They're wonderful," she said. "They're—lovely. That's not a word I ever use. They're *lovely*, Mark. They made a cake shaped like a lamb. They're terrific. I had a really nice time."

"Oh," he said. "Jules, I— That's great. I'm so glad. I thought so too, but you seemed—"

"You have the nicest, most normal family in the history of the human race." Maybe that was what annoyed her; maybe she was jealous of him and his lamb cake. Or maybe she was simply tired after bracing herself all night for an attack that never came.

"Well," he said, as though he clearly didn't agree. "I feel like there's something you aren't saying."

"Did you know there's a record for continuously rocking in a rocking chair?"

"Jules."

"You're all just—like, you seem to *like* each other so much," she said. "And it— That's not me, I guess. Where I come from. It's— Your parents play board games and mine are sociopaths."

"Jules," he said again, and she didn't like the pity in his voice.

"No. It's *fine*; I'm just saying—if that makes you feel any differently about me—"

"It doesn't."

"But if it *did*."

"Then what?"

"I don't know," she said.

He was quiet for so long that it almost seemed like he wasn't there, but she could smell the woodsmoke in his hair, feel his breath under the collar of her T-shirt.

"It always makes me a little depressed to be here," he said, and she stilled. It alarmed her that she hadn't been aware of him being depressed that night, with his laughing family at the dinner table.

"I feel invisible," he said. "It's been that way since I was a little kid, and it's still what happens, no matter what I've been doing when I'm away. That's the trade-off for having a nice time. I just have to accept the fact that they don't care what I'm actually doing with my life."

"Your parents seem really happy to see you."

"They are," he said. "But it's a very— We don't go too deep beneath the surface here, Jules. And I've always seemed a little strange to them, and they can't easily explain my job to their friends and I never want to own a house down the block like Drew does, and they don't know what to do with that."

"Strange how," she asked.

"Drew used to make jokes about me being the Unabomber," he said. "Before it was even—like, acceptable to make jokes about the Unabomber."

"Is it acceptable *now* to make jokes about the Unabomber?"

"Just because I liked to be by myself," he continued, rolling onto his back. "Just because I liked *science*, like there's something sinister about that. They all just regard me as this—anomaly, and they decided a long time ago that they didn't care about the details, and now they just kind of act like I'm not there, or if I am it's the me from twenty years ago. And that's better than— I mean, I know it's not the same as—"

"We're not in a contest," she said, and she took his hand. "And you don't have to say that just to make me feel better."

"I'm not. It's true. I have an— I don't know, a before and an after too, I guess. I'm just telling you that."

Wayne Gretzky grimaced down at them.

"You're not invisible," she said.

"I've never felt that way around you."

"Good." She traced her fingers over the hair on his forearm. "Good."

"How many rocks did the rocking chair person do?" he asked.

"They measured it in hours," she said. "It was in the hundreds."

He pulled her against him, pressed his face into her neck. "You aren't invisible either."

"Thanks," she said, and she rested her head against his shoulder easily, like it didn't mean that much to her, that she wasn't invisible and that she hadn't scared him off, or that if she had he wasn't letting on, this midwestern diplomat, and that he wasn't going anywhere, it seemed, holding her to him in a twin bed beside *The Guinness Book of World Records*, drifting into slumber because it was something he could do, as a person who'd always moved easily through the world. She'd told him more of the truth than she'd told anyone else and yet here he still was, and though she hadn't yet told him the entire truth she must have finally fallen asleep, too, absorbing through osmosis some of his ease, because when she opened her eyes next it was morning.

t is not just peonies Sunny has made her responsible for, but all flowers, table centerpieces and bridesmaid arrangements and what Sunny is calling *pocket square boutonnieres.*

"We thought you'd enjoy it," Sunny had said, like they were doing her a favor, before sending her a series of novelistic emails about color palettes and stem lengths, their text glowing blue with hyperlinks.

Julia scrolls idly through the latest one while sitting at the kitchen island sipping a glass of wine, clicking at random on one of the links and finding herself on a "luxe-rustic lifestyle" blog called Sincerely Shespoke, a post about the author's "barn-inspired" wedding. She closes her eyes, then the laptop. A night alone: less rare than it used to be and soon to be very common indeed, but today still rare enough for her to revel in; Mark and Alma are out and she should be taking advantage, a decadent roster of pedestrian indulgences including meditative perusal of the summer seed catalog and binge-watching a British mystery series that Mark finds *overly charming.*

But before she can get to either of those things, the doorbell rings, sending Suzanne into conniptions. This is not on her agenda, nor is the watery, distorted visage of Brady Grimes through the front door. She would like to ignore it, but Suzanne is so wildly losing her mind, popping up and down like something spring-loaded, that Julia is forced to open the door simply to get her to stop.

She's prepared to be short—the reticent give-and-take that has been characterizing her interactions with Brady since she met him—but the look on his face stops her, an almost comical sunkenness, puffy around the eyes.

"You'd think she'd recognize me by now," Brady says, stooping to pet Suzanne, who is engaged in a stern olfactory investigation of his shoes.

"She does recognize you," Julia says. "She just doesn't trust you."

He only half-smiles at her, which she finds worrying, because Brady always laughs too hard at her jokes.

"Mark isn't home," she says. She lifts Suzanne into her arms, feeling the dog's furious heartbeat through her tiny rib cage. "He took Ollie to the Cubs game."

"Oh." He looks crestfallen.

"Come in, though. What's going on?"

He comes past her through the foyer, leads the way to the kitchen. "Franny's gone."

For a second she understands this to mean that Francine has died.

"We fought," he adds helpfully. He lifts the bottle of wine from the island. "You mind?"

She wonders if he's already been drinking; there's a heavy-lidded slowness to his movements. She gets him a glass and watches as he eases out the cork, pours half the bottle into his glass and takes a long, greedy sip.

"This is nice," he says, looking disinterestedly at the label.

"Tell me what's going on, Brady."

He slumps down at the island like something that's been shot, dramatically more downtrodden than he'd seemed last month at Mark's birthday. He's usually one of those men who tries to over-compensate for his lack of height by constantly standing, but his posture is slouched, melting. She's known him for over twenty-five years, has witnessed dozens of iterations of him, like a basket of Barbie dolls—man-bun/Reiki cushion Brady, Italophilic Brady, very-enthusiastic-about-supplements Brady—but all of those versions were still governed by his characteristic blue-eyed arrogance, and she's never seen him like this. It makes her feel, possibly for the first time ever—she has wanted to drown him in a swamp more or less since she met him—tender toward him.

"I don't *know* what's going on. She's on her way back to Philly. Her family has a spare apartment in Rittenhouse; she's going to stay there—indefinitely, I don't know."

Her brain won't make the arrangements, Brady without Francine, this upstanding, impenetrable, smug, smug, *smug* pair of people who have towered over her own marriage for as long as she's known them: the proverbial perfect couple, her husband's ideal; there's not a universe in which she and Mark survive and Brady and Francine Grimes do not. "Tell me what happened."

"It's *been* happening, I guess," he says, taking a long sip of his wine. "She says we've been growing apart for years and I just haven't noticed." He picks up the wine bottle again, pouring another few inches into his glass and the rest into hers, decimating without second thought what had in fact been a fairly pricey bottle of Meritage.

"But there must have been some sort of—catalyst." She pictures a racketeering scandal, the apologetic outline of a mistress in the backseat of Brady's ludicrous European SUV.

"Nothing's changed," he says. "Everything's the same as it always has been; she says that's part of the problem. Which just seems *unfair*, don't you think? That she gets to suddenly change the rules without telling me?"

He downs his wine before asking, "Do you mind if I switch to something a little stronger?" He's already getting up, passing through into the dining room to the cluster of bottles on the hutch. He returns with the Blanton's a client gave Mark for Christmas. "I mean, is it offensive to say I think she's having a midlife crisis?"

"Yes," says Julia, though she has wondered the same about herself.

"We haven't been talking much," he says. "And then finally we just had one of those—where you're suddenly saying things you didn't know you were thinking, and you know you aren't supposed to be saying them, but you do it anyway? And it's like once we started neither of us could stop."

She feels edgy, listening to him, and gets up to putter around the kitchen, opening cabinets, the refrigerator. She pulls butter from the fridge, a block of mozzarella. The old Helen Russo impulse again, to entertain your way out of any crisis.

"What are you doing?" he asks.

"I'm making you a grilled cheese," she says. She has long since stopped feeling self-conscious about her hospitality toward Brady and Francine, who have been known to host parties with in-house valets and caught-that-day crab and live background performances by principals from the CSO, gatherings so sickeningly opulent that you couldn't attempt to match them, wouldn't *want* to match them, and so she doesn't. She, too, knows her way around the kitchen.

He smiles at her suddenly, bald admiration like a baby. "Thanks, Jules."

"Don't call me that."

"Do you think Franny's seemed unhappy?"

She frowns, sliding a pat of butter into the pan. *I try not to think about either of you when I can avoid it,* she does not say. She has never had any great understanding of Francine and her ilk, women who look like they rise with the sun and are always on time and get regular haircuts and bake allergen-free treats for not just their child's class but the entire grade. But it wasn't Francine's fault that she was the embodiment of everything Julia had resisted before she married Mark. It wasn't Francine's fault, either, that she was the embodiment of everything Mark had embraced before he married Julia. And it definitely wasn't Francine's fault that she'd seen what she'd seen the day Nathaniel Russo showed up at the house on Superior Street, as much as Julia wanted to resent her for being there.

"I couldn't say," she says. "Happy looks different on everyone. Maybe she just—needs a little time to herself."

"Do you think there's someone else?" he asks.

Something inside her stands up straight, hearing this. Francine's transgressing, Francine's having any kind of secret dalliance, has never entered her head as a possibility.

"God, I don't know. Do *you* think there is?" She'd always assumed that if someone was going to cheat it would be Brady; she's always assumed, in fact, that he habitually cheated, though it was a mystery to her how he could swing it, not the lying and sneaking but the actual acquisition of a person besides Francine who could tolerate his companionship.

"I'm not sure. I don't have anybody in mind, but I—I mean, it happens, right?"

His eyes on her are unreadable. She has never known exactly how much Mark told Brady about that time; she has never been sure exactly how much of her behavior during the Helen era is common knowledge in the Grimes household.

"Can I ask you something?"

The air in the room feels suddenly thinner.

"Have you ever wondered," he says, then stops.

She concentrates on flipping the sandwich. "What?"

"Just if—it always sort of seemed to me like we'd got our wires crossed. Or—that's the wrong phrase, like maybe we'd made some kind of—you know, cosmic error, the four of us."

"*Cosmic error?*"

"Mark and Franny have always seemed better suited to each other, don't you think? Than they are to either of us? And you and I—I don't know, that it might have made more sense?"

She leans back against the counter, feeling as though she's narrowly missed being hit by a bus just in time to be bowled down by a cab. "I have never once in my life thought that, no."

"No?" Brady seems unhurt by this, if genuinely surprised. "I've kind of always thought it. Francine and Mark are both so— They just have it *together*, always; they're the rule followers, the planners. Whereas you and I . . ."

"You and I *what*?"

"We're braver," he says simply. "And more interesting, maybe? I don't mean that in an asshole way, but it's kind of true, don't you think? I bet if you and I had gotten together instead we never would have gotten bored with each other."

"I'm not sure what boredom has to do with it."

"Really?" He glances up at her. "That's almost always the reason I stop doing things. I think that's what it comes down to for a lot of people."

"Actually," she says, "I consider myself pretty boring."

"Now, sure," he says. She lifts her eyebrows and his face relaxes into a little smile that—she can't help it—makes her laugh. "We all are *now*," he continues. "But back then? There's no way in hell Mark could ever have gotten bored with you."

"Back *when*?"

"Back at the beginning. Back when he met you. You were so—I don't know—brazen."

"It was all an act," she says, but there's heat in her cheeks.

"I'm just saying," he says. "I just always thought *I'd* be the one to fuck it up." His face is bleary with the bourbon; she'll make him take a cab home. "I mean—actively fuck it up. I just *do* things sometimes and I'm not always totally sure why. Do you know what I mean?"

During early talks about AllAboard, Brady had said to her husband, "You're the brains, and I'm the executioner." It had made her laugh at the time, but if the two are mutually exclusive then she supposes she, too, has been an executioner of sorts.

"Yeah," she says. "I do."

"That's what I mean," he says. "You get it."

"Eat this," she says, sliding the sandwich onto a plate. "Before you drink anything else."

He looks from her to the grilled cheese, then picks up a triangle and shoves half of it into his mouth. "Thanks," he says.

"Don't mention it." She sits down across from him at the table, feeling inexplicably tired.

Brady is chewing when he asks, "Your mom was a drunk, right?"

She stiffens. "What?"

He glances up at her, swallows. "What? Sorry. Wasn't she?"

"She—drank sometimes," she says tightly. "What does that have to do with—"

"I didn't mean to offend you," he says. "I was just wondering. About your mom. Franny says I'm drinking too much."

"Then you probably are." She rises from the table again, goes to the sink to wash the pan. "I'm not some kind of authority."

They're quiet for a minute, sponge scrubbing the bottom of the skillet and Brady compliantly chewing his crusts. She doesn't hear him get up, startles when she feels his presence behind her.

"Christ," she says.

"Sorry." He holds out his plate to her, and there's a beat before she takes it where she thinks of Nathaniel Russo, her first encounter with him in an arrangement not unlike the one they're in now, two uniquely misguided people in a kitchen, overly aware of the space between them.

She takes the plate and it slips from her fingers, clattering into the sink.

"I wasn't coming on to you," Brady says. "For the record."

"I know that," she says irritably. She brushes her hair from her forehead with a wet wrist.

"Julia?"

"For God's sake, *what*?" She turns off the water with her elbow, reaches for a dish towel.

"I don't know what I'm supposed to do," he says. "Without her."

"Oh," she says, and after a second she opens her arms to him, and Brady Grimes folds himself against her like a little boy.

She watches Mark in the bathroom mirror while they brush their teeth. He'd sat out in the yard with Brady for an hour after he got home from the game, finally putting him in a cab, and now she can tell her husband is a little buzzed too, though her own wine haze has worn off, leaving her feeling nervy and exposed.

"What do you think happened?" she asks, retrieving the special fancy moisturizer she has to hide from Alma in her underwear drawer.

Mark hauls himself into bed. "I'm not sure," he says. "It can't be as serious as he's making it out to be. I'll call Franny in the morning."

"What? Why?" She's never really been the jealous type, but the fact that her husband has a casual-phone-conversation type of relationship with Francine has always bothered her.

He looks at her with some accusation. "Because she probably needs to talk about it too? She wouldn't just pick up and walk out on her life."

It lands on them both at the same time. How many times has this happened to them over the years? A scene in a movie, a thoughtless turn of phrase. They are past this stage, or at least she thought they were, well beyond the point—they lived it for *years*—when there's a reminder at every turn.

"I just mean it's unlike her," he says, not an apology but also not combative. "Things like this don't just happen. I know they've been having problems, but not the kind that— Brady must be overinflating it. That's what he does."

"They've been having problems?"

"For a few months," he says, something evasive in the way he glances over at her.

"You didn't say anything."

"I didn't think you'd be interested," he says, and she decides— carefully, determinedly—not to take the bait. This was once well-trod territory for them; she has no desire to stomp around in it any longer. "I just feel like they— I don't know, maybe I should be trying to help in some way."

"Help *how*?" And there it is again between them, a flashing halogen bulb. Had Brady tried to *help* Mark, twenty years ago? And Francine, God—she has trained herself, over time, to look the woman in the eye again, a process aided by Francine's intractable patrician stoicism, but part of her has never been able to stop thinking about the day of the playdate. "What are you planning on doing," she asks, "staging an intervention?"

"This isn't funny, Julia. They're our best friends."

How many times has he said this to her? How many times has she bit back the statement *They're not* my *best friends*, and how many times has she slipped and actually said it, inciting his ire?

She stands up. "I forgot I've got laundry in the washer."

Mark frowns. "Right now?"

"What do you mean *right now*? You aren't the one who has to answer to Ollie in the morning if her jeans aren't dry."

He leans with exaggerated heaviness back against the headboard. "Fine, Julia."

She feels a prickle of defiance, that marital impulse to dig in your heels and get your way, even if your way is laundry.

"You aren't *mad* about this?" she asks.

"We're in the middle of a serious conversation," he says. "I don't see why the laundry is the first thing on your mind."

"These chores don't do themselves," she says. "And what's so serious about it? It has nothing to do with us." She doesn't mean to sound this way. She does feel for Brady; she, like Mark, is rattled by his visit. But it isn't their life, and she feels untethered enough as it is. It's a little annoying, frankly, that this news seems to have reopened the wound she and Mark have worked so hard to close, and that it has come at the time she most needs for them to be on solid ground.

"God," he says, "what's *with* you lately? It's like you've turned into this . . ."

"What?" She's genuinely curious; she would like to know what she's turned into.

"Do you have an ounce of compassion for anyone?" he says, and her genuine curiosity morphs into genuine surprise, surprise laced with hurt.

"Of course I do," she says, because he's supposed to know this; he of all people is supposed to know: that she isn't a bad person, just occasionally bad at *being* a person.

"You're so in your own head lately," he says. "It's like living with a teenager."

"There's a lot going on." She's trying to keep her voice level; she isn't a crier but tears feel close, and she feels familiar old defenses rising up, trying to stop them. An older iteration of herself trying to protect the current one. "Everything's changing."

"That's life," he says. "Everything changing is *life*, Julia. And normal people just roll with it. Normal people have no trouble feeling sympathy for their friends. Supporting their children."

She can't tell whether he intends for it to be as mean as it sounds.

"I'm *trying* to do those things," she snaps. "And since when are we talking about the kids?" Compulsively, she starts straightening the items on top of her dresser—such an underwhelming production, marital discord in the suburbs, in your fifties; part of her misses the athleticism of their early days, the slammed doors and heavily punctuated obscenities, the anticipation of reconciliation. Now she is *tidying*.

He drops his forehead into his hand. "I know you're trying," he says after a minute, and then looks up at her, heavy-lidded. "I didn't mean to— I know there's a lot going on. And I'm stressed about it too, and confused, and— Whatever you're feeling, Julia, I'm probably feeling it too. You can't just assume you're feeling those things more strongly than everyone else."

"I'm not," she says.

"It just seems like you're—pushing everyone away. You're barely talking to Ben. It feels like you're not really talking to me."

"I'm talking to you right now."

"You know what I mean," he says. "You aren't *engaging*. You're doing the thing where you're just—marinating in things but when it comes to actually talking about them you deflect, or you make a joke, or you just shut down. And it's— We know that doesn't work, Jules. It makes everything harder. On you, primarily, but also on the people around you."

"What am I making harder? I'm doing everything I'm being asked to do."

He looks at her like she's a particularly difficult toddler, like she's being intentionally obstinate, which she isn't, which she never truly is, at least not consciously.

"I'm doing the best I can," she says, but it comes out sounding a little defensive, which undercuts her credibility, which bothers her, because she's telling the truth, that her trying might not look like other people's trying but it is nevertheless *trying*.

Mark closes his eyes again. "I know, Jules," he says, and though she knows he's also being truthful, this statement is undercut too, by his gentleness—benignity, ammo of the congenial—and the placation nags at her, worms its way inside and lodges itself like a molar.

32

Brady and Francine Grimes had remained a distant, folkloric entity for the first year she and Mark were together. Mark and Brady had met practically as toddlers in La Crosse and remained inseparable until they parted ways for college. Brady was a venture capitalist, and she declined to inquire about what that meant because she was preemptively bored by the answer; he and his wife had been living in her native Philadelphia, and when Mark told her they were moving to Chicago she tried not to let it make her nervous. She'd tried to appreciate the fact that her boyfriend had a best friend, and she tried to find his loyalty and ability to maintain lasting friendships lovable instead of threatening. But every time he brought up Brady, she felt a kind of sibling rivalry that surely wasn't healthy but also couldn't be helped.

They'd bought a house deep in the suburbs of the North Shore, in a neighborhood Julia had not known existed in such proximity to her own and would have been content to remain ignorant of, houses with gables and wrought-iron security gates that looked like they had borne witness to dark eras of American history.

"Someone our *age* lives here?" she asked, watching out the window of Mark's car.

"Nice, huh?" said Mark, though that was not the word she had in mind.

"Moving to the suburbs is like getting a face tattoo," she said. "You're committing in perpetuity to a certain kind of lifestyle."

"It's not a lifestyle," he said. "It's just a place."

The other night they'd watched *Apocalypse Now;* as they pulled into Brady and Francine's driveway—lined on either side with light posts that were, if not heads on stakes, at least objectively phallic—she started humming "Ride of the Valkyries," only half-aware of the fact that she was testing him.

He smiled at her in a way she supposed was meant to be reassuring; she handed him the eighteen-dollar-bottle of wine they'd brought—a splurge—and tugged self-consciously at the hem of her dress as she got out of the car, boots crunching on rose-colored gravel. The front door opened before they'd reached it, revealing a blond woman with a buoyant, unmoving hairstyle and a beribboned maternity smock.

"Of course you're right on time," Francine said, putting her arms around Mark with an ease and familiarity that surprised Julia. "And we're about forty minutes behind."

"We're in no hurry," Mark said into the woman's hair, and when they pulled apart he was smiling.

"I'm moving a little slower these days," Francine said, turning to Julia, drawing attention to the unmissable fact that she was extraordinarily pregnant.

"Look at you," Mark said, that new goofy fondness still on his face. "You look fantastic, Franny."

Julia eyed him sideways. She wasn't sure she'd ever heard him use the word *fantastic* before, or the gushy voice he'd said it in, and neither seemed specifically applicable in this circumstance. *Franny?*

"Don't *start* with me," Francine said, swatting at him. To Julia, rolling her eyes, she said: "He knows I hate it when he calls me that. You must be Julia."

"Hi," she said, and then, clumsily, "Congratulations." It seemed there were babies everywhere lately—popping out of orifices, rolling grandly down the sidewalks in space-age buggies, rendering their contemporaries smug and distracted—and to be so close to actual gestation made her anxious.

Francine smiled at her. "We've heard so much about you."

She wondered what picture Mark had painted of her for them, his oldest friends, and she wondered how closely she was aligning with his rendering, standing on the front porch like a peddler in a slip dress under one of Mark's shirts and her motorcycle boots, which had seemed stylish when they'd left their apartment but now made her feel unkempt and slightly seedy.

"*Love* your dress," Francine said, and though Julia searched the words for a catty edge, some undertone of judgment, she was surprised to come up empty-handed.

"Yours too," she said, and followed Mark following Francine through the marble foyer. In the hallway, there was a framed photo on the wall, the couple in black and white, holding hands in a pastoral grain field. She reached to pinch Mark's elbow—it was the unspoken and cardinal rule of their socialization, that they would always have each other's backs, always find things for which to share disdain—but he didn't look back at her.

Brady was in the kitchen, wearing a cartoonish white apron and tending, disturbingly, to a forearm-length and gruesomely gutted fish; he turned to them and proved himself immediately to be the type of man whose gaze grazed a woman's body like it was just a routine part of making her acquaintance.

"She exists!" he said, and Julia preempted a hug by sticking out her hand to shake.

"Of course she exists," Mark said, and Julia watched the men hug, aware, in the simultaneous ease and ferocity of the embrace, that they'd missed each other.

"What is it about him?" she'd asked Mark once of Brady, mystified by the notion of maintaining such a long friendship, and he replied, sort of sheepishly, "I've just always known him. How many people can you say that about?"

But Julia had only ever felt this way about Mark—the relief at being reunited with someone you loved—and she felt her hackles rise, seeing him so happy to see someone else.

"It's so good to have you here," Mark said, and Brady clapped an arm around his shoulders.

"It's good to be here," he said.

"What smells good?" Mark asked.

"Brade's become quite the chef," Francine supplied, "since our trip to Italy last summer."

"Campania," Brady said fondly, with the faint hint of an affected accent, starting to pour wine from a bottle already open on the counter, one that had undoubtedly cost more than eighteen dollars. He began to tell them about the trip, an incomprehensible roster of dropped names, local landmarks, villas and vintages. Julia repeatedly tried to meet Mark's eye, but he wouldn't look at her, was instead listening to Brady talk; she saw him make eye contact with Francine and they smiled at each other like two tolerant parents listening to their hyperactive kid talk about summer camp.

"Maybe all four of us can go next time," Mark said, and smiled at Julia, like either of them could afford a gym membership, let alone a trip to Europe, like they were a *foursome* now, he and she and these two boring people she'd met eight seconds ago.

"There'll be six of us pretty soon, remember," Francine said, indicating her stomach, lest anyone had forgotten. Julia would have started a drinking game for herself, clocking the number of references to the pregnancy, but she'd already almost finished her glass of wine. Brady, who had all the finesse of a large adult rutabaga, sidled in close to her to refill it.

"Six?" she asked on a delay.

"Twins," Brady said, near enough for her to smell the basil on his breath.

"Oh," she said, momentarily cheered that the mystery of Francine's improbable enormity had been solved, but when she glanced over at Mark she saw he was completely unsurprised; he apparently already knew this.

"Speaking of," Francine said, almost a little shyly. "Julia, would you like to see the nursery? I've been decorating all month and Brady's reached his compliment quota."

And though she would much rather have endured another hour of Brady describing historic chapels, she agreed.

"You girls have fun," Brady said. "Mark, come see the pool."

Francine trundled off, and Julia trailed behind her, looking over her shoulder at Mark, watching him go with Brady, like something she'd accidentally dropped into a river.

There was another framed photo hung between two white cribs; it appeared to have been taken in the same sunlit wheat field and this time featured a recent image of Francine alone, lovingly cradling her belly. Now she walked Julia through what seemed to be every single element of the decoration process, some magical kind of caulk that changed color when it dried.

"Wait," Julia said. "You didn't do this yourself, did you?"

"Yup. Everything but the ceiling; Brady wouldn't let me get on a ladder."

"Wow," Julia said, and Francine seemed proud, and Julia decided that perhaps she'd underestimated her, at least in this particular respect. "It's fantastic," she said, borrowing Mark's word, and Francine appeared to glow a little, which was nice until the woman took their bonding moment as permission to veer into more intimate territory, guiding Julia with an equally disturbing level of detail through everything else about her life, including what she kept calling her *birth regime*, which featured intervention from Brady that bordered on pornographic.

"Wow," Julia said again. She felt a little sick. She was embarrassingly ignorant about all of it; she was pretty sure she never wanted to get pregnant and so had little interest in talking about anyone being pregnant, and she was starting to feel sort of diminutive and whorish alongside Francine's robust fertility, and aware of the fact that she'd brought wine into a nursery—red wine into a white nursery, no less—and also the stale smell of cigarettes.

"Sorry," Francine said, suddenly looking embarrassed. She laughed. "Can you tell I tend to get a little obsessed with things? I've been spending all of my time alone working in here, and Brady's— Well, like I said, he can only rally so much enthusiasm."

"No, it's exciting," Julia said. "It's—hard for me to conceptualize, honestly."

Francine eased herself into the rocking chair and gestured at a furry beanbag behind Julia. "Do you want kids?"

"Oh." Julia clumsily folded herself into the beanbag, careful not to spill her wine.

"Sorry, sorry," Francine said. "I'm nosy. You don't have to answer that." But she didn't move to change the subject, and Julia found herself scrambling to fill the silence.

"I'm not sure if I do," she said. "I'm not sure it's—in the cards."

"It isn't for everyone," Francine said, and though it didn't necessarily sound smug, it landed that way, considering its fecund, radiant source.

"Will you stay home with them?" Julia asked, unsure if she was allowed to be asking. "Or do you— I'm sorry, Mark didn't tell me what you do."

"I'm staying home. We went back and forth about it, but I decided it made the most sense. I actually really like kids, so I'm hoping that helps."

"How could it not," said Julia, smiling at Francine in a way that she hoped seemed supportive or sisterly or whatever she was supposed to be whilst trapped in an infant bedroom with a pregnant contemporary.

Francine smiled back. "Mark says you're a bartender?"

Any feelings of goodwill, compulsory or otherwise, evaporated; she felt a strange heat behind her breastbone. She'd never cared about things like this, never felt embarrassed or defensive about how she spent her days or earned her living, but coming from Francine's mouth, the word sounded like a swear.

"I am," she said tightly. "I'm also a librarian." She was not, technically, a librarian; her title was, quite literally, *Library Assistant*, but she was not about to get into the semantics with Francine Grimes glowing judgmentally over her.

"Really?" Francine raised her eyebrows. "Wow, that sounds interesting. Do you like it?"

She loved her work most days, in fact, sorting through materials in the tomb-like special collections room, surfacing occasionally to work the circulation desk. She wished it paid more, but it didn't, and a master's in library science was expensive and not a surefire path to more gainful employment. So she had worked it out, a system that made sense to her; there was nothing wrong with this, so why were her cheeks so hot, and why hadn't Mark mentioned to his friends the work that made up the bulk of her days?

"I like it very much," she said.

"Lucky," said Francine. "I was doing marketing in Philadelphia but I didn't like it enough to want to find something comparable when we decided to move. Hence—" And here she put her hands on her belly again, as though those were the only two options in life, procreation and marketing.

"Marketing what?" she asked, before Francine could ask her another question.

"Hotels," Francine said, and then, sounding almost defensive: "Creative direction, really. I was an art history major at Stanford."

Her footing felt so unstable that it took this a moment to register. "You went to Stanford?"

Francine laughed. "Yeah, that's how Mark and I met."

And before Julia could register, as well, the punch this delivered to her gut, Francine continued: "We were in the same dorm freshman year. We met during a fire drill."

"I didn't realize that," she said weakly, and immediately wished she hadn't; she'd never quite gotten the hang of female socialization but she understood that it had a lot to do with protecting your currency, and she could tell that by admitting this to Francine she'd just inadvertently relinquished some of her holdings.

"It was actually a fire *alarm*," Francine continued. "There was this *very* ditzy girl on my floor who—" She leaned forward conspiratorially in the way of people who'd had socially robust college experiences, always ready to spread gossip about the person a few doors down. "Once in a global studies seminar she revealed to everyone that she didn't know where Danish people came from." She paused for dramatic effect. "And then she started ranting about *Dutch* people, and how it should be more clear which of them was from Denmark, and also that it was confusing that *German* in German is *Deutsch*—my *God*, she was a moron. And—well, she'd read somewhere that you could burn off your split ends instead of getting a haircut."

"God," Julia said. "Was she—"

"She was fine," Francine said. "Just an idiot."

She wondered if the designation—idiotic but technically fine—wasn't rather applicable to herself at the moment, and Francine confirmed this for her when she smiled again, a moony, faraway smile that Julia was sure contained at least a modicum of malice.

"It's so funny you didn't know that. Mark introduced Brady and I."

Brady and me, she thought, clinging to a tiny vestige of superiority, even though she was sitting in a beanbag chair intended for a luxurious child who wasn't born yet and her opponent had a history with her boyfriend that he'd neglected to share with her.

"Mark seems happy," Francine said. She lifted a fuzzy throw blanket from the arm of the rocker and refolded it on the mound of her stomach. "It's good to see him doing so well."

"Uh-huh," she said. Was she hoping for a compliment, for the observation that Mark had never seemed as happy as he had since meeting her?

"Mark's really—rare," Francine said. "He deserves it." This proclamation seemed to apply to Mark overall, not necessarily his lowbrow bartending girlfriend, who'd brought the sullying musk of cigarettes with her into the future living quarters of opulent babies. "I just hope we can get him out of that job."

This surprised her anew. She had only a rudimentary understanding of Mark's work, but she knew it made him happy and that he was good at it, and she knew that finding something that fulfilled both of those criteria was rare.

"He loves his job," she said.

"Well, sure," Francine said. "But he never intended to do something like that forever."

She did not say *How would you know?* She did not say *Something like what?* And she did not say *He works at one of the best research universities in the country*, because she was embarrassed that this sort of pretentious defensiveness had even entered her head.

There was a barely audible ding from downstairs; Julia would not have noticed it had Francine not heaved herself up from her chair.

"The crostini's ready," she said, and she started down the hall.

Julia stayed in the beanbag for another few seconds, speechless. She could not imagine what it was like to be this woman, a woman so in control of her life, so confident of her place in the world that she could casually diagnose someone else's nonexistent problems while still keeping an ear tuned to the oven timer.

"Brade?" Francine called. "Time to poach the acqua pazza."

. . .

She'd gotten tipsy at dinner; in the car on the way home she held an unlit cigarette in her mouth, waiting to be smoked, because Mark didn't approve of her smoking at all and expressly forbade it in his car.

"They have a bidet." She shuddered; the cigarette bobbed as she spoke. "And there's a giant oil painting of one of their wedding photos in the upstairs hall? Like, life-sized? I wonder where that field is where they take all their pictures."

He barely smiled; she put a hand at the back of his neck.

"Probably also where the bodies are buried," she said.

He hummed, noncommittal, driving. The moonlight, through the trees, intermittently lit up his face, revealing at intervals something closed off and inscrutable. The air between them felt off, tinged with something she didn't like.

"She's really obsessed with being from Philadelphia, huh?" She was treading gently—perhaps not as gently as she would have had Brady not been plying her with Barolo all night—but she felt desperate, a need to realign herself with Mark, to reassure his status as her ally.

"Is she?"

"She must've brought it up a dozen times, and it wasn't like there was any context; there wasn't context for *anything* she was saying, just, like, ostentatious wealth, Philadelphia, cervixes, Philadelphia, faux-rustic wall sconces, Philadelphia, Philadelphia, Philadelphia. You know I'm suspicious of people who are too proud of where they came from."

"I do know that."

She glanced over at him, but he was fixedly watching the road. "Domestically, I mean. I don't mean, like—pining for your homeland is okay. Belarusians. Swedes."

"*Swedes*," he said evenly.

She wondered if he, too, had made fun of the girl who didn't know the difference between Denmark and the Netherlands. She boosted herself up and pretzeled her legs underneath her.

"You didn't like them," he said, half a question, his voice flat.

"I mean." She swallowed. "They aren't my *favorite* people."

Mark laughed dryly in a way that worried her.

"I mean," she said again. "Brady is objectively sort of—*oily*."

"Oily?"

"Fine," she said. "No, I don't like him. He's boring, for starters, but also just such a—*blow*hard; it's hard for me to understand how you've been friends with him for so long." She touched his shoulder. "That's a compliment."

"Jeez, Jules."

"I can't be the first person who's thought this." She felt affronted, and sort of nervous.

"I mean, I don't go around asking for reviews, because he's my best friend."

"I'm sorry, I didn't realize you were a twelve-year-old girl."

She remembered, in the quiet that followed, the feeling she used to get in bed when she heard her parents fighting. She and Mark didn't argue very often. He was conflict-avoidant to a fault and she, while a lifelong pessimist, appreciated his zen and was learning to adopt it, swallowing down her discontent in favor of a few hours of passive aggression if it meant they'd wake up the next morning on decent terms.

"He offered me a job," Mark said, which was not what she'd expected him to say.

"Excuse me?"

"I was going to tell you," he said, "as soon as you finished picking apart every single thing you don't like about them."

"I don't— What kind of *job*; what are you talking about?"

"He wants to hire me as his chief consultant," he said. "He's interested in biomed start-ups. I'll be doing the research and telling him whether or not I think we should invest."

"You're a *we* already."

"Hypothetically," Mark said gruffly.

"So you'll just be—what, reading about other companies and deciding whether or not to give them money?"

"It's a lot more complicated than that."

She sat with this for a minute, stewing, trying to pinpoint her reigning emotion, surprise and indignation amid a slurry of hurt. "But you love your job." It was important to her that her defense of him to Francine hadn't been for naught; it was critical to her to confirm that she knew him better than they did, that just because he hadn't turned to look at her when she pinched his elbow he still loved her more than he loved them.

"I do love it," he said. "But I— It's not—" He chewed at the inside of his cheek. "I wasn't— Look, Julia, I'm not—"

"Why are you calling me *Julia* like that?" she said. "Jesus Christ, I'm not interrupting you. Can you finish a fucking sentence?"

Francine had inherited a knack for soothing color schemes along with, apparently, a great deal of generational wealth; Julia had not taken much with her from her early life, but she had learned, by example, that it was easier to get mad at someone than to tell them you were scared.

"I just wonder if I shouldn't be thinking a little bit more strategically," he said.

"You just got a raise."

"I know that, but it— There's only so much ascendancy after this, if I stay where I am."

It dawned on her coldly. "You told him yes."

He didn't answer.

"You already took the job."

"I haven't—signed anything," he said.

"For Christ's sake. Okay. You— Okay."

"I was a little offended at first," he said. "I mean, he and Francine had clearly talked about it together, the fact that I'm probably not making a ton of money and the fact that we're living— You know."

"We're living *where?*"

"Just—an apartment. A one-bedroom."

"How many fucking bedrooms do we need? God, these snobby fucking dipshits. We're two functioning adults. With completely respectable jobs. And even if we *weren't,* for fuck's sake; what business of theirs is it to—"

"Look. If I got defensive it would just seem like I was trying to— justify that our lives are as legitimate as theirs."

"Our lives *are* as legitimate as theirs. Actually, you know what—we don't live in a diorama of the Hearst castle; our lives are a lot *more* legitimate than theirs."

"He just has a tendency to—everything's a contest with Brady, and he always—wins."

"Because he—" She stopped, hit belatedly by the remark. "Wait, that was *mean*."

"No, I didn't mean *you*— I just— It's a constant, like, *Oh, you got a raise? I started my own company*."

"*Your girlfriend's a bartender? Well, my* wife's—"

"That's not what I meant."

"What did you mean?"

"God, Julia, calm down. I just— Don't you just sometimes feel like our lives aren't as—real as other people's?"

"No," she said. "No, I have not once ever felt that way. What the fuck does that even mean? Like we'd be *realer* if we were married and took stupid photos in a field for our dumb suburban walls and you got me pregnant with giant babies who could inherit our non-existent fortunes? It's all her money, you know, by the way. She told me her grandfather invented—insurance or something."

"How is that relevant?"

"I just mean it's not like Brady's the big earner behind all of that hideous wallpaper. You didn't answer my question."

"I . . . don't know. Our life still feels a little bit—pretend to me sometimes."

"And you think it would feel less pretend if we—what, went through the motions?"

He came to a stop at a red light. "Maybe," he said. "I don't know. The motions seem to work for other people."

"They *appear* to work for other people, sometimes," she said.

"Would you—want any of that? Ever? With me?"

"*And then, reader, he proposed to me.*"

They lapsed into quiet; her face felt numb. She didn't know what she wanted. She never really stopped to think about it for too long, never identified anything beyond a vague desire for something good, some ephemeral notion of happiness, whatever that meant.

"Did you used to have a thing with Francine?" she asked.

She watched his posture straighten. "What?"

"Why didn't you tell me you knew her first?"

"I didn't know her first; I've known Brady since I was—"

"Why didn't you tell me you're the one who introduced them."

"I did tell you," he said.

"Mark."

"If I didn't, it was an oversight."

She stared at him until he looked over at her, a darting, guilty glance.

"I wasn't keeping it from you," he said.

"Did there used to be something between you guys?"

"No," he said. "Absolutely not. We were friends. We were in the same—"

"Yeah, I heard all about the fire drill. And the person who lit her own hair on fire."

"Oh," he said, and seemed suddenly a little sad. "Yeah, Heather. She was having a hard time of things."

She pressed her head back against the headrest. This was why she loved Mark, because he remembered things like Heather's name instead of how dumb she was.

"There was nothing going on with you two?"

"Me and Heather?"

She stared at him, again, until he caved.

"Francine's my friend," he said. "Nothing more."

"You still haven't answered me," she said. "You do want those things? Those things that we've never had a serious conversation about? Those things that you've never once expressed anything beyond a sociological interest in?"

"Is *cervixes* the right plural?" he asked feebly after a minute.

She looked at him lethally. "Can you articulate to me *why* you want them?"

"Isn't it okay to want something without fully knowing why you want it?"

"And you want—*that*? Whatever the fuck we just spent the evening with?"

"You don't have to be so critical."

She exhaled forcefully. "Ooh, boy. You know what, Mark? I'm not *fluent* in these passive Wisconsin semantics of yours, so how about you just say whatever it is you'd like to say?"

"I just mean— What's so great about your life? What makes it so much more acceptable than what Brady and Francine are doing?"

"It's *not* any more acceptable," she said. "It's the principle that there's such a thing *as* acceptable. We all have jobs, or don't, or make money, or don't, and it's *fine;* it's the insistence that one way is better than the rest of the ways that makes me homicidal. Who the fuck is Brady to tell you your job isn't good enough? Or mine? *That* was mean, too. What's so great about my life? God, you're being an asshole."

"No, I didn't— Jules, you're my favorite person ever. You know that. I've told you that a hundred thousand times. But you—make it kind of hard sometimes. You have this affected *something* that I just—I just don't *get* it; I don't understand what you're doing or why you think it's so much better than what everyone else is doing."

"I've never *once* said that I'm better than anyone else. Also, God, tell us how you really feel, Mark. What the *fuck.* I've apparently had this *affected something* since you met me, and I've never tried to force myself on you, or make you conform to me, or—"

"But I *have.* I've conformed to you in all sorts of ways and you haven't done a single thing to make room for me in your life."

"That's not true." She was at once grateful for the hardness in her voice and embarrassed by it; it felt like a vestige of earlier, worse times, times before she knew him, times when she didn't trust anyone at all. "What is it you'd like me to say to any of this? I'm— If you feel this way, Mark, there's no reason in the world for us to be together. I have no fucking idea what you're doing with me if this whole time you've felt like I'm just—"

"I've loved you practically since I met you," he said quietly, with an unfamiliar ferocity in his voice. "But you haven't— It's never felt totally reciprocal, like I'm— If I'm settling, it's for a woman who's never going to love me as much as I love her."

"I *do* fucking love you; God, I'm just— I don't have it as readily *available* as you do."

"But isn't that maybe a bad sign?"

"It's just how I *am.*" Maybe she, herself, was a bad sign. She didn't recognize the quietness of her own voice when she spoke again: "Are you settling? With me. Are you settling by being with me." Her body was taut, straight-spined, the rigidity itself a question.

It was something that had been following her around since they'd started seeing each other, the question of *why*. Mark had his faults—he was ornery, sometimes, and myopic, and gallingly uncomplicated—but he was by all accounts a catch, and she knew that if he weren't with her he could be with other women, women with fewer hang-ups, women who'd be happy to cozy up with him in a historic home in the suburbs and birth his standard-issue children without contemplating the futility of continuing to populate a dying race. She'd never fully understood his choosing her, and the fact of it, until that moment, had made her believe in something large and ethereal, proof of some divine construction, the corporeality of love. Before meeting Mark she'd trained herself to move through the world ready to be hurt, stooped like a boomerang against inevitable letdown.

"I don't know," he said, both a surprise and its opposite, and she cursed her own stupidity, indulgent belief in something beyond what was visible and likely.

He parked in front of their building and turned off the car. Neither of them moved.

"I'm not settling," he said finally. "It's more that I can't imagine anyone else. Not for lack of trying. I mean—not that I try very hard. I'm not saying this right. I don't, actually, Jules; I don't try; I don't *want* to try. I'm sorry I said—all of that. I don't— I'm sorry."

She futzed with the lock on the door. The next few moments could go one of two ways. She felt entirely in control, and she wasn't sure whether she resented it or not. She shifted toward him.

"I mean, you technically are settling," she says. "We all are, always, kind of, aren't we?"

"That's a pretty cynical way of—"

"Cynical's who I am," she said. "Cynical's who you signed up for."

"It is," he said finally.

"But I don't want you to ever resent me for the fact that you're settling, is the thing."

"I never said that I—"

"I just don't want that to be hanging over our heads. If it's just an accepted fact of our relationship, then fine. But I don't want it to surface in a year or twenty that you've been harboring any kind of—martyrdom. I don't need rescuing. I don't need a *favor*."

"I'm not doing you a favor."

"We'll see about that."

"Jules, I can't tell what it is you're trying to—"

"I'm trying to level our playing field. Do you want this? Genuinely. Absent of obligation or pity or lack of better options or— I don't know, buyer's remorse. Be honest, Mark. Christ. I can take it. Do you want to be with me?"

The things she was supposed to want him to say were not things she'd believe: *More than anyone. More than anything.*

"I'm ninety-eight percent sure," he said, "which is the closest I've ever come to a hundred about anything major."

A shutting of one door, then. A decision made to forget the last hour, because she was afraid, she realized, to be without him.

"It's my instinct, then," she said, "to not ruin a good thing."

"Mine too," he said, and it felt adult in a certain way, *real*, this complicit awareness of not wanting to ruin a good thing whether or not it was the *best* thing, because the best thing didn't exist. She was trembling, not entirely pleasantly, the aftermath trilling of a near miss. She thought of Francine in her nursery, in her stupid, enormous house; she thought of Mark getting through an entire dinner—and entire months preceding, she realized, probably the entire time she'd known him—sitting on the knowledge that he wanted what they had. And she thought of herself, so wildly out of place, an awkward outlier who didn't understand the rules; she thought of her life before she'd met him, its crisp solitude. She didn't know then, couldn't know, how much she'd come to miss her solitude, to crave it; she didn't know then that sometimes she would wish for it back, that sparse, easy life lived entirely on her terms. She knew only Mark, and the mere fact of him was a merciful kindness, someone in a sea of nothing. He put his arm around her; she turned her face in to his chest.

"Fine," she whispered. "Let's get married."

33

She and Mark are quiet in the car, on the way to the library's annual donor event. Julia is engaged in heated text negotiations with Alma, who is asking to use the Subaru this weekend to drive to Margo's parents' beach house in Michigan, a plan concocted in lieu of going to prom, which she has decided is beneath her. She and Mark have reverted to tiptoeing around her lately, reluctant to deny her anything because they both feel bad for her and fear her, but this is a bridge too far, her baby careening up I-94, the threat of the lake on one side and Indiana on the other.

Sorry, Julia writes, *but I'm not comfortable with that.*

And suddenly the phone rings, a photo of Alma as a swim-goggled toddler filling the screen. Her indignant and very untoddleresque voice blares from the speaker in Mark's car: "Mom, I could *just as easily* die in a car crash, like, backing out of the driveway."

"That's not helping your case, Ollie."

"You let me drive home from Iowa."

She does not tell Alma that at least, then, they could have died together.

"Ben and I need the Subaru this weekend," Mark chimes in.

An assist from an unlikely place, this harebrained *bachelor day* Brady Grimes has cooked up, Mark and Brady and Ben and Noah taking a ten-mile bike ride ending at a brewery on the Wisconsin border.

"Cycling and alcohol," Julia had said when Mark told her. "What could go wrong?"

Now she is glad for it. "A shame," she says. "Even though I was saying no anyway."

"Can you at least *pretend* to not sound so *happy* about it?" Alma asks. "God, Mom, you're so *mean*."

"Sweetheart," she says, but the word is punctuated by three forlorn beeps of a dropped call: Alma has hung up on her.

"It's very hard," she says. "Being this extravagantly adored."

But Mark hears the hurt in her voice—there she is, apparently, doing it again, *deflecting*—and reaches over to give her a comradely pat on the shoulder.

The library's fundraisers are always tepid, underfed affairs, boxed wine and waxy cheese and someone's teenage child nervously playing a string instrument. She cannot remember the name of the young woman she and Mark are talking to. She has identifiers for the constantly rotating roster of interns—*Overly Earnest Listening Face, Fictional Dietary Restrictions, Just Discovered Feminism*—and thinks of this one simply as *Gauchos*.

Mark is engaging the young woman in lively conversation about her upcoming summer plans as Julia scans the room. She sees, over by the fire escape, a primeval board member; she is talking to Melinda Wolcott, who helped get Julia hired twenty years ago.

The fact of the third woman these two women are talking to does not register in her mind as a logical possibility, though the rest of the room recedes and the trio pulls sharply into focus. Her brain sluggishly, stubbornly refuses to tie the knots that connect one piece of incontrovertible data to another: that the ancient board member has just very minorly choked on a canape, that Melinda Wolcott is patting her ineffectually on the back, and that the third woman has flagged down a waiter and commandeered a plastic cup of champagne, which she hands laughingly to the ancient board member, undoubtedly making a joke about how she'd never have made it in the Red Cross, but that someone should look into the logistics of Moët IVs in hospital settings. That the teenage boy playing an upright bass has just very, very loudly plucked the wrong note. That the woman with the champagne—radiant, scarf-draped, laughing in a way that bares her throat—is Helen Russo.

"Honey?"

She startles; Mark is smiling at her, a hand at the small of her back.

"We lost you," he says.

Gauchos is smiling too, the hint of a blush on her cheeks.

"Sorry," Julia says. "Sorry, I just—thought I saw John Cusack."

"Tara was just telling me what a great supervisor you are," Mark says.

"Just how you care so much," Tara says shyly, her blush deepening. "How you— Like, how important it is to you that we do justice to the material."

"That's very kind of you." Julia can still see the shape of Helen in her periphery, an undulating blue blur, like a cataract. "Would the two of you excuse me? Just for a second."

She doesn't even bother coming up with an excuse, though to her credit she does not say *I'm going to go walk sacrificially through a stained-glass window*, which is the option she is giving serious consideration. She starts for the exit, and then, feinting, turns to the sad assemblage of boxed wine and shoots herself some Cabernet from a plastic nozzle.

"Julia."

She turns; she has not yet taken a sip of her wine. She recognizes the scarf around Helen's shoulders, orange silk, patterned with gray and white horses, and realizes—feeling for a second very embarrassed, like she's been caught in her underwear—that she is wearing a similar one, smaller, the pattern more abstract, pale blue and dark brown.

Helen is smiling at her, and then she's leaning in and kissing both of her cheeks, and Julia recognizes her perfume, too, lavender that is somehow not fusty.

"Twice in as many months," Helen says. "What are the odds?"

"Astronomical," says Julia, who is unused to feeling her heart beat as hard as it is currently beating.

"I have to confess, actually," Helen says. "I get asked to one of these things every fifteen seconds and I almost never go anymore— I found them atomically tedious even *with* Pete—but the invitation showed up in the mail the day after I saw you parked outside of my house, and the happenstance seemed too compelling to ignore."

She lets it slip so easily that Julia does not immediately think to be embarrassed; she is distracted instead by the frankness of the statement, that Helen has come tonight specifically to see her.

"Whoops," Helen says, and mimes snapping a rubber band on her wrist. "My kids say I mention him too often. Apparently it makes others uncomfortable."

Julia frowns. "I don't know how you could be expected not to," she says. "When someone's been—for so long, when they've been—"

"My life," Helen says. "My half. Thank you, Julia. I suspected you'd understand that. See? You're still wise beyond your years. And wise beyond my daughters-in-law."

"I'm sorry," she says. "Again, Helen, about Pete, I—"

"I know you are, honey. Thank you."

And suddenly, looking Helen in the eye, the door opens up before her as it had the first time they'd met, the feeling that she'd known this woman for a very, very long time, that there wasn't anything she wasn't allowed to say. A generosity she'd never quite returned.

"How are you, Helen?" she asks. The question she couldn't ask in the grocery store; the question she didn't ask nearly often enough during those intense months they'd spent together twenty years ago.

"Oh, well," Helen says. "You know." And then she shrugs.

"How are you really?" Julia asks. Helen, all that time ago, handing over her scarf: *Should I ask?*

"How am I really," she repeats, like she's rolling the answer around in her head. She studies Julia for a moment. "*Really*," she says, "the first few months after were the worst of my life. And then without my noticing things gradually started to get less and less worse and now I've settled into—whatever I am now, something new, something not as good. It helped once I stopped expecting things to get *better*, because I've resigned myself to the fact that that's never truly going to happen." Her eyes are less sad than the tenor of her speech. "Honestly, Julia? This may sound terrible but I . . . Well, you'll understand this, too. There are days I'm *delighted* to be alone. Where I'm just bowled over by how unencumbered

I feel. My life is my own, my days are my own. I can do anything I want in the world, at any moment. The punishment for that, though, is—well, peaks and valleys. I can fly high for a good stretch but the longer I'm happy, the harder the comedown. I guess that's just—physics. If you'll allow me to mix my metaphors."

"So the comedown—"

"Makes me miss him more than I ever have before. Every single time." Helen smiles an unfamiliar sad smile. "And God, coming to something like *this* solo. As if these things aren't depressing enough."

"I can't imagine," Julia says softly.

"Oh, don't try," Helen says. "It's not something you can practice for; better to remain in ignorance for as long as you can, I'd say."

"I'm glad you're here," Julia says. "Tonight, I'm glad you came."

"Despite my singledom? I think I am too." Helen smiles at her. "Why didn't you come up to the door last month? That was Cal, in the driveway with me, by the way. It's eerie, really, how much they've all come to look alike. And *God*, how much they all look like *Pete*; I do a double take sometimes when one of them walks into the room. Except Francis. I always used to joke that he was the product of a dalliance with the mailman, but now I'm genuinely beginning to wonder."

"I wasn't— I'm not sure why I—"

"It would've been lovely to see you. And to let Cal show you what he's doing to the inside of the house; you won't be able to recognize the powder room. Or maybe that's— Is it presumptuous of me to think you'd have any recollection whatsoever of what our *bathrooms* looked like? Isn't it funny how when you're renovating you become so keenly aware of the most prosaic things and you forget that absolutely nobody else on the earth could care less?"

"I remember," she says, ridiculously, "what your bathrooms look like."

"Then you," says Helen, "are my ideal guest."

"I'm sorry," she says. "For—parking in front of your house." She says it like a joke, but her face is hot. "I was—"

But there is Helen, watching her patiently, that familiar, flattering laser focus.

"I was not in the neighborhood," she says. "I'm not exactly sure what I was doing there."

"I'm not exactly sure what I'm doing *here*," Helen says. "Particularly given what's on offer." She gestures to Julia's wine cup with her own. "I don't suppose I could lure you away for a glass of something nicer?"

It is, in the moment, all she wants to do, to be lured away by Helen Russo to the velvety dark of some candlelit Gold Coast wine bar; she cannot believe, really, how very much the notion appeals to her.

"There you are."

Mark alongside her again, and her loyalties shift back to something she recognizes: of course she will not be secreted away to a speakeasy by an eighty-year-old woman in a horse scarf; she will leave here, as planned, with her husband.

"Sorry to interrupt," he says, and Helen smiles at him.

"Helen Russo," she says, and holds out a hand.

They shake while Julia watches, wondering if this is what it feels like to wake up during surgery, anesthetized from the neck down.

"Mark's my husband," she says, and the looks they're both giving her indicate that she has likely just interrupted Mark telling Helen the same thing.

"She's been having hallucinations of John Cusack," Mark says to Helen. "Are you on the board?"

"God, no," Helen says. "I'd rather dig out my own organs with a blunt trowel than sit on the board of anything. Melinda and I were at UCSD together seventeen thousand years ago and she ropes me into showing up at these things every few years. I'm basically a census worker now, tallying up who among our ilk is still alive."

Mark is laughing—falling, already, she sees, under Helen's spell, because how could you not, and for an insane second she feels competitive, protective of what's hers, though she isn't sure if her impulse is to protect Helen or Mark.

"It's important to make yourself useful at these things, I think," Mark says.

"What's your contribution?" Helen asks. "Arm candy?"

Helen Russo is flirting with her husband.

"That's my contribution to every occasion, yes," says Mark.

Sweet Jesus, Mark is flirting back.

"I *like* him," Helen says to Julia, squeezing her arm.

"Yes," she breathes. Someone, cosmically, is fucking with her; some omnipotent squirrel-god is hurling acorns at her from the sky, just to watch her duck. "I'm fond of him as well."

She watches, numb, as Mark and Helen chat: about the construction around the Congress tunnel, about Mark's job. It is determined, through a boring round of six degrees of two people with ties to the corporate sector, that lawyers from Helen's old firm used to represent AllAboard.

"Small world," Mark says.

Julia agrees, vigorously; it is the tiniest world on the entire planet. And yet the conversation remains astoundingly innocuous; neither Helen nor Mark is letting on that they are two of only a handful of people on the earth privy to the fact of Julia's erstwhile indiscretion. They could be anyone, all of them; there is a possibility, she sees, growing larger by the second, that Mark will walk away from the exchange without giving it a second thought.

"What's Ben up to these days?" Helen asks, and Julia deflates, because of course she isn't going to get off scot-free; of course she doesn't deserve to.

But Mark doesn't seem to think this especially odd either. Bless men, with their nuance blindness! "What *isn't* Ben up to, is maybe a better question," he says. "His wedding's in three weeks."

"No," Helen says. "*Really?* Gosh, I remember him being knee-high."

Mark looks bemused; Julia feels a full decade get knocked from her life expectancy. "You—knew Ben? As a kid?"

"He was at work with me a few times when Helen was there to see Melinda," she says, and she meets Helen's eyes, pleading. She's a little scared of herself, of how easily the lie came to her after all these years of telling the truth.

"Ages ago," Helen says. "An unrecognizably long time ago."

"You'd be astounded," Julia says, trying to emanate gratitude.

Helen smiles. "I'm sure I would."

She hears a buzzing from Mark's pocket, and he hands her his wine as he fumbles for his phone. She can't tell if she's imagining his tilting the screen slightly away from her line of sight, but she's nevertheless grateful that this stuff-of-nightmares assembly is being interrupted by something other than her committing sacrificial suicide.

"Shoot," he says. "I've got to take this; do you mind?"

She shakes her head; Helen waves him away.

"Nice to meet you," he says to her, and then lifts the phone to his ear and hunches a little as he hurries from the room; she can't hear who he's talking to.

"Nice-looking man," Helen says, watching after him.

"Uh-huh," Julia says weakly.

"I always wondered what he looked like. He's not who I was picturing."

"Who were you picturing?"

"Well, I can't say for sure, exactly, now. Someone less agreeable? And I don't think I thought he had glasses."

"He wears contacts sometimes," she says.

"You're a cute pair," Helen says. "You complement each other."

"You think so?"

"You do. Or maybe part of it's just how much *lighter* you seem. A great deal more confident than you did way back when."

"Really?"

"In spades. Your posture's even improved. You've hit your stride, it seems to me."

She considers her spine. "It's all an act."

Helen laughs. "Well, sure. I mean you finally *learned* that it's all an act. You figured out how to play along like the rest of us."

It is, in characteristic Helen Russo fashion, precisely, incisively true; it seems suddenly undeniable how much playing along she has done in the last two decades, and how much that playing along has had a hand in getting her where she is; it reminds her, as well, of how she never felt like she had to play along when she was with Helen.

"I couldn't stop thinking about you after I saw you at the grocery," she says. "It brought up a lot for me. Seeing you."

"Me too," Helen says.

"Did it really?"

"Lord, of course it did," Helen says. "Why do you think I came tonight?"

She hasn't allowed herself to consider it as a possibility until now, that she perhaps has, after all, meant something to Helen too.

"So, would you like to get together?" Helen asks her. "Catch up properly?"

"I would," she says before she can give it any more thought.

"Would you really?" Helen smiles at her, searching her face.

"I really would," she says.

"Sounds like you have lots to catch me up on," Helen says.

"You have no idea."

What had happened in those eighteen years since that day they'd said goodbye at the library? Everything, nothing. The children had grown like weeds, Alma from her embryonic state; Mark's mother had died and his father had unceremoniously lost his memory. They'd redone their kitchen and, at the urging of an attorney, had wills drawn up; they'd traded in cars and gotten the gutters cleaned; they'd coaxed Suzanne into trusting them and Julia had been promoted at work. They'd grown up, in short, and yet standing with Helen Russo feels almost exactly how it used to feel: a muscle memory, and one that hasn't atrophied as much as Julia would have expected. She thought she'd stopped missing Helen—she had forced herself to stop missing Helen, all those years ago—but it turns out the need has been there all along, drowned out by her children and her colleagues, supplemented by her new friendships but there nonetheless, waiting in the wings. And now that she's had another taste of it—Helen's laugh, Helen's contemplative nodding, Helen's still-extraordinary taste in wine—she wonders how she survived without it.

"We'll set something up," Helen says. "Let me give you my number."

She had Helen's landline memorized when they knew each other; it took years for her to forget it. She pulls out her phone, punches in the number as Helen recites it to her.

"That sounds perfect," she says, and she can hardly believe it—any of this, like no time has passed at all—when Helen leans in to hug her again.

. . .

think she has a crush on you," Mark says later, when the event has ended and they're walking down Ontario to the parking garage. Julia, who had just been enjoying, for the first time in an hour, the sensation of being able to truly breathe again, nearly chokes.

"What? Who?"

"Tara," he says. "Or—what'd you call her, Jodhpurs?"

She relaxes. "Gauchos."

"I thought I'd have to fight her for you." He puts his arm playfully around her shoulders. "She's fallen under your spell."

"Who was on the phone?" she remembers to ask, and is sure, now, that she isn't imagining his arm stiffening a little against her.

"Work thing," he says, and she feels certain—the way one is just certain of things, sometimes, in a marriage—that he's lying, but she's equally certain that if she called him on it, she would seem like a psychopath, so she waits for him to say more, and when he doesn't, she lets it go. They can't tell each other everything. There aren't enough hours in the day.

"That woman seemed familiar to me," Mark says suddenly. "Have I met her before?"

It's her turn to stiffen. "I'm sure you haven't," she says.

"Maybe I just recognized the scarf," says Mark, who once failed to notice when Julia cut six inches from her hair, and she feels her heart in her throat.

"What?"

"I think I used a similar one recently," he says, his mouth near her ear, teasing.

"Oh." She relaxes against him. "Yes, God, you're right, it *was* similar." Then, like a true psychopath: "I'm glad she introduced herself to you, actually; I'd forgotten her name."

They walk for a block in a silence that's mostly comfortable, their respective untruths—whatever his is—softened at the edges but still there.

There aren't enough hours in the day to tell each other everything, and there's also, in a marriage, simply not enough *context*; there is not always enough common ground; there will always be spots where you don't align, pockets where you can't both fit. She can't help but think of the day she'd met Helen, how easily the woman had cut right to the heart of her problems, how freely Julia had told her everything. That wasn't the bad part; all of that happened before the bad part, and the thought of being able to do it again—share with an objective third party, an objective third party who apparently still cares about her—shimmers alluringly before her.

"How do you know what jodhpurs are?" she asks Mark.

"I wrote a paper in college on the political history of polo."

"Of course you did," she breathes.

"You want to get some dinner? What are you in the mood for?"

Xanax. An entire pack of cigarettes. Several horse tranquilizers. Suddenly the thought of sitting across from him at a table—the perfect occasion for a revival of their conversation last week, Mark and his abnormal wife, pushing everyone away—makes her feel terribly claustrophobic; she has half a mind to hightail it back inside and beg to see Helen Russo's bathroom remodel.

"Let's skip it," she says. "Can we? Let's just go home."

34

Babies had previously been a topic around which she and Mark had only loitered shyly, and Julia slightly resented Brady and Francine for forcing them into the headlines, but Mark, because he was a normal person, accepted Brady's two a.m. phone call with completely occasion-appropriate joy, dragging Julia with him the following morning to the hospital and stopping in the gift shop on the way.

"Are you trying to *seduce* them?" she asked, watching as he dubiously selected a bunch of roses, and when she saw him wilt—God, how *nice* he was, a niceness that shone more brightly beside her own lack thereof, like a new car parked next to an old one—she guided him gently over to the carnations.

In the hospital room, Julia started to feel weirdly jealous, jealous of the babies and Francine both, the babies for making Mark do that cute, skittish thing with his hand through his hair and Francine for smiling down tiredly on all of them like a dumb rich angel. Mark looked at once overcome and utterly content holding the babies, and she felt almost embarrassed being in the room, like she'd just wandered in to take out the garbage while everyone else was experiencing such extraordinary, intimate joy.

"They're beautiful," she said, and she was convinced everyone would be able to tell that she felt absolutely nothing. Because of course there was some deficiency in her, this complete inability to feel joy during unequivocally joyful situations. But in the moment she didn't like what Mark's quiet joy implied. She didn't like being made to feel deficient simply by existing.

"You looked pretty cute holding that baby," Mark said to her later when they were walking back to the Red Line. He looked so genuinely happy; his hand in hers, squeezing, felt so hopeful; his optimism, on the heels of meeting new life, seemed so *normal.*

"Well." Her voice strained against her throat. "Babies! They make them that way for a reason."

"You looked happy," he said, and it broke her heart, because she hadn't been, and he was the person in the room who was supposed to know that.

It had started happening gradually, a slow, subtle slippage, like freezing to death. And she watched it happening, little fissures forming, tiny bulbs of uninspired but logical ideas blinking over Mark's head at intervals, the house lights coming on: *Oh how about if we— Well if those people are doing that then maybe we should— Huh, I wonder if it would make sense for us to . . .* Tiny infidelities, each of these admissions: that he wasn't as content with their life as she was. Maybe this was how everybody's lives unfolded, just a series of *maybe we should* decisions made or not, succumbing to the silent lure of peer pressure without even realizing it.

They turned in to the stop at Chicago and State; he put his hand lightly on her back as they descended the stairs to the train, fed their cards into the turnstile. On the platform, they stood separately, leaning on either side of a painted column.

"Is it something you want?" he asked after a minute, and she couldn't pretend she didn't know what he was talking about.

"I'm not sure." She watched a rat saunter down the tracks with a cigarette butt in its mouth. "I take it I don't even have to ask you. Speaking of looking happy."

"Of course I'm happy for them. Aren't you?" The implication being *you are a woman of childbearing age; is some part of you not melting right now, because of all the cuteness?*

Was it? She wasn't sure. She certainly wasn't melting over the Grimes babies, nor was she moved by proximate babies she saw in the grocery store or on the bus. But she wasn't completely *opposed* to the idea, and this surprised her.

"I was very invested," she said, "when that baby fell into a well."

"Jules."

"I don't know, okay? I'm not sure how I feel."

"All right."

"One thing at a time, John Cheever," she said. "Could we?"

"Fair enough," said Mark.

"Let's have this wedding first," she said, and then, "Let's put a pin in it."

"You know," he said. "That actually has military origins too? World War Two."

And she came around the column and leaned against him a little. "I did not know that."

"Referring to hand grenades," he said, and then mimed pulling out the pin.

She was moved, of course, by his emotional generosity, his patience. He'd grown up lonely, with a family who loved him but didn't understand him particularly well. She could envision him being a good dad. Mark wanted it, and his wanting made her want as well, if not exactly a baby itself then the happiness he seemed convinced it would bring them, and she trusted him, had no reason not to trust him.

"We'll put a pin in it," she said again, and he put his arm around her shoulders, and she allowed herself, for the first time, to consider the possibilities.

Mark didn't ask her to, but she took *Ames* as her own, as much to acknowledge her new life as to commemorate the death of the old one, to seal up the files on Julia Marini, who had told her grade school classmates that her father was in the mafia, who had left and been left. And she liked being married to him. They'd become tenderer with each other, mindful of their good fortune, and the sex stayed good, and life felt like less of a free fall with him around. His new job with Brady proved to be annoyingly fruitful and so he was busy, invigorated, filled with a newfound sense of import—also fairly annoying—that came from making more money than most people; they bought a new couch, the first piece of furniture she'd ever owned that wasn't secondhand; and they were starting to talk about buying a place instead of renting, occasionally dropping in on open houses like wedding crashers, testing the faucets. Once you started making major life decisions, she realized, you came to see how dangerously easy it could be, their inherent magnitude some-how dwarfing their seriousness.

She stopped taking her birth control: a *let's just see*, a little experi-ment, trying without trying, because what, after all, was one more major life decision among a cluster of others? But of course she was one of those women who conceived on the first go, despite years of treating her body like it belonged to someone else, despite a fucked-up childhood and shoddy parental models and an as yet unfulfilled desire to understand what it meant to be an adult.

She regarded the pregnancy test with a sense of detached curios-ity, like she'd found it in someone else's trash can. She'd suspected it for over a week, a dragging feeling in her pelvis and a north-ward soreness and the unshakable sensation, even in the most mun-dane of moments, that she was about to burst into tears. So while the lines on the stick didn't surprise her, they did arouse a certain amount of fascination that was laced with terror.

She'd swallowed it down when her mother, citing the needs of an elderly neighbor who Julia was convinced didn't exist, did not come to her wedding. She'd swallowed down almost everything having to do with her mother, and she managed to keep it swal-lowed for the entire first year she was married. But for some reason, after she took the test on a warm Wednesday in early June, after she sat on the edge of the tub with her head between her knees for a few minutes—for some reason, when she picked up the phone, she did not dial Mark's work number but instead the one written on a sticky note stuck to the freezer door.

She boosted herself onto the kitchen counter as she listened to the ringing. She wondered if heart palpitations were ever consid-ered physiologically normal. When Anita answered, she was in the middle of trying unsuccessfully to take a deep breath.

"Hi," she gasped. "Sorry."

"What for?"

"It's Julia."

"I know that."

She pulled at a thread on her cutoffs and imagined she was six-teen again and they were having this conversation in the kitchen of the apartment on Fifty-Fourth Street, sucking on Otter Pops and

gossiping about her mother's coworkers at Dominick's, Anita sliding in with abject glee to tell her about some drama going down in
the deli or the married checker who was hooking up with one of the
warehouse guys. It was one of the only things that drew her mother
to full animation, the salacious details of other people's lives. But
her mother didn't even know where she was living, or where she
was working, and their last conversation had been the one in which
Anita had told her to "have fun" at her own wedding.

"How are you?" she asked. "Is now a bad time?"

"No," her mother said. "I'm fine. I just got back from the food
store."

"What'd you get," Julia asked.

A beat. "What did I *get*? Food, what do you think?"

"Right," she said.

"Why aren't you at work?"

"I'm off on Fridays in the summer."

"That must be nice."

She'd stopped bartending and worked thirty hours a week at the
library—Mark had urged her when he started making more money
and she qualified for his health insurance. But in a few words, her
mother had managed to make her feel like she was in high school
again, when she was only working a few afternoons a week at the
pharmacy because *she was in high school*, but Anita had a knack then,
too, for making her feel lazy.

"It *is* nice," she said, a little defiantly, and instantly regretted it;
she pictured the toxicity spreading through her veins and infiltrat-
ing her uterus and she tried to take a calming breath.

"Hot there?" Anita asked.

"A little," she said. "Low eighties."

"Here too," Anita said. "More like mid."

"We have ceiling fans," she said. "In our apartment."

She'd seen other people do this, imparting unbelievably banal
details about their lives for the sake of making conversation, with
the basic expectation that the audience would at least feign interest.
It was just what normal people *did*. Mark chatted with his parents
every Sunday and she marveled both at the tedium of the details he
shared and at how raptly his parents seemed to listen, responding to

his tales of car maintenance and road construction as though they were all huddled around a campfire. Last week she'd listened as he told them about a device they'd purchased on impulse that crushed aluminum cans.

She could have predicted, of course, that such a tack wouldn't work with her mother, but she forged on with something like desperation. She'd just thought maybe—possibly—enough time had passed so things might be less weird between them, so they could adopt a kind of mutually respectful détente, a silent agreement to compartmentalize the past and commune every other Christmas.

"Every single room, it's amazing," she said. "It only gets hot in here when it's *really* hot outside, but even then it's not so bad. Because of the air circulation."

Her mother was quiet on the other end. Julia was considering imparting the news of the can crusher when Anita spoke:

"You're pregnant," she said.

She felt her gut seize up. "What?"

"Aren't you."

Could she hear it in her voice? Did her mother perhaps know her better than she'd ever given her credit for? Was she aware of the molecular shift, the new presence inside her daughter on the other end of the line, and was this what motherhood *was*, being able to detect such a shift in your child over the phone, a thousand miles away after a ten-year hiatus?

"How could you tell?"

"I can't *tell*," Anita said. "I just can't imagine another reason you'd be calling me."

"Just to say hi," she said vaguely.

"So you're not pregnant?"

She paused. "No, I am."

The drugstore wedding card her mother had sent several weeks after the fact featured two cloying Precious Moments figures on the front alongside that stupid passage from Corinthians about love being patient and kind, and though that did not bode well in terms of sincerity—her mother was neither a collector nor an admirer of the spooky bug-eyed figurines, nor had she, as far as Julia knew, ever opened a Bible—she'd still held out hope that there might be something more momentous inside, some elusive morsel of wisdom Anita was sharing in lieu of actually showing up. But the inside only featured a preprinted message—*Wishing you a lifetime of happiness*— and, below it, her mother's signature, no note, not even a salutation. She'd thrown it out before Mark could see it.

"When are you due?" her mother asked, which was not congratulations but also, she supposed, not nothing.

"I just took the test," she said. *I called you first*, she did not say. "So I'm not exactly sure, but I think I'm— I don't know, maybe seven weeks?"

Her mother was quiet for a minute, and when she finally said, "So around January," Julia pictured her doing the math, ticking off the numbers like she used to when she balanced the checkbook, and for some reason the gesture brought tears to her eyes.

She cleared her throat. "Any words of wisdom?"

"*Wisdom*," Anita said archly.

She suddenly wanted to know everything about her own inception, all the questions she'd never thought to ask, or never thought she'd get an answer to. Her mother had been twenty and single when she'd gotten pregnant, making minimum wage and sleeping with a married man. How long had she waited to tell Lawrence? When had she first felt Julia move? How long had Julia taken to be born, and was her father there, waiting in the hallway to hold her?

How did you feel when you found out about me? Did you feel anything? Why don't I?

"Take whatever drugs they offer you," her mom said. "And hope to God it's a boy."

She stilled. "What?"

"I hear they're a lot easier."

She wasn't sure whether it was meant to insult her, but it did, even though she'd had the same thought when she saw the test result, a little signal flare of hope that she wouldn't be having a daughter, because the margin of error, with a girl, seemed so much larger.

"Is Mark excited?" her mom asked. She'd still never met him.

"Yeah," she lied, because she couldn't bring herself to admit how stupid she'd been, calling her mother before him, and because she knew the answer already. "He's thrilled."

"Great," her mother said.

"Yeah," she said again.

"Well," Anita said. "Keep me posted."

"Sure."

"I'd better go put the groceries away."

"Okay."

"Take care, Julia."

"Yeah," she said, "you too."

She listened to the dial tone for a while before she hung up. She'd intended to call Mark next, but instead she slid from the counter and lay weirdly on the kitchen floor, which she had mopped earlier and which was cool on the backs of her legs. She wasn't sure how long she'd been lying there when she heard his key in the door, and by then she felt somewhat hypnotized by the ceiling fan and was disinclined to move.

"Jules?" His shadow fell over her.

"Hi," she said.

"Are you okay? Did you—fall?"

"Did I *fall?*"

He knelt next to her and she tried to smile up at him like a normal person. He sat back against the cabinets, watching her. "What's going on?"

And after a beat she lifted his hand and pressed it to her belly, like someone who'd planned on something like this, like someone who was certain she wanted it, and in that moment the secret—that she wasn't at all sure how she felt; that she had, again, failed to be struck by any kind of cosmic certainty about any of it—implanted itself within her, and she imagined it growing, alongside the baby, their baby, into something else.

"January," she said, and his face went cartoonishly wowed, eyes huge.

"What?" he said, then, "Oh, Jules," then, *"Really?"* and she decided then that she would borrow, as her own, the unfiltered transcendent delight that appeared on her husband's face, because marriage was—wasn't it?—all about sharing, stories and tooth-brushes and feelings you were supposed to feel at the moment you were supposed to be feeling them. She would borrow liberally, she decided, for everyone's sake, and because it was on offer: Mark had love to spare.

35

Preparations for Alma's graduation descend on them, suddenly, like hail; instantaneously her daughter has shifted from caring about college to the far less fraught and more concrete problem of how she should wear her hair at the ceremony.

"Should I go blue?" She is sitting at the kitchen table, scrolling through her laptop while Julia makes dinner, and Julia turns to her, startled to be asked.

"Isn't there something they say about people who dye their hair blue?"

Alma glances up at her. "Something like what? Good or bad?"

"I can't remember," she says, though she thinks it may have had something to do with being crazy.

"Madison shaved her head over the weekend," Alma says, and because this is an act definitely associated with insanity, she says, "Oh, *cool*," knowing her approval will instantly deter her daughter from following in Madison's footsteps.

"How about these?" Alma asks, and Julia turns away from the stove to glance at her daughter's laptop screen, on which she has pulled up a pair of sandals.

Julia wrinkles her nose. "Are block heels back?" she asks. "And square toes?" She looks on as Alma continues to scroll, image after image of platforms and spaghetti straps. "God, are *all* these things coming back?" She returns to the counter, chopping kale. "That stuff was popular when Dad and I were dating."

"Back in 1840?" Alma says darkly. But then her voice brightens in the way it only does for people who aren't her mother: "Oh my God, *hi*."

She turns to see Mark in the doorway, just in from the airport, another overnight to New York; behind him is Ben, and at the sight of her son she feels a little swoop in her belly.

"Look who I found outside." Her husband ruffles Alma's hair, comes over to kiss Julia hello.

"Just came to pick something up," Ben says, squatting to pet Suzanne. "Hey, Suze, hey, Suze," he says, playing with her ears, and then, to his sister, "You never responded to my text, nerd."

"Some of us have *lives*," Alma says, even as she's pulling out her phone.

"What are you picking up?" Julia asks, to skate past the fact that her son has yet to acknowledge her.

"Just hoping I left this library book in my room earlier in the semester," he says. "They won't release my final grades until I return it or pay for it."

"Good that you're here, actually," Mark says. "I can give you a check for the last installment at the restaurant. You guys all set otherwise? Anything we can do?"

"I think we're good, thanks," Ben says. "Except— Oh, Sunny's dad called last night to say he's not going to be getting in until the day of the wedding," he says. "So he'll miss the rehearsal. But her mom *also* called this morning to tell us her grandma decided to come. So there'll be the same number at the rehearsal dinner."

Mark informed her last week—brightly, like she would be enthused about the development—that he'd offered for them to host a dinner for Sunny's family the night before the wedding.

"Her grandma?" Mark asks. "That's kind of a big deal, isn't it?"

"Sunny's grandma's, like, a big Jesusy weirdo," Alma says, to Julia's confused look.

"She was upset," Mark says more delicately. "About—the order in which things are—taking place."

"She's very conservative," Ben says, and Julia wonders when they all discussed this, and what else her family has been talking about without her knowing. "So it's a big deal that she changed her mind, yeah. Sunny's really relieved."

She can't tell if he meets her eyes at that moment on purpose or if it just happens; she looks into his, searching for—what? Accusation? Apology? Anything, really, that will set her more at ease than she is feeling.

"Let me go get you that check," Mark says, and disappears down the hall to his office, leaving quiet in his wake.

"I did ask her," Julia says, and both her children look at her uncomprehendingly. "Your grandmother."

Ben lifts his eyebrows. "You did?"

"Last month. I called her. She said no. Not because of— She was happy for you. But she couldn't get off work." She half-shrugs to acknowledge the same flimsiness she'd identified when her mother had given her the excuse in the first place. She feels Alma watching her.

"Why didn't you tell me?" Ben asks.

"I didn't want to hurt you." She hitches. "I mean—I know I can't control that, but I—still prefer to try when I can."

"Where does she work?" Alma asks.

"We didn't get that far."

Mark has returned with his checkbook. "What far?" He's distracted, leaning over the kitchen table filling out a check. He'd been sympathetic but unsurprised when she'd told him about her conversation with her mother.

"Dinner's almost ready," Julia says to Ben. "Why don't you eat with us, sweetie?"

How nice it would be, to be together again, the four of them at the table, Suzanne weaving figure eights around their feet hoping for scraps and Alma entertainingly expounding on her hatred of her class valedictorian and Mark telling them about some hidden gem sushi place in Midtown, Julia just sitting back, taking them all in, her people in their rightful places.

"I can't," Ben says, and she deflates. "Sunny had her stats final this afternoon; I want to be there when she gets home."

"Sure," Julia says. "That's nice."

"I'm going to go look for that book," Ben says, and then, after a beat—there's a little familiar glimpse of him, her compassionate child, the one whose eye contact she doesn't normally have to analyze—he says, "But thanks, Mom. For trying."

. . .

After midnight, Mark and Suzanne are snoring in tandem beside her, and she slips downstairs with the intention of going outside, but she hears the television and sticks her head into the den. Alma is curled up on her side on the couch, bathed in the blue glow of the screen, on which a bunch of people in chef's coats are frosting elaborate cakes. She doesn't move when she sees Julia, just meets her eyes with some amount of resignation.

"I *know* it's dorky," Alma says somberly, gesturing to the TV, "but I really, really love it."

Julia recognizes it, that edge-of-adulthood progression: tightly wound and hyperconscious teenage preferences—dictated for centuries, inevitably, by a tasteless few—giving way to the awareness that you're allowed to like some of the things that you're not supposed to like, that doing so may distinguish you, and that someone else might also like the forbidden thing, or simply witness you liking it and love you for it. Her daughter is piecing together her own interior rule book; this seems as marvelous a development as her learning how to crawl.

She takes Alma's admission as an invitation and slides in beside her. She learns quickly that she, too, loves the celebrity cake bust show, once she discovers its secret, which is that you are allowed to cry when you are watching it, no questions asked; emotions are allowed to be worn on sleeves during the baking show; you are allowed to wholly invest yourself in the struggles of eccentric British strangers; your blood pressure is allowed to rise when it looks like somebody's German chocolate Dusty Springfield might fall over.

"Mom?" Alma asks as another episode begins to play.

She looks down at her daughter, so close but not touching. "Hmm?"

"Why did you need to move away? From your mom?"

"Oh." It startles her. "Well, honey, I—" *Did something very stupid. Burned all of my bridges.* "It's hard to explain," she says, but her daughter looks up at her, watching with her big green eyes. "My mother and I reached a point where we— I mean, she and I never quite understood each other, I guess, or maybe it was that we understood each other too well, I'm not sure, but at some point we— I guess we both just ran out of whatever it took for the two of us to—coexist."

"But she's your *mom*."

"Yeah." She lets her eyes glaze, the celebrity cake busts melt. "Yeah, honey, she is, but that doesn't mean there can't be—complications."

Alma seems to meditate on this, and then says, "He'll come around. Ben."

"Oh," says Julia, glancing over at her.

"I think he's—like, he feels like he has to be super defensive about everything now because he's scared. He just wishes you were happier for him."

"I *am* happy for him," she says, and the look Alma gives her makes her laugh. "I'm coming around to it. It's a big thing."

"Didn't you tell me nothing's actually a big thing, though?"

"Kids are big things. Kids are the exception."

"You should call Sunny," says Alma. "Ask her to— I don't know what people like her do for fun, get towels monogrammed? You should ask her though, to hang out. It'll make Ben happy. I also do think you'll like her if you give her a chance. She's actually really nice."

"Maybe I will," Julia says. "Thanks."

Her daughter nods sagely, gaze now fixed indistinctly on the screen again, where a person is carving Mick Jagger's profile out of red velvet cake.

"Mom?" she says, so quietly Julia almost doesn't hear her.

She ventures to reach down and smooth some of her daughter's hair away from her forehead. "What is it, sweet?"

"I'm sorry," Alma says. "About—your mom. That it's like that for you."

There are suddenly tears in her eyes. "Oh, honey, that's—" But she isn't sure what to say, because it is not, really, all that okay, and it's too late in the day for her to explain why. "Thanks, Ollie," she says instead.

And Alma shifts, then, and—miraculously—rests her head in Julia's lap.

. . .

Alma falls asleep like that, leaving Julia to listen to her breath sounds. She sits there, afraid to move, and she thinks about the way her day has unfolded, an unusually good day, really, given how things have been going for her lately. Mark is home from New York, and before he'd fallen asleep they'd chatted very amicably about a ridiculous phone call he'd had with Blessing the Paleo from the restaurant where they're holding the wedding reception. Ben has thanked her for trying. Alma is—she watches it happen, more flattered than she should be—drooling a small dark patch onto her pajama pants. She has to admit that it feels better to be this person, the person who is trying and succeeding, the person with an intact family she never wants to lose. Her son is getting married in less than two weeks and her daughter is off to live in a dorm that, who's to say, could have almost been designed by Mies van der Rohe and her dog is unhealthily obsessed with her and she and her husband will be just fine in their empty nest; nobody is at risk of running out of what they need to coexist and it will remain that way so long as she doesn't burn it to the ground.

She picks up her phone and composes the *Moby-Dick* of indistinctly apologetic text messages to Sunny, *I hope all is well with you* and *I know the wedding is going to be great* and *If there's anything I can do, just say the word, really; I'd be happy to help.* She finally reins it in after her fourth semicolon and fires off the message.

And then, before she can stop herself, she goes into her contacts and deletes Helen Russo's number, because she is not supposed to have it; inarguably a thing she is Not Supposed to Do in her personalized Ledger of Trying is call Helen Russo again, and it seems, based on this good day she's just had, that she is perhaps, finally, past the point of needing Helen Russo, that perhaps she hasn't given herself enough credit, over the last twenty years, for getting by as well as she has without her.

36

Pregnant, she found herself incongruously, suspiciously happy, aswim in some mystical cocktail of hormones and carbohydrates and vitamin D. It took her a while to identify the feeling she was feeling—it was so subtle and so anomalous, and, ultimately, so short-lived—as happiness. It crept up on her quietly, not elation but *equanimity*. She was not inordinately happy—it was not crazy happiness, not full-throated wild happiness—but it was there, a *calm* she wasn't used to feeling, a sense of oneness with the world, with her days. She slept deeply and dreamed vividly; she floated through her workdays with serenity, having unearthed new reserves of patience and empathy and the ability to turn a blind eye to people she ordinarily wanted to murder. She observed, with a kind of blunted fascination, her changing body, tried to catch herself unawares in the mirror getting out of the shower. She began to observe the entirety of her life this way, in fact, from a point of curious remove: the husband, the future, the aquatic companion in her belly. And though she couldn't decide precisely how they made her feel—proud or defensive, claustrophobic or expansive, if those things were even mutually exclusive—she found she cared less, was spending less time in her head and more looking outward, preemptively scoping the landscape for whomever would soon be inhabiting it, the baby who wouldn't be inside her forever.

"We could go look at car seats after this," Mark said. They were at the garden store to buy a lawn ornament for his mother's birthday, stop one in a series of infernal errands, one of those depressing capitalist Saturdays where the day would end with their trunk filled with four thousand rolls of toilet paper and a giant tureen of laundry detergent and a box of Cheerios the size of a crib and maybe also an actual crib, or the car seat, something material for the child they'd yet to meet. She was wearing overalls, like a large adult in a child's educational program. She was still unused to this part of her life, the rewards membership, the exit ramp to a broad gray strip mall, the silicone, anesthetized air, but that day she was feeling buoyant, and somewhat entranced by the sensory overload of the fluorescent lights and the damp, chemical smell of peat moss and the sharp, dry smell of sawdust and the chlorinated wave coming from the greenhouse. She trailed her fingers over a series of hanging metal tools with gummy plastic handles.

She lifted one of the instruments from its hook, idly humming along to the instrumental Bee Gees medley playing wheedlingly from the sound system—*singing*, in *public*, like the easy-target victim in a fairy tale, but she didn't care, she felt untouchably blithe. She was twenty-two weeks pregnant; the world had, about a month ago, taken on a lush, pulsing, verdant quality, suffused with possibility and a three-dimensionality she could almost taste. She was almost always starving, and full of energy, and hornier than she could ever remember being.

She fitted her hand thoughtfully around the handle of the trowel.

"*Cause we're swimming in a world of pools*," she sang along, forgetting the words, the mesh strainer that was her memory the only current downside to her condition. She suddenly became aware of Mark just behind her, watching her.

She frowned, but it didn't last. "What?"

He shook his head, smiling, goofily, almost unnervingly. "Nothing," he said, nuzzling into the back of her neck with his nose. "Nothing, nothing, nothing," he murmured, the syllables warming her skin, and she felt a shiver from her sternum down to her groin.

She was unused to feeling the way she'd been feeling lately, a preoccupation with sex that outweighed nearly everything else, that came over her during wildly inopportune times, in the middle of meetings, on the train. The only time in her life that had remotely rivaled this one was during her final months of high school, and it troubled her to make this connection in her head, such a dark time arranged beside a joyful one, the innocent friskiness of her second trimester shaded by the dark and misguided desire that had preceded it.

He put an arm around her waist, pulled her to him.

"You make me so happy, Jules," he said, and she took him in— the creases at the corners of his eyes, the singularity of his gaze, the fondness all over his face, for her, and she was *entitled* to this, wasn't she; couldn't it be so that she *deserved* this joy, this man who looked at her like he'd never seen anyone better, this man who'd fathered the baby whose tenure inside of her was currently making her, in the middle of Frank's Nursery & Crafts, lose her mind with desire?

"What is it?" he asked.

"I," she said, and her throat filled.

"Hmm?" The sound buzzed into her neck. She shook her head and he pulled back to look at her. "Whoa, whoa, whoa," he said, seeing the shininess in her eyes, and it made her laugh. She was having a normal weekend in the middle of her normal pregnancy with her normal husband. Her life had improbably reached a stasis.

"I'm okay," she said, and she kissed him to prove it, and then kissed him again, harder.

A cleared throat: an older woman edged, scandalized, around them, excusing herself in a tone that suggested she was the one deserving of excuses. They were pregnant and cloying and blocking the path to the watering cans. Mark steered the cart with one hand and kept the other arm around her waist. She pressed closer to him and they clumsily navigated their way down the aisle, and she was thinking about how they must look, so smugly content; and then she was thinking about something else; she turned her wrist to veer their cart to the left, picking up speed, feeling his eyes on her—*Jules, where are we*—and thank God it was one of those places that had a big one-person bathroom; in a few months she'd have to be glad for the fact of a changing table but that day she still got to be relieved to lock the door behind them.

"Come here," she said, and fumbled with the straps of her overalls, grazing her own left breast in a way that made her whimper a little.

"Really?" Mark said, dubious but still kissing her.

"Be careful," she said, and he eased her gently up onto the sink while she forced herself not to think about how gross everything in there was, the smell of lemons and ammonia, something sinister beneath the surface.

She scrabbled with his zipper as he watched her, face alit with something—that familiar scandalization, that familiar fondness, that familiar unfamiliarity with her spontaneity. She put her hand between her legs, already seconds away, barely needing him.

"Oh fuck," she said.

Then she'd seen it, for just a second: something in his eyes that had ventured beyond the point of scandalization, a surprise further from joy than it was from dismay, and she felt a moment of disgrace that radiated down to her kneecaps, acute awareness of her own oddity, the edge to her newfound euphoria that was different from how it was supposed to be; she was not gentle Francine, cradling her belly in a field, but someone unseemly, someone wild and unmaternal. And though it apparently didn't deter him, or her—little could have, nothing could have; it was just her *body*, doing its thing; she couldn't *help* it; she wasn't *insane*—it was an expression that would make itself more at home on Mark's face in the coming months, the coming years, and Julia would grow more and more accustomed to it, come to accept it as fact, as just a part of how things were.

In the car on the way to the hospital, whizzing down Lake Shore Drive, she'd entertained the notion of opening the passenger door and simply letting herself fall out. When they arrived, Mark walked with her up and down eerie, darkened hallways and she stopped at intervals to bray against him and, once, throw up in a trash can hastily procured from the nurses' station. She forced herself to swallow down the sad fact that she wanted her dad, or her mom, the two people who had known her when she was as small as the baby in her belly, or anyone who had known her when she was smaller than she was now, really, anyone who might be able to offer some comfort; she felt she was overdue for it, and deserving, particularly under these circumstances, the sensory assault that was parturition, the overhead lights and the sound of her husband trying to soothe her and the smell of her own sweat and the remarkable, laughable pain. She kept saying no to the proffered meds, the epidural that the nurses had brought up more than once.

"You're progressing a little more slowly than I'd like," said the doctor, who had his hand inside of her vagina and who was not her preferred doctor but the one who happened to be on call because her preferred doctor was straight-facedly *in Anguilla*.

"Yeah, me too," she said, gritting her teeth as he continued his exploration.

"I'm tempted to try something to get things moving," he said. "Tell me, any family history of high blood pressure?"

"I have no idea," she said, and she hated the doctor's unsatisfied expression and the shame it made her feel, shame because she wasn't making progress and additional shame because she didn't know the basic facts of her parents' lives, let alone how forcefully their blood moved through their bodies. She hated the sympathetic pulse of Mark's hand squeezing hers and the nurse in the Snoopy scrubs rubbing with her cardigan sleeve at the dry-erase board in preparation for a shift change, all of them doing what they were supposed to do and Julia, somehow, not.

The doctor must have decided to proceed regardless of her ancestral ignorance, because suddenly, out of nowhere, things got worse than they'd ever been, pain like trying to walk down the street in a windstorm, broadsiding her from all directions.

"Jules," Mark said, looking young and terrified, watching her writhe and curse. "Come on, honey. Let them give you something, God, please."

She'd been propelled, until then, by the mantra that she couldn't keep out of her mind, a mantra that made her brush away the nurses whenever they offered her Demerol. Her mother's voice on the phone: *Take whatever drugs they offer you, and hope to God it's a boy.* It seemed ludicrous that you could lean so heavily on something so childish when you were doing something as inherently unchildish as having a child yourself, but there she was, remembering her mom's advice and actively combating it, even though she wanted to die.

"This is torture, Jules. Please, I can't watch you go through this."

It was the fear in his voice that finally did it. "Fine," she said, too exhausted to take issue with Mark's concern for his own mental health. "Fine, give me whatever, give me anything."

But the anesthesiologist was tied up, and plus it was too late, said the new nurse, who had Tweety Bird scrubs and her hand, now, as well, in Julia's vagina.

"Homestretch," the nurse said, and after that her memory went fuzzy at the edges; she supposed Mark had a clearer recollection but she had no desire to ask him; she didn't want, ever, to talk about it again, and she had already vowed, without telling him, that she would never do it again, that they would remain, in perpetuity, a family of three, because she—again, again, falling short—knew she couldn't handle anything more.

The first time she saw the baby she felt her brain sluggishly recalibrating as though the image didn't make sense, a horse head on a human torso or a tree growing upside down. Who was he, and where had he come from, and why did everyone else in the room look so euphorically happy, even the Tweety Bird nurse, who surely saw new babies all the time?

And so she just kept staring at him—let everything that wasn't Ben get fuzzy around the edges too, because everything that wasn't Ben seemed, suddenly, far too much to take.

37

She had fully expected Sunny to ignore her message like her own children do, but she received a prompt series of replies with far more than four exclamation points: *omg this is the most perfect timing* and *are you free tomorrow* and *emergency!!!!!!!* and about seventeen tiny emoji brides atop a line of police cars. She agrees, a little amazed at the response, to take Sunny to a dress alteration a week before the wedding.

"It fit me last week," Sunny says, seated beside Julia on a brocade fainting couch in a little hipstery boutique in Bucktown, not the fussy bridal emporium Julia had been expecting. "Perfectly. I don't understand how it's—just, like, overnight? I told my old roommate and she asked if she could borrow my bathing suits for her trip to Greece since they wouldn't fit me anymore. Which is disgusting, for starters, because who shares *swimwear* with another person?"

"Disgusting and—gauche, no?" She is surprised to feel protective of Sunny, who she notices is a nail-biter.

"Exactly," she says. "It turns out that it actually kind of sucks to be the only pregnant one out of your friends. Or maybe it's not just that I'm pregnant. It's—everything; nobody wants to spend seven hours watching me get a dress retailored when it's the end of the school year." Sunny exhales huffily. "Sorry, I'm in a mood."

"Is this? Going to take seven hours?" Julia asks. She prefers Sunny, she finds, *in a mood*. "Because I've got to get home and wash my hair."

But Sunny looks at her blankly, a blankness tinged with panic, and Julia supposes she can't blame her, supposes she has given

Sunny absolutely no reason to think she is a person who possesses a sense of humor or leniency or, God help her, basic human decency.

"That was a joke," she says. "I've got all the time in the world."

Sunny's holding a clipboard in her lap, a thick sheaf of papers pinioned to it filled with her looping scrawl in colored pens, *hard deadlines* and *ethereals* and *food!!!* underlined at the tops of the pages, a private glimpse into the more alarming crannies of her mind but not, Julia finds, entirely unrelatable—not, in fact, so different from her own brain when Ben was a baby, as she lay in bed making her lists, convincing herself that if she obsessively did the things she was supposed to do it would make up for her lack of desire to do them.

"We're almost finished," a severe woman says to them from across the store, where she is sticking pins into the dress of an impossibly tall, black-eyed brunette who looks like she rides horses and probably used to haze people at sleepovers.

"Thanks again for coming with me," Sunny says. "Ben said you were good at things like this."

"Things like—?"

Sunny shrugs. "Giving rides."

What does it mean, she wonders, to be good at giving rides? Not what it used to.

"Being on time. Showing up, was the gist. You and Mark continually outshine my parents as far as that stuff goes. Ben said the worst thing you ever did to him was forget to pick him up at school once."

It strikes her oddly, a bird landing on her shoulder. "What?"

Sunny's face is an interesting mix, someone trying to look amused but letting annoyance win out. "We were talking about— I don't know, whatever, our parents, and I was telling him all the horrible things my mom has said to me, and Ben— I mean, that was his one big bad memory. He said he was in preschool and you were late and he had to sit on a bench in a hallway that smelled like rubber boots with the art teacher, who apparently was, like, fiending for a cigarette and super jumpy, and then finally Mark showed up and Ben thought you were dead, but it turned out you'd just forgotten.

Or not— I don't know, maybe you just got stuck in traffic or something; he was, like, four, so who even knows if it really—"

"It happened," she says, and hearing her voice, Sunny looks at her with curiosity.

"You know what I'm talking about?"

"I do." *I was trying to forget. I was at a gas station, trying to abandon him. I was out of my mind; that happens sometimes.*

"He wasn't saying it in a bad way, Julia. It wasn't— Like, if that's the worst thing you can remember your parents doing, you're probably doing okay. My mom once told me I deserved to break my arm because I climbed a tree after she told me not to. I mean, I had some anger issues when I was little, so it's not like I was a model kid. But I think they were mostly reactionary, and even if they weren't, who says something like that to a six-year-old?"

The appropriate thing to say here, she thinks, is something along the lines of *I'm sure she's not so bad,* but Julia always hated when others assured her that her mother meant well.

"I'm sorry, Sunny."

"Can't wait for you to meet her next weekend!" Sunny intones, then, "She's only coming to see what she paid for."

"What do you mean by reactionary?"

"My little sister died," she says.

Julia stills. "Oh, God."

"I was five," Sunny says, that childlike tendency to orient oneself by proximity to an event rather than—who can blame her?— acknowledging the salient existence of the event itself. "She was two years younger. Leukemia."

"God," Julia says again.

"She couldn't pronounce my name. My mom used to call me *Bunny,* so Naomi started calling me *Sunny,* and it—I don't know— stuck. My parents started calling me that, too, when she got sick, I guess because I was super positive as a kid, but, like, how else was I supposed to be when everyone else was completely devastated? It's— Like, every shrink I've talked to says it's insane that they kept calling me that. They couldn't keep it together after she died, not surprisingly. My dad went a little—crazy. He's sort of a— Like, I love him, he's a good person, but he has a cabin way out in the middle of nowhere and he does IT stuff online and he pretty much never leaves his house. My mom had two new daughters with the guy she remarried and she became this— He has a lot of money, and it seems like she just kind of became obsessed with that, with controlling everything that way."

"That has to have been so hard," Julia says inadequately.

"It's behind me," Sunny says, shrugging, and Julia recognizes, for just a second, a hint of the lonely defiance she'd had in her twenties, the depressed person with the whispering roommates, insistent that she didn't need anything. "And I was— I mean, it's textbook, when you lose a child, for the remaining one to either be totally adored or resented for surviving. It's pretty obvious which one she chose. Anyway, I'm sorry in advance, for whatever she does when she's here. She and my stepdad aren't exactly—like, a joy to be around."

"I haven't been getting very high marks in that area either lately," says Julia after a minute. "I'm sorry about that, Sunny."

She sees the apology register on Sunny's face, sees her second-guess it for a beat before saying, "That's okay."

"It hasn't been—intentional."

"It's okay," Sunny says again. "Ben told me you had it—sort of rough growing up too."

It catches her off guard. "Well," she says. "I did, I guess, but that isn't an excuse for—"

But then a woman enters the boutique with a stroller and suddenly Sunny straightens to attention like she's just caught wind of a gas leak, watching openly as the woman sifts through a rack of blouses, idly rocking the stroller back and forth. She moves nearer, inspecting a row of sundresses, and the baby—microscopic, swaddled—comes into view. It's young, maybe a month, still inchoate and smashed-looking. Now that it's all behind her, now that her own babies are taller than she is and have no trouble taking her petty cash and enumerating her flaws, Julia understands the fairy-tale villain impulse to consume the babies of other people; she would like nothing more than to take this little invertebrate in her arms and smell its neck.

The woman sees them looking and she and Julia exchange polite smiles.

"How old?" Sunny asks.

"Six weeks," the woman says.

"Hi," Sunny coos, leaning over the stroller. "Hi, baby."

Julia is surprised to recognize in Sunny, too, the same kind of ineptitude she used to feel when interacting with children, misplaced enthusiasm and overarched eyebrows. She'd assumed Sunny would—like all other women, it seemed—possess that baby gene, or at least that she—being a *planner*—would have already taken some sort of course on socializing with the just-born.

"She's super cute," Sunny says. "Or—he, sorry, I—"

The woman smiles at her, too. "She's a girl. Lily."

"Lily was on our list of girl names for a while," Sunny says when the woman retreats, sinking back into the couch, chewing thoughtfully on her nail. She lowers her voice. "But I decided it was too basic."

"I thought you were sure it's a boy."

"Ben is," Sunny says, her gaze fixed indeterminately across the room. "Can I say something?"

"Sure."

"I really have *no* experience with babies. I was in middle school when my half sisters were born, and I really wasn't interested in them. And now, obviously, I'm the first one of my friends to be doing this. So I literally know . . . nothing."

"I didn't either, before Ben was born," Julia says.

"I just don't— I mean, people who say they *love babies*, do they mean—all babies? That just seems really weird to me."

"I've never understood it either."

Now Sunny looks over at her.

"When people say they *love kids*. It just seems so sweeping to me, and arbitrary. Like saying you *love adults*. Who loves all adults? I hate *most* adults."

"Exactly," Sunny says. "And some kids are horrible. My half sisters are *horrible*." She puts her thumb in her mouth; Julia fights the urge to swat it away. "I know I'm not allowed to say things like that."

"Sure you are," Julia says, thinking of Helen Russo, how refreshing she'd found the woman's outright rejection of conversational pretense.

"I'll love this baby, of course," Sunny says again, frowning over at a hat rack, and puts the hand that's not in her mouth on her stomach.

"You will," Julia says, and Helen is still on her mind when she adds, "But don't be worried, Sunny, if it doesn't—feel how you think it's going to."

"What do you mean?"

"I just mean that— I wish someone had said to me that there isn't— There's not a right *way* for things to look. Or for you to feel. It's okay if you—I don't know—if you don't think you're feeling how everyone else around you seems to be feeling. Or how you're expected to feel."

"Did you not feel—the right things?"

"I wasn't— I had this expectation that I was just going to be flooded with something transcendent and incredible the second I saw them, and I—wasn't. I had to—take a kind of inventory, I guess. And that made me feel wildly inadequate, that I wasn't just instantly over the moon like it seemed like everyone else was." She hasn't, she realized, said this aloud in nearly twenty years, not since she admitted it to Helen Russo. "But that's okay. It turns out okay. Of course I love my kids. And I did *fall* in love with both of them, crazily. It just didn't happen instantaneously."

She feels Sunny's eyes on her still, and she can't tell what she has just done, if she's transgressed by saying what she has, or hit the nail on the head, or achieved nothing at all, just a little bit of crackpot warbling on a fainting couch before the woman her son is marrying.

"I had—a hard time," she says. "When Ben was little." Perhaps Sunny knows this already. Sunny knows about the day she left him; perhaps she knows everything. Of course she has wondered— a fearful curiosity that borders on obsessive—about the extent of what Ben has shared with her, and the tone in which he's shared it, and whether or not her surrounding lore has become a point of bonding for him and Sunny, as tales of Anita had become for Mark and Julia. That unique skewed omniscience that comes with falling in love with another person, a crowded file room of every feeling they've ever felt, everything they've submitted for the record, mis-remembered or otherwise. She asks, with deliberate mildness, "Has he told you that?"

Sunny seems to be weighing out her answer. "He told me you two were close. Really close. When he was a kid."

A tug in her stomach. "We were. Claustrophobically, sometimes, I think."

"Yeah, I—" Sunny hesitates. "Well— I mean, he didn't say this, but I kind of wondered, based on how he was talking, if maybe he felt sort of responsible for you."

Before she can reply—what is there to say to that?—Sunny scrambles to continue.

"I think it caught my attention because that's how I always felt. Maybe I was projecting."

"No," Julia says, after a moment. "No, I think that's probably— somewhat accurate. Kids are perceptive. They pick up on—God— much more than I realized." Children, for all their selfish myopathy, were excellent at seeing through insincerity, could usually tell when someone was faking it; Ben had always had incredible radar for adult malaise. "I think I knew to temper myself better by the time Alma came around, but with Ben I was still—learning. And I was terrified to be away from him, so I almost never was."

"When did that stop?"

"It did eventually. It was a matter of—striking the right balance, I guess. And with Ben that's always been a little bit harder because he's so— Well, you know him. Better than I do now, I'm sure." It hurts her to say it. "It can be hard to tell when he needs help, or when you're overburdening him. Or it's always been hard for me to tell. He always seems so *happy*."

They are a family with a capacity for forgetting, or at least pretending to forget; they are a family with an inherited lineage of willful blindness.

"It drives me nuts sometimes," Sunny says. "That side of him. Especially lately. He's convinced everything is going to be completely fine, but he refuses to acknowledge that we have to *make* it fine, that weddings don't plan themselves and people—and *babies*—

are going to show up *expecting* things and you can't just—like, bury yourself in your dissertation and expect that when you surface everything's going to have been taken care of for you."

Julia is not clear on what the rules are in this situation, whose side she is supposed to be on or if she is supposed to, as a sage mother figure, be discouraging sides altogether.

"For the record," Sunny says, "I *know* a lot of this wedding stuff is ridiculous, but Ben's just— He doesn't realize what it takes to get from point A to point B. His attention to detail for stuff like this is nonexistent. You can talk to him for like six hours and he'll just glom on to one or two specific words and run with those. Do you know what I'm talking about? When he's focused on something, he doesn't notice anything but the thing he's focusing on. Did he get that from Mark?" she asks, then darkens. "Or—sorry, maybe it's you who's like that."

"I have the attention to detail of a homicide detective," she says. "Or a serial killer, as Mark sometimes says. Ben gets it from his dad." She has always found the trait more forgivable in her son than in her husband, because she isn't sure how much of Ben's head-down buoyancy formed out of necessity to combat the darkness she'd brought to his childhood. Self-soothing, like the monkeys with the cloth dolls, her boy in the backseat. "It's a kind of willed optimism, I think. Which can look a lot like—well, delusion."

"I'm sorry it was hard for you," Sunny says. "When he was little."

"Oh." She shifts, surprised. "Well—thanks, Sunny. I hope I didn't worry you."

"No, no, no, you didn't," Sunny insists. A verve has returned to her voice, energy that's unmistakably felicitous. "I'm *excited* about it, most of the time. This is the first time in my life where I feel like I'm actually doing exactly what I'm meant to be doing with the person I'm meant to be doing it with. I'm *happy* in a way that makes me feel—I don't know, sad for the person I was before. Does that sound insane?"

"No," she says, and she is thinking of her first months with Mark, the unrecognizable joy of them tinged just slightly with resentment that she hadn't previously known joy like that was available to people like her. "No, it does not."

"All right." The tailor is suddenly summoning them from the fitting area. "I'm ready for you."

Sunny rises from the love seat, lifting her binder to her hip like a baby.

"Are you Mom?"

Julia doesn't realize until she sees the woman staring at her that she is being spoken to. "Oh," she says. "No, no." She sees just a flash, *something* on Sunny's face, but it disappears before she can place it.

The seamstress seems unconcerned, directs her attention back to Sunny. "Have you decided on your lingerie for the day of?"

"I'm wearing it," Sunny says, smoothly all business, wiping her bloodied thumb on the inside of her jeans pocket. "I also brought my shoes."

"Marvelous," the woman says, and it hits her suddenly, Sunny's expression, and she stands up, takes a few steps toward them.

"I could be—mom-adjacent," she says, "in case you need me for anything." It was one of the reasons Helen meant so much to her—a person telling her, simply, whether she needed them or not, *I'm around*. Sunny looks to her with gratitude, and she recognizes this too. Sunny is not the gimlet-eyed nomad she herself had been with Helen Russo; Sunny is not Julia; Sunny has a *binder*. But what had been there, on her face, for just a split second is a feeling Julia knows well: panic, that out-to-sea desperation that flares up on occasion when you've fended for yourself for too long.

"Marvelous," the woman says again, clearly indifferent. "You can hold up her skirt."

The phone rings on her way home that evening, sudden surround sound: a number that she realizes she recognizes.

"Mom?"

There's static on the other end.

"Mom?" she says again.

"What?" Anita's voice is short, irritable, as though Julia's interrupted something.

"Are you—"

"Can you not hear me?"

She feels, for a moment, strangely nostalgic; her mother has always treated shoddy telephonic connections as personal failures and, too, abides by the faulty logic that yelling at a person with bad service will make any difference whatsoever.

"Just a minute," Anita says. There's a protracted scuffle, then a thump, then clear air. "How about now?"

She palms the steering wheel with both hands, exhales. "Now's good."

There's another long silence, so long she almost checks again to see if Anita's still there. It has always been the silences in their conversations that made her the saddest, their inability to fill in spaces like normal people, even if just with banalities.

Then her mother says, as though it has just occurred to her to ask: "How are you?"

"I'm fine," she says.

"Well, good," Anita says. And then, again, as though she's reading from a not particularly helpful phrasebook: "Have I caught you at a bad time? Listen, I won't keep you. I just wanted to— I wondered if it was too late to change my mind about the wedding."

"Change your mind."

"I just was wondering if the offer still stood. I know it's short notice."

"It— No, sure. Sure it still stands."

"And that offer has been—sanctioned? By the powers that be?"

"If you mean me, Mom, I've already told you you're more than welcome." *More than welcome*, it occurs to her, rings as far less welcoming than a simple *welcome*, but she doesn't make any moves to sound more convivial.

"I got tickets," Anita says. "Getting in Friday morning."

She can't think of what to say. "Midway or O'Hare?"

"O'Hare. Arriving at . . . eleven-seventeen."

"Would you like me to pick you up?" She asks it before she realizes that she's asked it.

"I— Well, sure, that would be nice, so long as you're not—"

"No, it's fine; I've got time."

"Thank you," her mother says formally.

Perhaps it's because she's just left Sunny, because she is high on the nearby fumes of successful familial accord, that she asks, "Do you have somewhere to stay?"

"I figured I'd just find a Holiday Inn by the airport." This, too, feels familiar, a familiar unwillingness to ask for help while making blatantly clear that help is desired.

"You could—stay with us, if you'd like."

Her mother is quiet for a minute. "I think you'd better ask Mark."

"I don't have to ask Mark," she says, though normally she would extend him this courtesy; the childish impulse to defy her mother is too strong.

"So the moratorium's been lifted?" Anita says archly.

"I'm not sure what you're talking about."

"I'd just like it repeated for the record," Anita says. "It's okay with you?"

"*What* record? Yes, it's fine with me."

"Because I can easily stay in a hotel. I don't *need* to stay with you."

"You can do whatever you want," Julia says. "But the guest room will be ready, should you choose to use it."

"Fine."

"Ben will be happy to hear you're coming."

"Well."

"Should you—send me your flight info? Do you text?"

"Yes, Julia, I *text*, for Christ's sake; I'm not a thousand years old."

"All right," she says. "Text it to me, then. And I'll see you Friday."

"Fine," says her mom. "See you then."

38

New parenthood was effluvia, and also the awareness of precisely how much fresh air there was to be inhaled at any given time. The three of them spent almost every waking second together, breathing in each other's breath, sharing the humid warmth of unwashed sheets. She and Mark felt like strangers, but also closer than they'd ever been, one feral, many-limbed cloud of halitosis and passive aggression. And between them, the baby—he was always *the baby*, or, occasionally and kind of hilariously, *Ben*, a name that still seemed too adult for him. Nicknames didn't come easily to Julia; she found herself calling him nonsense words, *Squirrel* and *Pinwheel* and *Applesauce*, some adorable wartime alphabet code. He filled all the spaces in the house, in her head; he was, impressively, everywhere.

And so was Mark, on generous AllAboard paternity leave and ceaselessly in the apartment but for grocery runs and his sleepy jogs around the neighborhood. Julia almost never left, on just a few rare occasions when she thought she might murder Mark and fabricated silly, hostile errands to run—"We're out of *Greek yogurt* again!"; "These library books are *almost overdue!*" But even during those errands she rushed, because being by herself made her anxious now; she'd spent two months in her apartment with her husband and her baby, and though she'd ceased being able to really *see* them, they were a comfort to her. A comfort, perhaps, in the way that shed-relegated kidnapping victims befriended pillows and dead leaves, but comforting nonetheless. His parents had come to town for a week after they'd gotten home from the hospital; they had intermittent visitors bearing tiny pairs of socks and ambiguous casseroles. She'd sent a small envelope of photos to her mother that she hoped wouldn't come back undeliverable. Otherwise it was just them, their little family, and there was something nice about it, even though it also kind of felt like they lived in a bunker. Time moved differently when you had a newborn, weeks of minutes, hours and hours and hours of yesterdays and tomorrows.

One evening she and Mark took Ben to Loyola Beach for a walk, Mark wearing the baby carrier on his front and both of them barefoot, holding their shoes, though the water, in late March, was still freezing. Mark had started work again and she was due back at Harold Washington next month, a time that seemed either very short or very long depending on her mood. There were many days she couldn't wait to get back—to adult conversation, to clothes that weren't crusted with spit-up, even to the familiar fresh-pee smell of the CTA, but then she would look over at Ben—his head, now, bobbing against his father's chest, his eyes drooping closed—and feel like she might die if she ever stopped looking at him. There were still periods of real joy then that popped up like gophers from the ground, moments when she looked down at Ben and fell in love with the world on his behalf, for all it had to offer him. It seemed like a trick, but she was too nervous to investigate it, because she had historically discovered that the more closely you looked at things, the more you found them wanting.

She felt sometimes like she'd gotten away with something by accident, slipped through, a bomb onto an airplane. It had been scary, before he was born, to think of babies with terrible afflictions, to consider all possible, horrible pitfalls—babies who never slept, babies who always cried, babies with murky, lurking darknesses just waiting to boil over. But instead she got a lovely, easy baby, possibly the best baby in the history of babies, she posited privately; she loved him so expansively, so unhingedly that she wondered sometimes if there was something wrong with her, because surely it wasn't healthy to care this much about another person, surely she couldn't be doing him any favors by being so obsessed with him. But she couldn't help it, and because her love for him was coupled with a considerable lack of instincts as far as his care, she committed herself fully to his proximity, singing to him dementedly— *a shady lane everybody wants one*—and holding him whenever she was not holding something else and sometimes then too; she developed an aptitude for multitasking, for doing nearly everything in her life with the companionship of her son. She felt sure she was supposed to be innately anticipating his needs in a way that wasn't coming to her naturally, so she spent all her time in a slingshot state, primed, crouching, prepared for the worst, though it never came; he remained easygoing and unperturbed, wide-eyed and pacific, gazing up at her with a kind of serenity that sometimes resembled resignation; she worried in these moments that she had inadvertently orchestrated a kind of hostage situation, a baby who knew how anxious his mom was and who, as a result, went against all of his own instincts to ensure she wouldn't completely lose her mind.

"It's okay" was the sentence she said to Ben most frequently, murmured incantation, *it's okay it's okay it's okay*, as much to herself as to him; sometimes when he was sleeping and she was alone in the house she'd say it, too, like how she'd taken to swaying her hips even when he wasn't in her arms.

Mark put his free arm lightly around her waist, like she was a cat he was trying not to scare away; they were slowly learning how to touch each other again, trying to be mindful of diverting some of their affection for the baby toward each other. She leaned a little awkwardly into him.

"Look out," he said, steering them around some broken glass. They stopped at a bench to put their shoes back on, and as they walked down Estes toward home, he took her hand. She squeezed his hand, studied him as they waited to cross the street at Ashland. He looked like himself, the Mark she'd met three years ago, walking her to work, but now he was reaching to pull the collar of their baby's jacket higher around his tiny neck.

He caught her looking and smiled at her. "What?"

"Nothing," she said.

A block later they were chatting amiably about the stray cat in the neighborhood who didn't have a tail but somehow maintained remarkable equilibrium when a woman came into view on the front steps of their building.

"Oh," Julia said, stopping in the middle of the sidewalk, still half a block away.

"Do you see him?" Mark asked, looking around for the cat, and all she could do was shake her head, though he wasn't looking at her, and keep walking, because they were still holding hands. "Who's that?" he said softly, noticing the woman on the stairs, who was suddenly standing, lifting a hand to wave.

"I thought maybe you were just ignoring the bell," Anita said.

"Is that—?" Mark asked, and she nodded.

"Don't worry, I can't stay long," Anita said like some ghostly prophecy, patting the bag beside her. "Just passing through."

"What are you—*doing* here?"

Her mother appraised her for a long moment. "Heading back to Columbus for a few days to sort some things out," she said. "Would you believe I haven't been here in over ten years?"

She did not say that she would in fact believe that; she did not betray any of the surprise she felt witnessing her mother traveling solo, her mother, who had never traveled anywhere until Julia left home. Her bag was a garish nylon color-block duffel, like something a child might pack when pretending to run away.

"Are you going to introduce me to everyone?" Anita asked.

"Sorry," Julia said. "I— Mark, my mom. Mom, my— Mark."

Mark let go of Julia's hand to offer his to Anita. "It's great to finally meet you," he said.

"Yes," her mother said, openly appraising him as Julia had just been doing, a block ago, three minutes ago, when everything felt normal.

Her mother was here. On her front steps, shaking hands with her husband.

"This is Ben," Mark said, indicating the baby, and Julia saw a flicker of irritation cross her mother's face.

"Yes," she said again, looking Mark directly in the eye. "I figured."

"We were on a walk," Julia said, like they all had something to be sorry for.

"Have you been here long?" Mark asked.

But Anita had turned her attention to Julia. "Either that's a deceptively flattering sweater," she said, "or you actually look pretty good."

It was a high compliment coming from her mother, especially

because she objectively—puffily postpartum and unshowered, sallow and blotchy and vacant-eyed, her hair inadvertently parted in the middle like Iggy Pop's—looked like someone who'd been lured successfully into a hard-core cult. She felt pinioned beneath her mother's gaze, a smarting mix of pride and embarrassment swirling somewhere under her breastbone, proud to be told that she *actually looked pretty good*, proud that she'd done this well for herself. And embarrassment for her body, which had recently produced a child; her body, which wouldn't exist were it not for her mother, whose own body had gone through the same things to produce Julia herself. Her body, which undoubtedly looked different to her mother, who hadn't seen it in years but who knew it better than most by virtue of the fact that she'd created it, lived under the same roof as it for nearly two decades.

"You too," she said, though her mother did not look particularly good either, in fact; she'd gained weight around her middle and in her face and the circles under her eyes looked carved out, the eyes themselves ringed with pink. "You should have called," she said. "If I knew you were coming I'd have—"

"Baked a cake?" Anita trilled, and then laughed in a way that seemed to make everyone nervous. Against Mark's chest, Ben began to fuss.

"I would have known, that's all," Julia said.

"It was last-minute," Anita said. "My bus leaves early tomorrow."

"Why are you going to Columbus?" Julia asked, as Mark was asking, "Where are you staying tonight?"

She looked over at him sharply. Registering this, Anita smirked.

"Ron died," she said. "I'm picking up some things he left me."

"Who's *Ron?*"

Her mother regarded her flatly. "The man I was living with there for three years, Julia, for Christ's sake."

"It's not like I ever met him," she said, hating the petulance in her voice, and seeing Mark hear it as well. "It's not like that name *means* anything to me."

"Well, it means something to me," Anita said.

Ben's fussing escalated to a low whine, and Julia reached for him, held him around his tiny waist and motioned for Mark to undo his straps. She lifted him to her and he pushed his little face insistently against her chest, rooting around.

"Shh," she said, and guiltily slipped a pinkie into his mouth. "I'm sorry," she said effortfully to her mother, calling upon the reservoir of magnanimity that opened every time she looked at Ben. Motherhood seemed to be making her gentler, or perhaps just too tired to hold her grudges very tight. With the baby in her arms her heart rate slowed; she pressed her nose to his head. "I'm sorry about—Ron."

"It happens."

"What did he leave you?"

"His car, primarily. Piece of shit, but it's better than nothing."

"You don't have a car?"

"I do now."

"You're driving back to Colorado?"

"If it'll make it that far."

"What kind of car?" She seemed incapable of asking anything beyond logistics, as though she could fill whatever void had just opened up inside of her with the mundanities of her mother's travels.

"You know me and cars," Anita said. Julia did, had witnessed her mother, on several occasions, attempting to get into the wrong car in a parking lot, convinced it was theirs.

"Is it—safe?"

"Have you started working for the Department of Transportation?"

"I was just asking."

"Not your problem," Anita said.

Julia bounced the baby in her arms, and Anita watched her.

"I was about to make dinner," Mark said, and Julia startled a little; she'd nearly forgotten he was there. "Why don't you join us?"

"Oh." She emitted the syllable without meaning to. Her mother looked at her and she looked down, at the baby, who was getting fussier, his face rubbing against her breast.

"What are you making?" Anita asked.

Mark, suddenly under the hot lights of her appraisal, reddened a little. "Well," he said. "Probably just some kind of pasta. Nothing fancy, but almost definitely edible. You should come in; we'll show you the apartment. It's sort of a mess, but as long as you don't mind clutter, we'd love for you to see it. And you can hold Ben once he— Well, we call him the Accountant, because he's so adamant about his routines, and also he makes this face when he's hungry where he looks *exactly* like my grandfather, who wasn't actually an accountant; he was a shoe salesman so I'm not exactly sure how we came up with . . . Do you remember, Jules?"

What sounded to Julia like overcompensation was in fact just who Mark was; he was playing by the only rules he knew, rules reliant on the expectation that parents cared where their children were living, wanted to hold their grandbabies and know the origins of their nicknames, rules that expected a certain amount of reciprocity and were built on the salient foundation of love itself. He wasn't aware that she and her mother were playing an entirely different game, one whose rules had never been written down and had also been known to change at will.

"I don't remember," she said. Ben began to cry and she boosted him up in her arms, her lips near the top of his head. "Sh-sh-sh," she hushed, but Ben flailed, pushing his wet little face into her neck, and she felt the tingling as her milk began to let down.

"You're welcome to stay over, even, if you want," Mark said. "The couch is pretty comfortable, or there's a futon in the nursery if you don't object to sleeping with—well, an accountant." He put a hand on Ben's back, trying to calm him down.

Julia imagined her son in a dark room, waking up with Anita sleeping beside him. She wasn't sure what it would mean to invite her mother into her house, whether or not it was against the rules of their current game and whether or not she cared, whether she wanted her mother in her house or whether her mother wanted to come in. When Mark's parents had come after Ben was born, Bonnie had so insistently complimented Julia's choice of bath mat that after a while Julia had started to feel genuinely proud of herself for picking it out. She imagined showing her mother around, Anita growing more and more underwhelmed with every step she took, snipping efficiently at the roots of Julia's pride, her enthusiasm, her

ownership of the life she'd arranged for herself. She imagined going
on, business as usual, after her mother had left the apartment, her
tobacco smell on the sheets and her hair in the drain, and she felt,
for a shameful second, sickened.

"I need to feed him," she said, and her mother stared at her;
Julia could feel her gaze again but she avoided it adamantly, and she
knew her mother knew what that meant.

"I'm staying with a friend," Anita said after a minute, and Julia
could hear the lie in her voice; it seemed likely that she *had* come
hoping to stay with them, and Julia wasn't sure what her nixing the
prospect meant for that plan, if she'd instead be forced to sleep at
the bus station.

"Could I drive you somewhere?" Mark asked, as though perhaps
he was thinking the same thing. She felt a tug of love for him, his
midwestern acuity.

"Wait," she said. "It's—fine. You can stay."

She predicted something snarky from her mother, *better get the
wheels checked on that welcome wagon*, but the quiet that followed was
even worse.

"No," Anita said, studying her. "I can't." She bent over her duffel and pulled out a crumpled yellow gift bag. "Here," she said, and
attempted to hand it to Julia, but Julia—feeling the beginnings of
desperation creep in, the same sensation she'd felt when she was
seventeen, after everything had happened—couldn't bring herself
to take it, so Mark interceded clumsily.

"Thank you," he said.

"Your wife forgot her manners," Anita said, and it was such a stupid, petty, *mean* thing to say that Julia felt—for the first time since
Ben's arrival, cocooned as she'd been in the muted miasma of new
motherhood—fury surge through her.

"Wait," she said. "Are you serious? Are you fucking *kidding* me?"

"Jules." Mark touched her back, his calm that grounded her and
drove her nuts. Her milk began to leak through her bra, bleeding a
dark wet amoeba onto the fabric of her T-shirt.

"You're seriously just going to drop off this—whatever this is and
say something like *that* and then just—leave?" The familiar indig-

nation, the fact that her mother saw fit to come breezing in for just long enough to let it register how long she'd been gone, and the fresh emptiness she'd leave in her wake.

"It's a stuffed giraffe," Anita said, sedate and sage, like a fucking swami. "You're leaking."

"I *know* that," Julia said. She watched her mother shoulder her ridiculous bag. "Mom," she said, and she hated how her voice sounded, shrill as her infant son's. "Mom, please; *really?*"

"You may want to lay off the pasta," Anita said, and she nodded at Julia's midsection. "It took me forever to lose the weight I gained with you."

"Please," Mark said. "Why don't we—"

"I'll see you," Anita said, ignoring him entirely. She leaned in, then, and kissed the baby's cheek; Julia smelled her same familiar breath, smoky and sharp, marveled at the gesture, at their closeness. Ben wailed, flailed, but Anita came in closer and slipped an arm around Julia's waist. She could not remember the last time her mother had hugged her, and she couldn't hug her back, holding the baby as she was. "Take care of yourself, Julia," Anita said, and then she was off at an impressive clip down Paulina toward Touhy, the hunch of her shoulders unreadable.

Mark stood watching her, but Julia brushed past him to the front door, fumbling with her keys.

"I'm sorry," she said to the baby as she hustled him up the stairs, both of them crying now. "Sorry, sorry, sorry, I'm sorry."

In the apartment, she closed herself into his room, began to nurse him before she even sat down. You were supposed to be calm when your baby was feeding; all the books talked about it. She settled into the chair and allowed herself a few ragged breaths, slowing her pulse. She pushed the sleeve of her shirt hard against her eyes until her tears stopped. Mark knocked gently on the door, and her voice was even as she replied, "I'm fine." And then she looked down at Ben, let him fill her entire field of vision, enough to edge out whatever it was that had just happened; and she felt, as she always did, overcome with a sense of calm, looking at him, and also a swell of affection that bordered on pain. Ben regarded her languidly, tired-eyed and trusting, incisive and wise, taking in her face how he did, the way that made her feel like he knew everything that was wrong with her and loved her anyway.

She never wanted her son to look into her eyes and see what she'd just seen in her mother's, that distance, that coldness, that could-have-been-anyone strangeness; she never wanted her son to feel the way she felt at the moment, an itchy, angry aloneness that persisted despite the fact that she was inches from him, a hallway away from Mark, the only two people in the world she'd figured out how to love.

"I won't leave you," she crooned to him. "It's okay, it's okay, it's okay."

She nursed him to sleep, put him in his sailboat pajamas and tucked him into his crib. In the bathroom, she changed her milk-stained shirt, stood in the tub to brush the sand from her feet, sand left over from a half hour ago at the beach, when everything was different. When she came out of the nursery, she smelled basil; Mark met her in the kitchen, pulling her into a hug, and she let him, leaned her weight against him until she was certain she could hold it up herself.

"I'm not sure what to say," Mark said.

"Yeah." She stirred the bow ties in their bubbling water.

"I'm sorry," Mark said, his hands on her shoulders.

"It's okay."

"It's not."

"*It is what it is,*" she intoned, one of their shared hated clichés.

"Jules."

"I don't want to talk about it," she said.

"All right," he said, and she allowed him to lead her to the table and pour her a glass of wine and stand, for a minute, behind her, stroking her hair.

"Maybe I shouldn't go back to work," she said.

His hand, on her head, stilled. "What? Jules—"

"I want to keep staying home."

"You—" She watched him collect himself. "Okay," he said evenly.

"I do," she said defensively.

"I heard you."

"But you think I shouldn't?"

"I didn't say that."

"You emanated it."

"Jules, maybe let's take a little time."

She looked up at him, Mark, who always wanted to understand, though she'd proven thus far to not be very good at explaining things to him. It seemed like it would be harder to fuck everything up if you were around all the time, but she wasn't sure how to tell him that.

"I want to," she said.

"You don't have to decide now," he said. "We should— Why don't we eat some dinner and then we'll— Let's talk about this, honey." He studied her. "Or not talk about it. Either way, for now, let's just—take a minute."

"I'm not going to change my mind," she said when he brought the pasta to the table.

"Okay," he said.

"I'm not crazy," she said, and his face softened in a way that made her wonder if she was.

"Of course you aren't."

"I just think it might be better," she said. "For everyone."

Mark cracked pepper over her pasta like a waiter, then touched her head again.

"You're nothing like her," he said quietly. "You know that, right?"

"That's not what this is about," she said, though of course it was.

She waited to cry until the next day, a few minutes in the laundry room when Mark was at work and the baby was napping; she cried for a number of reasons, but especially for the fact that when she'd called the station earlier, she was told there were no early morning buses to Columbus that day.

39

And then Francine Grimes comes home. Her hiatus from Brady has evidently been just that, and they are back, as though nothing has happened, to celebrate Brady's birthday the weekend before the wedding. Julia is stationed at the white marble expanse of the Grimes's kitchen island, where Francine has patronizingly tasked her with cutting the bristled ponytails off a bunch of radishes.

Julia studies her, looking for signs of unrest, but she seems the same as always, a billowy-sleeved eyelet blouse that looks a bit like a baby's christening gown, unmoving blond hair, dewy blush on her cheeks, and the annoying fact that all the details amount to something fetching. She has never seen the woman look anything but collected, never once gotten the impression that Francine Grimes does not have her shit together.

"So is everything—okay?" Julia asks carefully, and Francine smiles at her like a saint.

"It is. Getting there, at least. Glad to have a nice evening to unwind with friends."

It sounds like the caption of a photo she imagines Francine posting online.

"I feel unbelievably silly," Francine says then. "That it became this— God, we've agreed to move on from it but I'm mortified that Brady went running to Mark like he did. I hope it didn't— I know you have enough on your plate as is; I didn't intend to let our— whatever it is; we're working through it, I didn't mean for it to get in the way of what you guys have going on."

Julia wonders, dimly, what this means.

"We're looking forward to the wedding," Francine adds.

"Oh. Yes, we are too." She does not specify that at this point what she's really looking forward to is the wedding being *over*.

"I spent a few days with Lila recently," Francine says. "I don't think she's at all interested in marriage."

"Oh?" Francine, to her credit, has never been one of those moms who hands out her children's CVs at the start of every party, but also talk of the Grimes children has lessened significantly since the girls forayed, despite their parents' egregious wealth, into—from what Julia can tell—perfectly mediocre adulthoods, decent schools and fleeting interests and the same fumbling indecision as everyone else.

"She reminds me a little of you, actually," Francine says, and though her voice is chipper it's unclear whether or not the recall is favorable. "She's—alternative. Very don't-care, very cool; every time I went anywhere with her I felt like—well, someone's matronly old mother. We took the subway to dinner one night and I thought she'd die of embarrassment having me next to her in public."

Julia hitches for a second on the unlikely and enjoyable visual of Francine riding public transit, then says, "Ollie used to lie down in the back of the station wagon sometimes when I was driving her to school. Lest anyone witness the indignity of her beside me."

"Well, that's different," Francine says dismissively. "I mean Lila has this— She's twenty-six; this isn't teenage embarrassment, it's a kind of—I'm not sure. *Steeliness*. Like she figured it all out a long time ago and the rest of us are hopeless."

"Yeah." Julia lifts her wineglass. "Daughters are—skilled in that area."

"I felt that way when I met you, too," Francine says, seeming not to have heard her, her head in the fridge. She emerges with an arm-load of produce. "It was like you'd lived more than everyone else. Intimidatingly self-possessed. Could you start destringing these for me?" She drops a bag of snap peas in front of Julia and moves to her own station across the island with a bushel of kale. "You probably don't remember the night we met," she continues, "but I was pregnant with the girls and nothing fit me but these hideous maternity dresses my mother had sent me and you came stomping in in your combat boots and this sexy little— It looked like a *nightie*, and

Brady just about fainted over you; you were matching him drink for drink and he was so jealous because you and Mark had just gone to see some band I'd never even heard of and you just had this—*air* about you, that cool-girl air. Neither of the boys could take their eyes off you the whole night."

"They were motorcycle boots, actually," she says, uncomfortable, trying to joke, dutifully destringing her peas. "I wasn't nearly cool enough for combat boots."

Francine studies her for a moment, rolling the stem of her wineglass delicately between her fingers. "Mark hadn't dated much before you. We'd never seen him so excited about someone. And then you showed up and you were so different from what I was expecting, but I think it was more that— It was so clear to me that *we* weren't what you'd been expecting either; you didn't even try to pretend that we were." Francine tears kale into a salad spinner. "I cried after you left," she says, not looking up. "I just felt so oversize and silly and—small, at the same time."

"Oh, God, Francine."

"You didn't do anything wrong," Francine says. "You just didn't seem to care at all about the house or the babies or—well, any of the things that I cared about. After two *hours* with you I was suddenly second-guessing every decision I'd made, even though I'd put a lot of thought into making them, even though I was *happy* with them."

"I didn't—mean to do that. To make you feel like that."

Francine meets her eyes. "I know that, Julia. It was a hundred years ago. We weren't that much older than my girls are now; isn't that unreal? And I think I'd rather Lila be like you back then, rather than like me back then. Less rigid, more fearless."

"Mark and I almost broke up on the ride home that night."

Francine looks up at her with what appears to be genuine surprise.

"Mark cared about those things," she says. "The things you had, the things you were doing. And I—wanted to care about them, I guess. Or I felt like I was *supposed* to care about them, but I couldn't even seem to go through the motions. Nobody ever really taught me the rules. You seemed to know them innately. I was intimidated by you, actually."

It isn't quite true, not exactly. She hadn't been intimidated by the house, or the trappings of adulthood, but by the blithe, unyielding confidence Brady and Francine emanated. Nothing scared her more than seeing people who knew exactly what they wanted from life and knew how to go about getting it.

"I felt protective of Mark," Francine admits. "Of his—heart, I guess. He's so—not *fragile*, but—sensitive. *Good*. Generous, emotionally. And I could tell how much he liked you; he was over the moon about you. But I couldn't gauge how much you liked him back. Not at first, at least."

"Yeah." Julia smiles weakly. "I couldn't either."

"I was just worried about him getting hurt. We'd always looked out for each other. But then. Well. I knew— I mean, after I'd seen you two together enough, I could tell that you—*got* him. And I knew you were good for him."

And here she wants to ask—finally, finally, she wants to ask what she's wanted to ask for years, about that stupid, stupid playdate, what exactly Francine had seen, and what she'd made of what she saw, how it had changed her opinion of Julia. Whether it had remained between them as promised, whether it had anything to do with her recommending her therapist friend to Mark. She wants to ask, from this safe distance of nearly twenty years, if Francine had told Mark about Nathaniel Russo.

But Francine goes on before she can ask. "I wanted to thank you, too," she says. "For being so—understanding about— Well. All of it. I love my husband, but there are just certain things that— Either you've talked them to death, or you've *never* talked about them, so there's no context. We develop these languages, don't we? And there are certain times that we just lack the vocabulary. It seemed like I'd run out of ways to make Brady hear me. But Mark helped me to make sense of my own head. It's so much easier to run away from things than it is to try and fix them, but if you can fix them— ultimately you come out stronger, right? You must. You two did."

It takes her a moment to register this, and even when she does register it she doesn't fully comprehend it: she has been wondering about the wrong things. And this, she supposes, is what it feels like to reel; this moment, now, peeling stems from peas and watching them curl into efficient springs, is her real comeuppance, a tenth, perhaps, of how Mark must have felt the day she called him from the gas station, which is, of course, what Francine is referring to, the day she'd almost ended everything, the day she's thought, all this time, had remained between her and her husband.

She has been so worried about whether Francine said anything to Mark that it hadn't occurred to her that Francine didn't have to say anything. That Mark had gone to her.

Francine seems to register Julia's surprise. "Oh," she says. "I didn't mean—"

"He told you? What happened between us?"

Francine looks sort of pained. "Well," she says. "He just needed a sounding board, Julia."

This is, of course, the problem with transgressing as far as she had with Nathaniel Russo: she is not allowed to be feeling what she's feeling at the moment, white-hot hurt in the pit of her stomach. She deserves this hurt, and yet it nearly takes her breath away. Francine's face is twisted condolingly in a way that makes Julia want to punch her in the mouth.

"We've been able to—be that for each other over the years," Francine says. "Don't you have someone like that?"

"Of course," she says distantly, feeling like she'd felt in grade school, lying to fit in, *Of course I've kissed a boy, Of course I have a dad.* But she doesn't have someone like that, and never did, save for those few months twenty years ago.

"I just wanted you to know," Francine goes on, "that I didn't ask him to come see me at my parents'."

This brings on a specific sickness that she has always associated with betrayal; she has not experienced it since she was seventeen years old, that horrible, smarting betrayal, pitched at the highest level. Her face feels numb, and she's looking in Francine's direction but the only thing in focus is the Marchesi di Barolo sign hanging behind the woman's head.

"Fuck me *sideways*," she'd said to Mark after she first saw it, "if we ever own anything that can be even loosely described as *wine art.*"

And he'd laughed at her joke then; he'd laughed at her story, on the way here tonight, about her colleague who she thinks might secretly be a Scientologist; he has gone along as usual for who knows how long, not telling her that he had *gone to see* Francine Grimes at her parents' house, whatever the fuck that means; there are only, really, a few things that it could mean.

"I kept insisting I was fine," Francine says, as though she hasn't just dropped an anvil on Julia's head, "but I—wasn't. And he could tell, even over the phone. And he was in New York for a meeting— just a train ride away, he kept saying. It was so kind of him. Generous, like always. But I'd never ask him to go so far out of his way like that, Julia."

She feels defenses rising inside of her, neat little pickets that nudge her into compliance, that tell her to make her face neutral, her voice. She lately requires her self-preserving instincts so much less than she used to, but here they are still, ready to help her.

"Sure," she says. "I know."

"I just wanted to make that clear to you."

"Sure," she says again.

"He really helped," Francine says. "I'm not sure I'd— I mean, I'd've come home for the wedding, of course, but I'm not sure I'd be back for good otherwise."

"That's great," Julia says. She wishes Francine hadn't taken away her radish knife. "I'm so glad."

The voices from outside grow closer, louder.

"God!" Francine laughs out a big breath, drying her hands on a towel and taking a sip of wine. "Heavy stuff on an empty stomach, huh?"

The back door whooshes open, blowing in Brady, who deposits a grimy grill spatula in the sink; Mark follows him, holding a platter of swordfish, bottle of Rolling Rock balanced precariously on the edge and an easy smile on his face. Julia watches him for signs she's missed previously, little tells of his betrayal.

"We left yours on an extra minute," he says to her, taking a snap pea from her pile. It's a joke, an old one, from their early days when she was teaching herself how to cook and was constantly, awash in worries about undercooked meat, overcooking everything. She has known him for so long, since before she learned how to do so many of the things required of her to be a person in the world, and yet she doesn't quite recognize him; in this moment he is some alternate-universe version of himself, an evil twin, or someone else entirely.

"Thanks," she says, brightly, because Francine is watching.

"Ominously quiet in here," Brady says affably, like he hadn't, three weeks ago, been drunkenly pontificating to Julia about how things would have been if they'd married each other.

"Just finished up some Messianic chanting," she says, because this is the role she's supposed to play; cynical Julia with her dry sense of humor and her motorcycle boots, the anomalous outlier who's never quite fit but wedged herself in anyway, all those years ago, and is, somehow, still here.

She does not absorb much of what happens during Brady's birthday dinner; it takes her a great deal of effort to sit still. Her face feels hot and numb at once; she doesn't taste her wine, the bitterness of the radishes in the salad or the char at the edge of her swordfish.

"Jules?" Mark says at one point, and she becomes aware of all of them staring at her, glasses lifted, Mark wearing his earth-to-Julia face, smiling like she's just done something incredibly adorable, and she wonders what it would feel like instead to do something totally *insane*, throw a plate at his head or hold one of the lit taper candles to the base of his throat, wreak havoc in this ornate dining room.

"What," she says, unable to put any kind of socially appropriate apology into her voice.

"We're toasting Brady," says Mark. "Anything to add?"

After a minute she says, "To the unending forward march of time," and lifts her own glass. Brady laughs loudly; as Mark and Francine look on in confusion, he clinks his glass against hers.

What's the matter?" Mark asks in the car.

She starts to answer but finds, after hours of forcing herself into sociable submission, that it's difficult; it feels physical, a lassitude in her jaw.

"You went to see her," she says finally, and hates how it feels coming out of her mouth.

"Oh." Mark tenses, then sighs. "Shit. Jules."

"You took a secret trip? To go see Francine? When you were in New York?"

"Hang on," says Mark.

"The Columbia grad students?"

"They're real," he says, like that's the important part. "I actually was meeting with them."

"Before you went to Philadelphia. To see Francine. Without telling me."

"I— Yes, but it's not—"

"How it sounds? How's that? Like you lied to me?"

"I didn't, actually," he says. "I just didn't tell you. There's a difference."

"Why didn't you tell me?"

"It felt—like a betrayal of her confidence."

"*Her* confidence. As opposed to the fact that you took a secret trip to see Francine and she just told me, assuming that you'd *already* told me, which should be a completely safe assumption." Then it dawns on her coolly: "Unless she— Did you ask her not to tell me and she told me?" She's never taken Francine for crafty, but she's apparently been underestimating her all along, so it doesn't seem outside the realm of possibility.

"Of course not. She wouldn't do that. I told her you knew, okay? I lied to her too."

"She's not your wife."

"Believe me, Julia, I'm aware of that."

"What the hell does *that* mean?"

They're stopped at a light. She sees his jaw tense; he's gripping the steering wheel, elbows locked, staring straight ahead, a bluish cast to his face from the streetlamps.

"Brady asked me," she says, "if I ever thought we married the wrong people. Do you ever think about that?"

"When did he ask you that?" His eyes flash in her direction.

"That night he came over after she left. He said he sometimes feels like the four of us should have—I don't know, traded. Or chosen differently from the outset."

"How is that productive thinking?"

"I didn't say it was," she says. "Do you ever wonder, though? Why you didn't marry someone—" *Less like me.* She swallows. "More like Francine?"

He takes a long time to answer, and when he does, his voice is exhausted. "No," he says, and then, before she can take it as a good sign, "because that's a completely frivolous thing to wonder about. I married you."

And I'm so glad I did.

And I've never regretted it.

And look at us now, Jules; look how far we've come.

"Franny needed me," he says.

Of course it hurts.

"All right?" he says. "They both needed me to be there for them, so I did that as best I could." The measurement in his voice is infuriating. "I should have told you. I intended to tell you."

"But you didn't. You kept it a secret from me and I had to find out from Francine."

"Jesus Christ, Julia, it wasn't a *secret.*" He bangs his fist, once, against the steering wheel; she startles. "It's a thing I did that was separate from you. There's a difference. And the only reason I didn't tell you—truly—is because you've been acting so *strange* lately that I wasn't even sure it would register. You're so in your own head and so overwhelmed by everything and so—not like yourself. I was hesitant to pile on something else, okay? Because I thought you might take this the way you're taking it, and frankly I don't have the energy for that."

"I'm sorry if I'm acting *strange.* I'm fucking *sad.* One of our kids is getting married and the other one's moving away. I'm sad about that. And feeling *old.* That doesn't mean I'm some kind of head case. Everything's changing; am I not allowed to have feelings about that?"

"You're allowed to have whatever feelings you want," he says coolly. "Just like always."

And this hurts her more than anything, because it's not how she's ever seen it; she has never, in fact, felt in control of anything, least of all her feelings, and she hates the vantage point she's seeing herself from now, a woman who everyone rearranges themselves around, a woman who makes everything worse. But they are no longer thirty years old; she can no longer demand that he pull over so she can stomp home alone; her life is theirs now.

"Do you even want to know what happened when I went there? We *talked*. That's it. And I had dinner at four-thirty in the afternoon with her ninety-six-year-old mother."

"You're a saint," she says, finding her anger again. "Truly."

"I won't let you turn this into something it isn't."

"She told me you told her what happened. What I did."

She sees on his face that he knows immediately what she is referring to, only reinforcing this new vision she's drawing up of herself, the ruiner of everything.

"When did you," she asks. "Tell her."

"Not long after it happened."

"Does Brady know?"

"I don't think so," he says. "Franny told me she wasn't going to say anything to him."

For some reason this hurts her, too, more than she was expecting.

"I was embarrassed," says Mark. "Okay? I didn't want him to know because I was really fucking embarrassed that it had happened to me. That you'd done that to me. And I was—talked out about it. At the time."

She twists and untwists her hands together in her lap.

"You know what," he says. "I still *am* talked out about it. About all of this."

"We've only been talking about it for a few minutes," she says, though she knows this isn't true, that they've been talking about it for twenty years, for twenty-five, forever; it's possible that they've been here all along, stop-and-go on Lake Shore Drive, trapped together in the car.

"I don't deserve this." His voice is stony. "You know I don't deserve this. Give me some fucking credit, would you?"

"I do give you credit," she says. "I've always given you credit."

"And I've always *deserved* credit, Julia, so let's not act like that's you doing me some big favor. It's the least you can do."

He's not over it. Despite everything that's been said, everything they've agreed not to say; despite their affection for each other, the kindness they've shown each other, the salient fact of all the time that's elapsed, the fact that so much of that time has gone by without either one of them giving it a second thought; despite the dinner parties and the weekends spent making each other laugh while they did tedious projects like cleaning the basement and the nights when they fell asleep together in unflattering pajamas in front of *Frasier* reruns, despite Alma. Despite all of it, her husband is not over what she did to him, and she can't blame him for that, because he's right, he's always deserved credit; there is no amount of credit she can give him, really, that will match what he's given her. How long, she wonders, have they been this fragile?

She'd once feared being close to him but now they don't know how not to be together, even when they want to be apart; this is perhaps different, she sees now, than what she's always mistaken for intimacy; they have spent so much time, now, in the impenetrable haze of intuition and misunderstanding and willful blindness that is a long marriage, that she can't remember what it's like to be anywhere else.

40

Marriage in the aftermath of an affair: she hadn't known it was possible to feel so shitty; she could never have predicted that she could physically hurt because she was so sad, or that her own sadness would be secondary to Mark's. They talked around it, never referring directly to the day in Wisconsin or to anything that preceded it, and that had the effect that she knew Mark had intended: crippling loneliness on her end, the crushing weight of her shame and nowhere to off-load it, a dearth made all the worse by the fact that she'd simultaneously lost her only female friend. She missed Helen fiercely most days, would have loved nothing more than to discuss, over Muscadet, how it felt to be married to someone who sort of hated you.

She and Mark fought sometimes, never about what they actually needed to fight about but as a means, simplistically, of releasing some pressure. It was, she supposed, Mark's way of telling her he wasn't going anywhere, the fact that he still cared enough to pick fights with her about the thermostat. She saw this gesture and raised him sex, began finding her way back to him, and there was an anger in him when they were together that was not altogether unwelcome; she did not brace herself, and she did not have to fake it.

The smeary cumbersome mess of it all, tears and snot: crying during sex, swiping their noses with the backs of their wrists as they yelled at each other across the dining room, wet particles of meanness flying invisibly through the air. She supposed it was better than the alternative, and she supposed, as well, that beggars couldn't be choosers. She and Mark were still together, and Ben—though she *did* brace herself for this, staying up at night reading online forums about children from broken marriages who took to smothering their hamsters or peeing in the potted plants—was not exhibiting any signs of distress. She still had her good things, the skeleton of her good life, and she decided to take Helen's advice and try to embrace it.

Everything happened on a Friday night. Early, relatively, and following what had become for them a normal dinner, sterile and civil, their complete and collective focus placed on Ben. Mark took his time putting him to bed—she heard them, from the kitchen, laughing at Shel Silverstein. She built up her nerve as she listened, as she dried the dinner dishes, as she studied her ashen reflection in the window over the sink. Mark and Ben finished their bedtime routine with an off-key version of "Octopus's Garden," and she felt her heart break a little bit, listening to them singing.

She waited for him to come downstairs, but he didn't, and so she went searching for him and found him in bed already, though it was barely eight-thirty.

"Long week," he said.

"Can I—join you?"

He studied her. "If you want."

It was not quite the welcome she'd hoped for, but it was friendlier, she supposed, than his declaring their bed a free country.

"I was hoping we could talk," she said.

Mark looked at her warily. "Right now?"

"Yeah," she said. Then, less confidently, "If you don't mind."

"Is this going to be a whole thing?" he asked. "Because I don't really have it in me for a whole thing tonight."

"No," she said, beginning to second-guess herself. "Not a whole thing. Or not a— Nothing bad."

He sighed, closed his book.

"Please try to contain your enthusiasm," she said, and she saw the flicker of a smile on his face. "It's a good thing. The thing I have to tell you."

"Okay," he said. "Hit me."

She faced him, crossed her legs beneath her. "I think— Well. I'm not—" She took a breath, took his hands. It was the one thing she had to offer him. "I'm going to go off the Pill."

She had contemplated a variety of reactions, but none of them included Mark recoiling from her, pulling his hands from hers.

"Excuse me?" he said.

She couldn't read his tone. "I thought we should try," she said. "Now or never, right?"

Then he went as far as to get out of bed. "Julia, is this— Are you kidding me?"

She thought of his shell-shocked joy when she'd told him about Ben, on the kitchen floor, his hand on her belly. "Not kidding," she said, and she tried to smile at him. "It seems like it might be a good time," she said, which meant *I'm worried you're going to hate me forever.*

"Jesus Christ," he said.

"Perfect. Just what I was looking for." Her eyes filled hotly with tears.

"No," he said. "For fuck's sake, Julia, *no.* My God, are you *kidding* me?"

"No, I'm not kidding; we've established that I'm not kidding, could you— God, I thought you'd be *happy* about this."

"Did you? Honestly?"

"Of *course* I did; why else do you think I'd suggest it?" *Isn't this how you do things?* she wanted to ask. She'd made a list; she was checking things off: it was how Mark seemed to approach everything, with a plan, weighing logic against odds. Mark wanted another baby. Mark had always wanted another baby. She had not considered that his desire may have expired, been rendered void in the wake of her betrayal.

"What is this, a—consolation prize?"

"That's a horrible thing to say."

"Is it? Do you *want* to have another baby?"

"I'm—" She swallowed. "I'm coming around to the idea."

"You're— Jesus." Mark sat in the window seat, his head in his hands. His voice was hoarse when he spoke again, devoid of energy. "You know what I'm coming around to? The thing I can't get out of my head when I'm trying to fall asleep? That this guy is just out there, nearby. I've been thinking I want to get the hell out of here, out of this house, out of this *town*, because I could run into the guy my wife was fucking at the grocery store and I'd have no idea it was him."

She winced.

"That's where I'm at, Julia. That's as far as I can project into the future; that's as big a move as I can see myself making with you, literally *moving*, because you made it awful here."

"I'm sorry." She didn't know what else to say.

"I know. I know. I *know* you're sorry. God, I know you wish it hadn't happened, and I know you feel fucking terrible, and that makes *me* feel fucking terrible, and then I get mad at you all over again for making me feel that way. What kind of life is that, if we're both miserable all the time?"

"Are you? Miserable all the time?"

He looked at her tiredly. "A lot of the time, lately, yeah."

"Are you saying—that you—"

"I don't want a divorce," he said, and then, before she could feel relief: "I've already invested so much."

"*Jesus.*"

"Of fucking *course* I love you, Julia," he exploded. "This is the problem. That's never been in question. I've done everything I possibly can to show you that; I've done everything I possibly could to be there for you; every single thing I've done I've done for you and Ben and *us*, our family, *that's* how I show you I love you, and I do it constantly, and you still fucking did this to me. So it doesn't *matter* that I love you, and it doesn't matter whether you love me if the *way* you love me allows you to sleep with someone else, all right? So I'm trying to look at this from the only angle that makes sense to me anymore, which is the practical one, and from that vantage point I don't see how it benefits anyone if we split up, unless that's what you want."

"It's not," she said.

"You aren't fundamentally a selfish person," he said. "That's what galls me about this. I don't know how to make sense of it because it's so—unlike you."

"I wasn't myself," she said. "When it was happening."

"And now?"

"I'm not sure," she said. "I'm—more myself than I was, I guess. And I can't— I don't recognize the person that did it."

"What's to stop you from doing it again?"

"I just won't," she said. "You just have to— I'm *asking* you to trust me, even though I know that's going to be hard."

"It's not, though," he said softly, and with such sadness. "That's the other thing that I— I *do* trust you, second nature. Or I did before this."

And she thought, for the first time in a long time, of herself at seventeen, and of the moment she realized that there was such a thing as hurting someone beyond repair.

"Is it ever going to feel, do you think—like it did?"

Mark appraised her, not unkindly. "I'm not sure."

She nodded, looking down at her lap so she didn't have to see the answer on his face. "Do you want it to?"

She was preparing herself for the response she deserved, didn't hear him cross the room again, didn't know he'd moved until she felt him beside her on the bed.

"I do," he said. "Despite—God—all of this. Everything. Yeah, Jules, I do."

His hand in hers, suddenly, the fact of Mark wanting it, wanting her, wanting what they'd so haphazardly built together to remain intact. It hadn't all been horrible; just statistically speaking, it couldn't all be horrible.

She found herself, ludicrously, kind of jackknifing herself into his lap, straddling him, their foreheads nearly touching. "Then why don't we try again," she said quietly, her lips pressed to the hollow of his throat. "Didn't you want to try again?" Now she watched the mechanics of his face—always on display, his inner workings bald and unsubtle.

"What's going to make this time different?" he asked, but she didn't answer, was pulling at the drawstring of his pajama bottoms.

"We are. We can do it over. Let me do it over for you."

"Honey." He covered her hands with his, stopping her. "This can't be a thing you're doing for me."

She was willing herself; she was halfway there. That would be her concession, and Mark's would be to pretend it wasn't a thing she was doing for him. "Mark," she said. "Trust me, please."

And after a moment he kissed her, and after that they began to make over their life, a series of cosmetic changes that they hoped would—God, please, let them—permeate the surface. They moved to a century-old Queen Anne on the unobtrusively named Maple Street in another suburb, and Ben started kindergarten at a program run by aging folk musicians at around the same time Julia started back at work, all of these things cumulating, coalescing, step by step by step until she found herself, for the second time beneath the hypnotic whir of a new ceiling fan, marveling—there she was, Alma, darling girl, extraordinary product of so much bad decision making—over lines on a stick.

PART III

World of Fools

41

S he waits to call Ben and tell him that her mother is coming until she sees that her flight has actually taken off from SFO, the closest she can come to guaranteeing Anita will actually arrive, though there is still the possibility of an eleventh-hour escape from O'Hare.

"No way?" says Ben. He sounds, for a moment, teenaged.

She leans against the kitchen counter, feeling a rare moment of motherly victory. "I hope you won't mind an extra guest at the rehearsal dinner tonight."

"Of course not," Ben says. "It's great; I'm so happy she changed her mind. Did she say why?"

Julia has wondered this as well, what tipped the scales for her mother; the motivation behind her visits has never been clear, but she hopes this time might unfold more smoothly than past incidents, lacking the characteristic element of surprise.

"Or not that it— I guess it doesn't matter; the important thing is that she's coming. Sunny's been on the phone with the florist all morning; this is going to totally make her day."

"Is there a problem with the flowers?" She asks it sans irony, with genuine concern; she has worked with the persnickety florist to dream up what Sunny is calling a *rustic lavender vignette* for the cupcake sideboard and understated peony boutonnieres, and she's actually quite proud of them in addition to having spent an amount on them rivaling college tuition. "What's wrong?"

"I'm not— Sunny, what's—" She hears Sunny's voice in the background, rising and falling, and then Ben comes back. "Something with the centerpieces?"

"The lisianthus?"

"I'm not— I'll let you guys talk about it when we get to the house later. She's back on the phone."

"Tell her we'll sort it out," she says. "Whatever it is."

"Thanks," says Ben, and then, "Mom, listen, I wanted to— Just, I'm sorry if any of this has been hard on you. If there are ways I could have handled it better."

She opens her mouth, finds her throat uncooperative.

"I just wanted to say that. Before—all this stuff that's about to happen."

I am also sorry, she should say, *for absolutely fucking everything*. She should tell him what he means to her, that that's the reason she is the way she is, the reason she does all the things she does, some half-baked back-door bragging defense, *I just love my kids too much!*, but it's true, to a degree. She should enumerate all the times he's saved her without even realizing it, all the times he made her happy when nobody else could; she should tell him how sorry she is for abandoning him at Serenity Smiles that afternoon, and for all the other times she's abandoned him since then whether she was aware of it or not.

"Me too," she says instead of all those things, because it's all she can manage, and because she knows Ben—his father's son—will know what she means.

When she hangs up, Mark is standing in the kitchen doorway.

"Did I just—hear what I think I did?"

They have been, since Brady's birthday last weekend, interacting as needed—brief check-ins about the wedding, about Alma's graduation tickets and registration forms for Herzog, about the new tires for the Subaru—having graduated, apparently, from the silent treatment and passive aggression that characterized the tension of their earliest days to something more mature, or possibly just something that requires less energy, brisk, functional communication, smiles as necessary to save face. She's been waiting for some kind of a return to form, any cooling off at all, but at the end of each day she's surprised anew to realize that Mark seems as upset with her as he had been a week ago. She cannot quite assess whether the needle on her own scale has drifted down at all.

"Were you listening to my conversation?" She does not intend the slight bitchiness in her voice.

He ignores it. "Your mother's coming?"

"Evidently," she says. She's been keeping it from him, too, at first simply because she hadn't had the wherewithal to discuss it with him and then, since Brady's, because she hasn't been sure how to detonate it, whether she should use the news as some kind of ammo or if it might—God, please, let it—reunite them, give them a reason to brush aside what had happened in favor of shared adversity, a common enemy. Anita has historically, upon arrival, trumped whatever else was going on, and she realizes she has been expecting this to happen again, for her mother to sweep in with her mess and her murk and her bad humor and make them realize how lucky they are to have each other.

But that is apparently not the case; Mark's jaw is tense. "Were you going to tell me? Or ask me?"

"*Ask* you."

"It's courtesy, I'd say," Mark says. "At a bare minimum."

"Your standards have become a little hazy to me lately, actually," she says, "as far as *courtesy* goes." It's incredibly childish. She doesn't care; she has just made peace with her son and Mark has robbed her of the opportunity to bask in it, to rearrange her feelings into something resembling *hope* at the prospect of what's ahead of them this weekend, the whole family together plus a few guest stars. "I'm sorry," she says. "Jesus Christ, I was *going* to tell you once I knew for sure. I didn't want to get Ben's hopes up."

"Is she staying here?"

"Well," she says, and Mark laughs through his nose.

"That's great," he says. "That's gone over so well in the past."

She can see on his face that he immediately regrets saying it. One of those can't-take-it-backably *mean* moments in a marriage, a blip of incorrigible cruelty.

"I'm sorry," he says. "That was—uncalled for."

She brushes past him on her way out of the kitchen; she has lost track of who, exactly, is allowed to be the angriest overall, but she is content in the moment, given everything, for it to be her.

42

When she was in second grade, she was given a single line in the schoolwide production of an original food-groups musical called *Back in the USDA*, and she took her role seriously, practicing each evening, memorizing not only her line—"I sure could go for a nice, juicy cheeseburger"—but the ones before and after it, as well as the lyrics to all of the songs, which had been written by the creepy music teacher who chain-smoked in his Astro van during recess.

The day of the play she was focused primarily on those things, was not thinking about whether her parents would be attending. Gareth Drews, the boy stationed next to her, had wet his pants just before the show and was wearing their classroom's lavender pair of communal accident shorts, which smelled very strongly of fabric softener and only slightly less strongly of pee. So she was thinking about that, and her single line, and also how hot it was under the lights. She dutifully sang along to the opening number, which was about eggs, and tried not to watch as the music teacher creepily jitterbugged along with them backstage, mouthing the words. It was then her eyes drifted instead to the audience, scanning halfheartedly for her mom, who'd said that morning that she would try to make it but wasn't sure if she could get off work. She was looking for the white shirt of her mom's Dominick's uniform and so was surprised to spot her about ten rows from the front in a pretty blue peasant blouse.

She realized two things almost simultaneously: first, that her mother was wearing lipstick, deep red. And second: her father. There, next to her mom, the two of them together, in the auditorium, in her school, at one o'clock on a Wednesday afternoon. Her dad saw her see him and smiled, lifted his hand up in a conspiratorial wave, and then he leaned over and whispered something to her mother, who found and smiled at her too, the two of them *smiling, in her school*, and Julia smiled back.

Hers was the kind of father who swept in at unplanned intervals, each new arrival either a holiday or a tornado, defined by ferocious hugs or conversations through the walls that awakened her in bed, bass notes hitting the ceiling that thumped alongside her heartbeat. She knew him less as *Dad* than as *Lawrence, Loor-ants*, coming from her mother's mouth through the insulation of the house, *Loor-ants, how dare you; Loor-ants, I told you*. He in fact felt more like a visiting uncle, floating through their lives unexpectedly with gifts ranging in opulence from stuffed animals to, once, a slightly scuffed but nevertheless alluring pair of roller skates. He worked a lot, so he never showed up to her school things, and she almost never took it personally. She'd conditioned herself not to anticipate his visits, because it was better to be surprised than disappointed.

But here he was, and she was smiling so hard her face hurt. She was smiling so hard, in fact, that she missed her cue, which she didn't realize until an electric silence settled over the stage and she saw the music teacher gesturing wildly behind his velvet curtain and the other kids looking at her, and she opened her mouth to speak but found she couldn't bring herself to say it, couldn't stomach the embarrassment of everyone staring at her *plus* the ridiculous cheeseburger line, especially now that her parents—*her parents!*— were watching, so she just shook her head, and the teacher, bugging his eyes at her in outrage, moved on to the next kid.

But she couldn't stop smiling. She didn't care that she'd missed her moment, didn't care that Linda Greely, who everyone thought was beautiful just because her dad owned a Burlington Coat Factory franchise in the Grand Boulevard Plaza, was laughing at her, didn't care about the pee smell or the hotness of the lights; she didn't care about any of those things because *her dad was at her school*, her handsome dad with his black swoop of forehead hair and the tattoo on his forearm from when he was in the Navy and the little rectangle on his shirt pocket where he kept his cigarettes, all of it was there in her actual auditorium, not even in the back like Linda Greely's dad, who had shown up late and was looming in the doorway, but right in the middle, on the aisle next to her mom—who looked so pretty, *beautiful*, twists of her dark blond hair pulled back on the sides to reveal her face—*her parents were there* and she was so happy that she started bouncing a little, but she had to get through the entire rest of the play before she tore over to her dad and threw herself into his arms, split between her joy that he was there and her hope, hope, hope that everyone else was witnessing what was happening.

"You're *here*," she said, just to say something, because once she was in his arms she felt a little embarrassed; it was not a place where she spent a lot of time.

"As we live and breathe," her mother said dryly, but there was a smile on her face, her trademark smile, twisted downward but lipsticked today, and she was watching them with something that might have been pride, a cousin of contentment.

Her mother had always told her that her father got home late and left for work early. This seemed to track, based on the fact that she almost never saw him; because of this—coupled with the fact that she was seven years old—she accepted their lifestyle at face value, had never known anything different, relished the Thursday evenings and occasional Sunday mornings when he *was* home. There was a safety in that kind of knowing, the confidence in the particulars of your circumstances, that stretch of childhood before the broader world fully showed itself and threw everything else into relief, that spell before other people slipped in and made you realize how weird your own life was. They simply were the way they were: her mom worked in the bakery at Dominick's and came home with the slightly chemical smell of icing soaked into her clothes; her father read her *Goodnight Moon* on Thursday nights before tucking her into bed. But today was a Wednesday, and here he was.

"Were you expecting someone else?" her dad asked, and he smelled like tobacco and Trident gum, and he boosted her up a little higher in his arms. "You were great up there."

She glanced around to see if anyone was watching. She never got to be this person, this person with this life, with parents who had good hair and showed up to things on time and told her she was great up there. She noticed that Linda Greely's dad had brought flowers, but they were ugly, droopy daisies and baby's breath. She snuggled a little closer to her dad and her mom reached out and smoothed Julia's hair away from her face. It was as if they all understood that the rules were different today, that everyone was pretending to be someone else, Julia a person with this other, better life and her mother a person who affectionately took a bobby pin from her own hair and pinned back her daughter's bangs because they were driving everyone crazy. And her father: a person who asked if *his girls* were free for ice cream, even though it was December.

"I'm playing hooky," he said, and as they walked out to the car, Julia still riding high in his arms, he reached over and hooked a finger through her mother's belt loop.

In the backseat, she sat beside a case of Dr Pepper; her father oversaw a warehouse for a beverage distributor and sometimes, in addition to his roller skate and toy offerings, brought home castoffs, cans of soda with dents or misprinted labels or expiration dates from last year. Her father's arm was up across the back of the seat, not around her mother but not *not* around her mother either, his palm brushing her hair.

"I could cook tonight," said her mom, who never cooked, and Julia saw her lean back her head a little, pressing it against her dad's hand.

"Oh." Her dad patted her head a couple of times. "No, that's— all right, Anita, thanks."

Her mom turned to look at him, moving her head away. "Why not? We won't eat late."

"I've got to clock back in at three."

Julia saw her mother deflate as she felt herself do the same.

"You just said you were playing hooky."

"Only for a couple of hours. I can't just take a whole day off right before the holidays."

Her mother snorted, and Julia could tell she was trying to sound less hurt than she actually was. "Right," she said. "That Fraser fir's not going to buy itself."

"Anita, please."

"Doing it all for the Christmas ham."

"I took off as much time as I could."

"*I really can't stay,*" her mom sang, like Ella Fitzgerald.

"Do you want to go or not? I can just drop you guys off at home right now."

"No." It came out of Julia as a yelp, the dread filling her stomach. "No, can we, please?"

Her father looked at her mother; the car was silent for several seconds.

"Fine," Anita said, flicking her hand at them, turning to look out the window. Her father's arm seemed to wilt on the seat back, drooping like Linda Greely's daisies. Julia wondered if they were going out to celebrate too, the whole stupid Greely family in their Burlington Coat Factory coats, or if their car, too, was filling with the black smoke of a bad mood.

She boosted herself up on the Dr Pepper to be taller, trying to gauge whether or not she could still make it okay. Slowly, carefully, she reached up over the back of the front seat and pinched the papery skin of her dad's elbow, rubbing it between her thumb and forefinger. After a beat he turned back to her and winked, and something inside of her relaxed.

It was a game they played: no matter how hard she pinched him or pulled his arm hair, he never let pain show on his face. She leaned forward more and pinched his forearm.

"Does this hurt?" she asked.

"Nope."

She pinched harder. "This?"

"Not a bit, Julia Grace."

Her mother sighed and they both ignored her.

"How about now?"

"Are you pinching me?" he asked. "I didn't even notice."

She leaned farther over the seat back, her head now level with her mom's, trying a new angle, getting into it, pushing her fingernails into his arm.

"Now?" she said. "Now?"

She did not notice—did not let herself notice—that her mother was growing irritated beside her. She kept doing it, all the while watching her dad's expression, even and unchanging, the hint of a smile at the corners of his mouth.

"*This?*" she asked, trying hard, screwing up her face with the effort, and when she finally let go, her elbow bumped into the side of her mom's head.

"For Christ's *sake*," her mother said, whipping around.

Her father's arm retracted; Julia sank back onto the case of Dr Pepper.

"Sorry," she said.

"Why do we even try," said her mother.

"Anita," said her father.

"Let's just forget it."

"No," Julia said again, desperate now. "Please, sorry, can we just—"

"Anita, come on."

"I'd like to go home, Lawrence."

Loor-ants. Julia sank back against the seat.

"She didn't even *say* anything," her mom said. "There's no reason for us to *celebrate* her."

"Honestly, Anita," her dad said, but he changed lanes and turned right, toward home. She listened to the engine as he accelerated.

"You've been practicing nonstop all month," said her mom. "How could you forget one line?"

43

Alma never wants to come with her anywhere, but she's asked to come with her to the airport, and Julia—seizing the opportunity for some forced togetherness—lets her, so her daughter is beside her in the passenger seat, the two of them stalled in short-term parking at O'Hare like people awaiting the news of a grim surgical procedure. Her mother's plane is late.

"I used to have a skirt like that," she says to Alma, indicating a severe chignoned woman teetering by in stiletto boots. The skirt is a dark floral print and she fears, if she were to inquire, that she would learn it to be considered *vintage* now.

Her daughter glances up from her phone, appraising. "Okay," she says, unimpressed.

"See, trends *are* cyclical."

"Apparently," says Alma.

Should she bring up the purloined Jesus and Mary Chain T-shirt? *Speaking of cycling, I noticed something went freewheeling out of my closet directly into yours.*

"Stop looking at me," Alma says.

"I wasn't," she lies. She leans her head back against the headrest, and it's precisely the second she allows herself to relax that Alma asks, "Why haven't I ever met her?"

She opens her eyes. Her daughter has harbored mild curiosity about Anita over the years but seems to have come to accept her grandmotherless state as a point of fact; it even, during a third-grade "celebration of elders," lent her some cachet as an exotic.

"She actually showed up just before you were born," Julia says.

Alma looks over to her sharply. "*What?* I thought you never saw each other." There's bald accusation in her daughter's voice, as though she's discovering that her entire lineage is a lie, and Julia feels it grating at the back of her neck; she has, already, quite enough to grapple with this weekend without being unjustly indicted by someone ironically wearing a Lisa Frank scrunchie.

"We *don't* ever see each other," she says. "We haven't. She's just had a couple of—guest appearances. They never ended well."

"Hence my not being allowed to meet her for seventeen years."

Julia inhales slowly. "It's not that you weren't *allowed* to; she's just not the most—"

"You've never made an effort to get us together."

She sighs. "That's right, Alma, I haven't."

"But *Ben* got to meet her."

"Lucky Ben," she snaps, and then, "Meeting Ben wasn't planned."

"Even so. Don't you think that's kind of fucked?"

"God, Ollie. Do I? Yes. I do think it's *kind of fucked* that I haven't seen my own mother in seventeen years. It's a lot more complicated than you know, all right? I could stand to not have you talking to me like you're talking to me."

Alma, surprisingly, seems adequately chastened by this. "Sorry," she says. And when her daughter speaks again, she's quieter, less accusing: "She just showed up? Before I was born?"

"Out of nowhere," Julia says. "It was technically your due date."

"Why haven't you ever told me this?"

"Because it made me really sad," she says simply. She is too tired to pretend otherwise, and too wired by the encroaching nearness of her mother. "It was— I thought she was going to stay; she said she was going to stay, and then she didn't. It was a hard time for me, honestly, Ollie. And having babies tends to—heighten emotions. Dredge things up."

"I'm never having babies," Alma says.

She glances over at her, wondering if she should take this declaration personally.

"What did you guys do?" Alma asks. "When she was here?"

"It was very—normal, actually. We did some touristy stuff. We went to the movies."

"What movie?"

"One of those— That horrible actor with the eyeliner, that— about the pirates?"

Alma wrinkles her nose. "God, really?" she says, as though this reveal bears great weight on her existence. "Is that why she left?"

Unexpectedly, she finds herself laughing, and sees Alma suppressing a smile of her own.

"I'm not completely sure why she left," she says. "But I also wasn't completely surprised that she did." She can't explain this without both going more deeply into her past than she's willing to and without implying somehow that Alma will never understand because she herself has *had* a good mother.

"She just bailed?" Alma says. "Like, without telling you?"

"Note on the coffeepot." She says it more jauntily than she feels; she can still remember how it had felt to find that note, knees weakening so she'd had to sit down hard in a kitchen chair, shame and stupidity knotted hotly in her sternum. She swallows with difficulty. "And a few hours later, my water broke."

"Gross," Alma says, and it snips kindly at the tension stretched taut between them. Alma, the baby inside her that morning in the kitchen, steadily kicking as if to console her, as if to remind her that there was something more, that the borders of her world had broadened, that her hurt had to share real estate with other, better things, that it could no longer fill every square inch. Had Alma saved her life? No. But also, sort of.

"Indeed," she intones. "Then you showed up, Ollie, and here you are still." She ventures to reach over and tug her daughter's earlobe—those tiny ears, with their whorled mollusk innards; she used to stare at them until her vision blurred—and Alma, kindly, only flinches a little bit.

And then her phone dings with a text from her mother, who apparently shares her granddaughter's tendency toward monosyllables: *Here.* She starts the car again, angles down the ramp out of the lot and makes the loop to reenter the arrivals queue.

"Did something," Alma asks, and there's a rare hesitancy in her voice, "between you and your mom, did something—happen? Like I'm just curious why— Like, how you could never want to see each other."

This feels, too, like an indirect compliment. "It's not that I haven't wanted to see her," she says. "People fall out of each other's lives sometimes."

"But what happened?"

She does not, after all this time, know how to answer the question. *Everything*, she cannot say, but *nothing* is inaccurate as well; she can't tell Alma, at this point in her daughter's life, what had happened when she herself was seventeen, but to omit it seems to implicate Julia in a way that doesn't feel fair, that has never quite felt fair. *A child.* The designation seems inapt, though, seated as she is beside Alma, who is many things but not, anymore, a child.

"She's not a bad person," she says. "She could be pretty fun, actually. And she's got a good sense of humor. She was always more—exciting," she says. "Than I was. Am."

"Exciting how?" Alma seems to make no objection to the notion that her mother is currently and historically uninteresting in any capacity.

"I don't know," she says. "Maybe that's the wrong word."

She never viewed it as exciting at the time. It had been occasionally exhilarating, in a purely physiological way, the verbal calisthenics in which her mother repeatedly engaged with boyfriends, with employers, with anyone, really, who she felt was slighting her. And it had been—how is it she's meant to couch it now, years later, from a point of safe remove?—*character* building, she supposes, when they were forced to reassemble at a minute's notice. Anita would have, in another world, in a highbrow comedy series, been a rich eccentric, but she wasn't rich, and she wasn't, when it came down to it, all that eccentric either, just wanting, and creative about how she filled in the gaps.

Julia slows down by United and sees Anita right away, a twofold surprise: first, her smallness, dwarfed not only by the passage of time and an enormous pink suitcase but also by the presence of the second surprise, a broad, tanned older man in a baseball cap. He leans to Anita and says something; she smiles, a hand on his forearm. Julia pulls up in front of them and, because her mother is now scowling, either at the car or against the sun, she leans up over the steering wheel and waves through the windshield. Anita's face relaxes slightly in recognition, and Julia puts the car in park and climbs out. She sees Alma hit the button to turn on the flashers. She has never known how to be reunited with her mother, has always wondered what it would feel like to incite the kind of joy she's seen on the faces of other people's mothers. Her own, as usual, looks underwhelmed.

"You made it," she says, and after a beat she opens her arms, trying to emulate Mark, someone to whom affection, genuine or otherwise, has always come easily.

"Sure did," Anita says, and she steps awkwardly into the embrace, bent bird-wing arms keeping their bodies at a distance. The man stays where he is, watching them smilingly. Anita waves a hand between them as though she's casting a spell. "Marshall, Julia. Julia, Marshall."

He holds out his hand and after a second, Julia takes it.

"Your parole officer?" It just comes out, seemingly unconnected to her brain, but the man laughs, a big booming laugh that ricochets off the cement awnings.

"Marshall Torres, Julia; it's great to finally meet you." And he leans to kiss her hand, and she's surprised to hear herself laugh as well.

"How about we take it down a notch," Anita says, frowning, again, in the direction of the car, having apparently made out Alma's shape in the passenger seat.

"I didn't realize you'd be—accompanied," Julia says, and she immediately feels bad, particularly because it's evident from the look on Marshall's face that he's been under the impression Anita had made clear he'd be joining her. "I mean—"

"He's very low-maintenance," Anita says. "Is that Alma?"

Her daughter's name sounds strange coming from her mother's mouth.

"It is." Julia drums on the window with her fingers in a way that she hopes her daughter interprets as friendly, and after a second the door opens and Alma gets out. Julia notices, for the first time, that she's dressed slightly less like a miscreant than usual.

"Hi," she says, and Julia touches her shoulder. To see her daughter and mother side by side like this is jarring, Alma projected far into the future and Anita catapulted backwards; she supposes she herself is the logical midpoint.

"Mom," she says. This comes out strangely too. "Ollie. Ollie, Mom."

"Nice to meet you," Alma says, and Julia feels protective, her mother's gaze attuned sharply on this person she created.

"How tall are you?" Anita asks.

Alma flushes, unconsciously stoops her shoulders even more than usual. "Five-ten."

"Good Lord," Anita says.

"Mom," Julia says, not sure what she's policing.

"Like Larry Bird," Anita says. "Well, your father's a giant, I guess." She glances back at Marshall, who's barely taller than Julia, and says, "Good thing you've never had a complex." She gives Alma another once-over. "You're quite pretty."

"Oh. Thanks. Um—you too."

Anita laughs at this, genuinely, it seems. "A liar," she says. "Just like your mom."

"We should get going," Julia says. She watches Marshall load their luggage.

"Word on the street used to be that only lesbians drove Subarus," Anita says.

"*Mom*," Julia says, just as Marshall's saying, "Honey," and it strikes her, the casually tender admonishment in his voice, the easy way he touches between her shoulder blades.

"You aren't allowed to say things like that anymore," Alma says, the hardness in her voice directed, for once, not at Julia.

"Aren't I?" Anita sidesteps Alma and usurps her place in the passenger seat. "Why's that?" She closes the door behind her—hard, like always, that great hollow *thwack* of the driver door of the Oldsmobile, the one that had exploded in the White Hen parking lot—and regards them all expectantly, like she's been ready to go for hours.

44

There was a particular nervousness she felt in the pit of her stomach whenever her parents fought, an involuntary tensing of her abdominal muscles as she lay in bed listening to them from down the hall. Sometimes she sensed that it was coming, the way dogs and old people with bad knees felt rain in the air, and when she got that feeling she picked up the stuffed hippo her dad had given her when she was born and clamped her fist tight around his neck, the fur worn from years of such handling; she did it not to hurt the hippo but because she knew he could tolerate it.

A month after the play her father came home shortly after she'd gone to bed; she was still awake, flipping through the pages of a book she'd taken out from the school library on the history of the United Nations. She'd chosen the book because of its cover, a smiling likeness of Eleanor Roosevelt, who looked like someone's nice grandmother so she thought maybe the book would be some kind of nice-grandmother story, but instead it was about World War II and people having meetings and was in fact quite boring. She closed it when she heard the front door, and the tenor of her mother's voice, already agitated—Julia had put herself to bed early because her mom had started drinking at dinner, from the squat green bottle, and was in one of her moods that seemed upbeat but had a hard edge to it, a faraway meanness in her eyes that made Julia avoid her gaze.

The walls of the house were thin, but she'd found that if she folded over the soft parts of her ears and then very tightly shoved her head between the mattress and the pillow she could drown out a lot of the noise. She had made the mistake in the past of listening to the substance of their arguments. That night she pressed her earlobes in too, and as she lay there, hearing the close rushing-water sound and, more distantly, the rise and fall—more rising than falling—of her parents' voices, she thought about last week, when Gareth Drews's mother, who was a nurse, had come to talk to them about staying healthy, and one of the big things she said was that you should never put anything smaller than your elbow into your ear. She wondered if earlobes were included in this rule, and she shifted a little under her pillow, leaving the tops of her ears folded over but freeing the lobes.

"You don't get to have an opinion," her mother was saying. "You can't show up once a week and tell me how the hell I should be living my life. I'm *here*, aren't I? Christ. If you had any idea what it was like to be *here* all the time, Lawrence, you might also want to blow off a little steam."

Loor-ants. She pressed her earlobes back in and held them there lightly with her fingers. Mrs. Drews had talked to them about getting enough vitamin D and covering your mouth when you coughed or sneezed, which seemed funny to Julia because Gareth Drews never covered his mouth and was also constantly picking his nose and wiping the boogers on the underside of his desk.

From beyond her pillow she heard her father say *so goddamn selfish* and then, more clearly, "This is what we agreed on, Anita. I don't know what you want me to do."

At this, she lifted her head from beneath her pillow to listen, and her stomach tensed in preparation for something bad.

"I don't want you to do anything," her mom said. "I don't know why you even bother showing up when you do."

"I *bother* because she's my daughter."

"Ladies and gentlemen, the father of the year. You just make everything harder, you know that, right?"

"What the hell does that mean?"

She pressed the pillow down again, chewing on the insides of her cheeks. Mrs. Drews had a high red ponytail and a shiny little Scottie dog pinned to her uniform and she was someone who smiled with her whole face, and you could tell she was proud of Gareth in spite of the boogers and the communal accident shorts, just because she was his mom. She'd had them all line up at the teacher's desk so she could test their reflexes, and Julia, watching her classmates go up one by one, started to feel very nervous that she'd get it wrong. Linda Greely's knee had kicked out, and then Gareth's—his mom had kissed his head after she tapped him with the little hammer— and Julia felt her heartbeat in her neck thinking about all the times her mother had knocked on her head like it was a door and asked *Anybody in here?*, thinking about the day she'd forgotten her line in the play and how it hadn't felt embarrassing until later that night when she was trying to fall asleep and she played it over and over in her head.

The person behind her had nudged her, and she realized she was now at the front of the line, Mrs. Drews smiling at her with her tiny hammer ready, and she'd climbed onto the desk.

"Ready?" Mrs. Drews had asked, and she'd squeezed her eyes closed and kicked out then, hard, just wanting to get it right, get it right like everyone else had gotten it right.

She heard Mrs. Drews laugh and she opened her eyes.

"I haven't even tapped you yet," she said.

"Oh," Julia said. Her face burned; she heard a few people behind her laughing.

"It's okay," Mrs. Drews said, leaning in close to her. She smelled like soap and vanilla. "I get nervous too. Just try to relax."

She closed her eyes again, felt a tap on her knee and, like magic, her leg kicked out just like it was supposed to, her heel clanging back against the metal desk. Her eyes widened, and she saw Mrs. Drews register her expression and laugh again, a nice, friendly whole-face laugh, and she wondered what it would feel like to have that face be your mom's face.

"See?" Mrs. Drews said, leaning down again and cupping a hand to her face. "You're a natural."

And without thinking she'd reached out and put her arms around Mrs. Drews's neck and hugged her, and after a second she felt Mrs. Drews hugging her back, and she buried her face against Mrs. Drews's chest, the Scottie dog pressing into her forehead. Linda Greely made fun of her for it later, calling her a baby, but it hadn't bothered her because she was preoccupied with something else, the noise she'd heard Mrs. Drews make before she'd hugged her back, a soft *oh* that was full of surprise and kindness but also of pity, a single syllable that reminded her, almost chasteningly, that this mom was not her mom.

In bed, she took her hands from her ears again and lay on her back, the pillow lightly covering her face, absorbing her breath in a damp circle.

"Don't bother," her mother was saying. "We'll be just fine."

Oh, Julia thought, and then *no, no no no no no*.

"Keep your voice down," her father said.

"This is my house."

"Is it? Because the last time I checked—"

"Oh, spare me, Lawrence."

Loor-ants.

"For cripe's sake," she heard him say, and then there were footsteps down the hall and a gentle knock on her door as he twisted the knob. In the doorway her father was tall and tired, his face smiling and sad. "You're awake."

She watched him rub his face with both hands, lightly close the bedroom door behind him, and she felt the rhyme in her head, folded it over and over like a piece of paper getting smaller and smaller—*for cripe's sake you're awake*. He sat on the edge of her bed.

"I thought you were sleeping," he said, and patted her knee over the blanket. "I'm sorry."

"For what?"

He blinked, his face blank, as though he found the question truly baffling. "I'm sorry," he said again, and then shook his head like he was trying to get water out of his hair. There was a crash from the kitchen and then the sound of the television, louder than it needed to be, the tinny itch of canned applause. Her father squared his jaw. "What're you reading?" He gestured to the United Nations book. "You want me to read to you?"

"I finished that one," she said, hastily shoving Eleanor Roosevelt to the floor and retrieving her stack from the nightstand. "Let's do these instead."

She handed over the books, avoiding his eye contact in the hope he wouldn't notice there were four of them in total. When she dared to look at him again, his face had relaxed into an actual smile, scanning the titles on the spines before meeting her gaze, roughly ruffling her hair. "Why not," he said, and motioned for her to scoot over so he could sit beside her.

She snuggled against his side; his forearm was dry and scratchy. She began pulling at the hair on it and then, tentatively, she pinched him.

"Does this hurt?" she asked, and he didn't answer right away. She tried again. "This?"

"Not tonight, okay?" he said. His voice wasn't mean, just tired, but it still hurt her feelings, started up that nervousness in her stomach again. He put his arm around her and she relaxed a little, sat silent through the entirety of *Frog and Toad Together*. He moved on from that to *Amelia Bedelia* and *A Bargain for Frances*, reading methodically and without his usual voices for the animals, so boring that it might as well have been the United Nations book. He started in on *Goodnight Moon*—always the last book he read to her before bed—in the same monotone, and she placed a finger on his wrist and pressed.

"Daddy," she said, and he stopped, sighed.

"I'm sorry," he said for a third time.

"It's okay."

He looked down at her and smiled, then flapped closed the book, one arm stretched under her head. "Goodnight Thursday," he said, sighing. "Goodnight January seventeenth."

She felt his breathing as a round of applause came from the living room.

"Goodnight Continental Packaging Solutions," he said. "Goodnight timecards; goodnight bureaucrats; goodnight union goddamn dues."

She snuggled against him, pressed her cold feet under his knees beneath the blanket, not entirely sure of the rules of the game. "Goodnight night-light," she said, to the half-moon plugged into the outlet by her door.

Her father laughed, *Loor-ants*, and it flooded her with pride. "Goodnight backpack," he said. "Goodnight doorknob."

"Goodnight rug," she said, "goodnight school shoes, goodnight bookshelf."

"Goodnight Washtenaw," he said.

The TV blared.

"Goodnight Mommy," she said.

A beat, then a laugh, gruff and hollowed out. "Yeah, goodnight Mommy is right."

She felt now that something was at stake, that something was expected of her, but she couldn't ascertain the details because she didn't understand the rules of the game.

"Goodnight . . ." she faltered. "Goodnight pillow."

He was quiet for so long that she worried, though she could feel his presence warming her cold toes, that he had evaporated, disappeared like he so often did.

"Or," she said, nervous now, "or not— Pillow was stupid." She thought somewhat desperately of the hallway, the living room, the kitchen: her plate of fish sticks and her mother's green bottle catching the light. "I meant—goodnight—goodnight Tanqueray."

She would remember, forever, that she'd pronounced it the way it always looked in her head, like *sanctuary* but with a *t*, and she would remember the way her father laughed, the saddest laugh she'd ever heard in her life. *Oh.*

She would remember the stillness, then, how he'd worried her hippo between his hands like a hot potato. "God, kid, you've got your work cut out for you, don't you?"

"What?" She could tell she'd misstepped, but she couldn't tell exactly how. "No."

"What'd we do to you? Jesus."

"Daddy," she said. "No, Daddy." She petted his arm. "Did you see my spelling test? On the kitchen table? I got eleven out of ten."

She counted four breaths before he asked: "Eleven out of ten?"

"Extra credit," she said.

"What was the word?"

"*Which.*"

"Which," he repeated, then held out his hand for a high-five. "Nice work, Julia Grace."

She hit his hand with her own. "Like *which one*," she said. "Not like a *sorceress.*" She'd recently read the word in a book of fairy tales; she loved the feel of it in her mouth.

Her father laughed the sad laugh again. "Where did you come from?" he asked, and he rubbed at her forehead with his rough fingertips, and she could feel the affection of the gesture, but it was tinged with pity, even more pity than Mrs. Drews's, and her stomach started up again, tensing itself, waiting for something to happen. "How the hell did we get so lucky?" His voice was thick-sounding, full of something.

"Goodnight *feet,*" she said, wiggling them, desperate to make him laugh again, but he didn't laugh, and he put his hand over his face again for a long minute.

"You are a marvel, Julia Grace Marini," he said finally, and he got up from her bed and bent down to kiss her forehead, but then he leaned over again and lifted her up from under the blankets into his arms, hugging her tight.

"I'm sorry," he said, four sorries, and instinctively she wrapped her arms and legs around him like a koala, smelling his cigarette smell.

"Daddy?"

He laid her gently back in her bed, pulling up her covers and smiling down at her.

"Goodnight, Julia," he said, and then he was gone.

Despite the fact that he was almost never around, she found she missed her father quite a lot when he was fully gone, felt her anxiety rise and then crest when he failed to show up for four requisite Thursdays in a row. Each of the four nights she'd lain awake for as long as she possibly could without falling asleep, reading aloud to herself and then, to stay awake, quietly singing and dancing in her bed, understated prostrate versions of "Y.M.C.A." and "The Hustle." But each of the four subsequent mornings she awakened to a quiet house, padded into her parents' bedroom to find her mother sleeping alone and deeply, a snoring, sticky sleep induced by the gin whose crashing aftereffects Julia's singing had muffled the night before.

"Brush your hair," her mom said when she inquired after his

whereabouts, pushing herself stalely out of bed, eyes spidery and red-rimmed. "You look like Jim Morrison."

All of the cigarettes in the kitchen ashtray were her mother's brand, but that wasn't so abnormal. The shaving kit he kept in the medicine cabinet was still there, as were, by the front door, the funny rubber galoshes he put over his shoes when it was raining. She supposed it was possible he was just working lots of overtime. She preferred to think that he was coming in after she eventually succumbed to sleep, like the tooth fairy, kissing her on the forehead and then tiptoeing out to join her mother, shaving when he woke before sunrise and forgoing the galoshes because it was February and everything was frozen, not wet.

But a feeling began to pool in her gut, not the nervousness she felt when her parents were fighting but instead a nagging kind of dread, and she began to wonder if that was what she'd been waiting for all along, if all those nerves she'd felt lying awake in her bed at night had simply been the opening act for this inevitable main attraction; she began to wonder if part of her had always known that their fights were leading up to something, that they would stack up, one fight on top of another until they finally imploded, a poof of smoke and her father disappeared, reduced to traces in the medicine cabinet.

On the fifth Thursday, she crept down the hallway well past her bedtime and found her mother sitting with a near-empty bottle of red wine, smoking out the front window on the living room couch. She sidled into the room, paying attention to the feel of the air, trying to gauge her mother's mood. The red wine suggested a sad one, which was definitely better than an angry one if not necessarily an ideal one for extracting information.

"Mom," she said.

But her mother's face, when she turned to her, was not sad but soft, heavy-eyed and contemplative. "Come here," she said, and opened her arms, and Julia, who hadn't sat in Anita's lap since she could remember, found herself climbing aboard, resting an unpracticed head against the bony protrusion of her mother's sternum. She tucked her nose into the fold of her mother's robe to avoid the smoke and was surprised by the warmth of her skin.

"Where's Dad?" she asked.

She waited until her mother had drained the bottle of wine into her glass.

"Julia," her mother finally said. "I want to tell you something."

She expected—even then—some divisive moment of adult honesty, and the notion frightened her, the idea of being forced to concretely acknowledge the mature world. She felt suddenly protective of an ignorance she hadn't been previously aware of having. She fought the urge to feign a stomachache.

"If you remember anything I ever taught you, let it be this, okay?"

She scrambled to think of what she *did* remember: that sweaters should be folded by the creases in the shoulders; that you should never open your knees when wearing a dress, even if you were also wearing tights; that putting milk in your coffee was a sign of weakness. The living room was a haze of smoke; the wine in her mother's glass smelled yeasty and sour; it was snowing that evening and out the window a car drove past their house with abandon, coasting black over the powder, its brakes grinding before the stoplight at the end of the street.

"Nobody," her mother said, "is entitled to anything."

She pondered the word *entitled*. Her mother brought the glass to her lips and held it there, not drinking, her eyes squinted. "We don't *deserve* anything. You understand? It doesn't matter what we do or how good we think we're being or if we feel like we've earned some kind of—of—*medal*. Nothing's certain. Nobody's a guarantee."

She squirmed, wished she had stayed in bed.

"It's easier to just not count on anybody else, all right? You'll save yourself a lot of time and energy."

"Anybody like who?"

"Anybody like anybody."

"Can I count on you?" She couldn't bring herself to inquire about her father.

Her mom was quiet for a long minute. "Yes," she said finally. Then: "Sure."

"Okay, but Mom." She began to feel like she was going to cry. She suspected that she would have nightmares about this conversation long into the future, imbued with an acrid cigarette musk, set to a soundtrack of antilock brakes, *nothing's certain*.

And she suspected, curled against her mother, throat burning, heart beating like it did when she ran the mile in PE on Tuesday mornings, absorbing the sad gray glow of the living room past her bedtime, that they would end up donating the galoshes to the Salvation Army.

"He loved you," her mom said, and it landed square in the middle of her chest, the past tense, the thing she hadn't known she'd been waiting for all along. "For what it's worth."

"Wait," she said. "Mom, wait."

"Things happen," she said, "and we get over them. All right?"

She didn't answer, partly because she wondered if it would help at all if she didn't say it was all right. She listened to another car go by, watched a streetlight flicker. And then she felt her mother's breathing slow, warm on the part in her hair as Anita's chin dipped forward in sleep.

"Mom," she said. "Mom."

But Anita didn't wake, and so Julia carefully removed the lit cigarette from between her fingers and stubbed it out in the ashtray her father was apparently never going to use again. She moved to go back to bed but her mother's arms tightened around her and one of her hands pressed Julia's head again against her chest. It made her want to scream a little bit, the arms around her, the hot skin, a thick haze of smoke still in the air; she wanted nothing more than to slip out of her mother's embrace and go back to her bedroom, her bedroom where her dad would never come again to read to her about frogs and toads, but because normal people hugged their mothers, because she felt the desperation in her mother's body, because she had a suspicion that this may be the first and last time they'd ever sit like this, she stayed—though she felt, suddenly, finally, tired, more tired than she'd ever been, and wanted nothing more than to be alone in her bed with her hippo and her night-light, she stayed, because nobody was entitled to anything.

45

She is cooking elaborately, so as not to have to be stationary anywhere for too long, and, just in case, so she'll once again have the excuse to flee to the store in pursuit of some obscure forgotten ingredient. How much she would like to have another produce-adjacent rendezvous with Helen Russo instead of what actually lies ahead of her: Sunny's family descending from Connecticut in just a couple of hours, everyone communing for a prenuptial meal, and Julia has yet to determine whether this will help or hurt things; the extra bodies could help to diffuse tension, theoretically, but they could just as easily yield an atmosphere that's oppressive and foreboding. Mark hustled Marshall off to his office down the hall the second he expressed marginal interest in wearable technology. Her mother and Alma are sitting at the kitchen island, awaiting coffee. Suzanne is sitting at Anita's feet having recently sidled into the room with her stuffed taxicab in her mouth. It is the only toy whose existence she deigns to acknowledge; it came with her from the shelter and is nearly the same size as she is, and she has only ever before shared it with Julia, but now she keeps looking up at Anita and then back down at the taxicab as if to draw her attention to it. Julia is trying very hard to not feel threatened by this.

"Sugar?" she asks her mom, and Anita shakes her head, watching Alma getting oat milk from the fridge, still not paying mind to Suzanne.

"I guess you don't have to worry about it stunting your growth," she says.

"Mom," Julia says.

"It's okay. I *am* objectively tall," Alma says amiably. Her daughter's allegiances have shifted a few times in the past hour; she has forgotten, too, how often this happens with her mother: Anita tends to either attract or repel. She can't decide, looking between her mother and her daughter, plucky satellites on either side of the island, whether it warms her to see them getting along or makes her nervous; it's a complicated mix of the two, some inborn satisfaction at seeing harmony among kin coupled with an equally cell-deep fear that her mother is going to hurt Alma, or rub off on her.

"Where did you say Ben was?" Anita asks. "The *florist?*"

"Apparently there's a problem with the lisianthus."

"Lisianthus," Anita says, not exactly a question.

"Lisianthuses?" Alma tries out. "Lisian*thi?*"

Julia wonders if this is what it feels like to go insane. She brings over mugs of coffee and stoops to give Suzanne a consoling pat on the head. "Should I see if Marshall wants some?"

Anita shakes her head. "He only gets one cup a day. Bad for his heart." Then: "I hope he isn't throwing a wrench in your dinner plans."

It's the closest Julia knows she will come to an apology. "No," she says. "Not at all."

"No shortage of room in this house, I figured. Unless her family's staying here too? The bride of ill-repute?"

"Her name is Sunny. And no, they're staying downtown." Julia stands at the sink, watching two ruddy brown cardinals competing for a spot at the feeder. "Why didn't you mention you were bringing someone?"

"I'm sure I did," Anita says.

"I'm—almost positive you didn't."

"We'll have to agree to disagree, I guess."

Julia bites down on her molars. "She's trying to say hello to you, you know," she says shortly.

"Who is?" Anita asks.

"Suzanne," says Julia, and Alma supplies, "The dog. They're obsessed with each other."

"We are *not*," Julia says. "I'm just saying that she's trying to get your attention and you're ignoring her."

"I didn't *see* her," Anita says, and leans over to offer her hand to the dog. "She's about four inches tall."

Suzanne takes to licking Anita's hand with a lot more enthusiasm than Julia is comfortable with, so she asks, irritably, "How long have you been together? You and Marshall?"

"Oh, God, I don't know. Awhile."

"What does he do?"

"He was a public defender," she says. "He's been retired for about ten years."

"He seems nice," Alma says.

"He doesn't hate himself," Anita says. "Which is more than I can say for almost everyone I know."

Julia turns around, surprised. "Present company excluded, I'm sure," she says.

Anita glances at her. "Sure. Of course."

She can't get over, really, how well her mother looks. She's always been slight but what once could have been called scrawniness has morphed into something lithe, the silhouette of small, strong shoulders through her batik-printed wrap. Her hair is bottle-dyed dark, and her smudged eyeliner seems deliberate rather than residual; she seems *present*, alert, blinking around the kitchen like the children did as babies, no piece of stimuli too small for their notice.

"What's her story?" Anita asks, and there—in this glowing, leveled-up version of her mother—is a glimmer of something recognizable, her morbid and near-rabid curiosity about the lives of others. "*Sunny.*"

"She's studying contemporary Baroque painting," Julia says, knowing, sadistically, that this will amuse Anita as well—it's both pathetic and involuntary, this desire to please her mother—but Alma is shaking her head.

"No, she's an art *minor.* She's majoring in sociology. Or—some, like, specific kind of sociology; I don't remember."

"Is she?" Julia frowns.

Alma nods, stirring honey into her coffee. "Right now she's doing research on whether or not the rise in digital technology is contributing to an increase in drive-offs."

"Drive-offs?"

"When you drive away with the gas pump still in your car," Alma says sagely.

Julia frowns, trying to determine if sociological research about gas pumps feels any less nebulous than the study of an imaginary art form. And then she wonders, suddenly, if she'd been the one— distracted, as ever—to mishear Ben in the first place; and she wonders what else she's potentially missed, letting her head get in the way.

"Well?" Anita says, and Julia and Alma both look to her. "Does it or doesn't it?"

"Oh," Alma says. "Well—I don't know; I think she's still collecting data."

"We'll be waiting with bated breath," Julia says, meaner than usual. Her mother snorts, and it bathes her for a few seconds in warmth.

"You must be heading off to college soon," Anita says then, to Alma, surprising her further. She cannot recall a single instance during which her mother instigated conversations regarding Julia's own academic matriculation.

"In the fall," Alma says. "To Herzog."

"It's a very good school," Julia supplies, too enthusiastically. "In Iowa."

"I know where it is," says Anita.

"You do?" Julia asks, and both Alma and Anita—it's eerie, really— narrow their eyes at her.

"Yes, Julia, I've actually heard of a lot of things." To Alma, less acidly, she says, "Marshall's daughter went there."

"Marshall has a daughter?" Her voice sounds too loud.

"Two," Anita says. "And a son. You talked to Lydia on the phone, actually. When you called me last month."

Julia blinks. "You said that was your coworker."

"Well, she is, technically. My boss, really. She runs a school for the deaf in Rio del Mar."

"You work at a school for the *deaf*?" Julia is saying, as Alma intones, "*That's* cool."

"I keep the books," Anita says. "Sometimes I sub in if one of the aides is out sick."

"Do you speak sign language?" Alma asks.

"I'm getting better at it," Anita says. "Lydia's husband and daughter are deaf, so I'm around it a lot of the— What is that *face* you're making, Julia? Jesus, it's like I just confessed to a triple homicide."

"I'm just—surprised, is all."

"Yes, that's obvious. What exactly is so surprising to you?"

"I'm—not sure," she says.

Alma looks anxiously back and forth between them. "You live in California," she says to Anita, who slowly refocuses her attention.

"I do, yes."

"Why?" Alma asks. "I mean—what made you go there?"

It's a question Julia has never felt brave enough to ask herself.

"A lark," Anita says. "I was working for a drugstore chain in Fort Collins and they offered me a transfer to Santa Cruz."

"I've heard it's really pretty there," Alma says. "It would be cool to come visit sometime."

If Julia's had trouble loving at all, her daughter loves too easily; it seems unequivocally clear that the former is worse, but it makes her nervous, seeing Alma exposing her heart like this to someone with such a grisly track record for emotional injury.

But her mother answers easily, around a sip of coffee: "Sure. Anytime."

Alma looks over at Julia with a hint of accusation: *All we had to do was ask?*

"That would be cool," she says. "I've only ever been to San Francisco. My dad went to college in Palo Alto."

"Yes, I'd heard that," Anita says. "Your mother mentioned it about seventeen times when she called to tell me she was getting married."

"That's not true," she says, feeling her face getting hot.

"It was like he'd been knighted or something," Anita goes on. "The *gushing.*"

"I didn't *gush,*" she says, "and I'm surprised you even remember this conversation. You got off the phone after about thirty seconds because you said you had to work, even though it was Columbus Day."

"Indigenous Peoples'," Alma says reflexively, but her daughter looks nervous again, and it occurs to Julia that Alma is unused to seeing her like this—combative, a little unstable; she has become, she realizes, unused herself to *being* like this.

"A *biologist*, you kept saying," Anita says. "With a degree from *Stanford University*, as though I'd never heard of it."

"I don't *talk* like that," she says. "And he's an engineer."

"Oh, calm down," Anita says. "I'm just teasing. You're still a little grouch, then?" What her mother used to call her when she woke up grumpy; she hasn't heard the phrase in decades. "Since she was a baby," she says to Alma. "Never happy about anything."

"She's happy about things," Alma says, and her defense feels like a great kindness.

Anita holds up her hands, an overdone showing of defeat, as though she's the only one not overreacting.

When Ben appears in the doorway, he reminds her not of Mark, but of her own father, perhaps owing to the context Anita provides, sitting in front of him; it takes her breath away for just a second, how much he looks like Lawrence, *Loor-ants:* the tired broadness of his shoulders, the dark hair on his forearms and the way his left eye appears to be just a few millimeters higher than his right.

"Honey," she says, and Anita has evidently been expecting Mark, because when she glances over her shoulder and sees Ben she straightens a bit to attention, then gets up from her seat; Julia sees her adjust her wrap and tuck her hair behind one ear, the nervous gestures of someone awaiting inspection. When Ben smiles, it's his father's smile, though Mark's reception of Anita had been chilly at best.

"We're so glad you could make it," says her son, and Julia watches with something like awe as he opens his arms and dwarfs her mother in a hug. Sunny has come in behind them, and she catches Julia's eye and smiles.

"You're a bit bigger than the last time I saw you," Anita says, almost shyly, when they separate, and Julia sees that she's flustered. "Thanks for inviting me."

"Thanks for coming," Ben says, and she loves him so full-heartedly, for his generosity, for his considerate shape-shifting, for his ability to make anyone feel welcome. He looks up and bestows his smile on her, and then—as though he's already clocked the dynamics in the room and knows that she needs it—comes over to hug her too.

46

Alone, she and her mother lived like two people sharing a hospital room, perfectly civil but never—out of some combination of politeness and fear of what they might witness—looking at each other head-on. Not long after her father had stopped showing up, they had been forced to leave the house on Washtenaw; they'd packed up the car hastily and left in the dark hours of a Sunday morning—Julia suspected her mother's parting with their landlord had been less than amicable. They then lived in a series of cramped apartments in Hyde Park, only about twenty minutes east. Later, Julia would be surprised by the closeness—and how near her father had been, too, without her knowing and evidently without his caring—but at the time it may as well have been another country, a new neighborhood, a new school with new people and a new narrative at home: her mother had stopped, without preamble or any further explanation, referring to her father at all. She'd also started dating, a questionable roster of men who'd appear like library books, to be returned a few weeks later. Anita started working the early shift at the bakery and so left during the night and got home during the day when Julia was at school, was home all afternoon to drink and watch *General Hospital* or entertain women from the neighborhood, women who'd be giggling like schoolgirls into their gin and tonics at the kitchen table when Julia came home.

But it was her life, the thing she was used to. There was need, but not dire need, and it was punctuated occasionally by upticks in prosperity when her mother got a Christmas bonus or a tax refund. And Anita vacillated as well, rapturous highs or droning lows, silences that radiated from her bedroom like dog whistles or theatrical fights with the men who inevitably disappointed her. Her mother wasn't the kind of drinker whose drinking repeatedly crescendoed into chaos; her bad habits were steady, at times impressive in their functionality, simply a part of who she was; in addition to working at a bakery and dating men who Julia liked to armchair-diagnose with personality disorders and reading issues of *Good Housekeeping* she stole from the hair salon, she drank. And Julia maneuvered accordingly, aided by the predictive abilities of her gut, which had only improved since she was a child in her bed, listening to her parents fight.

She could tell—she had radar so keen for her mother that it sometimes felt unseemly—that she was not supposed to comment on the men, that she was simply supposed to take in stride the occasional guest at their dinner table. She didn't begrudge Anita her happiness; it was more that it was strange to see her mother opening up, and every time Julia heard her overdone laughter, saw the effort she made to dress nicely and stay half-sober and act interested in whatever the men—who were, across the board, objectively uninteresting—were saying, it hurt her feelings, because Anita never did any of these things for her. Her mother didn't have the patience for hurt feelings, though; she had so consistently and aggressively rejected any kind of emotional indulgence that Julia had learned to simply deny herself it, except when she couldn't, when she was feeling tired and unreasonable, but on those occasions her mother simply chose not to engage with her.

Her mother had many infuriating traits, but this was arguably the most infuriating one, and indeed the most hurtful, her ability to dismiss Julia with a handful of words, to reduce her to nonexistence simply because she felt like it.

"She's like a lamp," Anita had said of Julia once, and for a moment Julia had gotten her hopes up, entertained for just a few seconds the possibility that her mother was about to get poetic and profess that her daughter was a beacon of sorts. But Anita had tacked on, "Easy to pack up and take with you," which had disappointed Julia on levels both literal and emotional, because in fact they had never brought their lamps with them when they moved from one place to another—the shades and the cords were a pain in the ass, and cheap replacements were easy enough to find at Goodwill—and because, yes, though by age ten she had developed the ability to squash down any inkling of inconvenient feeling that rose to her internal surface, she was hurt, and because she knew that her mother had intended it that way.

In ninth grade, she got a scholarship to the Lab School, and when she was a sophomore, she tumbled in, quite by accident, with a moody, cosseted group of kids, many of whose parents worked at the U of C and all of whose parents owned homes much nicer than Julia and Anita's apartment on Fifty-Fourth Street. Julia spent her free time with these classmates in the carpeted basement of her sort-of boyfriend, a blithe, squat boy named Neil, whose parents were geology professors. They would get high and talk about politics or listen to jazz, all of which she found unbearably tedious, but it was preferable to the alternative, and felt most days like a kind of sociological study, Julia content to sit back and observe what seemed like an entirely different species.

"This is *wild*," Neil's beautiful friend Catherine said one afternoon, lying in the middle of the floor, her feet elevated on the coffee table and a hardback copy of *The Joy of Sex* propped open against her chest. "Did your mom actually go out and buy this?"

"My dad got it for her for her birthday," Neil said. "They had it in their bedroom for a while." *Their bedroom.* Parents who bought books for each other as presents. It enthralled her.

"*Mouthwork for him,*" Catherine read, and did an exaggerated wink at Julia and Neil, who both colored. Neil was on the wrestling team and had a morbidly fascinating case of cauliflower ear, florets blooming from either side of his head that she avoided looking at or touching when they were together. He was otherwise relatively datable, given the low bar for teenage boys—he had good hair and a weed hookup and a whole finished basement to himself—and she suspected his physical anomaly was in part why Neil had settled for her from the girls in their friend group; she was not the best looking—that was Catherine, who was pale and waifish, cadaverously pretty—nor was she the most sexually experienced—hands-down

Kitty Schultz—nor the most interesting. She was arguably the *least* interesting member of their group, in fact, in large part because she kept so much of her life a secret from them. She sometimes wondered—as they lay around ironically listening to Fleetwood Mac (who Julia secretly liked, unironically) and, once, as Neil fingered her under a blanket in his father's La-Z-Boy with a faraway look on his face—if they'd forgotten she was there.

"Do your parents still fuck?" Catherine asked her. Julia had long suspected that Catherine didn't like her, and she didn't particularly like Catherine either, didn't trust the perfect arches of her eyebrows and could never assess the level of malice in her voice.

"Ick," said Kitty.

"It's *perfectly natural*," Catherine intoned, like the narrator of the pedantic video on sexually transmitted diseases they'd recently watched in health class. "Mine do on major holidays."

"I walked in on my mom blowing my dad on his birthday," said Simon, and Kitty said, again, "*Ick.*"

She had come to join this group mostly because she and Kitty had bonded freshman year over a remarkably stupid honors English project where they were forced to dress up like Rosencrantz and Guildenstern. But she had only ever felt marginally like she fit in with them, this group of people who had the luxury of rich, present parents, the dubious gift of years and years of attention and analysis and assurance that they were unique, destined for things, worthy of unlimited inward-looking. Nobody in Neil's basement had ever for a second worried that things wouldn't work out for them broad-scale, and yet they were constantly in tatters over what Julia considered to be ridiculous problems, botched travel plans or arguments with their parents about Michael Bilandic or what kind of car the family should buy. Once Catherine had stormed in almost in tears and declared, as though announcing a recently uncovered genocide, "Oh my *God*, my mom is thinking about opening a *boutique*." Julia both envied this and found it terribly annoying, sometimes wanted to take Catherine by her lovely shoulders and remind her that some people had real problems, that some people's moms didn't remember what grade they were in, let alone think to inquire after their opinions on a mayoral election, that some people didn't have the luxury of overanalyzing every nonproblem that got foisted in their direction.

But of course she never did; she instead allowed herself to fade into the background, lamp that she was, and settle into Neil's parents' soft basement carpet, the quiet, comfortable, safeguarded space of a home that wasn't her own.

"I think I've seen your mom," Catherine persisted. "She's always wearing the Dominick's uniform, right? She's pretty. She looks super young; is your dad young too?"

Julia took this as it was meant to be taken, as a full-throated insult. "No," she said tightly.

"He's old?"

"He's not—around."

"Oh yeah?" Catherine asked, a deliberate innocuousness in her voice. "Where is he?"

She would consider later that if Neil actually cared about her he might have sensed her discomfort and stepped in at this moment, but instead he and Simon had commandeered *The Joy of Sex* and were cracking up over the part on anal beads.

"He's just not," she said.

"What does he do?" asked Catherine, whose dad was—it was always the kids of shrinks or writers, she would later assess, who turned out to be the most fucked up—a psychology professor.

When she was in middle school, she'd started responding to queries about her father with increasing allusions to the fact that his absence might have ties to something of intrigue.

"I'm not really allowed to talk about it," she'd say, casting her gaze mournfully downward. "For security reasons."

The legend built in her head as well; the roller skates—which she kept, still, now many sizes too small, in a box on the high shelf in her closet—were scuffed because they'd tumbled off the back of a truck in the middle of a clandestine goods transfer; the cases of Dr Pepper actually contained not soda cans but fat, tight rolls of ill-gotten cash. Her last name was, after all, *Marini*, and a mobster dad lent more cachet than the truth did.

But by the time she got to high school she'd outgrown this narrative, and having a father in the mafia did not account for the fact that her mother was home and drunk on Swiss Colony most afternoons, nor for the string of underwhelming men that passed through their apartment like tides. Having a father in the mafia did not account for how little money they had, how unwilling her mother was to acknowledge the injustice—the *sadness*—of the fact that Lawrence—*Loor-ants*—had evaporated overnight and never looked back.

"He's dead," she snapped, just to shut Catherine up, and she regretted the words as they came out of her mouth, sending her father to his death—her father who'd read to her, her father who'd loved her, her father who wasn't dead or in the mafia, just electively gone.

"Whoops," Kitty murmured, peeling apart a strand of her hair.

"I didn't know that," said Neil, who knew almost nothing about her, who had once, in a note passed in algebra, written her name as *Julie*.

"It was a long time ago," she said, trying to sound at once nonchalant and traumatized, but she could already see the interest fading from the faces around her, see Catherine's shame quickly wearing off and Neil's focus returning to the anal beads and Kitty's hair swinging in perilous proximity to the joint she was trying to light; even a dead dad was not enough to make her worthy of their attention for longer than a few seconds, and she couldn't blame them, really; you could only count on people to stick around for so long when you didn't give them much to work with, and she simply didn't have much to *give*; she felt like she'd been deprived of some critical lessons in socialization right out of the gate, and trying to make friends, when you'd skipped those lessons, was like learning a new language relying solely on a handful of reticent subjects, in this case subjects who'd already decided you were never going to be fluent.

"I want fries," Catherine said, boosting herself up from the floor. "Let's go to Morry's."

Neil and Kitty and Simon joined her without a second thought, abandoning *The Joy of Sex* and the tiny pile of split ends and Julia herself, though she stood up and followed them, the hanger-on, the lost cause, the lamp, because, at the time, it seemed better than being by herself.

47

The house is alive again, artichoke tarts fresh from the oven and Wilco on the stereo and optimistic floral napkins wrapped around each place setting at the dining room table, but the conversation isn't flowing as it has at previous, less stressful gatherings; there aren't enough people, maybe, or there are, simply, the wrong people. Nobody is interacting, really; everyone seems to have staked out isolated territories at safe distances from each other. Sunny's tween-aged half sisters are deeply bottle-tanned and glued to their phones and radiating unpleasantness; camped out by the crudités like they are, they could easily be putting curses on everyone by way of the baby carrots. Her stepfather is a quiet, lumbering man in a sweater vest who is seated alone in the middle of the living room couch, thumbing thoughtfully through Julia's seed catalog; her mother and grandmother are frowningly study-ing the wall of family photos like people disappointed by the size of the *Mona Lisa.*

Anita and Marshall had retired upstairs for an hour before the party began, emitting a suspicious quiet that Julia had tried to over-power with David Bowie and an early glass of Viognier as she'd worked in the kitchen grating Gruyère, chopping artichoke hearts, pulling some puff pastry from the fridge. She'd wondered what they were doing—actually sleeping? The silent calisthenics of some alternative religion? Not having sex, surely? Perhaps they'd been debriefing, at length, the insufferable pretention of Julia and her family, with their French press and their Stanford legacy.

They'd nevertheless compliantly come back down when Sunny's family arrived, Anita chic and Californian in a linen wrap dress and Marshall smelling very faintly of an earthy aftershave, a handsome couple, really; Julia had done a double take at the sight of them. Now Marshall is laughing with Alma as she feeds snap peas to Suzanne, and Ben and Anita are in the middle of what looks like a very animated conversation. Sunny, leaning against the dining room radiator picking at her cuticles, looks very sad and very pretty, her hair braided back from her face like it had been the day they met. Her interactions with her family have seemed strained to say the least, and Julia knows Sunny is preoccupied as well with the last-minute details of the wedding—the *lisianthi*, Sunny informed her earlier, have been delayed and need to be picked up from the florist first thing in the morning ("I will buy the flowers myself," Julia had intoned, but Sunny had just looked at her blankly), and there is some sort of issue surrounding the forks at the restaurant that Julia couldn't quite follow. She is about to go over to her again, but Mark beats her to it, saying something that makes Sunny laugh. She feels his distance and wishes they hadn't fought, or at least that they'd timed their fight differently, considered in advance that it may have behooved them to wait for a time when they might need each other less than they do this weekend.

She turns away from him, going alone back into the kitchen, where she tops off her wineglass and stirs her risotto, prods the steaks around in their marinade. She doubts Helen Russo's dinner parties have ever featured this particular dim, dry din; she hears Sunny's sisters break into a brief fit of pealing, murderous giggles. She has, a few times since Brady's birthday, allowed herself to regret deleting Helen's number from her phone. There are few people on the earth to whom she could explain why she and Mark are in the place they are in right now, and Helen is one of them; she also allowed herself to wonder earlier—once she's opened the gates to this kind of thinking it's difficult to prevent other things from slipping through—what Helen would think of the menu she's come up with for dinner. The Bowie has gotten dark, his last album, trippy and echoic, *Way up, oh honey, I've got game.* Defiantly, she scrolls until she finds the Bee Gees, sinks onto one of the stools at the island and inhales deeply.

"Are we interrupting?"

She turns, startled. Sunny's mother and grandmother are named Melissa and Joyce and they are both dressed like Daughters of the American Revolution, or the florid mother-of-the-groom women Julia found on the internet last month; Joyce has a sharp-shouldered tweed jacket and Melissa has clearly had something injected into her forehead so that it doesn't move when the rest of her face does and Julia, in her sweeping black wombat dress with her unedited frown lines on bare display, feels a bit like she used to around the Serenity Smiles moms, uncultured and underdressed and, ultimately, uninvited, even though she is in her own kitchen.

"Not at all," she says, standing up. "Can I get you two anything?"

"Everything's lovely," Melissa says, and then, with the put-upon but superstitious stiffness of someone passing along a chain letter, "I appreciate your hosting tonight."

"It's our pleasure," Julia says. "It's so nice to finally meet all of you." She cannot quite bring herself to add something about how she's heard so much about them, because she hasn't, not really; she knows that Melissa married into money and once yelled at her daughter for falling out of a tree and she knows, of course, that she lost a child, but beyond that the women are mysteries to her, and she lacks Helen Russo's mystical ability to connect with anyone who happens to cross her path.

"Sunny's very fond of your family," Melissa says. "You're all she talks about."

"Oh." She's very touched by this. "It's— We're very fond of her. I—Mark and I. And Alma. And—Ben, of course." She wonders, nervously, if she should just keep listing people: *and Suzanne, and my mother, and her unusual boyfriend.*

Melissa smiles tightly, Joyce lurking at her elbow like a goblin.

"Obviously none of this was what any of us wanted," Joyce says, and it takes Julia a moment to parse; she thinks, at first, that the woman is referring to the rehearsal dinner, to her risotto, which she is supposed to be stirring.

"Sunny's always marched to the beat of her own drum," Joyce continues, clawlike hand on her daughter's arm. "But we never thought that she'd be marrying her *teacher.*"

"TA," Julia says reflexively.

Melissa arches her eyebrows, which Julia is surprised her forehead allows.

"I just mean that— He didn't pursue her when she was his student. She asked him out, and they— That's not what this is."

"What would you say it is, then, dear?" Joyce asks.

"*Mom*," Melissa says, and Julia feels just a split second of solidarity, because she's spoken to her own mother in the exact same tone several times today.

"Ben's very mature," Julia says. "And he— I mean, of course I'm biased, but he's really a wonderful—" She stops herself before saying *kid*. "He's a good man. And he loves her a lot. I was skeptical at first too, but . . ." She isn't sure, exactly. And she's a little startled to be making these arguments after she's attained such eloquence, in the last couple of months, in the semantics of the other side. "I think they'll be okay," she says, and is startled anew to realize that she believes it. "They seem to make each other really happy."

"*Happy*." Joyce emits a squawking sound that might be a laugh. "What does *happy* have to do with any of this?"

Melissa pries her mother's fingers from her arm. "Mom," she says. "Could you go check on the girls for me?"

Joyce seems to contemplate protest, but then she huffs once in Julia's direction and sets off back into the dining room.

"I'm sorry," Melissa says. "She's—upset about this, understandably. We all are. Life's been unfair to Sunny. And yet she still seems fairly—unprepared for it. I'm always just waiting for her to trip over something new."

"I get that," Julia says. "But she seems—steady. To me. Sunny does. For what that's worth."

Melissa smiles faintly, a small, unpracticed smile, and Julia wonders how she looks to this woman, her unworried proclamation, seventies pop on the stereo now, and her family comparatively carefree.

"I'm very sorry," Julia says. "About your—other daughter."

Melissa looks so surprised that she worries she has overstepped.

"I hope you don't mind me saying that."

"No," Melissa says after a moment. "No, I don't— Yes, of

course; thank you. Sunny told you? About Naomi?" She seems to absorb this. "It's funny. I— This will sound crazy, but I forget sometimes that—not that it happened, of course, but how much it has to do with everything that's happened since. It didn't occur to me that some of this must have to do with her. The decisions Sunny makes, the things she decides are important to her. Things would probably look very different if her sister were still here."

"I've had that thought before," Julia says. "About a lot of things. Who's to say, I guess?"

Mark, whose timing is usually impeccable, appears now, seeming to clock the gravity in the air a second too late.

"Sorry to interrupt," he says. "I just came to— Is it about time for me to start the grill, Jules?" He smiles at Melissa.

"Now's good," she says. "Remember to throw a veggie burger on for Ollie."

"Roger," he says, and touches Julia's waist lightly as he slips past her to the yard. To any outside observer—to Melissa, probably, hopefully—they'd seem affectionate and well oiled; Julia is the only one who can feel the remoteness in his touch, hear the hardness around the edge of his speech. She takes a swallow of wine, too cold; her temples pulse a few times as she feels it go down her throat.

"Your mom," she says to Melissa, searching for some good-natured entry into a less loaded conversation. "She seems— It's nice that she's as protective as she is of Sunny."

"That's one way to look at it," Melissa says, and she laughs, lusty and surprising, a laugh full of things Julia both does and doesn't recognize, private griefs and savage disappointments and lifetime scrutiny of inscrutable daughters.

48

When Julia was seventeen, her mother started dating a man named Jonathan. He was a few years younger than Anita, and his arrival was a bang, a bird against glass; Julia watched with fascination as her mother invited him in, felt her fascination grow as he continued to stay, filling their house with his music and his cooking smells, a floating haze of dog hair and a wheezing but infectious laugh.

Her mother was changed around him, younger-seeming and almost worryingly upbeat; these facets seemed to pale slightly whenever he wasn't around, but they never left her completely, leading Julia to believe that there was something genuinely different about him. They'd met at the bakery when Jonathan had come through to order a birthday cake for his sister; they had a whole story now, whether people asked to hear it or not, about how Anita had talked him out of putting a hundred candles on it as a joke, because some women, she said, were sensitive about their age.

"Are you one of those women?" Jonathan was reported to have asked.

"Do I *look* like one of those women?" was Anita's alleged reply, to which Jonathan had supposedly drawled, "I can't tell yet, but I'd sure like to find out," and they'd both laugh every time they told it while Julia stood by, so frankly captivated by the show that she almost forgot how embarrassing it was.

Jonathan had a ponytail and a fondness for Rush and his dogs were named Flash and Gordon; he taught comp at a community college in the south suburbs. He came for dinner once or twice a week, and Julia found herself sticking around instead of retreating to her bedroom like she usually did; she had, by then, made her quiet parting from the group who met at Neil's house, and from Neil, who hastened the process by cheating on her with beautiful Catherine. She got a job at the local pharmacy and had, too, in the last months, applied to four colleges, which she and her mother never discussed, though Jonathan had offered to proofread her application essays.

The house felt more festive when he was there; he compensated for his lackluster culinary abilities by cooking with copious amounts of garlic, so the kitchen always smelled good, and was warm, and he'd play music for them, the Velvet Underground and the Talking Heads—bands that would later inure Julia to the too-cool men she dated after college, men who viewed a woman with good musical taste as a statistical anomaly—until Anita whined in the background about how she wanted *her* kind of music, and then he'd switch to Frank Sinatra or Sam Cooke and sway her mom around the apartment, her head tucked under his chin, and again Julia would watch in wonder, this tableau of her mother in a state of contentment, a bleary kind of happiness on her face, her eyes closed as she pressed her cheek to Jonathan's chest. On one occasion Jonathan caught her looking and winked at her, like they were in on it together, and it made her wonder what it would have been like to have had a stepdad, to have had some good company during all those lonely years, someone who made her mom happy and looked at Julia as something other than a nuisance.

It wasn't Jonathan's fault that what happened that night happened, but it was likely it wouldn't have happened if he weren't there, if her mother hadn't been relaxed by his presence and Julia relaxed by extension, both of them again falsely lulled into the sense that they were other people. It was an evening in early February, frigid and sallow outside, and Jonathan was making spaghetti; the garlic smell was atomic, the radio played softly in the background, and Jonathan and Anita were sipping judiciously on glasses of Chianti—Anita still, months into their relationship, exercising most of the restraint she usually only pulled out for the first few weeks—and Julia took all of these things in concert as a signal that she too could loosen up a little. The primary thing she appreciated about the periods when Anita was dating someone was the fact that when the men were over, Julia got to clock out, stop worrying because for a couple of hours someone else was, if not always looking out, at least paying attention to her mother.

Julia was doing her French homework at the kitchen table, conjugating verbs while Jonathan and her mother chatted idly over her head, innocuous, white-noise, end-of-day chatter that served to soothe rather than distract her.

"Give her a little wine, Jon," Anita said, swaying to the music. "Just don't spill any on your homework," she said to Julia, "or they'll have me sent to Twenty-Sixth and California."

Jonathan poured her some wine, raising his eyebrows at her in question.

"*Jail,*" Julia translated, and shyly took a sip, feeling in their presence more like a seven-year-old than a high school senior. It wasn't unpleasant, feeling like that, and she relished it, leaning back in her chair, pulling a knee to her chest, adding an accent aigu to an *e* on her paper.

"What's this?" her mother asked, tapping at a form sticking out of the back of her notebook. She pressed her finger down and slid the form toward her. "Cap and gown rental?"

"For graduation," Julia said. She had already decided not to ask; she wasn't required to walk in the ceremony. "I'm not going," she said. "I still get my diploma."

Jonathan spoke up from by the sink: "You have to go."

They both looked over at him in surprise.

"It's really not a big deal," Julia said.

"Of course it's a big deal," he said. "You're graduating high school."

She wondered, fleetingly, if Jonathan was one of those incredibly suspect adults who insisted that high school had been the best time of their lives, but before she could make her assessment her mother said, "He's right."

Julia turned, studied her face, which was defiant, the kind of obstinate what-do-you-mean-I'm-not-always-like-this expression she wore when Julia caught her behaving anomalously for the sake of impressing a boyfriend, when she lied about regularly going to church or "not really caring for" booze. But this time her change in behavior benefited Julia in addition to making Anita more attractive to her boyfriend, and there was something flattering about that, and could it possibly be true as well that her mother *wanted* to see her graduate?

"It's something to celebrate," Jonathan said, coming behind Anita, and she looked up at him.

"Get my checkbook," she said to Julia, eyes still locked with Jonathan's.

She would wonder later if Anita had orchestrated it, or at least if she'd intended the eventual discovery. Julia went down the hall to her mother's bedroom and opened her desk drawer. The square of paper was affixed by static to the plastic cover of the checkbook: a torn piece of newsprint folded neatly along the edges to make a tiny rectangle, barely an inch long. Womack & Womack's "Love Wars" was playing from the kitchen as the paper detached itself and fluttered back into the drawer. It was unusual in that it was there at all; her mother had no patience for, among many other things, clutter. Julia assumed it was garbage and was about to crush it in her fist when she saw the tiny print.

She absorbed the information with a peculiar lack of feeling, as though she'd determined that the paper was indeed garbage. But after a moment she recognized the neat creases as her mother's. The edge where the paper had been folded over at the top revealed the clipping to be from the *Daily Southtown*, not the *Trib*, which was the paper they bought on the very rare occasions they did buy the newspaper. She spent an inordinate amount of time—standing there, bile in her throat, the music pulsing jazzily from down the hall—wondering how her mother had come to obtain the clipping. It was nearly six years old.

MARINI, LAWRENCE M., 49, of Berwyn, died Wednesday of complications from pancreatic cancer. Born in Cicero, Marini was a veteran of the U.S. Navy and spent over 20 years as a production manager at Continental Packaging Solutions. He is survived by loving wife Lorraine (nee Leary) and daughters Cindy and Amy.

She noted, dazedly, the lack of an accent aigu in *nee*, and she sank onto the edge of her mother's bed, the ugly maroon quilt she'd had since the house on Washtenaw, the quilt that her father had occasionally slept under. She snagged, hard, on the fact that she had never known his middle name. The number of possibilities was overwhelming—*Martin, Marvin, Melvin, Maxwell*—as was—her pulse quickened at this—the fact that she might never learn the right one. Was there some sort of naval database?

The rest flooded her a few seconds later, in ascending order of comprehensibility: first, the pleasing alliteration, accent or no, of "*loving* wife *Lorraine* (nee *Leary*)"; then that she apparently had two half sisters she had never met; that when she'd lied to her classmates in order to garner sympathy, she'd inadvertently been telling the truth, because her father was dead, her father *had been dead* for six years and prior to that he'd been living just a half hour's drive away, but no longer, because her father was dead, and he had two daughters, neither of whom was she; she apparently didn't exist, but neither did he, her father, because he was dead. She stood up from the bed, did a lap from one end of the frame to the other, three neat steps and back. *Cindy and Amy*. Fussy names, girly names; she wondered if her father had approved of *Julia*, hard-edged and vowel-laden by comparison; she wondered if he'd been there when she was born; she wondered if his wife—his *wife!*—had known; she wondered what their house looked like and whether or not they had a copy of *Goodnight Moon*, and she wondered—this made her sit down again, hard—whether her roller skates had previously belonged to his other daughters, his real daughters, if *Cindy and Amy* had been the ones to scuff them up gliding around the streets of suburban Berwyn; she wondered if he'd gone to their school plays; she wondered if he had another pair of galoshes. She wondered how her mother had found out he was dead, and she wondered if Anita had seemed different that day and Julia—eleven, then; she had been eleven years old when her father died—just hadn't noticed, had chalked it up to one of her moods; she wondered if Anita had cried, even though Anita never cried.

And then before she knew what she was doing she was back in the kitchen.

"As if I don't give that school enough of my money already," Anita was saying, reaching out for the checkbook, but her smile faded when she caught sight of what was in Julia's hand.

She would have accepted a number of reactions, she realized a few moments later, when she was sitting on the curb in front of their building, shaking with cold and—could this be shock? There were a number of expressions she would have permitted to cross her mother's face, among them surprise, remorse, or even regret over having been caught.

Instead, Anita listed, her face slackening with weariness and with wine and with—Julia could not forgive her this, never would— a flicker of irritation.

"Oh, for Christ's sake," she said. "Please don't start with me."

That reaction—she could see it, branded onto her brain, as she crouched over the cold curb, rocking a little—was not among those accepted, and so she'd admittedly lost it, thrusting the scrap of paper in her mother's face, catching one of Jonathan's prepared plates of pasta with an elbow and sending it crashing to the kitchen floor.

"Don't *start* with you?"

"We have company, Julia."

"Maybe I should—" said Jonathan.

"No, stay," Anita said. "Julia, this isn't the time."

"He's dead." She tried out the words.

"I'm aware of that," Anita said, and then, defensively: "Nobody told *me*, either. His old busybody secretary sent me the notice a month after it ran."

"He's been dead for six *years*."

"I figured there were a number of things in there you might find upsetting," Anita said. "Which is why I chose not to share it with you."

"You didn't do this to protect me," Julia said, though she wasn't entirely sure she believed it. "You don't get to pretend that you did this so I wouldn't get *upset*; I was upset when he *left* and you didn't do anything about it then; I was *already* upset so you don't get to act like you cared whether or not—"

"What exactly was I supposed to do to keep him from leaving? Chain him to the walls?"

"If you hadn't been such a trainwreck he wouldn't have felt like he had to stop coming. And you were always fighting with him; you were always so *hard* on him."

"Watch your mouth," Anita snapped. "You try making it work with a man who only finds time for you after he's taken care of everything else. Christ. He left us because he cared about them more. Plain and simple. You wanted me to spell that out for you when you were seven years old?"

She took a moment to comprehend this, and felt it turn, as she did, into venom. "He didn't leave *us*," she said. "He left you."

Anita studied her for a long moment before replying, almost brightly, "You know something, you're right. Thanks for that."

"Who came first?" she asked. "Us or them?"

"Would you like to call me a *whore*, Julia? Go ahead. He didn't tell me he was married at first, okay? Not that it's any of your business."

Jonathan had retreated into the far corner of the kitchen, perched on the windowsill watching them nervously.

"How is it not my business?"

"We never intended it to be anything long-term," Anita said.

It dawned on her belatedly. "So I was an accident."

"Let the pity party commence," her mother said, and Jonathan said, softly, "Anita."

"She's embarrassing herself," her mom said, pouring herself more wine, several more fingers than was socially acceptable, her façade of moderation slipping. "Most of us were accidents," she said. "It means nothing. I raised you, didn't I? You're *alive*, aren't you? And growing into such a *theatrical* little thing, my God."

"You just let me believe this whole time that he didn't want to see me," she said.

"He *didn't* want to see you, for Christ's sake," her mother exploded. "He's only been dead a few years, Julia; do you think he was banging down our door before then trying to spend time with you? He wasn't. He never sent a dime. He never picked up the phone and checked to see how you were doing."

"You scared him away," she said, but she could hear the weakness of her own voice. "He didn't call because he knew you'd be the one to answer."

"You want to tell yourself that? Go ahead and tell yourself that." Anita lit a cigarette, dragged deeply. She looked up at Julia as she exhaled, and her eyes were frankly full of pity. "It was a bad hand," she said. "Okay? I know. I get it. But what else is new. It happened and it's over. What's the sense in dwelling on it?"

She hadn't brought her coat with her, and the cold of the concrete ate through her jeans, started a trembling from her thighs down to her feet. There was snow in the forecast and someone had staked out the parking space in front of where she was sitting with two woven plastic lawn chairs. She'd accidentally stepped in a puddle of slush; she had chemistry homework; she would get frostbite; her father was dead.

"Jesus Christ," a voice said behind her, and before she could register what was happening, there was a coat over her shoulders. "You must have a death wish."

There was warmth, suddenly, from the space beside her; she could smell the Prell and spearmint scent of Jonathan through his coat. There was something very appealing about a man pretending not to be cold on your account; she hadn't experienced it until that moment, and she pulled the coat tighter.

"Poor choice of words," he said.

She laughed a little, dryly, aware of herself in a way she hadn't been a few seconds earlier; she heard, in the laugh, her own unconscious efforts to sound adult and world-weary.

"I'm still not entirely clear on what happened in there," he said. "But I got the gist, I think. I'm sorry for your loss."

Nobody had ever been sorry for her loss before. "Thanks."

"Your mom— You know, she doesn't— She has a—"

"Please don't," she said, and he seemed relieved.

"Are you okay?" he asked. It was a stupid question, both because no, of course she wasn't okay, and because she'd barely had a moment to take stock of what had just happened. "Sorry," he said, the perfect thing again, and this time, stilling her shivering, he put his hand on her leg.

49

The first thing she notices at dinner—regrettably, after she has uncorked several bottles of a lovely Provençal rosé purchased specifically for the occasion—is that her mother isn't drinking. She has a radar for it, still. It's unreal, really, the things the body recalls when it's so content to forget others. She can't even remember her own *age* sometimes, but she can easily conjure the wool scritch of the tights she wore the year she went to Catholic school, and the bone-deep chill of the walk-in freezer of the coffee shop in the basement of the Hancock, and Mark coming to pick her up sometimes, their Red Line ride home together, knees bumping, that confidence-inspiring warmth of another leg pressed to her own. And the feeling she's feeling now, the feeling she's been feeling since she laid eyes on her mother in airport arrivals, the internal tenseness that was active in her for the first eighteen years of her life, a barometer for her mother's moods, for the directions the moods were headed in and at what speed they were traveling and to what degree they were being amplified by the ingestion of nicotine or alcohol or sometimes just *sugar,* which had a tendency to make her mother childlike, prone to wild giddiness and subsequent crashing sulks. It's been in her, latent, she realizes now, ever since she left home, and it's one of the reasons she's so edgy this evening—one of about a dozen reasons, to be fair—and, arguably, drinking her own wine at a less than leisurely pace.

But her mother—newfound wellness guru, sun-kissed Californian, *aide to the deaf,* for fuck's sake—is sipping demurely on soda water, and so is Marshall; Marshall is talking to Ben about the erosion of the Pacific coastline and her mother, sainthood-eligible, has somehow coaxed Suzanne into her lap and is stroking her one-handed, the dog's little eyes growing heavy as Anita eats her salad.

It's at that moment that she notices her mother's left hand, her third finger encircled by a dainty ring, silver with an opalescent cluster of stones, and she feels it spreading—a cold, sure kind of certitude—down the bones of her wrists, knows it—this, too; she once knew her mother so very well—before she looks at Marshall's left hand and sees a chunky band of what looks like hematite. It could be nothing—he is also wearing some kind of hemp wrist-let and a hoop through one ear—but she knows, somehow, that it is not.

"How did you two meet?" she asks, and though she doesn't intend to, she halts the conversation all around the table—Sunny's family, huddled together at one end as though for warmth, regards her, five wide, startled pairs of eyes.

"I mean," she says, and glances to Mark, wanting to feel less alone than she does at this moment. Quizzically, he lifts an eye-brow at her. "Sorry. Mom, you and Marshall. I was just curious how you met."

Her mother looks at her steadily for a long moment before she says, "Through friends."

The mother she knows never really had any friends, which had a hand in exacerbating that tense feeling in her gut, which was, she supposed, the reason for her internal activation in the first place: there was almost never a responsible, certifiable adult around to pick up the slack; there was almost never another adult around, period. It had just been the two of them, Julia and Anita, both of them too young, really, to make sense of anything.

"How long have you been together?" she asks, and Marshall smiles at her, his arm loosely around Anita's shoulders now, that gunmetal band innocently glinting in the candlelight.

"Four years next month," he says, and she can tell by the way he says it that he's under the impression she already knows they're married. He has every reason to believe that Anita told Julia, three Junes ago, that she was getting married to someone, because *why wouldn't she tell her*, because Julia is her daughter, because that's what you do when you marry someone, at a bare minimum, you inform your daughter of the development unless you consider her undeserving of the update, unless you have decided that she simply isn't worth telling.

She wonders what their house looks like. She wonders what they do together in their spare time. She wonders if his kids came to their wedding, and if they love her mother, and if her mother loves them back. She wonders if they got sober together or if they were both already sober when they met, another thing her mother has undergone without her knowing, another thing she isn't allowed to feel surprised by or proprietary of, even though it's a behavior that had a hand in shaping who she's become, a person who didn't trust anything until she met a man who proved himself trustworthy, and not even exactly then: the ball of nerves, the little grouch.

"Time flies," Anita says dryly.

"We've got nothing on you two," Marshall says, nodding to Julia, and she thinks, for a second, that he is referring to her and Anita, before she hears Mark beside her.

"Twenty-six in September," he says, but he isn't looking at her, and he sounds a little strained, and when he tells the story of the parking meter, she wonders if she's not imagining the detachment in his voice, like the two of them could have been anybody.

50

She got her letter from Northwestern on a Wednesday in April, an evening when she'd finished her shift at the pharmacy and come home to the smell of frozen pizza in the oven and the sound of the WGN evening news from the living room as her mother folded laundry on the couch. She took it straight to her room and slit it open even as she was pulling the door closed, so she read the first line just as the latch clicked and was kneeling on the floor to steady herself when she read the second paragraph about the scholarship. Not a full ride but close to it, close enough that her going there felt feasible. She wanted to scream; she wanted to do whatever it was people did when they were excited about something; she couldn't remember the last time she'd been excited about anything.

"Dinner," her mom called, and she smoothed the creases in the letter, read it over again twice to make sure she hadn't gotten it wrong. She thought—she'd been allowing herself thoughts like this recently not because they floated freely to the surface of her psyche but because she knew they would annoy her mother—about what it would be like to tell her father, to let him know that she'd received a substantial scholarship to Northwestern University.

It hadn't surprised her that things had almost immediately gone back to the way they were after she discovered his obituary. Anita, as she'd always known, had an impressive ability to bounce back; her mother seemed to think, as she'd maintained all along, that Julia was undeserving of her indignation, her hurt, her confusion, and so she simply refused to acknowledge them, starving them into nonexistence, and after a few days of that they'd settled back into something recognizable, the rhythm of their shared household.

Jonathan had been coming over less frequently since that night, and when he was around, Julia usually made herself scarce.

"Coming," she said, and carefully folded the letter back into thirds, tucked it into a notebook and checked, just once more, to make sure it hadn't evaporated before going to join her mother in the living room. The pizza was on the table; her mother was using the flattened box as a serving tray and Tom Skilling was predicting light rain. Julia took a slice and a paper napkin and curled up on the opposite end of the couch from her mother.

"I have good news," she said, and instantly regretted it. She could sense her mother was in the wrong mood, her most common mood, where she couldn't bring herself to be generous; her mother did not have patience for the happinesses of others, even if the others were her daughter. She wondered what it would be like to have a mom who forced herself to snap out of it for the sake of her kid, but instead she had this mom, who wasn't interested in snapping out of it, who cast her a flat sidelong look across the couch.

"What?"

Just a few minutes ago, she'd felt a little sad being alone with the good news—it was even sadder, she thought, than being alone with bad news—but to tell her mother and get a tepid reaction would be the saddest of all; she couldn't stomach having it get ruined yet.

"Marissa McNeal got fired," she said. "So I get to take her Saturday shift."

And Anita's face suddenly brightened, brightened for the misfortune of others in a way that Julia knew it wouldn't have for her daughter's victories.

"Fired for what?"

"I'm not sure. She was always late."

"She's the ugly one, right? With the braid?"

"That's mean."

"Isn't she?"

"She doesn't *always* wear a braid," Julia conceded, and Anita cackled.

In a few months' time she'd be coming home to a dorm room instead, a dorm room with a smart roommate and no TV on which to watch stupid local news; she would eat her meals in a dining hall, not off of a cardboard box, and she'd be surrounded by people who actually wanted to talk about real things, not just pettily delight in the adversity of others.

"It's just a fact," Anita said, an impish smile on her face. "It's not mean to say, because she looks exactly like that skeevy little bastard from the cereal box, the one . . ."

"Count Chocula," Julia said, because it was just true, and her mother laughed, and she laughed too, feeling hot unexpected tears in her eyes, because in a few months' time she and her mother would no longer be like this, like they had been forever, and the thought at once thrilled her and made her tremendously sad.

She went for a walk after dinner, just to stretch her legs, she said, and Anita called after for her to pick up a pack of Winstons. She walked with forcible nonchalance, no hurry at all, her hands shoved into her pockets. It wasn't until she was a block from Mr. G's that she allowed herself to break into a jog, all the way to the pay phone. Before she picked up the receiver she glanced around furtively.

He answered on the third ring, one of his dogs barking in the background.

"I need to tell you something," she said. "Can I tell you something good?"

There was, at first, a hard edge to his voice when he asked, "What is it?" and she panicked, because she wasn't sure she could handle it if she found in Jonathan the same kind of emotional reticence she'd just avoided in her mother.

But as soon as she said it, he whooped so loud she instinctively pulled the phone away from her ear, and both his dogs started barking, and she felt herself laughing, a release of all the euphoria she'd forced herself to sit on throughout dinner, the smile she'd made herself suppress as she walked the darkening stretch of Blackstone to the store.

"Hell yes," he said, and "Of course you did," and "I'm really fucking proud of you, Julia; is that weird to say?"

And she glowed, felt certain she was illuminating the whole block. She fantasized, sometimes, about what would happen if her mother overheard one of their exchanges, the affection in her boy-friend's voice directed full force at Julia.

"Thanks," she said, and "Thanks, Jonathan," and "No"—as she rested her forehead against the plexiglass of the phone booth, light-headed with pleasure, phosphorescent, *proud, proud, proud*—"No, that's not weird at all."

They'd been having sex for over two months by then. It didn't occur to her until much later—years later, long, long after she'd picked up the cigarettes for her mother and walked back home with the secret of his joy still pulsing beneath her breastbone—that he may have sounded nervous at first lest she was calling to tell him she was pregnant.

51

Her mother follows her into the kitchen when she goes to ready the dessert. Though Julia can feel her presence—and smell her, a smell both familiar and not, a new scent like coconut beneath skin and baby powder and, deeper still, a hint of anise and cigarette smoke—she doesn't turn from the counter, where she's whipping heavy cream in the stand mixer.

"I had no idea you were so culinarily inclined," Anita says.

"Well, why would you, I guess."

"Dinner was delicious."

"Thank you."

"And your hair looks nice tonight."

She looks over her shoulder to her mother's nunlike benevolence. "Thanks," she says, with suspicion.

"Have you put on a little weight?"

Now she spins to face her. "In eighteen years? You know, yes, I'm comfortable copping to that."

"I didn't mean— I was asking because I think it suits you. You look healthy, I'm saying. You were such a slip of a thing when you were little. I remember one of the neighbors on Fifty-Fourth asking me once if you had scurvy."

She's watching the whisk spin when she asks, "Do Marshall's kids know you're married?"

Her mother sighs. "Julia."

"Do they?"

"Honey, please." The endearment seems to startle them both; Julia is now, helplessly, envisioning her mother doling out such easy affection to the Torres children. She's not sure she can remember, at least until she met Helen Russo, ever being called *honey* in this particular, exasperated maternal way.

"I think it's reasonable," she says, "for me to be surprised. That you didn't consider me important enough to—"

"It wasn't about *you*," Anita says. "We barely told *anyone*; it was for *tax* purposes, mostly, not that that's any of your business."

This hurts more than she expects it to. She turns back to the mixer. "Right," she says. "I guess it isn't."

"I just *mean*, Julia, that that isn't the type of relationship you and I have. When's the last time you ever told me anything that was going on in your life?"

"I reached a point of diminishing returns," she says. "It starts to become clear that the other person doesn't care after the ninety-seventh time they show utterly no interest in whatever it is you're telling them."

"I'm sorry you feel that way," Anita says.

"What a heartfelt sentiment," Julia says. "Not remotely disingenuous."

"Oh, Julia, this really isn't the time to—"

"I *agree* it's not the time to," she says. "For the record, I agree with that, though you always seem to be the one who decides what the right time is."

Anita is quiet for a long minute, the kind of quiet—fermented, fizzy with vitriol—that made Julia very nervous as a child. "Perception," she says finally, "is a funny thing."

"Oh, for fuck's sake," Julia breathes. "Okay, Mom." She goes over to the fridge but feels Anita watching her still. "Was there something else?" She regrets her tone of voice, if not its acid then the fact that she sounds theatrical and petulant, a great deal like her teenage daughter.

"I just came out to see if you needed any help with dessert."

"No." She squares her jaw. "Thank you." Defiantly, to the point of violence, she begins washing a plastic carton of raspberries.

"Because you seem a little . . ."

"I seem a little what?"

"Just you might want to slow down on the wine."

She stiffens, turns to face Anita, raspberries dripping water onto the floor. "You're *kidding* me."

Her mother's face is soft, noncombative. "It can be easy to lose track," Anita says, prim, suddenly, a portrait of controlled urbanity. "Of—how much you've had to drink."

"For you, yes, it certainly can."

"I haven't had a drink in eight years, actually."

And while she genuinely does, for a second, feel happy about this, happy for her mother, *proud* of her mother for doing something that must have been incredibly difficult for her to do, that sentiment is replaced by the one she used to feel when Anita cleaned up her act for new boyfriends, the distant, childish sensation of *Why them? Why now? Why not for me?*

"That doesn't make you an authority," she says. "That doesn't mean *anything* when you compare it to the other *fifty* years." Because she's embarrassed, of course; because she actually *never* drinks like this; because she learned before she was even conscious of learning that she couldn't slip up, given the high likelihood of slippage by those around her; because isn't she *allowed* to slip up every once in a while? Because she's angry with herself for letting this atypical time happen in front of her mother, and angry with her mother for making her feel so fiercely protective of her own defenses.

"I'm sorry you're angry," Anita says.

"You understand that that's not a real apology, right?"

"I'm not the one going off the rails here, Julia."

"I'm not going off the *rails*. I've never gone off the rails, Mom, because I've never been *allowed* to go off the rails. You don't get to just keep showing up here and judging me and then leaving before you've had a chance to clean up everything you've—"

"I'm not judging you."

"I'm overweight," Julia says. "And I'm drinking too much."

"I don't know what your habits are normally, Julia; I'm just saying that—"

"My habits normally are *normal*, Mom. My whole *life* is normal, despite your best efforts. I'm drinking because every single time you've come here—*both* of those times, over the course of twenty-five years, have ended disastrously for me."

"You have trouble," her mother says carefully, "accepting blame, Julia, do you know that?"

"I didn't *do* anything. I won't accept blame because I didn't do anything *wrong*."

"You're the one who left in the first place," Anita says.

"What are you— I didn't *leave*. I went away to college; that's not the same as—"

"I'm not talking about that," Anita says. "Though you did seem particularly thrilled to tell me you were getting as far away as you could."

"But you let me go. You just let me leave for college and you never even— You didn't do anything after that to suggest that you even remotely cared about me."

"Oh, I *let* you go?" She hears the venom in her mother's voice and realizes that she's been prodding around for it all along, searching for that recognizable ire beneath the new landscaping. "Is that what happened, Julia, because I seem to recall your just *announcing* to me that you were leaving. You told me in no uncertain terms that you were going, and off you went. How could I have prevented you from doing that?"

"I don't mean literally; I'm talking about the nuance."

"*Nuance*." Anita laughs. "I don't abide by whatever touchy-feely bullshit parenting philosophies you've had the time and the means to adopt, Julia. I fed you and I clothed you and I kept you alive, by myself, and that left me with very little time for *nuance*, all right?"

She's never been able to articulate to Mark how it had felt to arouse such anger in another person simply by existing. She almost never lets herself look back on it, how ambivalent her mother seemed to feel toward her; she had fought so hard against that same instinct of ambivalence toward her own children, fought it until it ceased fighting back, until loving them became the default.

"You could have at least—made it clear that you cared one way or the other," she says. "If I went or not."

Her mother's mouth is a thin line. "You made it abundantly clear, Julia," she says, "that you didn't care at all about what I thought of you."

She wilts back against the counter. "I was seventeen."

"You were an old seventeen. Old enough to know what you were doing," Anita says.

She can't believe she's saying it; can't believe that they're finally talking about it, *now*, on the eve of her son's wedding. "But I wasn't old enough to—understand what it meant."

"That was my responsibility? To explain it to you?"

"It was your responsibility to be aware of the—of how complicated it was, and how—confused I must have been. You could have made me feel less—terrible about everything."

"You did a terrible thing. Why should I have helped you feel good about that?"

She has always known this is how her mother feels; she has always known that this—a blunt string of words, nothing softened at the edges—is Anita's official version of events, but she has not, in forty years, heard it spoken aloud, and it hurts like something molten in her stomach.

"Everything all right in here?" Mark is in the doorway. She watches her mother tense in his presence, possibly the only person on the earth who Mark makes nervous. "Your voices are carrying a little," he says softly.

Her mother rolls her eyes, leaves the room without another word.

"You okay?" Mark asks, and she wants to say *Not especially*, wants to go to him, across the kitchen, but she doesn't, just nods once.

"Fine," she says, and Mark studies her for a beat longer before nodding back, turning to rejoin their guests.

52

Jonathan had a busted-up Jeep with a backseat roomy enough for both his chocolate Labs and the evenings Julia spent alone with him, and some afternoons he'd pick her up from school in it and she would take her time as she approached him, hoping pathetically that her classmates might see.

They went for drives and hikes and once made love on a tree stump, like elves, and he continued to school her in obscure rock bands, knowledge that would later endear her to Mark, and she'd pet his dogs until her hands came away tacky with their grime. Together she and Jonathan would fog up the inside of his Jeep, which was a thing she thought only happened in movies. She never got tired of the power she had over him, that mystical transaction, something enchanted—one strategically placed hand and he liquefied before her. She did feel bad about it occasionally; she regretted it, after the fact and, actually, frequently, during the act itself, but she'd fully intended for it to happen: it was, in some ways, her most major act of assertion yet.

Jonathan was sixteen years older than she was—almost exactly twice her age—and he was also, not that she told him this, the first person she'd ever had sex with, having gotten only so far with Cauliflower Neil and the upright bassist who stood behind her in music class and also the delivery boy at the pharmacy, a cowlicked high school dropout with whom she smoked cigarettes and occasionally made out when she was supposed to be signing for his shipments of Sudafed. She tried hard not to let on her inexperience, and it worked in her favor that Jonathan was fairly unobservant in this respect; he was simply happy, it seemed, to be with her, and very comfortable giving her pointers, which she took, at the time, with gratitude, figuring they would only help her out in the long run.

She didn't clock that anything was wrong the afternoon he picked her up from school a few weeks before her graduation.

"What a ridiculous day," she said gleefully, hoping that she had an audience of her peers, lolling her head back against the seat. Jonathan fancied himself an outdoorsman, and the weather was finally warm, so they lately spent their afternoons in the Dan Ryan Woods or Calumet Park, tromping around like people looking for a place to bury a body before eventually settling somewhere shaded, where no one would give them a second look.

They drove fast down South Shore. It embarrassed her, later, to remember how oblivious she'd been to his mood at first. He didn't say anything as they exited the car. She noticed, then, that he hadn't brought the dogs.

"Where're the boys?" Her mother did not like his dogs; he rarely made comparisons between the two of them, but that was one thing he had pointed out, that she had a way with Flash and Gordon that her mother didn't, and they brought her additional satisfaction for this reason.

"I left them at home."

"You're being so quiet," she said, tugging his hand so he'd look at her. His face was boyishly troubled in what she briefly let herself acknowledge was an unattractive way. She was filled with a sudden panic that he might be breaking up with her. She'd known things would end eventually, but she didn't think it would be so soon; she'd envisioned whatever it was they were doing lasting at least through the summer; she was holding out for the possibility that she'd be lonely her first semester and he might come visit her occasionally at Northwestern. She pushed her hips into his. "Are you okay?"

Then he smiled, just a little bit, and kissed her. "I'm okay," he said. "Just wanted you all to myself."

And she allowed him to lead the way, rubbing the back of her hand with his thumb in a way that made her feel like he loved her, and they ventured off-trail into a copse of trees and he pulled her down with him onto the ground and she felt the chill of the soil through her skirt and then on her thighs as he pushed the skirt up. The lake breeze in the air, the way his body fit against hers, the minute possibility that someone would see them and call the cops; when he came he shuddered against her, and though she hadn't quite gotten there herself, she made herself make a moaning sound.

"Let's walk," he said a minute later, rolling off of her, but she held on to his arm.

"Just a few minutes." She burrowed against him and was surprised to feel the new stiffness in his body. "Come on, I'm cold."

He didn't yield to her touch. "Remember to check for ticks when you get home."

"You want to check *for* me?" she asked, wheedling, nuzzling his arm with her nose.

"Jesus, knock it off," he said, and he didn't push her away but the force of his voice made her move back from him.

"What the fuck?" She tried to sound indignant instead of like she was about to cry.

"Your mom knows," he said.

"That you're a total grouch?" she asked, but halfway through the sentence she realized her error and the last word—Anita's word—came out of her mouth like sludge: *grouch.*

What was worse—the realization itself, or the fact that he'd allowed her to be so glib for so long, to sing along to Van Morrison in the car and tell him a story about her physics teacher throwing a chair across the room in an effort to conceptualize gravity? The fact that her skirt was still pushed up over her hips, because he'd just fucked her in a pile of peat moss? Like they were raccoons; like she was subhuman.

Which was worse: these things, or the fact that she felt, for just a second, *thrilled* to hear that her mother had found out?

"How?" she asked. "Since when?"

"We met for lunch earlier."

She leaned heavily against the tree behind her. What could she have expected, really? She knew she was not allowed to feel this way—especially not now—but the fact that Jonathan had been with her mother just hours earlier filled her with something akin to jealousy; she tried, generally, not to think about the two of them together. And she wondered if he'd fucked Anita first too, before she found out what he'd done; she wondered if her mom had walked away from the exchange feeling as filthy and humiliated as Julia felt now.

"I wanted to tell you in person," Jonathan said in his new stiff voice. "But this has to be it. I'm sorry."

"How does she know? What did she say?"

He sighed, suddenly impatient. "I slipped up. I mentioned you."

Of course this had been her intention all along—to hurt her mother, to provoke her mother, to get her mother to pay some fucking attention to her, force her gaze in Julia's direction—but the thought of Anita actually finding out made her feel like someone was sitting on her chest. "What do you *mean* you—"

"I said something about how I'd seen you over the weekend. It just came out. And she— I don't know, she just knew."

"That doesn't make sense."

"She's your mom."

"Yeah, but she's not . . ." She didn't have the kind of mom who intuited things, who *just knew*. "That doesn't make any sense," she said again.

"We shouldn't have— I know better, Julia."

"Don't patronize me."

"Let me give you a ride."

"I think you already did," she said, and amid all the pain she felt afterward, all of the regrets, the loneliness and the confusion and the disappointment in herself for who she'd become—or who, perhaps, she had been all along, the unshakable feeling that she was fundamentally flawed—she would always, always remember saying this line, and what a very, very stupid line it was, and the embarrassment she felt about that burned brighter than nearly anything else.

She took two buses home after Jonathan told her, and she kept her wits about her on both rides, because she figured that crying on the bus would make her even more susceptible to perverts than usual. She tried to think about it rationally, forcing herself to replay her conversation with Jonathan verbatim, but it filled her with such sickly shame that she had to stop. She hugged her backpack in her lap, trying to predict what would be waiting for her when she got home.

She wasn't used to having to defend herself to her mother, because she had never been prone to misbehavior. Her scoldings for minor infractions consisted of the occasional spanking when she was a child but mostly psychological warfare, masterful feats of inattention, stints of silent treatment or incisive character assassination. She could recall, in fact, only a single occasion on which her mother had actually punished her for doing something wrong, and that had been several months after her father left. They had been at Montgomery Ward—her mother had dragged her there one afternoon because her new school required uniforms—and Julia recalled feeling not quite like herself, tired from a day of brand-new fellow third graders and achy deep in her left ear and annoyed about the uniforms, which were not plaid like she'd seen on television but plain navy. Tension fed off tension when you lived closely with another person, and she and her mom could sense it in each other like weather; her mother had been annoyed too, her generalized foul mood giving way to something harsher, a mood that caused her to tug impatiently on Julia's hand, pulling her through the aisle of saddle shoes, across the shiny linoleum to the blouses. The display of sewing patterns caught Julia's attention midway to the hosiery section and she managed to slip her hand out of her mother's without attracting attention, stood there gazing at them, rows of big-eyed, small-waisted cartoon ladies with candy-colored outfits; she did not know exactly what they were but could, regarding them, think of no more satisfying object to own, nothing more glamorous in the world than these women with their square-necked dresses and high-waisted trousers; she could hang them in her room, she reasoned, and possibly bring one to her new teacher, who had a smiling lipsticked mouth and swishy skirts. She chose the best one, featuring a green minidress, and took it gently from the rack.

"Oh for Christ's *sake*." Her mother's hand was suddenly gripping her upper arm, jerking her away from the display. "What are you doing?"

"Could I get this?" she asked shyly, holding up the envelope.

"Could you— No, Julia, you can't *get that*. How many times have

I told you to stay where I can see you? God. Do you even know what that is?"

"Paper dolls," she said reasonably.

"It's to make a dress," her mom said. "Which you can't do, the last time I checked."

She didn't remember exactly what happened after that, just that she'd kind of crumpled to the floor when her mom tried to pull her back to hosiery; she remembered how waxy and cool it had felt on her face, and how it had smelled like rubber and a sick-sweet popcorn scent from the mall that sort of made her want to throw up, and how once she started crying she found she couldn't stop, and the harder her mom pulled on her wrist, the louder she cried, louder and louder until it started to feel both necessary—her ear hurt; she wanted the paper dolls; she hated when her mom talked to her like that; plus the more she cried the more impossible it seemed to stop—and almost kind of good, like itching a mosquito bite until it bled. She distantly remembered her mother abandoning her armful of uniforms on a chair and picking Julia up under her armpits, other customers watching as she carried her out to the parking lot.

By the time they reached the car, she'd calmed down, run out of steam. She was not conditioned for tantrums. She clicked her seat belt and rested her head against the armrest, closing her eyes, which felt hot and itchy. It wasn't until she felt the car moving that she became aware of her mother's silence, and of the way that she was aggressively not looking over at Julia, not turning her head a fraction of an inch in her direction. She would not recognize it until later as one of Anita's tactics—she showed her anger most patently by ignoring you—but she knew, then, on a gut level, that it meant something for them to be driving in complete silence, complete absence of anything, the radio or her mother's running commentary on the substandard abilities of her fellow drivers, and she knew that it was bad.

"Mom?" she said. "Sorry. I'm sorry. I didn't mean to."

Her mother stared straight ahead, blinking almost lazily as she looked through the windshield. They zipped along on the highway, the silence seeming to increase the pressure in her ears, and it seemed like a possibility, then, that her mother might never speak again, that they would persist in this silence forever, all because she'd done something stupid, something she hadn't even *meant* to do, something that had just *happened;* she began to worry that she'd ruined everything just by making a dumb mistake, just by getting tired.

She couldn't help it: she started crying again, and she could feel too her mother's silence getting louder, her irritation radiating off of her like something chemical.

"Mom," she said, and then, more desperately, "*Mom.*"

Her mother flicked on her turn signal, slowly turned right onto an unfamiliar side street. She pulled to a stop at the curb halfway down the block. Still not looking at Julia, she reached across her and pushed open the passenger side door.

"Get out," she said.

"Where are we?"

"Now."

"Mom." Panic rose in her, something liquid.

"Out of the car," her mom said, and because she sounded like she meant it, Julia undid her seat belt and climbed out.

When her mother yanked the door closed behind her and pulled away from the curb, she watched it happen like she was watching someone else's mom drive away and leave her standing in front of a brownstone with chrysanthemums in big pots on either side of the front door; she watched it happen like it was some other wet-faced little girl with saddle shoes and a wicked ear infection, someone she could distantly pity. She watched until her mother's blinker flipped on again and the car turned slowly left at the corner, and then she stepped back inside of herself and registered that her mother was gone.

It felt like she was standing there for at least an hour, though it was in fact no more than a minute or two. But a minute was long enough for her brain to spiral into the scariest place, for her to experience a dull, cold terror like nothing she'd ever felt, for her to reach the conclusion—frank resignation—that she was someone worthy of being left, by one parent after the other.

Her crying had stopped making any sound when her mother

pulled up again. This time she did not open the door for her. Julia approached tentatively and reached for the handle.

"Are you ready to stop acting like a baby?" Anita asked.

She nodded, and Anita indicated that she could get in, and she climbed up and redid her seat belt, and when they stopped at Dominick's to pick up some things for dinner, she gripped her mother's hand so hard her knuckles turned white, so hard that her mother had to pry her fingers away in order to pay for the groceries. They proceeded after that, as always, as usual, except that when her mother came to say good night that night, she leaned over and hugged her so tight she almost lifted her from the bed, and Julia allowed her to do so, hanging sort of limply from her mother's arms but feeling the fierceness of her grip and understanding, somewhere, that it was an apology.

"Oh, please," Anita said when she brought it up a few years later. "I just drove around the block. And it was a really nice neighborhood. Who knows; you may have been better off if you'd gotten kidnapped from there."

Now, the bus stopped by the law school and a man with his hands suspiciously shrouded inside his coat pockets settled in across from her. She pulled the chain for the next stop and walked the rest of the way home. How would normal people handle this type of parental confrontation? She considered shame-filled obsequiousness; she formulated a half-assed speech, soliloquizing, calling upon the free-love rhetoric of her mother's formative years. But both of those thoughts were quickly extinguished by a third, truer one: that normal people wouldn't need to prepare for this kind of conversation. Normal people wouldn't have done what she had.

When she came in the front door her mother was sitting placidly at the kitchen table, hands around a mug of tea.

"You're late," Anita said.

"Sorry," Julia said, and she opened her mouth to lie, but as she did she met her mother's eyes, and closed it again. She waited, but nothing came; her mother continued to stare at her, but she didn't say anything. Julia hung her jacket on the coatrack, slipped off her shoes. When she turned around her mother had fixed her gaze on a spot near the refrigerator, so she went, nervously, to her room, eager to get out of her skirt, still moss-damp. If she'd been a less pragmatic person, she might have thrown it in the trash.

Her mother started speaking before she'd made it back to the kitchen, as she was walking down the hall from her room.

"I can't for the life of me imagine what you were thinking," Anita said, almost pleasantly. "I never in a million years would have expected this of you."

She was startled by the fact that they were already talking about it. But she was more startled by the admission of expectation, that her mother had expected anything of her at all. Of course she had always been relied on to be self-sufficient, to be compliant and quiet, to not throw tantrums in Montgomery Ward. But it had never occurred to her that her mother also might be holding her to higher, more refined standards, the standards of decent human behavior. It had never occurred to her that her mother might trust her.

She felt the impulse to say it again, what she'd said in the car years ago: *I didn't mean to.* Because she hadn't, not really; of course she'd wanted to hurt her mother, but Jonathan had happened for other reasons too, many of which she didn't understand and so couldn't enumerate.

"Mom, I didn't mean to—"

Had she meant to? She wasn't sure anymore.

"Didn't you?"

"I didn't mean for it to—*hurt* you; I—"

"Oh, I'm not hurt. This isn't hurt."

This stilled her, and then a surprising anger surged in her chest. "It— Of course it is. You can't just pretend you're not feeling something when you're clearly feeling it, Mom; you can't just say you aren't hurt by something when you clearly—"

"When you've clearly done something incredibly hurtful? I'm fucking furious, Julia, make no mistake about that. But I'm not giving you the satisfaction of *hurt*, all right?"

"Satisfaction? You think this makes me *happy*?"

"I don't have any idea what it makes you," Anita said. "I don't even know who you are."

"I'm not sure how it happened," she said quietly. "I'm not— He just—"

"Don't worry, I'm holding that scumbag amply responsible. Were you careful?" Her mother smiled then, her familiar dry, down-turned smile. "Did you use protection, I mean."

She lowered her eyes. "Yes."

"Well, Lord, let this be the only time I have intimate knowledge of your sexual partner's venereal health, but you should be free and clear." Then, such aggressively disgusting phrasing: "I'll let you know if anything crops up on my end."

"I don't have an STD."

"Brava." Her mother raised her mug in a toast, sipped deeply. "You know, I don't even have it in me to be disappointed in you?"

This caught her off guard. "Why? Why can't you— Like, just *feel* something?" It was pathetic, she realized, her desire for something more, for some kind of fallout, proof that her mother cared about her in some capacity, but she couldn't help the hysteria creeping up her throat.

"We're done here," her mother said, rising from the table, and when she passed by with her mug, Julia caught the telltale licorice whiff of gin.

"Mom, please."

"Go to bed, Julia." Her mother started down the hall and she began to feel the panic setting in again.

"Mom," she said, desperately, going after her. "Wait."

She followed Anita into her bedroom, where she'd already started calmly going through the motions of getting ready for bed, resuming her familiar game of inattention.

"Mom, you can't just ignore me."

Her mother met her gaze in the mirror. "Can't I? Why's that?"

"We can't just— We need to *talk* about this."

"We already did. I'm finished talking about it. You win, okay, Julia? You want out of this? Door's right there." She gestured vaguely toward the hallway.

"What do you— What do you *mean*, want out? I never said that I wanted *out*; I don't know what happened, Mom; I don't know why I did it."

She hadn't realized she'd been testing her mother, but she saw now that her mother had failed. She watched Anita calmly rub Pond's cream onto her face, and she shuffled through the familiar deck of cards in her head, all the possibilities of what other people—normal people—might currently be doing with their mothers: watching *Dallas*, having deeply felt heart-to-hearts about healthy sex with age-appropriate boys or simply existing, in different areas of the house, without the strangeness and animosity that had characterized Julia's home life since she could remember; she wondered what it would be like to just be lying on her bed right now, doing nothing, never having been at risk of behaving badly enough to push her mother away forever, never having entertained the notion that her mother might be okay with her not being around. "Mom, please."

"Please what?" In the mirror, she watched Julia evenly, expectantly.

"I'm sorry," she said.

"Yeah, I'll bet you're sorry."

Anita brushed past her en route to the bathroom; Julia heard the ordinary sound of running water, her mother casually brushing her teeth as though this were any other Thursday.

She, too, went to bed. And the next day she called the registrar at Northwestern and told them she was withdrawing her enrollment for the fall; it was a better school, but Kansas State had given her a full ride and was ten hours away, and though she'd learned by then that it didn't matter how far you went—that you could live thirty minutes from your dad and not even know it; that your dad could live thirty minutes from you and not even care—she decided she would go there, because it seemed like the best thing, to put as much physical space as possible between her and her mother. She did not attend her graduation. She stopped by the school the week after to collect her diploma, and when the cheerful woman in the front office asked her what her plans were, she told her Northwestern, just so she could say it once, like it was true, like anything was happening how it was supposed to have happened.

53

When Sunny's stepfather lurches up from the table just as she's set out the dessert and sat down herself, she worries for a few seconds that he's having some sort of medical episode. It occurs to her that she can't remember his name; she is trying to determine whether anyone has actually told her his name when he taps on the edge of his water glass with a fork.

"I'm sorry," he says. "Forgive me; I'm just wondering if I could have—a moment."

He is not, it seems, accustomed to attention; there are mottled red patches blooming from beneath his shirt collar. He clears his throat. Sunny looks to her mother, who looks, with some desperation, to the tweens, who have abandoned the muted videos they've been watching on a phone beneath the table for the entirety of dinner and are watching their father, wide-eyed, with gleeful, car-accident horror.

"I just hoped I could have a minute," he says, fumbling in his pocket before producing a folded square of paper. "I'm told it's customary for the fathers to say a few words."

Mark looks to her, panic in his eyes.

Sunny's stepfather clears his throat again as he begins to read; his volume has increased a few decibels, and beside her, Alma startles. He proceeds, to Julia's astonishment, to tell them that love is patient and kind, the same Corinthians verse that had appeared alongside the Precious Moments figures on the wedding card her mother had sent to her all those years ago. The reading is too common for it to qualify as more than a coincidence, but she still feels bowled over. She looks up to see if her mother remembers—of *course* her mother doesn't remember—but Anita is just listening, Marshall's arm around the back of her chair and Suzanne—the traitor—again in her lap.

"Good luck," says the man—it's ridiculous that she still can't think of his name—tucking away his paper. "And thank you, Julia and Mark, for your hospitality." But he hasn't lifted his glass; he suddenly gestures at Mark like he's randomly selecting a member of the studio audience.

"Oh." There's a beat, then Mark rises. "Sure, I— Phillip, for starters, Julia and I want to thank all of you for making the trip out here." *Phillip.* This is Mark's nightmare, she knows, but she's also very glad that it's he who's been summoned, because it is her nightmare too, and she's reached her quota. "I have to admit I wasn't prepared to give any sort of— But it's— We're so happy. Julia and I."

She feels his steadying hand on her shoulder, and she reaches up and covers it with hers. Maintaining a partnership wasn't easy, but relying on it publicly was, and its benefits in social situations could not be overstated, hiding behind the protective barrier of plurality, the royal *we*, the buffer that another person provided. She's trying to think of a way to step in and help when suddenly Mark starts speaking again.

"I wish I could truly express how much we love this kid," he says. "From the minute he showed up; it was— We were done for. And it's been— Since then, it's been— Certainly not without—*speed* bumps, but Ben's— You've just been steady, kid. The constant line. I'm so proud to be your dad."

She thinks of her son's eyebrows in those first hours, and of her husband beside her, noticing them too; Mark doesn't always clock details but he tends to see the ones that count.

"And we're so happy you've found Sunny," he goes on. "That you found each other. That you get to know what it feels like to find that—*thing* with another person. Because it's—a pretty great thing to find."

She feels his hand pulse a few times on her shoulder and she looks up and meets his eyes, finding in them if not quite forgiveness then at least a little bit of give. She weaves her fingers through his.

"We're really proud of the two of you for—forging your own

path like you are. It's no small thing." He seems to relax, then; the worst is, perhaps, behind him. His voice is more confident when he goes on: "We love you both, and we're here for you, and we're going to miss you, Ben, coming over every fifteen minutes to eat our groceries."

Laughter. Julia slips her hand from her husband's and sips her wine, feeling disembodied.

"To Sunny and Ben." Mark lifts his glass, and Julia participates fully in the clinking, and then drinks more wine. She watches, seated, as her husband and her son hug each other; she watches Alma dab at her eyes with a napkin; she wonders if she, too, should be standing, hugging, crying, but instead she's fixed to her seat, thinking about Ben, the tiny, obliterating entity he'd been at the outset, her mystifying companion in arms.

She has always vacillated between feeling things too deeply and not feeling them at all, so she learned, at a young age, how to steel herself; she could stop herself from feeling, she found, if she tried hard enough. It became a muscle she could flex, hardening herself against any unwanted onslaught of disappointment, and it works, too, to prevent crying in public. She feels others watching her, and she resents these impromptu performances for putting her in the limelight as well; her silence in the wake of Mark's effusion feels conspicuous, and she keeps taking little sips from her glass to give herself something to do.

When he sits back down, she squeezes his thigh under the table. The music takes over again, a helpfully jaunty "Everybody Needs Somebody," and she sees her mother watching her; looks away, over at her son, who isn't going far, true, but who, God, they're really, really going to miss.

After everyone leaves, Julia slips out for a walk with Suzanne, hoping the chill in the air will clear her head. She's halfway down the block, the dog nose-down in the neighbors' peonies, when she hears footsteps behind her. Perhaps she'll be murdered tonight, she thinks idly; perhaps all of this has been leading not to a wedding but to something much larger, a much simpler end, really, compared to everything that has preceded it. She's had much too much to drink.

"You mind?" her mother asks. She's wrapped in Mark's windbreaker. "Jesus Christ, how do you stand it? Isn't it *May*? I don't know how I stuck it out here as long as I did."

Julia eyes her warily. Suzanne, who believes in quiet sanctity during her walks, huffs from beneath the peonies.

"I come in peace," her mother says. "I lost my cool in the kitchen."

She's so surprised that she can't think how to respond.

Anita pauses to light a cigarette. She waves it at Julia, smoke streaming from her mouth as she asks, again, "You mind?"

"It's fine."

"I know I need to give it up," her mother says. "But it's my only earthly vice. Anymore, at least. Even if it's turning me into one of those— Remember those dried apples they used to make around Halloween?"

"You look good," Julia says grudgingly.

"I *feel* good. I'm probably the healthiest I've ever been. Better late than never, I guess." She shivers in Mark's coat; Julia imagines him pulling it on in the morning, smelling the cigarette. "The warm weather helps. I never thought you'd come back here, to all this—winter."

"It's my home," Julia says.

"It's just that you were so eager to get away."

"I wasn't trying to get away from the city," Julia says, and she feels it strike her mother.

Anita sighs. "I'm sorry if you didn't want me to come this weekend."

"Are you on some kind of nonapology tour? Is this a twelve-step thing?"

"Don't belittle that," Anita says sharply.

"Sorry," Julia says, feeling fourteen. "Mom, I'm—" *Proud of you,* she cannot say.

"I'm sorry I came," her mother amends. "If you didn't want me to come."

"I *invited* you. You're the one who said it wasn't a good idea." She picks up her pace to match that of Suzanne, who is hunting some invisible prey, her belly low to the ground.

"My curiosity won out, I guess. I wonder about you. All of you."

"Forgive my skepticism," Julia says.

"You don't have to believe me. That doesn't mean it isn't true; that doesn't mean I don't think about you. For Christ's sake, Julia, why do you think I'm here? Why do you think I came last time?"

"I have no idea why you came last time," she says. "You left before I could figure it out."

"I *left*," her mother says after a moment, inhaling like Julia does when Alma is being particularly trying, "because I felt—extraneous. Do you have any idea how it felt to show up at your house and find out you were about to have a baby and that you hadn't told me?"

"Your number was disconnected. What was I supposed to do, send out some kind of signal flare?" At Julia's raised voice, Suzanne looks back at them, ears flat against her skull.

"Being here, I felt— You obviously didn't need me; you clearly had this whole *life* built for yourself, Julia, and I was just—extra."

"*I* didn't make you feel that way," Julia says. "You can't—*turn* this on me; I welcomed you into our home and I invited you to stay with us and you said *yes*." She's surprised by how accessible her indignation is, by how easily and fully formed the sentiment springs from her. "You moved into our guest room and you told Ben you'd come to his soccer game and you told *me* you'd be here to help out with the new baby and then you just—ab*scon*ded in the middle of the night. To who the fuck knows where. When I was about to give birth. When I hadn't seen you for more than ten minutes in fifteen years."

"Mark didn't want me there."

"Mark was fine with you being there because *I* wanted you there."

"He insisted that I was *on* something," her mom says. "Which I wasn't, for the record. I'm not saying I was sober at that time generally, but I was when I was there visiting you. I was just *happy*, Julia."

"He insisted—when? What are you talking about?"

Anita studies her. "I've been trying to decide if you genuinely don't know."

"For God's sake, Mom, don't know *what*?"

"You've always been a good liar," Anita says, and then, as if making up her mind, she shrugs. "Mark called me. A few days later, when I was back home. He told me you'd had the baby and everyone was fine and if I ever showed up at your house again he'd turn me away at the door."

She stops walking; this time Suzanne stops too, leash slack, looking up at them as though she also doesn't know what to make of what Anita has just said.

"He really didn't tell you?" Anita asks, and Julia has, just barely, the presence of mind to shake her head. "Huh," her mom says. "I'd wondered, all along, if you'd asked him to do it."

"I didn't."

"Maybe he has more balls than I thought," Anita says. Then: "You two look out for each other, don't you? That's good, I guess."

"That's why you left? Because of Mark?"

"No." Her mother looks at her with—there it is again—something like pity. "No, Julia, I left because I saw how afraid you were I was going to ruin things for you again. I don't even think you realized it yourself; you were trying so hard to convince yourself that it would be a good idea for me to stay."

She doesn't respond to this, either, because it's true.

"I didn't want to be around someone who was trying to make herself want me there," Anita says.

"But I'm— You're my *mother*, ninety percent is being there regardless of whether your kids want you around. And you treated *me*— After what happened, it was like you didn't care if you ever saw me again."

"God, I've spent so many years trying to put all of this behind me. What do you want me to say, Julia? That I blame myself? Of course I blame myself. If not—exactly for what happened, then for—what you did. What you thought was okay to do. I was responsible for you; I *made* you and you turned out to be capable of that kind of cruelty? Of course it felt like my fault."

"I didn't do it to be cruel. Or I mean—I guess I did want to hurt you initially but then it turned into something— He was a predator, Mom, he took advantage of me, even if I *let* him take advantage of me."

"Jesus Christ, you think I don't know that?" Her mother's voice is sharp and clear. "You think I didn't feel *sick* about that part of it?"

"It didn't seem like you did," she says, not to be mean, just because it's true. "It seemed like you hated me."

"Of course I don't hate you," Anita says, suddenly sounding tired.

"You haven't been a part of my life," Julia says. "At all. My entire adult life."

"Not all mothers are close to their daughters, Julia," Anita says thoughtfully after a minute. "Not like how you are with yours."

She turns this over in her head, trying to determine whether it's a compliment, whether Alma—she misses Alma suddenly, even though she's half a block away, at home in her bedroom for not much longer—would embrace the assessment or stagger theatrically away from the notion of their being close.

Anita continues: "Something that I— Something Marshall has helped me to see, over the last few years, is when it makes sense to just call something what it is. It's never been easy for us. You and me. And that's— It has to be okay. We can't go back and change any of it."

"So that's just— That's it? You're just giving up?"

"I'm giving *in*," Anita says. "I'm calling it what it is."

"And what it is—"

"We are who we are."

"Are you just going to spout fucking clichés at me until you short-circuit?"

"I do care about you, Julia, even if you don't believe me. We just see things differently, I think, on a fundamental level, but that doesn't mean that I don't . . ."

She's about to turn up the front walkway to the house, her mother behind her. She stops and turns to face her. "Don't what?"

It doesn't mean I don't love you is what she'd say to Alma, to Ben; she has spent years making sure they know what they mean to her, telling them without telling them that she may not understand her feelings about most things, but that she knows, like nothing else, how she feels about them. She waits for it; she can't help it; some part of her, despite everything, has always been waiting for it.

Her mother falters. "It doesn't mean," she says, "I'm not glad to be here."

54

Ten minutes later, Julia is on her knees in her bathroom, vomiting violently. Mark, who is made squeamish by bodily emanations, is standing in the doorway, head turned away, offering platitudes and idly making motions as if stroking her hair.

"It's okay," he says, and "You'll feel better when it's all out," and, nervously, "God, I hope it's not *E. coli*."

When the exorcism seems to have run its course, she sits back on her haunches, breathing athletically. She lifts her head to regard the burgundy flecks on the shower curtain.

"Why did you let me drink so much," she says, and he snorts.

"I didn't see you eat much. Did you eat *anything*?"

"Not really." She rises tentatively, reaching for her toothbrush. "Some arugula."

She starts brushing her teeth and Mark, coast clear, joins her. She watches him in the mirror, his threadbare Sebadoh shirt and enough dental floss to string a harp. It's something of a fashion to lament moments like this one in a marriage, such unsexy oral unity, tartar buildup and mouthwash and, thanks to her, vomit, but she's always been soothed by the steady simplicity of proximity and routine, the workaday comfort with another person's body.

"You all right?" Mark asks, and she nods, rinsing her mouth.

"I think so."

"Deep breaths." There's warmth in his voice, and she meets his eyes in the mirror. He wets a washcloth and holds it out to her. "Come on, Miss Arugula," he says, and puts an arm around her waist, guides her to their bed. She lies flat on her back, staring up at the ceiling until it stops spinning. Mark stretches out beside her, propped on an elbow.

"You never drink like this." He dabs the washcloth at the base of her throat.

"I didn't mean to. I guess I was nervous."

"Big night," he breathes.

"Ben looked really happy," she says.

"Yeah, he did."

"Are we," she starts to ask, but she isn't entirely sure she's ready for the answer. "I missed you tonight," she says instead.

"Oh, Jules." He sighs. "You want to do this now?"

"Why not."

He rolls onto his back, covering his face with a forearm. "I can think of a few reasons why not. Several."

"There isn't ever going to be a time we *want* to. Shouldn't we just— Out with it?"

"Fine," he says after a minute. "But will you let me talk? First?" He moves his arm away, meets her eyes.

"Sure."

"I've been trying to—figure out how we're supposed to talk about this. I wasn't expecting that we were ever *going* to talk about it again."

"Me either."

"I thought I'd put it behind me."

"But you haven't?" she asks, and then, when she realizes she's supposed to just be listening, "Sorry."

"Francine's my friend," he says.

"Okay," she says, and "I know," and then, again, "Sorry."

"I told her what happened between us because I didn't know who else to tell," Mark says. "And I didn't tell you I'd told her because I—honestly, I felt like after what you did—I was allowed to have something that was mine too. And wouldn't it just have hurt you if I'd told you I talked to her?"

"Yeah," she says. "It would have."

"I *wanted* to hurt you back then, but not in that way. That seemed—just needlessly cruel." As needlessly cruel, he does not say, as her telling him about Nathaniel in the first place. She meets his gaze, good old agendaless Mark, who is more complicated than anyone—than she—has ever given him credit for.

"I wasn't ready to forgive you," he says. "Back then. I wasn't sure

I could ever forgive you. But talking through it with her—made a difference. It helped me look at things from further away. She convinced me I should. Forgive you. She helped *save* us, Julia."

And years ago it would have killed her to hear this, that he'd chosen to repair their marriage not because he wanted to but because Francine Grimes thought it would be a good idea, but here she is, beside him, very much alive, and this in itself feels extraordinary, that some things—this thing, and very probably other things—might possibly be too far in the past to hurt them anymore.

"That's why I went to see her in Philly. Because she and Brady both mean a lot to me, and I felt like I owed it to her. To be there for her the way she'd been for me. I love her, Julia." He turns his head to look at her; she feels a strange, cold sensation in her hands, tingling down to the tips of her fingers. "I love her like— I'm not sure. Not like a sister, but also not— I mean, not at all like *you*, but also not— I admire her, and I like being around her, and I care about her. It's its own thing. It always has been, and it has nothing to do with you."

She thinks of Helen Russo beside her at the botanic garden, Helen Russo, whom she has always loved too: love that she'd never quite been able to define, love that wasn't specifically anything, familial or sexual or aspirational, parental or romantic or platonic, but also wasn't specifically *not* any of those things: love that was simply a point of fact, its own entity.

"I understand," she says.

"I'm sorry I didn't tell you I went to see her," he says. "I do regret that now, seeing how much it upset you. But honestly it seemed like more trouble than it was worth. And also— I don't know, Jules, our lives are so—*ours*. Is it always such a bad thing, having our own things? My intention is to not have secrets from you, but it— We've been together for almost thirty years; shouldn't we trust each other enough by now?"

"We should," she says. "We—do, don't we?"

Mark is frowning at a spot on the bedspread, his fingers worrying a loose stitch.

"I do," she says. "Trust you. But I understand if you— If that's not . . ."

He looks up at her, his gaze steady. "I do. Now I do."

"Thank you," she says quietly, because it is perhaps the kindest thing anyone has ever said to her; it is, perhaps, the most generous thing Mark has ever done, trusting her, after everything. Perhaps it is possible—could her mother be right?—for things to happen and be gotten over.

"You're welcome," says Mark, and reaches for her hand.

"I'd kiss you," she says, "except."

He leans over and kisses her forehead; she is just beginning to relax against him when he asks, "What happened with your mom?"

"I'm not sure how to answer that," she says, straightening. "She told me I've gained weight. We talked about—a lot of things, actually." She does not look at him when she says, "She told me you called her and told her not to come here."

A beat. "Oh," he says. "God, Jules, I'm—"

"Full of surprises," she says, shifting gingerly, "aren't you."

"I wasn't— I was so *angry*. And we were trying so hard to make things better. And the fact that she had the gall to—God—do that to you again, whether or not she knew how much it had hurt you the first time; it made me want to kill her. And I was envisioning her doing it again, and again, just this endless cycle of her coming in and knocking you down. I knew the hold she had over you—*has* over you, even if— I think you're too close to it to see it sometimes, but it's always there, even when she's not. And after you told me what she did to you, what happened to you, I—" He shakes his head. "I didn't want her anywhere near you. Near *us*; I just kept looking at Alma and thinking— I know it's a cliché, to have your own kids and assume you're going to do a better job raising them than your parents did raising you, but I just kept thinking of how *vulnerable* she was. And how vulnerable you'd been as a kid. And how vulnerable *we* were then, our family, and I—didn't think we'd survive it. Her showing up again. Hurting you again."

He studies her; they are both assessing the same thing: how, precisely, she feels about this.

"You're mad," he says.

"No." She shakes her head thoughtfully. "I think I'm— Part of me feels like you should have told me, because it seems preferable, thinking she stayed away all those years because you told her to, but then— I mean, is that really any better? That you felt you needed to tell her in the first place? And God, that she *listened* to you? Can you imagine someone telling us to do that? And our actually doing it? Jesus."

"That's about her, though. You know that, right? It's about her, Jules, not you."

"It's about a lot of things."

"Maybe I made the wrong decision." He rubs his forehead. "Maybe— I don't know, I was so angry, and maybe I didn't think it through."

"You probably did," she says evenly. "You usually do." He looks out for her, Mark does; her mother, at least, is right about this.

"I'm sorry," he says. "For not telling you."

"I'm sorry for—" *Everything* feels overly generous; *everything else* not generous enough. "Projectile vomiting," she says. "This isn't how I'm supposed to be doing this. Shouldn't I be—what, bagging Jordan almonds with Sunny's mother right now? Shouldn't I be drinking tea?"

"Do you want some tea?"

"No. But I *should* want it. My God. We're *old*. And I'm— This is sophomoric. I'm *el*derly. This isn't how I'm supposed to be doing any of it."

"Jules," he says. He seat-belts his arm around her waist and she presses back against him. "You're doing just fine."

"Really?" she asks. "I haven't— Have I—"

"Shh," he says. Then, into her ear, teasing: "Bagging Jordan almonds. Is that a euphemism?"

"No," she says, closing her eyes, resting her head on his chest. "No, Mark, it's from the Revolutionary War."

55

She hopes—owing to emotional distress and far, far too much wine—that she might sleep deeply, and late, but she finds herself in a familiar arrangement early the next morning, wide awake at five a.m. while Mark slumbers beside her. She shifts on her side to observe him. It's astounding to think that she used to rue his presence in bed; more astonishing still is the fact that she has this thought set to the cacophonic soundtrack of his snoring, which blares discordantly from the dignified landscape of his face. She touches his cheek, pulls the comforter up around his shoulders and then slips out of bed.

The light in the kitchen is gray-blue, not yet pink, a light she's always enjoyed very much, now because it helps her think and, long ago, simply because of the quiet that came along with it, because you were seldom actively accountable to anyone at five in the morning. She gets a sweatshirt—Mark's, huge—from the mudroom and wraps it around her shoulders. She's hungover, her teeth and her nerves trilling from the wine. She notes the already-made coffee at the same time her senses register the airy musk of nearby cigarette smoke. She's pouring herself a cup when she sees Marshall in the yard, sitting at the bottom of the back steps. She stands on tiptoe, trying to take advantage of this unfettered access to his private self when he doesn't know she's looking. She's not sure what to make of him, this man who wears blousy short-sleeved button-downs and touches her mother's elbow as he passes her, like a reminder that she still exists and someone loves her.

She sips the coffee—much stronger than she makes it, bordering on acrid—and heads for the back door, knocking on it gently from the inside so she doesn't startle him.

"Morning," she says, and he waves at her with his cigarette.

"Hope I'm not disturbing you."

"Not at all. Thanks for making the coffee."

"Your mother says I make it too strong."

"Apparently she and I have a few points of commonality after all."

"Join me, if you'd like," he says, and after a second she does, pulling the sweatshirt tighter around her shoulders. "You mind my smoking?" he asks.

"Not unless you're smoking menthols."

"Whew." He exhales away from her. "That would've been a difficult one to fake."

"My mom's still asleep?"

"Yep."

"Good for her," she says, not quite nicely.

He drags on his cigarette before responding. "At the risk of overstepping my bounds," he says, "you don't give her enough credit."

She laughs loudly, theatrically, and she imagines the birds awakening overhead in their nests. "Yes," she says, "that's always been the problem, a hundred percent."

"I don't mean—" He clears his throat. "I don't presume to know what it was like for you, growing up. But she thinks about you more than you'll ever know. Worries about you."

"I'm fine," she says.

"It's not always *rational* worry." He smiles. "You're a mother. You know that."

"If she spends one *hundredth* of the time I spend thinking about my kids—"

"Things are different for you, Julia."

She pauses. "If you reveal yourself to be some sort of pyramid schemer, I'll have no qualms about calling the feds," she says.

"You get your sense of humor from her, you know," he says.

"Maybe she gets hers from me."

"I'm not talking about money," Marshall says. "I'm talking about— You've had options. Opportunities. A husband who loves you, friends, a job you like."

"I worked for those things," she says. "I had to *find* those things."

"I know that. I'm just saying you're living a whole different kind of existence from what your mother had to go through."

"*Chose* to go through," she says.

"You think it's that simple?"

Her cheeks burn. "Of course I don't."

"She's happy you have those things. For the record. She's told me that many times. And I'd like to tell you that I am too. Happy for you. I've heard so much about you over the years that I feel like I know you. And I'm rooting for you. Your mom and I both."

"Okay, Father Christmas," she says, uncomfortable.

"I love your mother, Julia. And I love you by extension. I'd just like for you to know that."

"Well, I— Thanks."

Marshall smiles. "Don't mention it."

He leans back and lifts his face up toward the sun, smoking like someone who takes the time to enjoy every cigarette. She leans back too, and closes her eyes, the sun hard on her skin, black constellations blooming behind her eyelids.

"She hadn't told you we were married, had she?" he asks.

She blinks her eyes open. She must like him, because it is her impulse to lie.

But he seems to register her hesitation. "It's all right," he says. "I was just curious. Something about the way you looked at dinner last night made me wonder."

"She didn't tell me, no. Did she— Did you have a wedding?"

"Nothing big."

"Your kids came?"

Now Marshall hesitates.

"She didn't want me there," Julia says.

"She didn't think you'd want to come."

"You must have thought I—" She forces herself to laugh. "God, you guys all must think I'm just this awful *shrew*." But it hurts her to say it, and the bitterness in her own voice almost makes her flinch. She remembers, of course, the pity on the faces of Mark's family members when she'd explained to them that her mother was alive but simply not attending her wedding; she used to lie awake imagining what conversations transpired between Bonnie and Skip behind closed doors, midwestern judgment couched as bafflement, *Now what kind of mother does that?*

"Nobody thinks that about you, Julia," Marshall says. "I've never for a second thought that, and your mother's never said a word to suggest it."

"Has she told you a lot about me?"

"She has," Marshall says. "As much as she knows, I imagine."

She cannot bring herself to ask if Anita has told him what she did, what had happened when she was seventeen. She studies his expression, looking for some sign of it, but his face is, upon examination, not all that unlike Mark's: contented, preemptive mercy in the eyes, not a trace of malice to be found.

"About your kids, I mean, Julia," he says. "Your job. The pictures you send her. That's the stuff she talks about. How funny you were as a little girl; how you used to leave ice cream out for the neighbor's cat in the summer."

"I don't remember that," she says softly.

"She does," Marshall says emphatically, forcing her to meet his eye. "I know things are complicated between the two of you. But that's not the stuff she talks about. And I haven't pressed her on it. When you find a partner later in life— I don't know, I guess you just accept the fact that there are going to be parts of the past you don't get access to."

She is surprised to feel tears in her eyes; it's plausible, of course, that Anita never told Marshall what happened because she's embarrassed by it, but it feels more—she does know her mother; she knew her so well for so long—like an act of loyalty to Julia, not passing on to anyone else that dark time in their shared history.

"I know she feels like she doesn't know how to be a mother to you," Marshall says.

Her anger wins out again. "Nobody ever knows *how*. Jesus. That's— Isn't that just part of the game? But you have to at least *pretend* that you care about your—"

"You've progressed beyond her understanding," he says. "Our kids are always, one day, going to progress beyond our understanding; don't you think?"

"Mine did before they were even born."

She can see, in the easy way Marshall's face lifts in a smile, that he does care for her, even though he's only known her for twenty-four hours. He cares for her in the generous, compliant way you're supposed to care for the people a person you love cares for, the way she has come to tolerate Brady Grimes, the way she's grown fond of Sunny.

It's strange for her to think of someone loving her mother, equally strange for her to think of her mother loving anyone else; Anita's life, for the most part, lacked the context for it. It was easier for people who'd known care, what it felt like and how to give it back; it was much easier—she has learned this, too, after years and years of study—to dredge up affection when you had some idea of what it looked like.

"Is she happy?" she asks.

"I think so," he says. "I hope so." Then: "Are you?"

"I'm old enough not to care."

"You're so much like her," he says.

"How can you say that? You barely know me."

"I hope that changes," he says. "For what it's worth, I hope we'll have a chance to get to know each other better. You should come visit us sometime."

She tries to smile at him.

"I mean it," says Marshall. "She'd love it. Have you seen the Redwoods? Monterey Bay? We could make a whole family thing out of it."

"Maybe we could," she says. "She—" She clears her throat. "She's close with your kids, isn't she?"

"She is, yeah. My daughter Lydia especially."

"Close how?" Like prodding at a broken tooth. "Like—just from day one?"

"No, not at all." Marshall smiles faintly. "There was a bit of a learning curve. My kids are very loyal to their mother, which I don't blame them for. They were resistant to my marrying someone new. And she's not always the easiest person to get along with, your mom."

"No," Julia says. "She isn't."

"But then neither is Lydia. I think maybe that's why they've ended up being as close as they are. They've met their matches. Lydia's the one who convinced her to come this weekend, actually. She gave her a real dressing-down about it, that she'd be crazy not to come when you'd invited her."

She has never felt strong enough to dress down her mother herself, or her mother has never seemed strong enough to withstand it; she can't imagine what this might look like, having a casual spat with Anita, a spat that didn't risk ending everything.

"It's easier," Marshall says gently. "When people aren't your own kids."

"Yeah," she says. "It is."

And she thinks—of course she does—of Helen Russo.

t hadn't all been horrible. Just statistically speaking, it couldn't all be horrible. She and her mother would watch *Fantasy Island* and *Emergency!* and late-night local access programs of troubled people doing karaoke. They'd wander down to Symphony Lake to feed stale brioche to the ducks. They'd heat up olive oil in the microwave and comb it through their hair to prevent split ends; they'd flip through the Sears catalog and choose the most desirable objects on every page. This was the white noise, the gray matter that made up their life together, shared rolls of Life Savers and winter jackets and hair conditioner, a mutual obsession with the woman in the third-floor apartment across the street who had a full set of inflatable pool furniture in her living room instead of a regular sofa and chairs. They shared everything, for a time. They used to dance in the kitchen for the length of full albums, *The Supremes A' Go-Go* and *Runaround Sue* and *Hunky Dory;* her mother would come home and Julia would be able to feel something good in the air she brought with her from outside, and they'd start in on some recipe together—because there always needed to be a context, something to get them in the same room, brownies or banana pudding—and it would quickly fall by the wayside, her mother, nerves stripped from a day at work and an evening looking, however shoddily, after a kid, would start singing along to the music, and then Julia, after a minute, would join her, *I love you and nobody else,* and if the right song came on—it had to fit specific criteria, an inarticulable formula, the right balance of whimsy and heartbreak, earnestness and stamina, passion in the vocals but not so much that it was un*seem*ly, and then suddenly they'd both be dancing, *Yes indeed, all I really need;* when she was little enough Anita would lift Julia into her arms, and the hollow of her mother's collarbones would smell like sweat and sugar and something else, something she'd never find again. They would shimmy and twirl and lunge across the kitchen, sometimes laughing uncontrollably but just as often with studied, sacrosanct seriousness, her mother moving with an athletic grace, and like it was her job, like there was nobody else in the room, like all this movement was going to *get* her somewhere; it never was clear to Julia whether she was welcome to come with or not, so she danced just as hard regardless, eyes squeezed shut, tiny toddler body doing the Twist and waving her arms.

"*There* you go," her mother said to her once, lifting her into the air, burying her face in Julia's belly, and she remembers feeling loved then, wholeheartedly, loved just for existing.

They'd stopped doing this together at some point, but she couldn't remember which time was the last time; she kept doing it herself for a while, after they'd gone their separate ways, and she has always wondered—she will always wonder—if her mother did the same.

57

The florist—of course it is—is only about a mile from the old house on Superior Street. She stands by as a cadre of sleepy-eyed teenage boys load eight hundred dollars' worth of lisianthuses into the back of the Subaru, and then she tucks, beside her in the passenger seat, a bright bouquet of poppy anemones, picked up on impulse; they watch her with their black eyes as she drives the familiar route to Helen Russo's house.

Walking up the front path, she is overcome by a bit of respiratory paralysis; there seems to be a shimmering, misty quality in the air before her, though it's certainly her imagination, imposing something cinematic onto ordinary circumstances, like cotton cobwebs for Halloween. She touches, lovingly, a pane of stained glass on the front door before she rings the bell.

Until the door opens, she forgets to be nervous, but the person who answers the door is a man, her own age, decidedly not Helen Russo.

"Hi there," he says. He has a trimmed, pale beard and deep laugh lines around the eyes, which are—here she relaxes—a muddy brown. Otherwise his resemblance to Nathaniel is almost uncanny, aided in part by the fact that she has to add twenty years to her memory of him anyway, but lo, this is decidedly Not Nathaniel, some pale facsimile. "Can I help you?"

"You must be Cal," she says. Around her she notices the detritus, evidence of a man deep in a project, detached gutters laid out before the lilac bushes and a small hill of gravel to her left.

He smiles at her. "You looking for Mom?"

She has always been distrustful of adults who refer to their parents conversationally, to unrelated parties, as *Mom* and *Dad*, instead of *my mom* and *my dad*, the unconscious suggestion therein that whoever is being addressed is just supposed to know the speaker's parents. It implies, too, that the speaker still considers himself or herself to be entitled to parenting regardless of their age. Sunny's frequent and ingratiating repetition of *Baby* feels somehow more excusable, a preemptive effusion of parental love instead of this odd manifestation of arrested development, a sixty-year-old man still umbilically tethered to his mother.

Or perhaps she's being unfair. Perhaps it's envy she's feeling, at this man's ability to speak so easily of the woman he came from.

"Helen," she says. "I was looking for—Helen."

"She's out back," he says. "Come on in." And he's already opened the door wider, waving her in behind him as he heads down the foyer to the kitchen. She takes a step inside, then another, and then, uncertainly, she clicks the door closed, wiping her dry shoes on the worn rug.

They don't happen very often, but moments like these of sensory recognition are some of the most potent she's ever lived, the transportive effect of a whiff of perfume or pencil shavings. The Russos' house smells just like it used to, buttered toast and wood varnish and damp fresh air, the close collegial quality of somewhere lived in and well loved, and it hits her tangibly. She loved this house like a person, so much more than her own home.

Little has changed. It's messier, cluttered with more evidence of Cal's renovative efforts—a tackle box of drill bits, a plastic curtain hung over the entryway to the living room—but otherwise the same, the chaotic mail table and the big kitschy pendant light overhead, painted with flowers, a jumble of shoes spilling forth from a wicker basket. It had struck her back then so forcefully, how lived in it was, the inhabitedness of it, but her own foyer has been similarly trod on now, filled with its own clutter, Alma's four thousand interchangeable pairs of Converse and Mark's dorky Yaktrax and Suzanne's array of outerwear, do-gooder commemorative tote bags and mismatched communal accessories, garden gloves and earbuds and tea towels for drying the dog's paws. All stuff, only stuff, but evidence nonetheless of life, the clunky but functional life that's improbably hers.

Cal leads her through the kitchen. She sees the familiar table in the breakfast nook; she can feel, in the tips of her fingers, the slightly gummy surface of the wood, decades of coffee rings and jam and baby food rubbed into the grain, how, at Helen's house, what might seem grimy elsewhere was simply *textured*. She hears the distant strains of a radio-fuzzed Johnny Cash song she can't quite place, *I grew up quick and I grew up mean*. She's a little desperate to see some vestige of herself here, some mark she's left, proof of existence; she searches in vain the motley collage on the refrigerator door for something, anything—her own phone number on a faded Post-it, the Christmas card she'd sent Helen the year they'd met, not that she remembers what it looked like. The side of the fridge is blanketed with children's artwork, a tessellated installation of scrap paper and pages torn from coloring books, mixed media of crayon and marker and the spiking EKG of a ballpoint pen, and she contents herself with the notion that it's possible something of Ben's made it into the mix, that some of his indistinguishable blues and greens, generous interpretations of dogs and dinosaurs, are buried beneath the surface.

"I didn't catch your name," Cal says.

"Julia."

"You're Julia?" He looks at her over his shoulder, smiling. "She's mentioned you a few times."

"Has she?" The pride this floods her with is familiar too.

The back deck is the same, faded floral cushions on the chairs, and Helen is leaning back in one of them, sunlit and regal, her feet up in front of her on a wicker ottoman.

"Ma," Cal calls. "You've got a visitor."

Helen sees her and her face opens in a smile. "Do I," she says, and ushers Julia out. "Julia Ames," she says, "are you *courting* me?" She holds out her arms; Julia can't tell if she's soliciting a hug or the flowers.

"Don't get up," Cal calls over his shoulder as he goes back inside.

Helen rolls her eyes, accepting the anemones. "I twisted my ankle this morning tripping over one of his power tools," she says. "I think he's worried I'll sue him if it gets any worse."

"Are you okay?" Julia asks. "Can I get you anything? Is it a bad time?"

"Lord, I forgot what a *nervous* thing you are. It's a perfect time. I'm wonderful. Sit down and tell me what brings you by."

"Here to serve you with a summons," Julia says, taking a seat across from her.

"You'd be good at that, actually," Helen says. "Enigmatic. Light on your feet." Helen studies her. "Unpredictable, to a degree. I confess I wasn't sure I'd see you again."

"I wasn't sure either, I guess."

"What tipped the scales?"

"I was in the neighborhood," she says, because this time it is at least partially true. "I've got a carful of flowers. Ben's getting married this afternoon."

"And you're *here*?"

Her face warms. "I— Well."

"I'm not complaining," Helen says. "It's very flattering, actually. I'm just surprised you aren't in the middle of a million logistical things."

"Ben's—Sunny, she's a planner. Very little left to chance."

"A *planner. Tell* me. Do we hate her?" Helen sounds exactly how she used to, wicked delight that never felt entirely mean-spirited.

"We don't." Julia smiles. "She's growing on us."

"That bodes well, I'd say. I never faced down any of the boys' weddings without some pretty significant expostulation. Though I do wonder sometimes lately if I wasn't a bit ungenerous."

Julia lifts her eyebrows.

"I have a lot of time for *ponderance*," Helen says. "Wizened hag that I've become, here in my crumbling manse."

"You aren't a *hag*," Julia says.

"See?" Helen says to an invisible audience. "She is courting me."

She suppresses a smile. "You look the same," she lies. "So does the house. Almost exactly how I remember it." But that's not entirely true either; she had identified, immediately, something missing when she'd walked in the front door, the life a person brings to a household whether they're home or not. There is a new pervasive stillness in the house, a kind of *stale*ness, the molecules having rear-ranged themselves around the absence of Pete.

"A bit quieter though, wouldn't you say?" Helen says, reading her mind. "And much dustier, too, without him. I can't quite fig-ure that one out. It used to drive me insane; I'd come down in the morning and the coffee table would just suddenly be covered with this fine layer of dust, and it seemed so unfair, like half my life gets taken away and I still have to *clean*?"

She'd noticed this without realizing it as she followed Cal out-side, motes floating lazily through the air, backlit by the sun, and wonders now if it has anything to do with the basic kinetics that come from having multiple people in a house; there is doubtless the same *amount* of dust in her own home, but more people to stir it up, prevent it from settling on the surfaces.

"Then I discovered, though," Helen says, "that I could just stop dusting. It's been quite freeing, actually. So that's one upside. Apol-ogies in advance if you're prone to allergies."

"I'll survive," she says, and Helen smiles at her. "I'm sorry I didn't know," she says softly. "When Pete— I would have come to the service."

Helen raises her eyebrows. "Would you?"

She colors. "I would have—sent a card, at least, or— I mean, not that a card would have— I know it wouldn't have made a difference, but— Not that it's *about* me, not that you needed *me* around, but I—just really liked him."

"He liked you too," Helen says. "I mean, he didn't dislike too many people, to be fair, but you were popular in our household. Ben too. Is he a hundred feet tall now?"

"A hundred and ten."

"And getting *married*, my God. Isn't that unbelievable? I'm too old to be as completely wrecked by these developments as I always am."

"So am I."

But the way Helen is looking at her unnerves her; she rises, uncomfortable, and goes to the railing of the deck, leaning over to look at the garden plot below.

"Celosia," Helen says. "Like little Dr. Seuss heads, my grandson used to say. Also known less elegantly as *cock's comb*."

"They're beautiful."

"What did you mean," Helen says, "when you said I didn't need you around?"

Julia turns back to face her. "Oh. Well. I just mean— I know we haven't seen each other for years, but I still . . ."

"What?"

"I'm just sorry. I wish I'd been a better friend to you. You were so kind to me. You didn't have to be. The least I could have done was be kind back."

Helen studies her. "Just because I have a lot of people in my life, Julia, doesn't mean that I *like* a lot of people. I liked you a great deal. You were terrific company. It's a chemistry thing, isn't it? Don't you sometimes just *feel* something for another person? Like you were meant to have found them? That's how I felt about you when we met. Like I already knew you."

She sinks down across from Helen, that same fluttering in her chest she used to feel every time Helen opened the front door, every time Helen laughed at one of her jokes, every time she said something that terrified her to say and Helen took it in stride.

"Lord, I wasn't kind to you because I felt like I *had* to be, Julia. I was kind to you because I liked being around you. And because you seemed lost, sure. But plenty of people are lost. I didn't go around inviting all of those people over to my house. I invited you because it seemed like we could both use a friend. Isn't that part of what defines every relationship? That mixture of how much you need someone and how much they need you back? It's never an equal amount. And it fluctuates—ideally it does—because both of those things are exhausting in their own right. You needed me more than I needed you then, maybe, but that doesn't mean that I didn't need a friend too. That I didn't benefit from having you in my life. Of course I did."

"But—"

"I confess," Helen goes on, "that there is a particular type of satisfaction that comes from a younger person paying you heed, and all my kids were gone by that point, so there was something kind of lovely about your coming in to fill the void. But mostly I just liked talking to you, Julia. I felt very connected to you. And honestly, is it such a bad motivator? *Pity?* Some people are simply having a harder time than others; why is it so wrong to acknowledge that? To acknowledge that you have something to offer that they might be lacking? Isn't that better than just leaving them to run circles around the inside of their own heads?"

"It is," Julia says, because she knows firsthand that this, at least, is true.

"I have a few friends in assisted living now whose kids have hired these—well, paid companions for them, I guess you'd say," Helen says. "Not nurses, just people who pop in to play cards or do the crossword. And it used to make me so sad, even just conceptually, but now I can't decide if it's the most or least generous thing I've ever heard. Loving someone so much that you'd buy her a friend? It's the sort of thing I would have done for my boys when they were little if I could have; how you'd do anything for your kids to make sure they never feel alone."

She can still feel, when she lies in bed some nights, the ghosts of Ben's and Alma's bodies pressed against her, their warm backs against her chest as she stroked their foreheads, hoping to stave off bad dreams or psychosomatic stomachaches; she has lost count of the harmless lies she's told to spare them undue heartache or early exposure to the less palatable parts of the world.

"A couple of them have really grown to *like* these people," Helen says. "They've become friends, regardless of how the circumstances came about. And you can argue that their kids should be visiting them more often—of course they should—but who's to say they aren't benefitting even more from spending time with a friend instead? Can we really indict anyone in this scenario?" Helen shrugs, leans back again. "This being said, if my boys don't come to visit me after we sell the house, I'll have them killed."

She's always been annoyed by people who pine over their childhood homes—she remembers one of her old roommates crying like someone had died when her parents downsized to a condo—but she can't identify the emotion bubbling up inside her as anything else, territorial nostalgia for the sun-bleached wood of the deck beneath them, the drip of the gutters, all the things that make this house itself, this house she hasn't set foot in for twenty years but that still means so much to her.

"You're selling?"

"Oh." Helen's studying her, her face soft. "You get it; of course you get it. I'm being glib because I can't stand to think about it, to be honest. This place getting snatched up by a securities trader or a plastic surgeon with one kid and a wife with no taste; they'll immediately gut the kitchen and all the bathrooms and add on a hideous addition for a squash court or a panic room and within a year we won't recognize it from the place next door. Of course it's silly to be attached to something so—well—material. And the *privilege* of me, God. But it makes me very sad, Julia, if I'm telling the truth."

"Does that— But where will you go? If the house . . ." She can't separate them in her head, Helen from her backdrop, her trappings, and she feels a strange panic, as though Helen will cease to exist without her surroundings, that old campfire story—Ben used to be afraid of this too—about the woman whose head was attached to her neck by a silk ribbon.

"Cedar Knoll," Helen says, and for a second Julia snags on this, envisioning an actual cedar knoll in which Helen will be taking up residence, like a gnome or a dryad, but then remembers the sprawling retirement complex that went up in a neighboring suburb a few years back in regrettable proximity to a landfill. It's hard to imagine Helen living somewhere like that, somewhere not here; it is impossible to envision someone as glamorous and autonomous as Helen Russo living in something that could be called a *complex*.

"Your *face*." Helen laughs dryly. "See, I keep telling my kids how depressing it sounds. God, maybe they *should* buy me a friend. But I made the decision two years ago; it's just now that a spot's opened up. Lord, listen to me. Speaking of depressing. A *spot's* opened up."

What had she thought would happen? Helen may well be the spryest eighty-five-year-old in all of the Chicagoland area, but she is nevertheless eighty-five, and Julia feels unbelievably foolish for not seeing this until now.

"It's just a place to live, right?" Helen says.

"I'd like to come visit you," Julia says. "If you'll have me."

Helen opens her eyes, smiles. "So you *did* talk to Cal. Has he put you on the payroll yet?"

"Very little money will change hands," Julia says, because she knows it will make Helen laugh.

"You have a standing invitation," Helen says. "Come by anytime."

58

For the wedding, Alma is wearing utilitarian funeral garb, a black dress with long-sleeved lace and Doc Martens, the ends of her hair now a striking white-blond.

"You all set?" Julia is watching her from her bedroom doorway. Alma regards her derisively in the mirror over her dresser, where she is not studying her own reflection but scrolling through her phone.

"Margo's still coming, isn't she?"

"Yup."

"That's good," says Julia. "I'm glad."

And there is not a hint of irony in her daughter's voice as she replies, "Me too." They won't be staying together; Margo is a "fourth-generation legacy" at Brown, Alma has told her matter-of-factly, and they've decided to go their separate ways come September, but she seems to be accepting this with serenity, now facing down her graduation with something that at least looks more like optimism than its opposite.

"You look lovely, sweetheart."

"Thanks," says Alma. "Is that what you're wearing?"

She looks down at her clown pants. "I'm just about to get ready."

"Oh," Alma says, reaching across the dresser. "Isn't this yours?"

Her last tube of Power Raisin. She takes it from Alma's outstretched hand, uncaps the lipstick, twists it up then screws it back down. "Keep it," she says, tossing it back to her daughter. "It suits you."

"My stupid bangs keep falling in my face," Alma says, which Julia takes as an invitation, inching her way into the room. She arrives behind her daughter and rests a hand on her head.

"Can I help?" she asks. "So they won't drive you crazy all day?"

Alma, miraculously, angles her body to give Julia free rein over the cluster of bobby pins on the desk. She dips her head back like she used to do in the bathtub, a tiny girl amid an ocean of tugboats and rubber octopi. Julia runs her fingers through her daughter's hair, Alma's skull now so sturdy and concrete. She twists a lock away from Alma's face and pins it back near the crown of her head and then—taking a chance—she bows her face to kiss her daughter's part.

"Or I could do a braid, if you wanted," she says.

"Whatever," Alma says. From her, this may as well be a wrapped present.

Alma's hair united them when her daughter was tiny and tempestuous and still clinging to their failed attempt at attachment parenting. Hairstyles were their currency—Princess Leia buns in exchange for a peaceful pre-K parting, a crown of braids if Alma promised to entertain herself during afternoon quiet time. Now she takes advantage of her daughter's unexpected seventeen-year-old acquiescence and attempts a French braid, dipping into her own adolescent repository for the muscle memories that allow her to plait Alma's hair into an intricate landscape across the back of her skull. She squats behind her daughter in a way that her legs no longer willingly accommodate and holds herself there, breathing in her girl, a faint dermatological smell that reminds her of Mark. Alma enjoyed it as a child, she knows, almost drifted off sometimes while Julia combed through her tangles, twirled dark locks into odd swooping shapes.

She holds the squat until she's woven Alma's wild dark hair into a braid. She rises with a grunt and regards Alma again in the mirror, the face that's at once unmistakable and unrecognizable. "When did you stop being a baby?"

"Fourscore and seven years ago," Alma says, rolling her eyes.

"Oh, my love," she says, a hand on either of her daughter's narrow shoulders. It may well be, her relationship with Alma—fraught though it is—the least complicated one in her life, or at least the one, after all, whose terrain is the most familiar to her. She studies

Alma's face below her own, so like her own, so much better than her own. "Beautiful girl," she says. "How very much I love you."

"Oh, God, please don't get weird."

She kisses Alma's head again. "I can't help it," she says.

Later Alma comes in to borrow Julia's tweezers and when she emerges from the bathroom she's wrinkling her nose.

"What's all over the shower curtain?" she asks. "Did one of you puke?"

Mark walks in when she's getting dressed, flitting around their bedroom in her nylons and bra, an obscene display of beige constriction she wouldn't wish on her worst enemy.

"Oh, God," she says. "Don't look at me."

"Too late." He chastely pats her ass as he passes by her en route to the closet. He's not ready yet either, unzips his jeans as he peruses his meager assortment of ties.

She steps into her dress and shimmies it up her body. Mark catches sight of her in the mirror and smiles, comes over and kisses her shoulder through the lace.

"You look gorgeous," he says.

"Thank you," she says. "I expect you'll look very handsome when you put on pants." His pale blue dress shirt hangs endearingly long over his briefs, skinny legs ending in black socks, and she is thinking, suddenly, of their own wedding, not the ceremony itself but the two of them getting home to their apartment after the party in the park, tipsy, slap-happy, pushing into their front door like it was any other night, *PBS NewsHour* blaring from the unit next door and a note from the super letting them know he'd had the plumber in to look at their garbage disposal, everything the same but for Julia in her vintage dress, Mark's tie askew, both of them loaded down with shopping bags full of cake and wedding cards, and once inside, they'd looked at each other, still the same but also entirely not, and she'd started laughing, and Mark, looking at her, looked suddenly so filled with earnest adoration that she wondered if he was about to start crying—he, not she, had gotten a little choked up during the vows—and he bent over, his face buried in her clavicle, and she very tenderly touched the back of his head. They were delicate, shy: married, suddenly, to each other.

In their bedroom, nearly twenty-six years later, he kisses her again.

"Zip me, please." She turns away from him, feels his fingers going nimbly up her back. When he finishes he holds out his wrists for her to do his shirt cuffs.

She looks up at him as she fastens them. "We're doing this, huh?"

"Seems that way."

She's aware of the slight weight at the back of her neck, something like dread. She forgets to worry about the big things sometimes, the massive potential for peril that exists beyond the tepid roster of nonproblems with which she usually concerns herself. It's easy to grow complacent, to allow yourself to dwell in the dull dramas of the everyday and lose sight of your own unimperviousness. There'd been a bomb threat in Mark's building when Ben was a baby; he'd once been very minorly involved in a midwinter pileup on the Eisenhower; it feels as though they spent the entire first decade of the century falsely reassuring the children of their safety.

"Stop," says Mark.

"Stop what?"

"Fatalizing," he says, and she presses her forehead into his chest. And perhaps it is true, what everyone else accepted months ago: that it could be worse, that there are far more terrible things, that this—like dental procedures and childbirth and tedious dinner parties, like arguments and betrayals and misunderstandings, like joy and sex and love so strong it makes you want to run away—will happen and it may or may not work out, but today, at least, the odds are more in their favor than they are against it.

"It's going to be fine?" she asks.

"You need to relax."

"Mark, tell me it—"

"Come here," he says, and leads her over to their bed, where they lie together, entwined, a complicated and well-heeled twist of weight and body.

"It's going to be fine," he says.

She sinks into brief contentment, the kind of contentment she's only ever found with him. They don't make love—of course they don't, impeded by decorum and formal wear—but for a number of reasons it may as well be the same thing. They're two people bonded by something extraordinary: surviving a nuclear explosion or seeing the Beatles live—or just loneliness, loneliness at their respective outsets that colored everything else; or proximity, or passion; or hurting each other, or watching both their children leave the nest, or deciding to keep coming home to each other at the end of the day. Closeness and distance at the same time, antipathy and affinity, love and exhaustion. The way time moves, glacial and breakneck, the way two people fit together in a bed, in the hours after their son is born and the hours before his wedding. Unbelievable things, really, and so many of them; she'd like to stay here with him, making a list, but there isn't time; they have to go.

59

The church is on the South Side, a lenient Unitarian venue not far from the old apartment on Fifty-Fourth Street. She finds Ben in what appears to be a storage closet, perched on the top of an old tablet-arm desk. His friend Noah is seated across from him on a windowsill and Julia remembers the two of them as preschoolers, tiny orb-headed humans with chubby knees and knowing eyes.

"Mom," says Ben.

"Mrs. Ames," says Noah.

"Julia," says Julia. "Am I interrupting?"

"Of course not," Noah says. He goes to Ben and Ben rises and they grip hands, pull together in that kind of hard strange masculine hug—men, now, the two of them, Jesus Christ; Noah about to set off for New York, and she finds she isn't jealous anymore on Ben's behalf because he looks *happy*, her son, truly happy, about to set off on an adventure of his own, and her eyes have filled when they part so that she thinks but can't be sure that both of them are a little emotional, too. "Hey, Mrs. Ames," Noah says, stopping to kiss her cheek on his way out. "Congratulations, huh?"

She nods a little toward Ben like *Congratulations to that one*.

"See you out there," Noah says, and he disappears, leaving them alone. The sight of Ben by himself stops her in the doorway. She's seen him in a suit before—a smattering of Nordstrom dressing rooms, graduations and job interviews—but something about it now strikes her, a blow to the gallbladder. His knees are spread wide, his shoulders hunched, a barely touched glass of champagne in hand. He smiles at her, and suddenly there's a song in her head, the theme from *The Muppet Show*, his warm tiny body in her lap, *It's time to light the lights.*

"Are you accepting visitors?" she asks.

"Yeah, of course. Just—taking a minute."

"Take as many as you need," she says. "They're unlikely to start without you."

She goes over to him; in lieu of throwing her arms around him and attempting to absorb him back into her body, she starts futzing with his tie, ineptly, because she'd never learned how to tie one; Mark rarely wore them, never needed her help when he did.

"Are you all right?" she asks.

"Yeah," he says. "Totally. Good."

She looks up into his face, so like Mark's but for a second's hesitation in the eyes that you can only catch when you're looking at precisely the right instant, a little flicker of skepticism—not the worst thing in the world, really—that had to have come from her.

"I really am," he says. "I'm not even really nervous. Is that weird?"

She hadn't been nervous before she got married, in part perhaps because the whole day had a slightly artificial feel to it, everyone costumed and smiling. But Mark hadn't made her nervous either, not really, not that day and not in the way that almost everyone else in the world did.

"No, honey, that's not weird at all." She gives a final, ineffectual tug to his tie. "You're great," she says. "You know that? You always have been great; you will be great."

His eyes crinkle up at the corners. "Mom," he says.

She shakes her head. "You know how much I—" Her voice breaks.

Her partner in crime, Ben. The one who'd accompanied her complicitously through the darkest and most shameful moments of her adult life: cradled in her arms as she wandered woozily around the apartment at night, entertaining thoughts of disappearing while she slowly hummed him pop songs; strapped into the backseat while she wept in the parking lot of the Whole Foods; taking over when she got too tired to finish reading to him from Harry Potter, too young to read but making up the story as he saw fit—*then he found a werewolf in the woods, and it was really funny and then really scary but mostly funny ha ha ha and then everyone went to bed, the end, Mama. Mama?*

"Mom," he says now, and she wonders if he ever remembers the late-night times of his toddlerhood when she would creep in and lift him from his bed and rock him back to sleep in the glider, *Mama's nuts about you, chipmunk. Mama wouldn't understand the world without you in it.*

"Love you," she finishes. "You know how much, right? If I ever— If it ever felt like I wasn't—what you needed me to be, honey, I'm sorry about that. I'm sorry if I didn't always—know the right things, or understand what I was—"

"Mom," he says, and puts his arms around her. "I love you too."

A few weeks after he was born, a very early morning on that futon in that bedroom in the apartment on Paulina, she sat with Ben, considering the weight of him in her arms, the way he fit so snugly against her chest. She traced his cinnamon swirl of hair and drew a line with her finger across his forehead, still wrinkled like a wizard's, and she wondered if her own mother had held her like this, had contemplated the nuances of her face and envisioned all the ways it would change. She wondered if her mother had felt her heart break for all the things she couldn't control and for all the things she could, for all the ways her child would come to know the world while not wrapped in her arms, and she wondered if her mother had touched foreheads with her like they were ponies, because that's what she was doing with Ben, this person who was inexplicably hers.

And then he opened his eyes, her son, and fixed them on her face, and she saw him recognize her.

Oh, she thought, and there it was, shining before her suddenly like a soap bubble, having taken longer to arrive, surely, than it was supposed to, but better late than never: a love so strong it made her sick, a transcendent gut punch. The first easily articulable feeling of her life, love, *love*, for this tiny, tiny person, and she felt, then, such wonderful relief, that finally something had worked the way it was supposed to.

She holds him to her now, though it doesn't look like it anymore, dwarfed as she is by his frame, and she breathes in, tries fruitlessly to catch a vestigial whiff of milky infant sick-sweetness.

"Any parting words?" he asks when they've pulled apart.

She dabs at her eyes. "We're not *parting;* you live in the same *county.*"

"Mom, come on. Word to the wise? Inside baseball?"

He is asking her outright, seeking her counsel; she can't have done everything wrong, if some part of her son still thinks she could have answers. Her eyes fill again but she swallows it away, and then she begins to panic, because she cannot, immediately, think of any words to the wise, but then she looks up at him, her son, his patience, his openness, his *sportsmanship*, really, sweet boy, little love, how the hell did they get so lucky?

"Try to be happy," she says, and he seems to be waiting for more, but it's the best she can do. "That's my advice. Try to count on her, try to be there for her. If you're trying, it means you care."

"Okay," Ben says.

"That's it," she says. "Try." She holds his face in her hands, the face they created together, her own eyes looking back at her, startlingly mature. "That's all I've got."

She and Mark walk their son down the aisle. She dissociates a little, a coping mechanism, and she's surprised, as they make their way, by the crowd that's been drawn. There's a handful of Ben's friends—boys whose traces of baby fat have melted away to reveal strong jaws; and some of Sunny's—artsy girls with middle-parted Ali MacGraw hair and tight satin dresses; a smattering of extended family; Brady and Francine Grimes are in the third row, and they both, disturbingly, wink at Julia when she catches their eyes across the church. And her mother and Marshall are together a few seats down, a perfectly respectable grandparently showing; her mother gives her a short nod as she passes.

When they reach the front of the church, she accepts her son's kiss on her cheek and then watches him hug his father. Mark whispers something to Ben before he lets go, and Julia will never know what it is that he said; she will forget, repeatedly, to ask him. The music starts—she recognizes the strains of something—and Sunny appears in the doorway on the arm of her stepfather, whose name Julia has again forgotten. She's wearing her elf braids and her wedding dress makes it clear, now, that she's showing, and Julia is surprised to find herself feeling moved. She chalks it up partially to the fact that the song, she recognizes after a few more seconds, is by one of Alma's maudlin indie bands. *You May Find Yourself Verklempt Before a Pregnant Undergraduate. And You Will Put on Your Game Face, Julia Ames.*

The couple has not written their own vows, and when they get to the part about "all the wonders life has to offer," she happens to glance over at Alma and sees her discerning daughter's artfully distorted smirk, and she feels some relief. Still, she cries a bit, against her will, and Mark rubs his thumb over and over again in the little bowl at the small of her back, soothing her like you'd soothe a dog during a thunderstorm.

They convene afterward in the closed-for-the-occasion Lettuce Pray, forks present and accounted for and lisianthuses on the tables. Ben and Sunny's first dance is set, blessedly, not to "Wonderful Tonight" or "Just the Way You Are," but "Waiting on a Friend"—bless these youths, with their vintage taste—and though Sunny's entourage of shiny-haired coeds emit little lascivious hoots at *Don't need a whore,* Julia feels a wetness behind her eyes again, and she looks over at her husband—the man with whom she shimmied with suggestive abandon, twenty-five years ago in their rented-out park, to "I Just Want to Make Love to You"—and he takes her hand under the table and squeezes it.

She leans into him as Ben and Sunny canoodle for their audience. Ben bows to whisper something to Sunny, and Sunny looks fondly at him for a beat before she kisses him.

She and Mark had more time for indulgences, of course, when they were young.

"Favorite Talking Heads song," she remembers quizzing him on one of their early dates. Then, narrowing her eyes: "There is a right answer."

You got to spend time on that stuff before all of the mire slipped in. You got to argue the merits of different tracks and ignore the big picture: kids and mortgages and which pieces of your motley ethical and religious upbringing survived the journey through life. You got to sit back and consider—in that liminal space before everything accumulated all of its weight—the substance of the other person.

Mark puts his arm around her. "It's nice, isn't it?" he whispers.

She nods.

"Oh, youth," he continues, teasing her now. "Oh, maturity."

She tries not to smile.

"Come on," he says, wheedling, nosing his mouth up near her ear as their son has just done to his new wife.

"Am I interrupting?"

They both look up, like they've been caught making out under the bleachers, to Anita standing over them.

"No," she says, straightening. "Sure, no, sit down."

"That's all right," her mother says, and—even despite everything, the mason jars of flowers and her husband's hand on her leg and her daughter and Margo Singh dancing, in her periphery, to the Spice Girls, all this revelry—she feels her heart sink.

"Are you leaving?" she asks. She's embarrassed by her voice, hope and dejection laid bare on the table like Sunny's rustic bouquets. She feels Mark shift beside her and knows he will never rub in her face the fact that he was right, that he knew all along her mother would just take off again. "It's still early," she says; "we haven't—" But what is she supposed to say here? *We haven't packed up the cake yet. Nobody has yet danced the Electric Slide. You can't go, Mom.*

"We're both exhausted," Anita says. "And I figured Suzanne could use some company."

Julia studies her.

"Alma mentioned she might make French toast in the morning," Anita says.

"She does sometimes," Julia says. "On Sundays."

"Well, I told her to count me in," Anita says. "She's quite persuasive. As long as that's— If it's okay with you. Both of you."

"It's okay," Mark says. "You should stay."

She watches her mother watch her husband, the person who used to know her best in the world and the person who does now.

"Fine," Anita says finally. And then, turning away, "We will."

She watches her go; she feels Mark's gaze parallel to hers.

"Thank you," she says, still watching—Marshall helping her mother into her jacket; her mother tucking a napkin-wrapped cupcake into the jacket's pocket.

"For what?" he asks, and she leans against him again, but she doesn't have time to answer, because Ben comes over at that moment, bows gallantly before her and asks her to dance.

She will remember the few moments that follow repeatedly in the time she has left, which turns out to be quite a lot of time, an incalculable amount of time, really, or at least an amount that she never allows herself to attempt to calculate. She will remember them when recounting the wedding to her colleagues on Monday, and when she drops off her mother and Marshall at the airport several days later than she expected them to leave, and when she is attempting to liven up the conversation at a dull dinner party. She will remember them when Alma graduates the following week, and when she and Mark wave goodbye to her in the rearview mirror outside her dorm in Iowa, neither of them daring to look at each other until they're thirty miles or so into the country, until they can trust themselves to hold it together and she says, observing a billboard, "Well. Do you need to buy any fireworks before we cross the state line?"

She will remember them when she holds her grandson in her arms for the first time, and when she holds Mark's elbow, after, when they're alone walking to the lakefront, and when Ben calls her in the middle of the night to ask her how high a fever is too high. She will remember them when she and Mark are babysitting the boy as he takes his first tentative steps, the two of them side by side on the floor with their backs against the couch, her knee resting idly against her husband's and both of their arms outstretched toward the baby, anticipating a fall that doesn't come until he reaches them, tumbling proudly into their overlapping legs.

She will remember them two and a half years from now when Mark, six weeks on the heels of his retirement from AllAboard, dies unexpectedly of an aortic aneurysm and is found by fellow joggers in Forest Glen. She will remember the moments frequently, then, and with a level of detail that makes others uncomfortable, that makes her children reach out imploring hands to her and ask *Is everything okay, Mom?* and she will bite her tongue to keep herself from replying as she wants to—*No, no, no, there's nothing worse than this, my sweet things*—and try to conjure her husband's knack for numbers— *I am, statistically speaking, the most alone on the loneliness gradient; I am alone, just when I'd started to truly appreciate the company*—and instead she'll hug her kids and assure them that everything's copacetic, look for Mark in the slope of Alma's nose and in Ben's astonishing conscientiousness; she will focus on those things instead of the endless stretch of hours that lie before her, hours for which she cannot bring herself to feel gratitude, a hundred thousand solitary hours of aimless forward motion and invalid existence. She will remember them while showing Sunny around her garden, when Ben walks into the kitchen and she thinks—just for a minute—that he's his father; she will remember them in the moments that follow that second of misrecognition, moments of such cavernous aloneness— such unbelievable pain—that she almost starts laughing. She will remember them when she accidentally makes an extra piece of toast in the morning and when she turns on an album he doesn't like and when she turns on an album he does like and when she awakens unnerved in the night and feels with scissoring legs the cool pitiful bounty of space in their bed. She will remember them when she finds herself, on certain days, bowled over by how unencumbered she feels, a return to form, to the quiet days before she met him; she will remember them, too, during the subsequent comedowns, each one lower than the last.

She will remember them when Helen dies, too, when she stands at the back of a packed church and when she remembers, an afterthought, to wonder which graying head in the front pew belongs to Nathaniel, when she leaves before the reception and cries in her car, cries for being the lone woman lurking at the back of a funeral, cries for the fact that Mark isn't there, cries for the fact that he wouldn't be there even if he were still alive, cries for Helen Russo, who pitied her just the right amount and who is ultimately responsible for far more good things in Julia's life than she is for the one big bad thing that she happened to be there for.

She will remember them when she does the crossword on the El on her way to work and when she pays a teenage neighbor to edge the lawn and when she takes her lunch break along the riverfront by the douchey Irish pub where he used to walk her to work, which is now a Sephora. She will remember them when Alma graduates from college, and when she sees her off at the O'Hare security line before she catches a flight to Accra, and when she talks to her daughter, on a pixelated video line, about her experience teaching English and digging wells on the side, catching the notice of her ten-years-older fieldwork supervisor, with whom she will embark on a yearlong love affair. She will remember them when Alma returns from the trip at once someone new and the same as she's always been, and when she moves back home for six months, filling the house with sounds again, stirring up the dust, stomping downstairs in the morning and watching *Gold Beach* reruns until three a.m. and wearing her father's careworn gray pullover when she goes out to walk Suzanne and— once—her mother's faded teal Jesus and Mary Chain T-shirt as she passes by Julia in the hallway.

She will remember them when she thinks she feels her heart skip a few beats while she's volunteering at the arboretum and when Sunny graduates from college, then from a graduate program in something called Strategic Design and Transformative Thinking, which nobody is semantically able to explain to her but with which Sunny seems very happy. She will remember them when her second and third grandchildren are born—three magnificent, baffling boys; the odds!—and she will remember them at school plays and grandparents' days and Halloween parades where the boys dress up as increasingly unrecognizable characters. She will remember them when she realizes that Mark will exist to them only in folklore, as a kindly magical presence, like Santa, someone whose existence is contingent on belief.

She will remember them when Alma announces that she is getting married and then, a few months later, announces that she is not; she will remember them when her daughter, the head of an international education nonprofit, is profiled in a local magazine as one of twelve Women to Watch, and then when the nonprofit in Denver, owing to the underhanded investments of the man at its helm, folds, and Alma asks her what she should do, and she says— even while, out of loyalty to her husband, wiring her daughter two months' rent—that she'll just have to figure it out.

She will remember them when she pulls up in front of her mother's house in Capitola, and when she meets Marshall's children and their spouses and feels, for just a moment, like she had when she was fifteen, getting afterthought introductions to Anita's boy- friends. She will remember them, too, when her mother's memory starts to go shortly thereafter, pulling odd bits of sediment to the surface and letting other handfuls slip through her fingers; when she asks Julia how the biologist is doing, if they're thinking of hav- ing kids, and good luck if so.

And she will remember them when her own mind starts to worry her, words streaking by just beyond her grasp, iridium flares or the distant searchlights of a mall's grand opening, memories missing in action only to materialize later, when she's falling asleep, a flash of how the impatient nurse at the hospital when Alma was born kept calling her *Juliet* or how many miles per gallon (twenty-seven) her car is supposed to get.

She will remember them when she observes her friends tiptoe- ing around her, when she can feel in the guilty darting movements of their eyes and their hands that they are pitying her. She will remember them when Francine brings her a photo she finds of Mark in their freshman dorm, or rather she will remember them later, when she is alone and trying to conjure generosity, because the photo—intended, surely, to evoke pleasant nostalgia—will send her spiraling, thinking about all the years she didn't know him, back when he wore glasses like the ones he is wearing in the photo, all the different ways his life might have branched off had he not met her at the parking meter.

She will remember them when she remembers Mark's absence, which is almost always, and on the four distinct occasions she for- gets he's gone, three of which happen immediately upon waking, before she realizes his shape beside her is in her head, and once when she picks up the phone to tell him she's going to be late. She will remember them when she's alone, the house making its house sounds, Suzanne warm against her side—*thank you, tiny lady*—and she will remember them when she's surrounded by other people and their deafening noise. She will remember them when she is feeling bad, or when she wants to feel bad, or when she wants to feel good, depending on her mood, depending on the lighting, depending on whether she has had one or two glasses of wine with the dinner she eats alone. And she will remember them sometimes when she is already feeling good, those rare moments of gratitude for being alive.

She will remember them lastingly, wistfully, imbued with hindsight advantage, backlit by a rosy glow. She will remember those few moments so often that after a while she'll begin to doubt that they ever happened at all.

When their grandson is born—indeed a boy, a tiny man riding a bike with a more conventional name than she was expecting—they will drive to the hospital to meet him, but Mark will suggest, afterward, taking a walk to the lakefront—the lake that whipped their hair into their faces the afternoon he accidentally told her he loved her, the lake that glittered eastward through the windows of his car the night she asked him to marry her, the lake into which, in two and a half years, she and the children will be scattering his ashes in a ritual that feels hollow and overdone, but at the time she'll just be thinking that it's a pretty day and the breeze feels nice and they've got the whole afternoon ahead of them and then some.

Mark will reach over, when they're waiting for the walk sign on Chicago to cross Lake Shore Drive, and brush away some hair that's blown into her face.

"We did it," he'll say, and hold up a hand for a high-five, which Alma has repeatedly informed them is a thing that nobody does anymore. She'll slap her palm against his and then twine their fingers together as the signal changes and they start across the street, the wind high.

"So what do we think?" he'll ask.

She'll be feeling a little older than she's comfortable with, and a little bit like she's underperformed before Ben and Sunny and the baby because—it's true—she will not have felt all that much, holding her grandson in her arms; much of the feeling, in fact, will have come from seeing the baby with Mark, her husband's easy affection, his effortless wonder over wonderful things; she will have borrowed his wonder as her own and she'll be feeling a little guilty about that, fifty-seven years old and still without a complete toolbox of human emotions.

"He looks," she'll say carefully, "sort of like Eleanor Roosevelt."

And Mark, the diplomat, will consider it for a few seconds, and in those few seconds she'll panic a little, but before she can backpedal, he will say, "You know, he actually kind of does?"

"He's beautiful," she'll protest. "Of course he is."

And her husband will shrug. "So was Eleanor Roosevelt."

Then he'll put his arms around her, and kiss her hair, and she'll slip her own arms, against the gales, inside of his coat.

She will remember it just as it happened, or maybe not exactly, who's to say: the four of them, dancing, Julia in Ben's arms, Alma twirling around on Mark's raised hand—Sunny sitting on the sidelines watching them pridefully like she's the mom, like they're her bunch of unruly children—and then Ben dips her suddenly and she's so startled that she honks a little and they both start laughing, cracking up like when he was a toddler and she'd drive down dips along the highway, really getting into it, holding her hands over her head like they were on a roller coaster and Ben would just be beside himself, intoxicated by the abundant charms of his tiny life, *ha ha ha Mama again again*, great deranged baby laughter, the infectious kind, stereo on loud, *Got the wings of heaven on my shoes*—but wait, no, that's now, that's the song playing now, Alma gorgeously uninhibited, tipsy, probably, doing the *Saturday Night Fever* thing with her finger, busting up laughing with Mark, *live to see another day*, and Ben fans her out on his arm and then pulls her back in, his chest a man's chest now, and when he spins her out again she and Alma trade places, and she finds herself against Mark, tired suddenly, pleasantly exhausted—so like love—and she leans her weight on him and looks up into his sweet spent open face, and he bows down to kiss her full on the lips.

Again Mama again, ha ha ha, and she'd tell him to wait, my sweetheart, you'll have to wait, because she can't control the placement of the hills along the road.

Acknowledgments

First things first: dogs are the best people, and Renee is the best dog. To the tiniest girl and hugest source of joy, the brightest light, keenest eye and most steadfast companion, who found me right when I needed her most and has remained within four feet of me at all times ever since: thanks for rescuing me, tiny lady.

I stop to consider, at least once a week, "What would Ellen Levine do?" and am worlds better for it. To my absolute dynamo of an agent, for your tenacity and your acumen and your advocacy, for your humor and humanity, for reading about seventy-three drafts of this book: thank you for seeing whatever you see in my work and fighting for it as fiercely as you do.

To the best editor on the entire earth—oh my God, oh my God, oh my God: THANK YOU, LEE BOUDREAUX (yet another proposed alternate title). This book would not be itself without you; nor would I: thank you for your brilliance and your grace and your patience, for asking all the right questions, for always being willing to talk to me (even—nay, *especially*—when all I want to talk about is paint colors), and for bringing infectious joy and light to everything you do. There's truly no one smarter, funnier or better at what she does; I am the luckiest ever.

To everyone at Doubleday for allowing me to remain in the best place in publishing for a second book, especially Bill Thomas, Maya Mavjee, Todd Doughty, Vimi Santokhi, Jess Deitcher, Kristin Fassler, Milena Brown and Maya Pasic. And to Elena Hershey, whose patience and insight and organizational prowess are the stuff of legends. To marvelous Emily Mahon, for reading this book on vacation and then devoting an unreal amount of time to finding it a cover, and to Kelly Blair and Cassandra Pappas. To production editor extraordinaire Ellen Feldman, whose brain astounds and eye is unmatched: thank you for reading this novel so many times with such incredible care, and for being the Noticer of Everything. Thank you as well to your unbelievable proofreaders, Susan VanOmmeren and Carla Benton, for quite literally not missing a trick. To Ruth Liebmann, for your enthusiasm and your generosity. To the KDPG sales reps: thank you; you're wonderful. And special thanks to Jason Gobble for the Bee Gees Golden Book, for noticing when Anita discarded twice in a row, and for being my friend.

To lovely, lively Lettice Franklin at Weidenfeld & Nicolson, for writing me the most extraordinary twenty-two-page letter I've ever received: thank you so very much for your smarts and enthusiasm, and for helping me to see this book with fresh eyes. And to the wonderful team at W&N: thank you for believing in Julia in her early days and welcoming her across the pond.

At Trident Media Group, my abundant thanks to Martha Wydysh and Audrey Crooks, for more help and patience than I deserve. Thank you, thank you, Ana Ban, for finding homes for Julia et al. around the globe. And at the Gotham Group, thanks to the wonderful Rich Green for seeing this book in 3D.

Thank you to brilliant, dogged early readers, at the Iowa Writers' Workshop, of Julia's early antics, including but not limited to Lan Samantha Chang, Margot Livesey, Maria Kuznetsova and Drew Calvert. Special and enormous thanks, as ever, to Ethan Canin for helping me find my way.

Thank you to the unendingly generous Rick Russo, in Key West, for early, green-inked encouragement. Gigantic thanks to Alexa Stark, for years of keen insight and advice. And to Rich Zabransky, who was effulgent, and who I will remember, always, laughing—I thank you, and I really miss you.

To the Fairhope Center for the Writing Arts, especially Skip and Barbara and Archie Jones—thank you for a magical month in a truly special place; I'll be back soon whether you like it or not.

Thanks to Erin Goetz for being there for me from the get-go, and for bringing so much humor and color and wild intelligence into my early years—or, actually, all of my years.

To so many writers I am fortunate to call my friends, for making this world less lonely and for support, commiseration, advice and great company, thank you: Julia Claiborne Johnson, for finding light everywhere and making the world feel way better than it is, and for letting me camp out on your couches, proverbial and actual; Regina Porter—I am so glad we have each other to keep tabs on; trusted pen pal and billowing champion Anton DiSclafani, who makes me lol many times a day; Kevin Smith, the gentlest pal—I breathe easier knowing you're across town; my New Friend Tracy Towley, and Beck Dorey-Stein, Julia Drake, Kate Russo and De'Shawn Winslow.

Thanks to Sue Anzaldi for always understanding and humoring me, even when I was sixteen and at my most incomprehensible and least amusing—your friendship is one of the greatest gifts I've gotten. Thanks to Wanda Raiford, my running buddy and the bright light across the street; and to Robbie, the most handsome and deep-feeling boyfriend I've ever had. To Ruth Hesseltine, my partner in neighborhood surveillance and the appreciation of tiny objects. To Jane Van Voorhis and Kurt Anstreicher, my Covid family. And to David Rubin, whom I've now officially known for longer than I haven't, thank God.

To my sister Heidi, and my brother Adam; and to my sister Molly, who was endeavoring so much more than writing while I was writing this book—I am really fucking proud of you, pal.

To Jan Weissmiller, Bookseller Extraordinaire and uncanny rememberer of birthdays, for your great company (and delicious gossip) at the information desk, and for giving me a place to land. And thanks to Prairie Lights Books (with special thanks to Kathleen Johnson), my local indie and beloved employer, for being the beating heart of a wonderful community of writers and readers.

On that: thank you to all independent booksellers and librarians for literally everything, for being safe havens and light sources even in the worst of times; for your zeal and your compassion and all you do on behalf of writers and readers and words.

To Tony Lombardo, my dad, whose heart and humor and humility have been guiding me since before I even knew it. To brave, strong, resplendent Sally Lombardo, my mom and my dear friend—I'm sorry for being a seventeen-year-old lioness (or maybe just a narcissist), but thank you so much for seeing me through it and continuing to always be there for me.

Thanks to readers, all, who have given any time to anything I've written—my God, I am continually amazed you exist, and so grateful.

And to all of the Helen Russos in my life—you know who you are, or maybe you don't, but I am much better for knowing you.

A NOTE ABOUT THE AUTHOR

CLAIRE LOMBARDO is the author of *The Most Fun We Ever Had*. She lives in Iowa City, where she has taught at the Iowa Writers' Workshop and works as a bookseller at Prairie Lights Books.